THE VAMPRESS GIRLS

Witches of Cazador
Book 2

THE VAMPRESS GIRLS

Witches of Cazador
Book 2

JACY NOVA and NICK NOVA
MANUEL CADAG

KENSINGTON PUBLISHING CORP.
www.kensingtonbooks.com

KENSINGTON BOOKS are published by

Kensington Publishing Corp.
850 Third Avenue
New York, NY 10022

All Kensington titles, imprints, and distributed lines are available at
special quantity discounts for bulk purchases for sales promotions,
premiums, fund-raising, educational or institutional use.

Special book excerpts or customized printings can also be created to
fit specific needs. For details, write or phone the office of the
Kensington Special Sales Manager: Kensington Publishing Corp., 850
Third Avenue, New York, NY 10022. Attn: Special Sales Department.
Phone: 1-800-221-2647.

Kensington and the K logo are Reg. U.S. Pat. & TM Off.

ISBN-13: 978-0-7582-2529-0
ISBN-10: 0-7582-2529-6

First Kensington Trade Paperback Printing: October 2008

10 9 8 7 6 5 4 3 2 1

Printed in the United States of America

Jacy Nova:

This book is dedicated to Nik and Boris,
the two muses in my life. Much love.
A special thanks to June Clark and the Kensington team.

Nick Nova:

This book is dedicated to my Mom, Dad, Grandma,
Nessa, Todd, Derek, and Greg.

LOVE

TRIBE: VAMPIRE

ZODIAC SIGN: CANCER

TITLE: HIGH PRIESTESS OF THE VAMPIRE CLAN

THE MOTHER OF THE VAMPRESS GIRLS SHE IS THE SOLE PROTECTOR OF THE DREAMERS AND THE VAMPRESS CODE. DO NOT BE FOOLED BY HER KIND AND LOVING HEART; SHE IS CONSIDERED ONE OF THE MOST POWERFUL VAMPIRES TO WALK THE EARTH.

SHADE

TRIBE; DEMON

ZODIAC SIGN; SCORPIO

TITLE; HIGH PRIEST OF THE DEMON CLAN

A FALLEN VAMPIRE. HIS GREED AND LUST TO POSSESS THE VAMPRESS CODE CONSUMES HIM. WOMEN FIND IT HARD TO RESIST HIS MAGNETIC CHARMS. INTENSELY SECRETIVE, HE IS AN INTIMIDATING FORCE AMONG THE DEMONS.

PASSION

TRIBE: VAMPIRE

ZODIAC SIGN: LEO

TITLE: THE VAMPRESS GIRLS

INSTRUMENT: VOCALS

THE OLDEST OF THE FOUR SISTERS, PASSION ENJOYS BEING THE CENTER OF ATTENTION. SHE IS CREATIVE AND PASSIONATE. QUITE THE FASIONISTA. SHE IS CONSIDERED THE HEART BREAKER OF THE GIRLS.

SWEET

TRIBE: VAMPIRE

ZODIAC SIGN: PISCES

TITLE: THE VAMPRESS GIRLS

INSTRUMENT: DRUMS

AN OLD SOUL, SWEET IS SHY AND QUIET. HER UNCANNY PSYCHIC ABILITIES COME IN HANDY WHEN PROTECTING THE WORLD FROM THE DREAM SUCKING DEMONS AND THE WITCHES.

RAVEN

TRIBE: VAMPIRE

ZODIAC SIGN: TAURUS

TITLE: THE VAMPRESS GIRLS

INSTRUMENT: GUITARS

THE MOST OUTSPOKEN OF THE GIRLS. RAVEN IS PERSISTANT AND DETERMINED IN ACHIEVING HER GOAL. DESPITE HER WICKED SENSE OF HUMOR, SHE'S A HOPELESS ROMANTIC AND IS WAITING FOR 'THE ONE' TO SWEEP HER OFF HER FEET.

PAGE

TRIBE: VAMPIRE

ZODIAC SIGN: VIRGO

TITLE; THE VAMPRESS GIRLS

INSTRUMENT: BASS

THE RESIDENT FAMILY GEEK, PAGE IS SENSITIVE AND SUPER-SMART. MORE OF A HOMEBODY, HER KEEN INTUITION OFTEN KEEPS THE GIRLS OUT OF STICKY SITUATIONS.

BRANDY

TRIBE: DEMON

ZODIAC SIGN: SAGITTARIUS

TITLE: THE DEMON GIRLS

INSTRUMENT: LEAD VOCALS

BRANDY IS A FREE SPIRIT WHO NEVER TAKES NO FOR AN ANSWER. FUN LOVING AND ALWAYS OUT-SPOKEN. SHE IS FIERCELY INDEPENDENT AND DETERMINED TO TAKE THE BAND TO NUMBER ONE ON THE CHARTS.

JADE

TRIBE: DEMON

ZODIAC SIGN: ARIES

TITLE: THE DEMON GIRLS

INSTRUMENT: BASS

JADE'S NON-STOP ENERGY IS CENTRAL TO THE PUNK SOUND OF HER BAND. HER BIG EGO CAN BE OVERBEARING AT TIMES. HER ARCH NEMESIS IS RAVEN. WHO STOLE HER MAN DAMIEN. WHAT REVENGE WILL SHE BESTOW ON THE VAMPRESS GIRLS?

EVE

TRIBE: DEMON

ZODIAC SIGN: AQUARIUS

TITLE: THE DEMON GIRLS

INSTRUMENT: GUITARS

EVE PRIDES HERSELF ON BEING UNIQUE AND UNCONVENTIONAL. SHE IS ORIGINAL IN CREATIVE EXPRESSION AND GETS BORED EASILY. SHE IS INTENSELY JEALOUS OF THE VAMPRESS GIRLS SUCCESS.

SPAZ

TRIBE: DEMON

ZODIAC SIGN: GEMINI

TITLE: THE DEMON GIRLS

INSTRUMENT: DRUMS

SPAZ LOVES TO TALK AND HAS A GREAT SENSE OF HUMOR. THE IMPULSIVE MEMBER OF THE GROUP, SHE HAS A SECRET CRUSH ON SHADE. SHE IS JADE'S SIDEKICK IN WREAKING HAVOC IN THE VAMPRESS GIRLS LIVES.

LUCY FUR

TRIBE: DEMON

ZODIAC SIGN: CAPRICORN

TITLE: PRINCESS OF DARKNESS.

AN EXTRAORDINARY BUSINESS WOMAN. LUCY FUR IS SUPER CONFIDENT AND IS CALCULATING IN HER WAYS. CUNNING AND SMART. SHE IS SHADE'S GIRLFRIEND. TOGETHER THEY ARE BOTH DETERMINED TO POSSESS THE VAMPRESS CODE.

DAMIEN

TRIBE: DEMON

ZODIAC SIGN: LIBRA

TITLE: PRINCE OF DARKNESS

DAMIEN IS LUCY'S BROTHER AND HEIR TO THE THRONE OF THE DEMON EMPIRE. HE IS OUTWARDLY CHARMING AND FRIENDLY, BUT IS MADE OF STEEL UNDERNEATH. WILL RAVEN'S LOVE MELT HIS HEART OF STONE?

THE VAMPRESS GIRLS

Witches of Cazador
Book 2

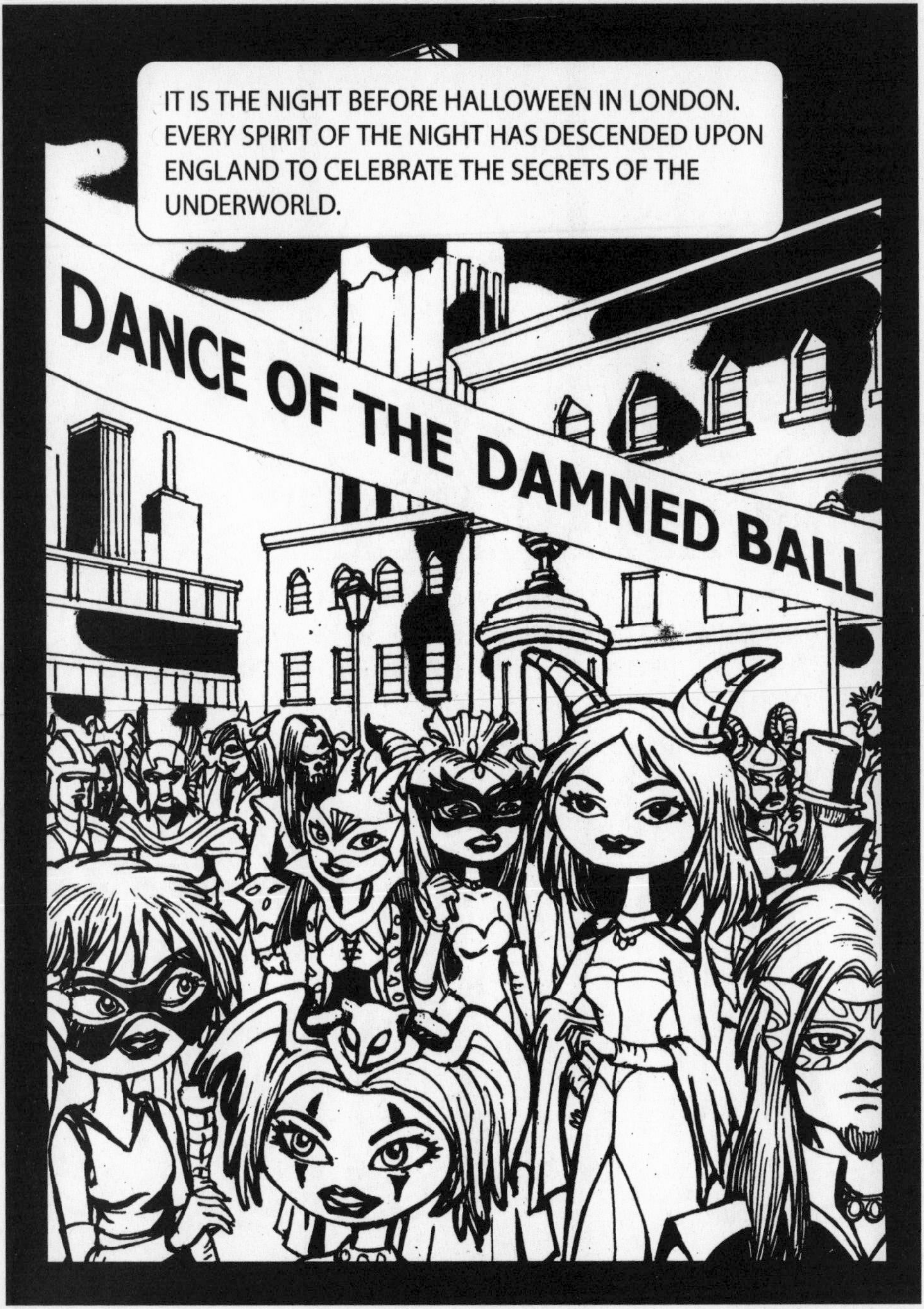
IT IS THE NIGHT BEFORE HALLOWEEN IN LONDON. EVERY SPIRIT OF THE NIGHT HAS DESCENDED UPON ENGLAND TO CELEBRATE THE SECRETS OF THE UNDERWORLD.
DANCE OF THE DAMNED BALL

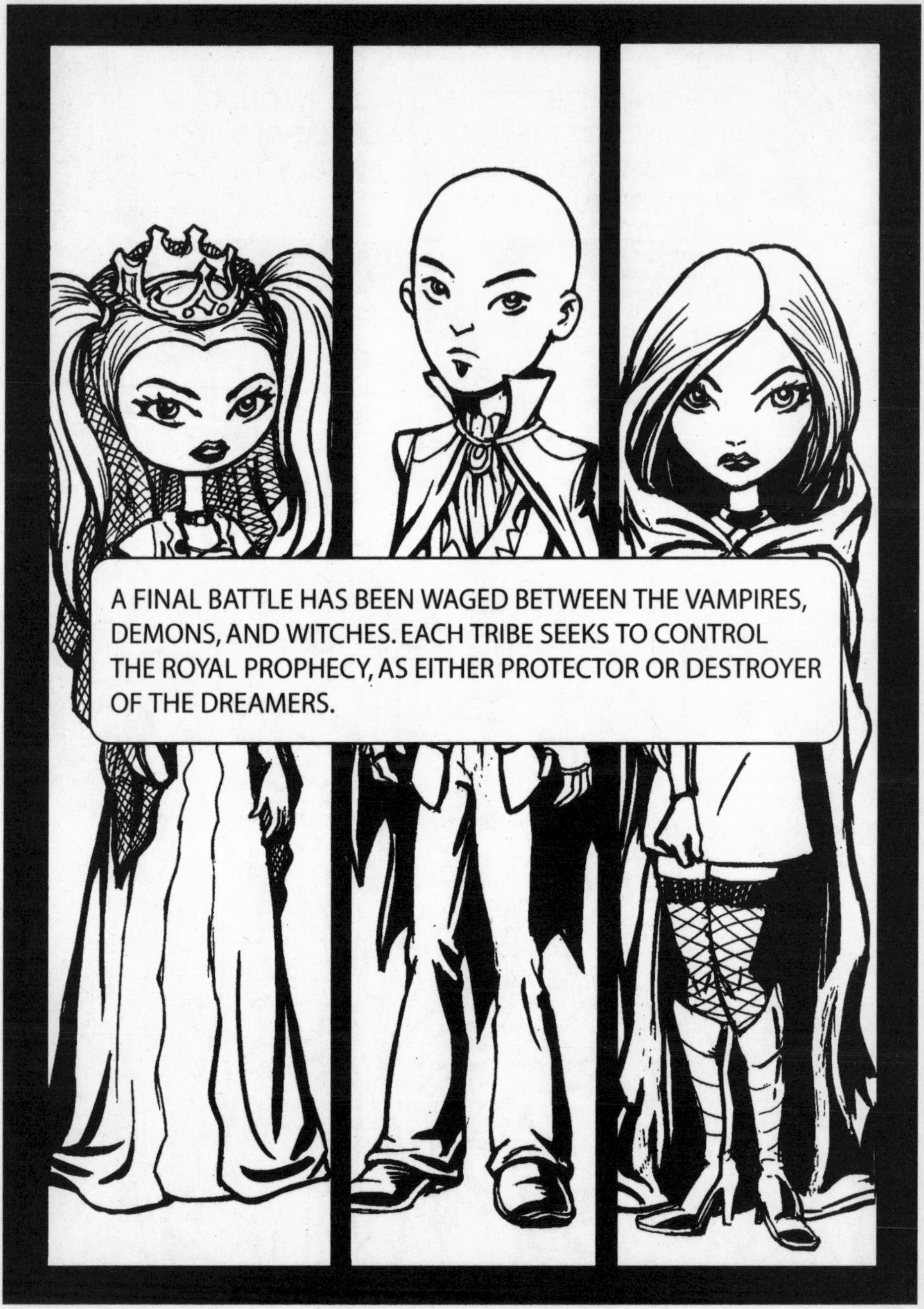
A FINAL BATTLE HAS BEEN WAGED BETWEEN THE VAMPIRES, DEMONS, AND WITCHES. EACH TRIBE SEEKS TO CONTROL THE ROYAL PROPHECY, AS EITHER PROTECTOR OR DESTROYER OF THE DREAMERS.

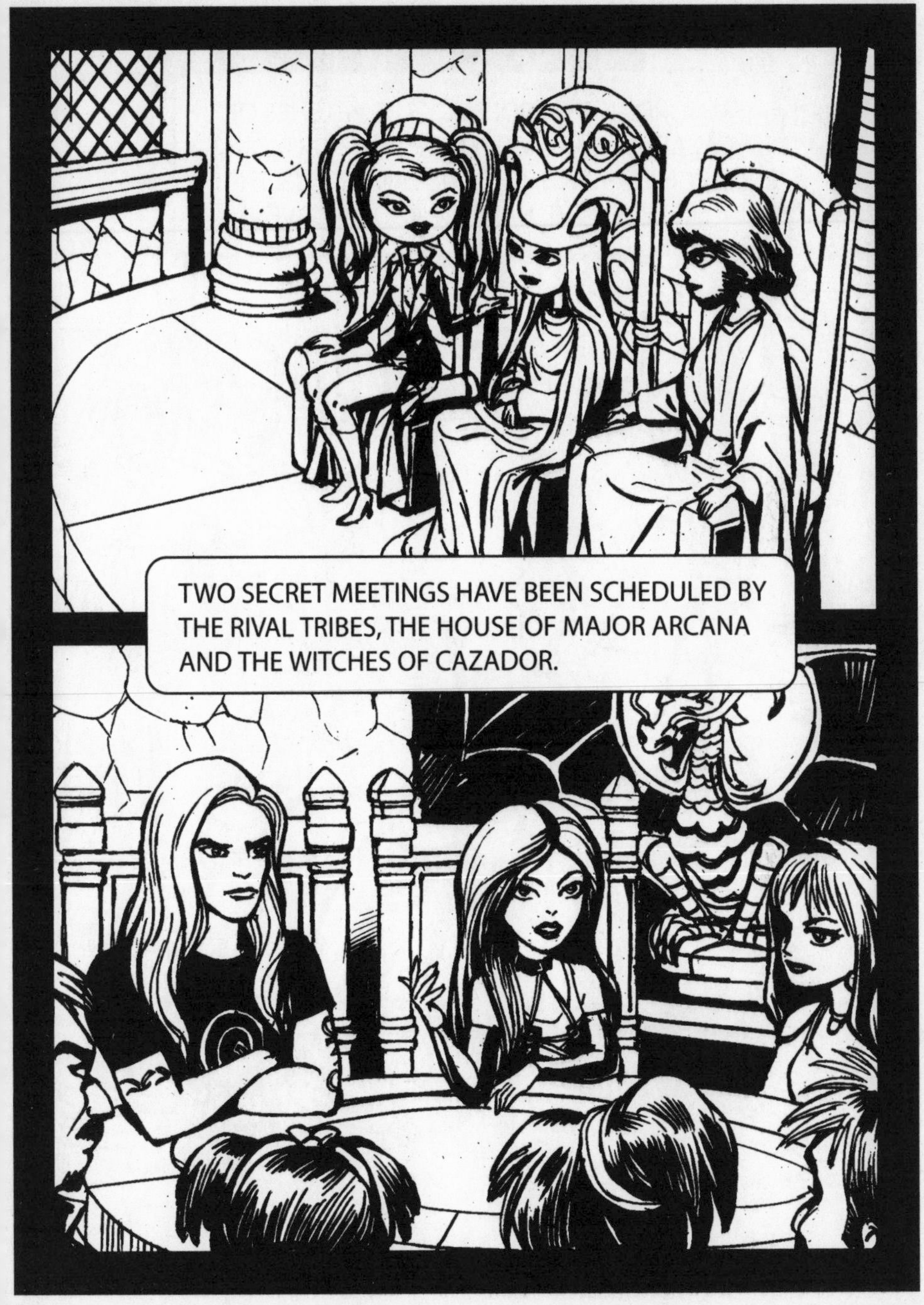
TWO SECRET MEETINGS HAVE BEEN SCHEDULED BY THE RIVAL TRIBES, THE HOUSE OF MAJOR ARCANA AND THE WITCHES OF CAZADOR.

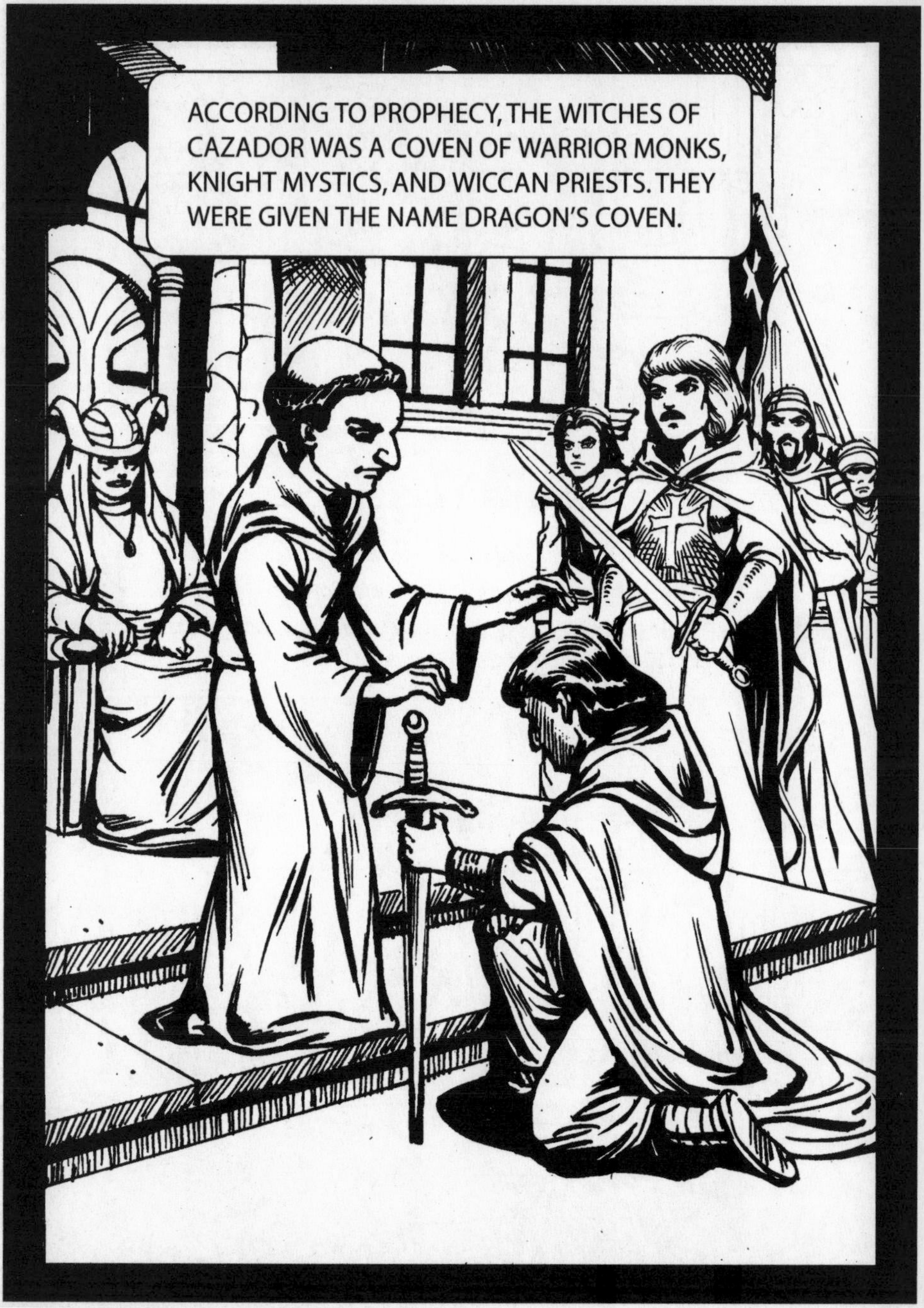
ACCORDING TO PROPHECY, THE WITCHES OF CAZADOR WAS A COVEN OF WARRIOR MONKS, KNIGHT MYSTICS, AND WICCAN PRIESTS. THEY WERE GIVEN THE NAME DRAGON'S COVEN.

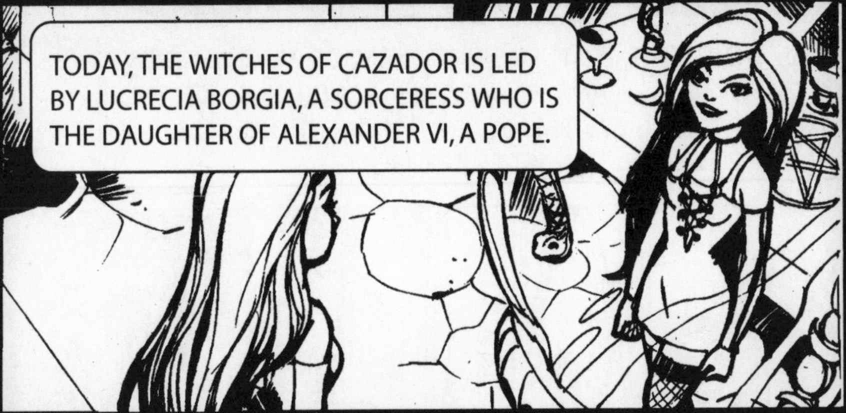
TODAY, THE WITCHES OF CAZADOR IS LED BY LUCRECIA BORGIA, A SORCERESS WHO IS THE DAUGHTER OF ALEXANDER VI, A POPE.

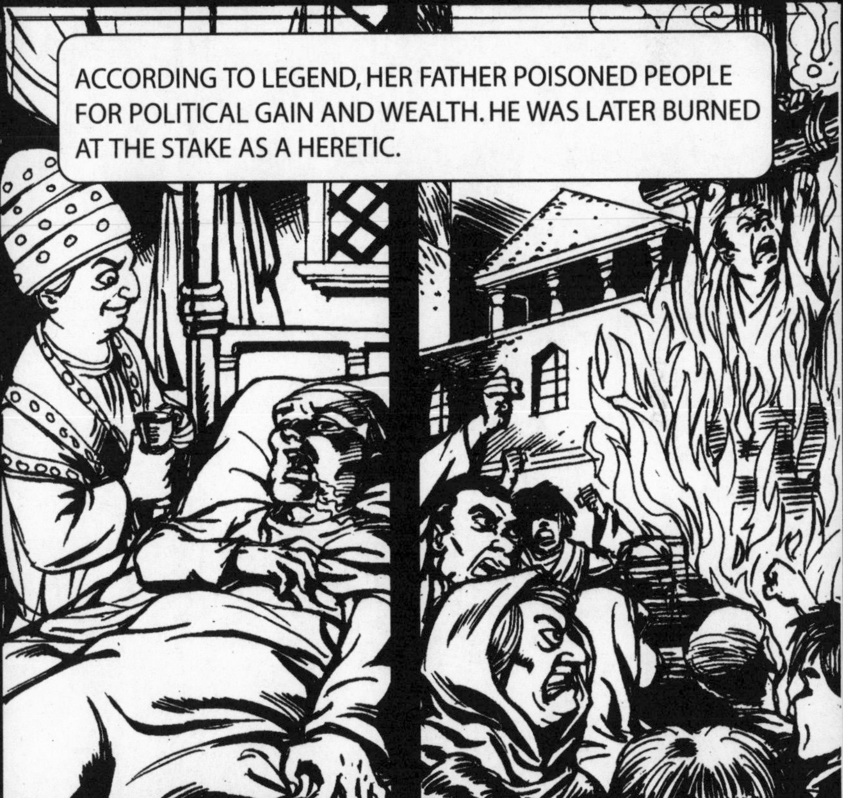
ACCORDING TO LEGEND, HER FATHER POISONED PEOPLE FOR POLITICAL GAIN AND WEALTH. HE WAS LATER BURNED AT THE STAKE AS A HERETIC.

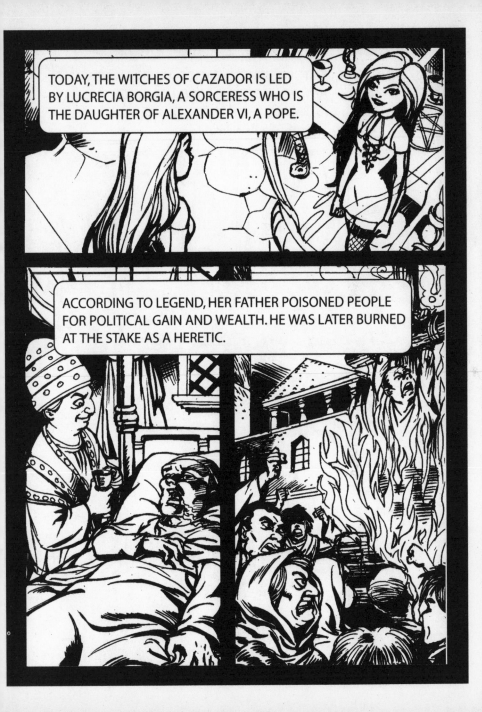

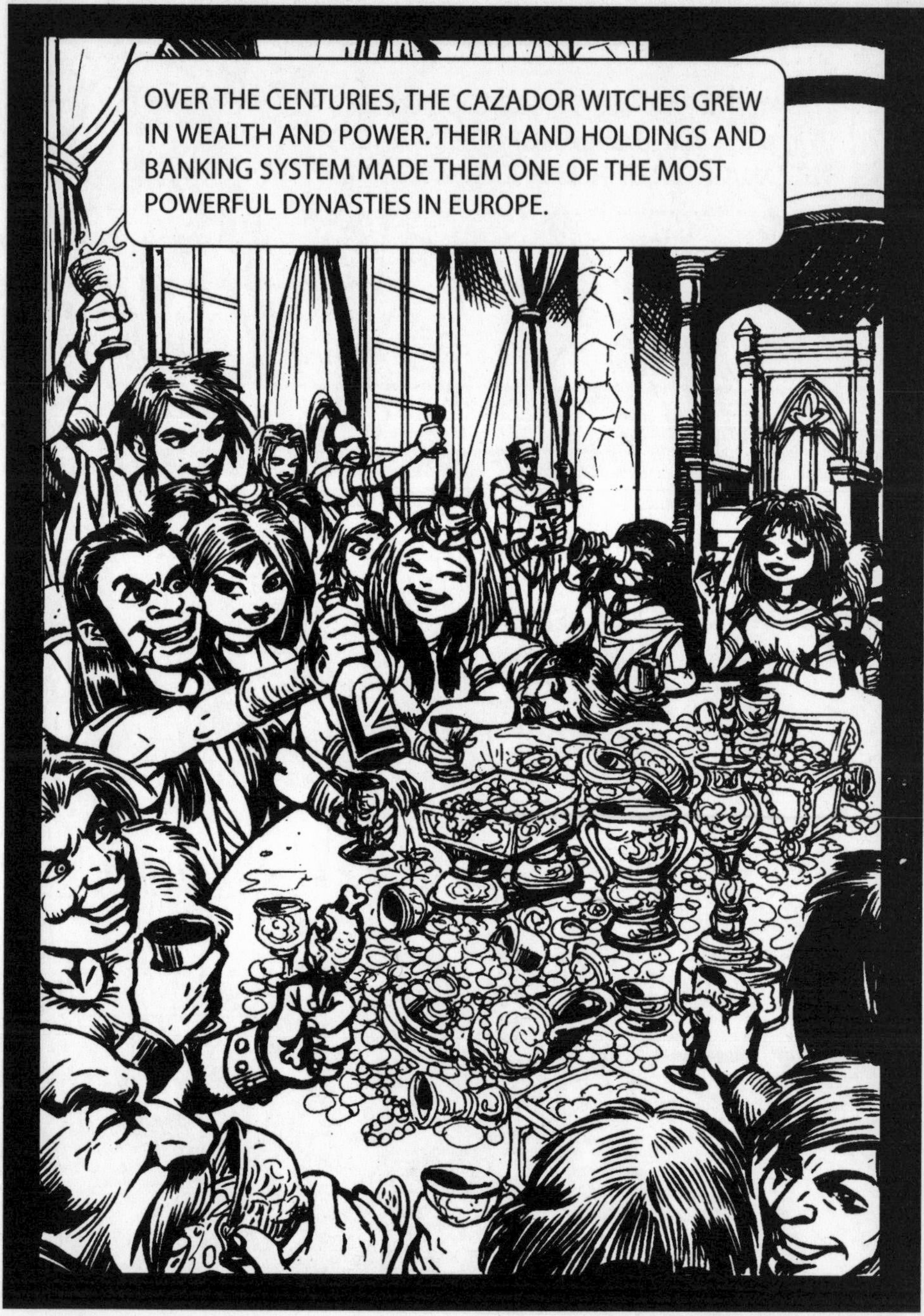
OVER THE CENTURIES, THE CAZADOR WITCHES GREW IN WEALTH AND POWER. THEIR LAND HOLDINGS AND BANKING SYSTEM MADE THEM ONE OF THE MOST POWERFUL DYNASTIES IN EUROPE.

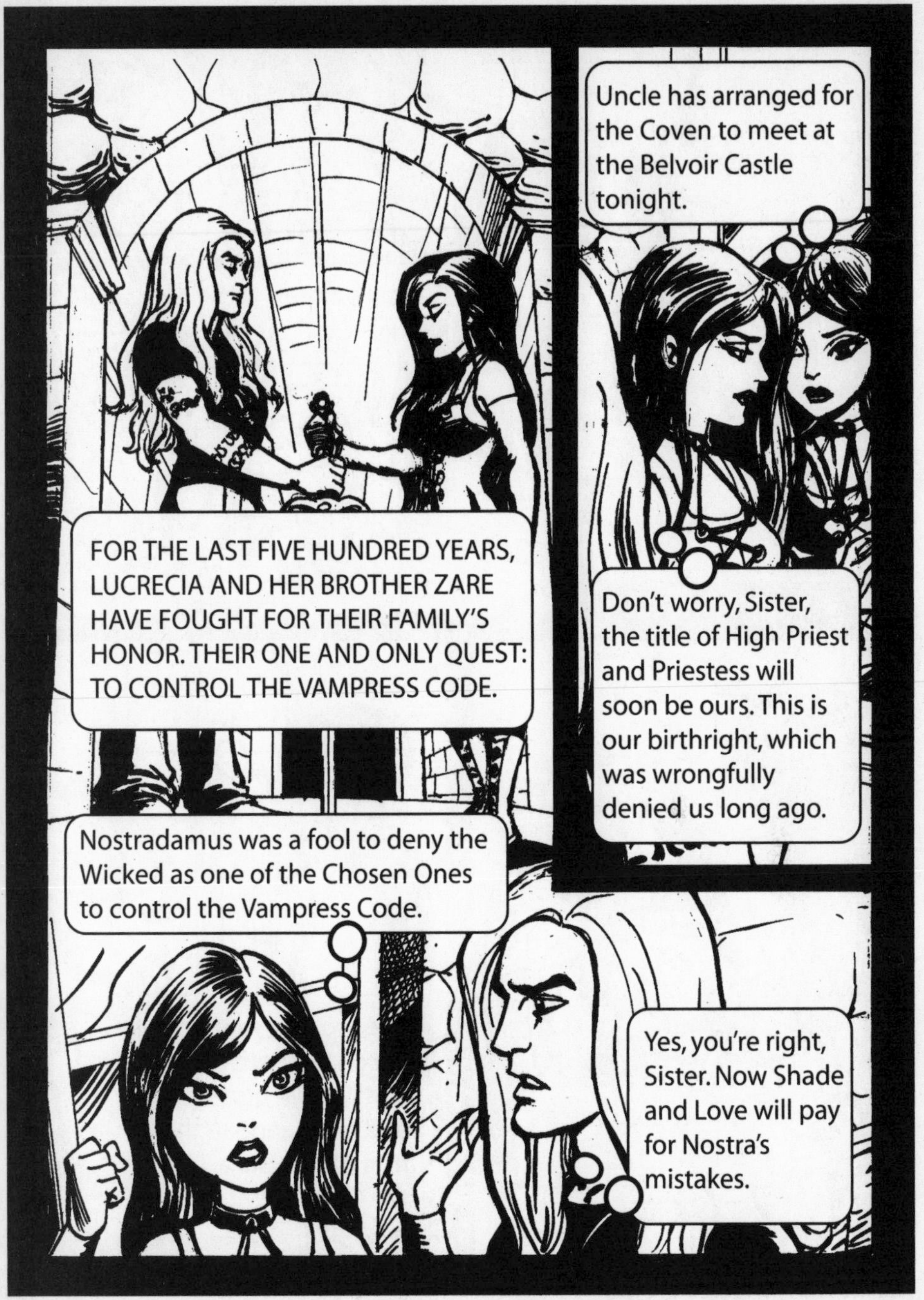
FOR THE LAST FIVE HUNDRED YEARS, LUCRECIA AND HER BROTHER ZARE HAVE FOUGHT FOR THEIR FAMILY'S HONOR. THEIR ONE AND ONLY QUEST: TO CONTROL THE VAMPRESS CODE.
Uncle has arranged for the Coven to meet at the Belvoir Castle tonight.
Don't worry, Sister, the title of High Priest and Priestess will soon be ours. This is our birthright, which was wrongfully denied us long ago.
Nostradamus was a fool to deny the Wicked as one of the Chosen Ones to control the Vampress Code.
Yes, you're right, Sister. Now Shade and Love will pay for Nostra's mistakes.

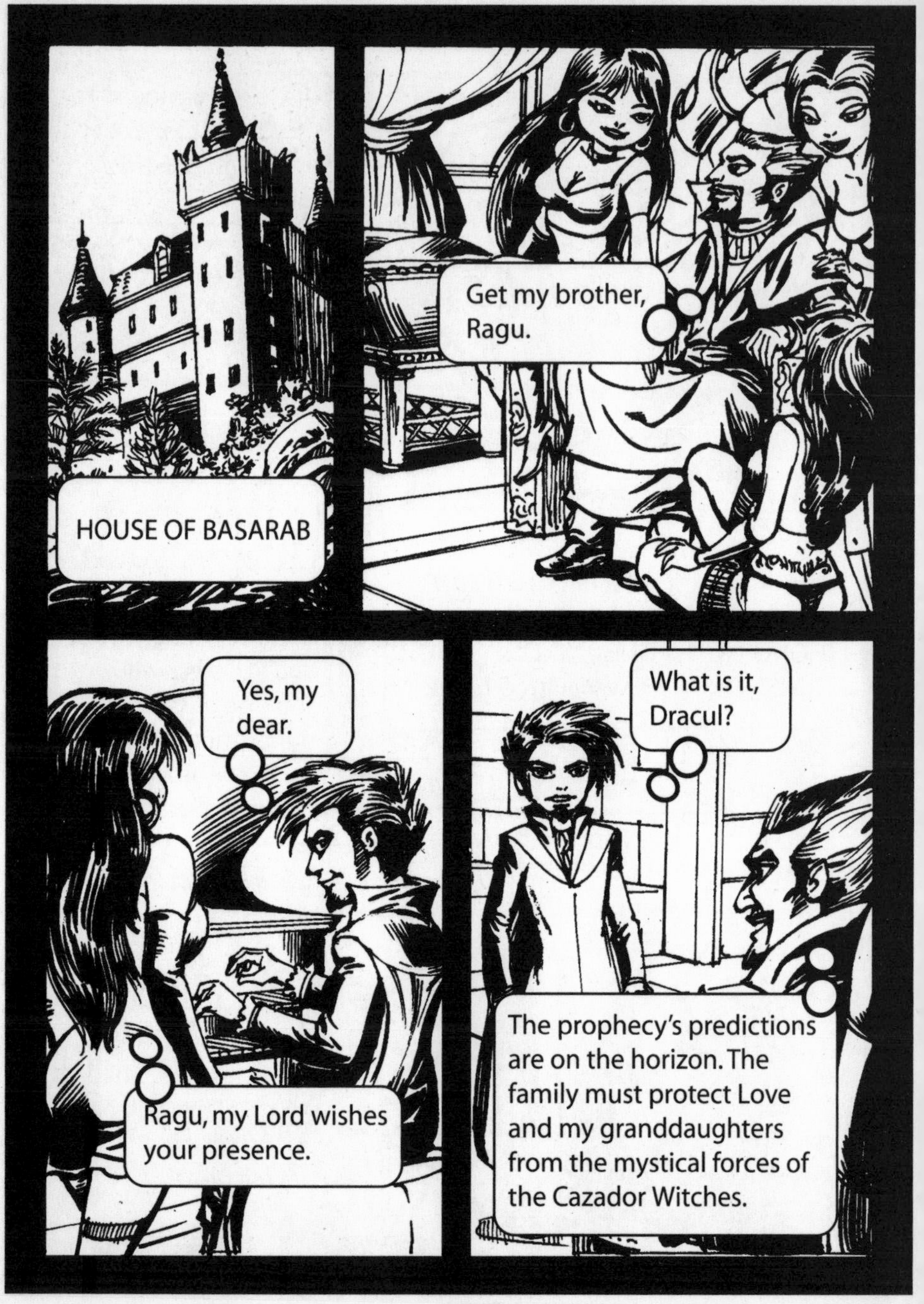
HOUSE OF BASARAB
Get my brother, Ragu.
Yes, my dear.
Ragu, my Lord wishes your presence.
What is it, Dracul?
The prophecy's predictions are on the horizon. The family must protect Love and my granddaughters from the mystical forces of the Cazador Witches.

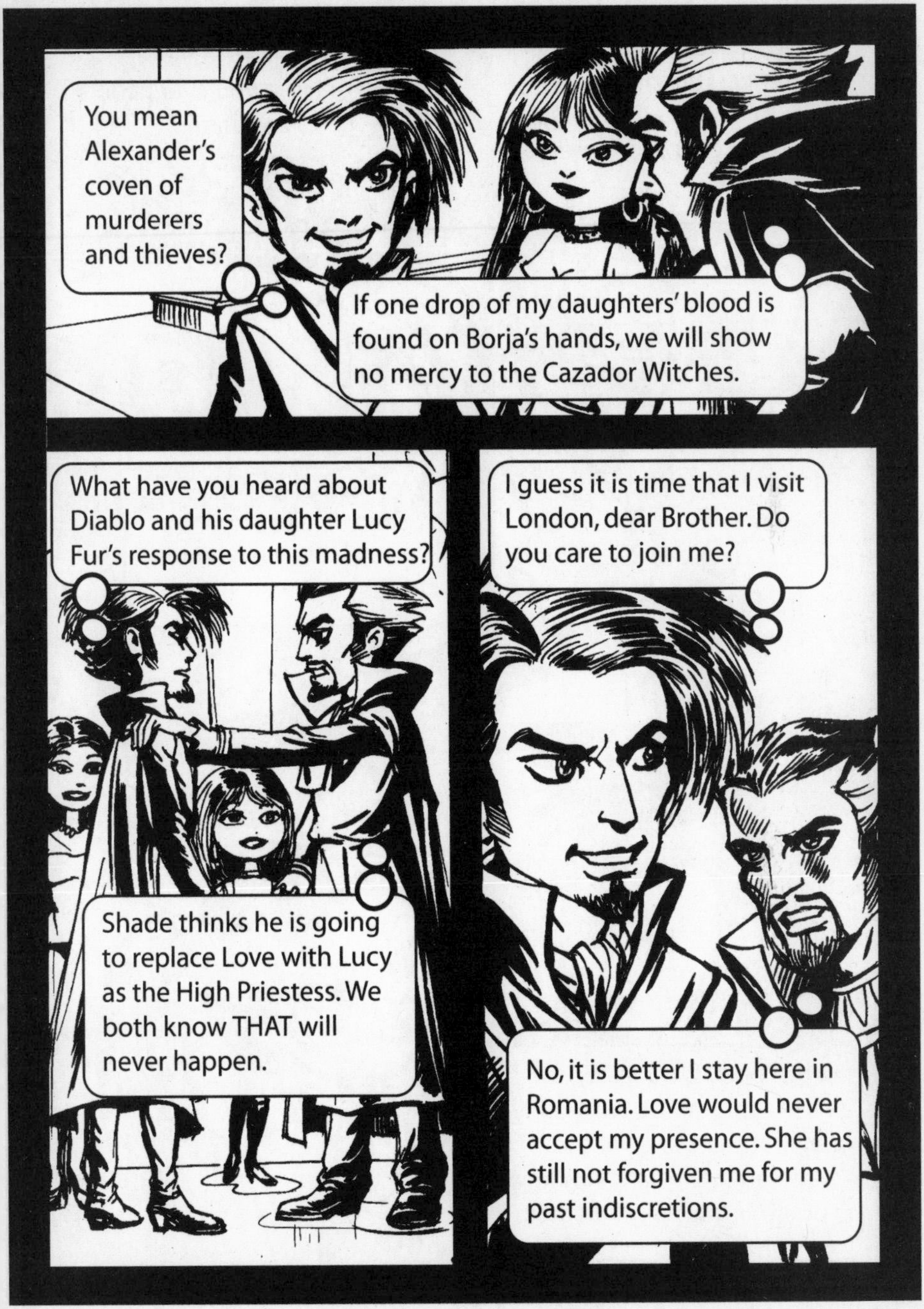
You mean Alexander's coven of murderers and thieves?
If one drop of my daughters' blood is found on Borja's hands, we will show no mercy to the Cazador Witches.
What have you heard about Diablo and his daughter Lucy Fur's response to this madness?
Shade thinks he is going to replace Love with Lucy as the High Priestess. We both know THAT will never happen.
I guess it is time that I visit London, dear Brother. Do you care to join me?
No, it is better I stay here in Romania. Love would never accept my presence. She has still not forgiven me for my past indiscretions.

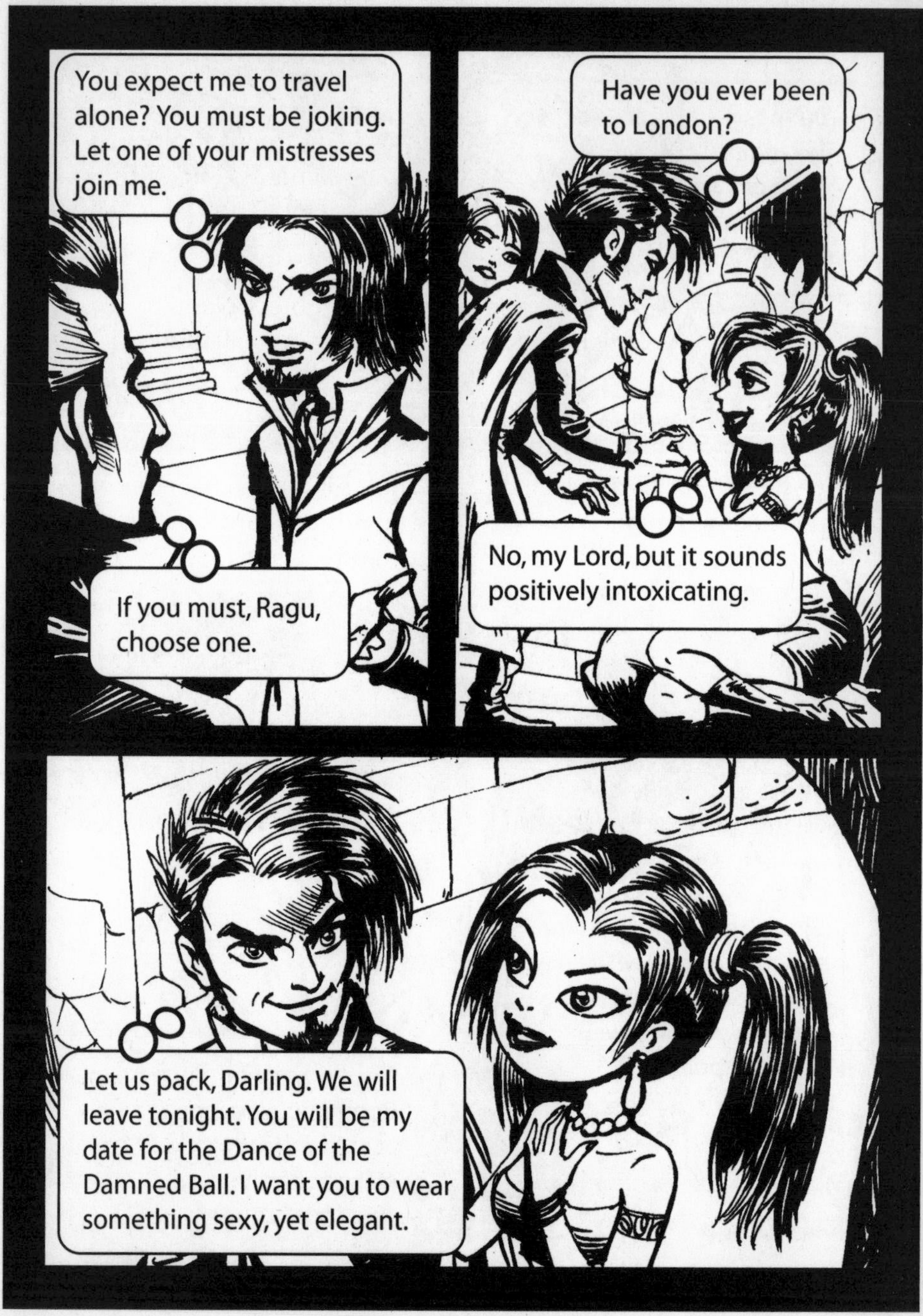
You expect me to travel alone? You must be joking. Let one of your mistresses join me.
If you must, Ragu, choose one.
Have you ever been to London?
No, my Lord, but it sounds positively intoxicating.
Let us pack, Darling. We will leave tonight. You will be my date for the Dance of the Damned Ball. I want you to wear something sexy, yet elegant.

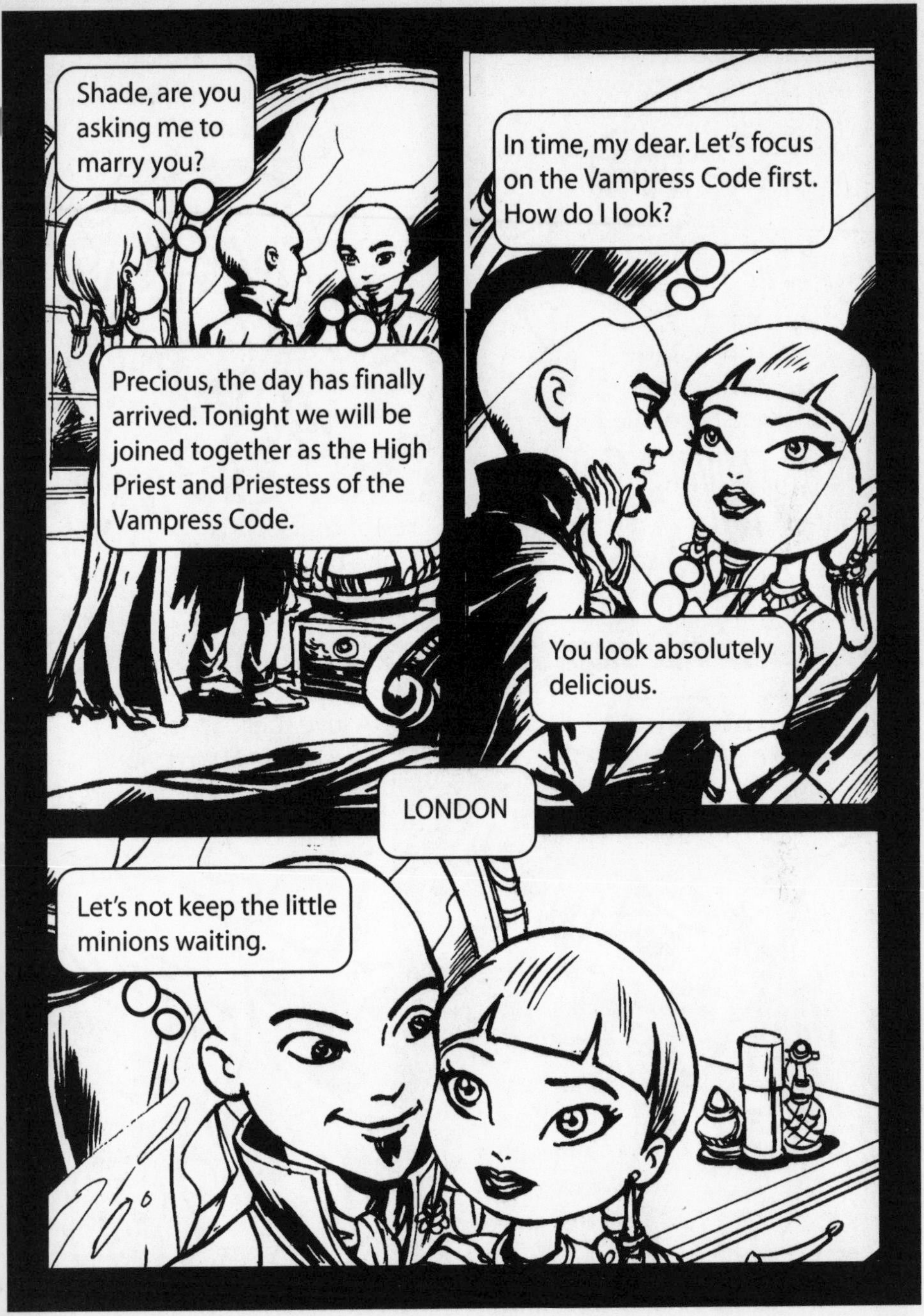
Shade, are you asking me to marry you?
Precious, the day has finally arrived. Tonight we will be joined together as the High Priest and Priestess of the Vampress Code.
In time, my dear. Let's focus on the Vampress Code first. How do I look?
You look absolutely delicious.
LONDON
Let's not keep the little minions waiting.

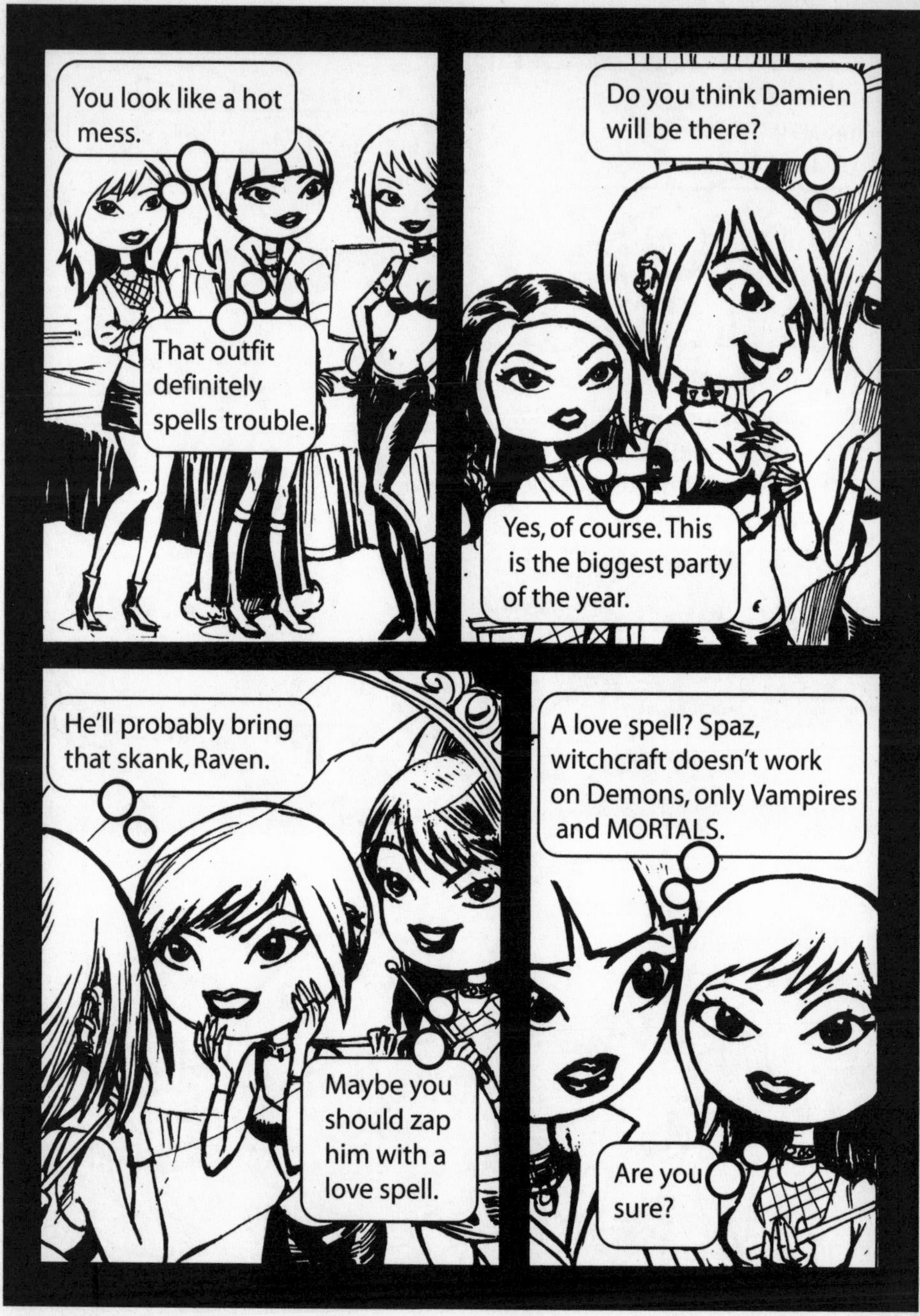
You look like a hot mess.
That outfit definitely spells trouble.
Do you think Damien will be there?
Yes, of course. This is the biggest party of the year.
He'll probably bring that skank, Raven.
Maybe you should zap him with a love spell.
A love spell? Spaz, witchcraft doesn't work on Demons, only Vampires and MORTALS.
Are you sure?

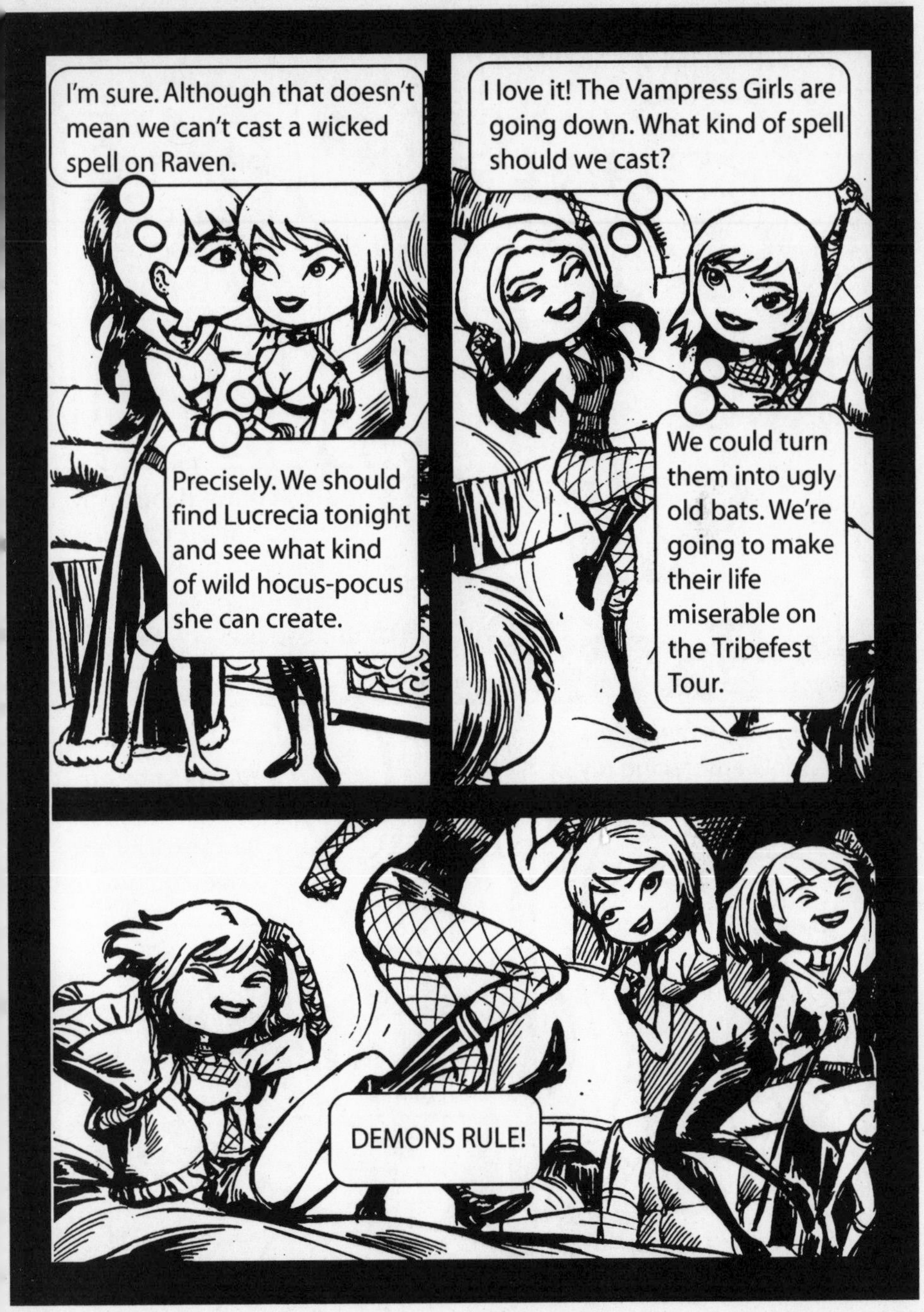
I'm sure. Although that doesn't mean we can't cast a wicked spell on Raven.
Precisely. We should find Lucrecia tonight and see what kind of wild hocus-pocus she can create.
I love it! The Vampress Girls are going down. What kind of spell should we cast?
We could turn them into ugly old bats. We're going to make their life miserable on the Tribefest Tour.
DEMONS RULE!

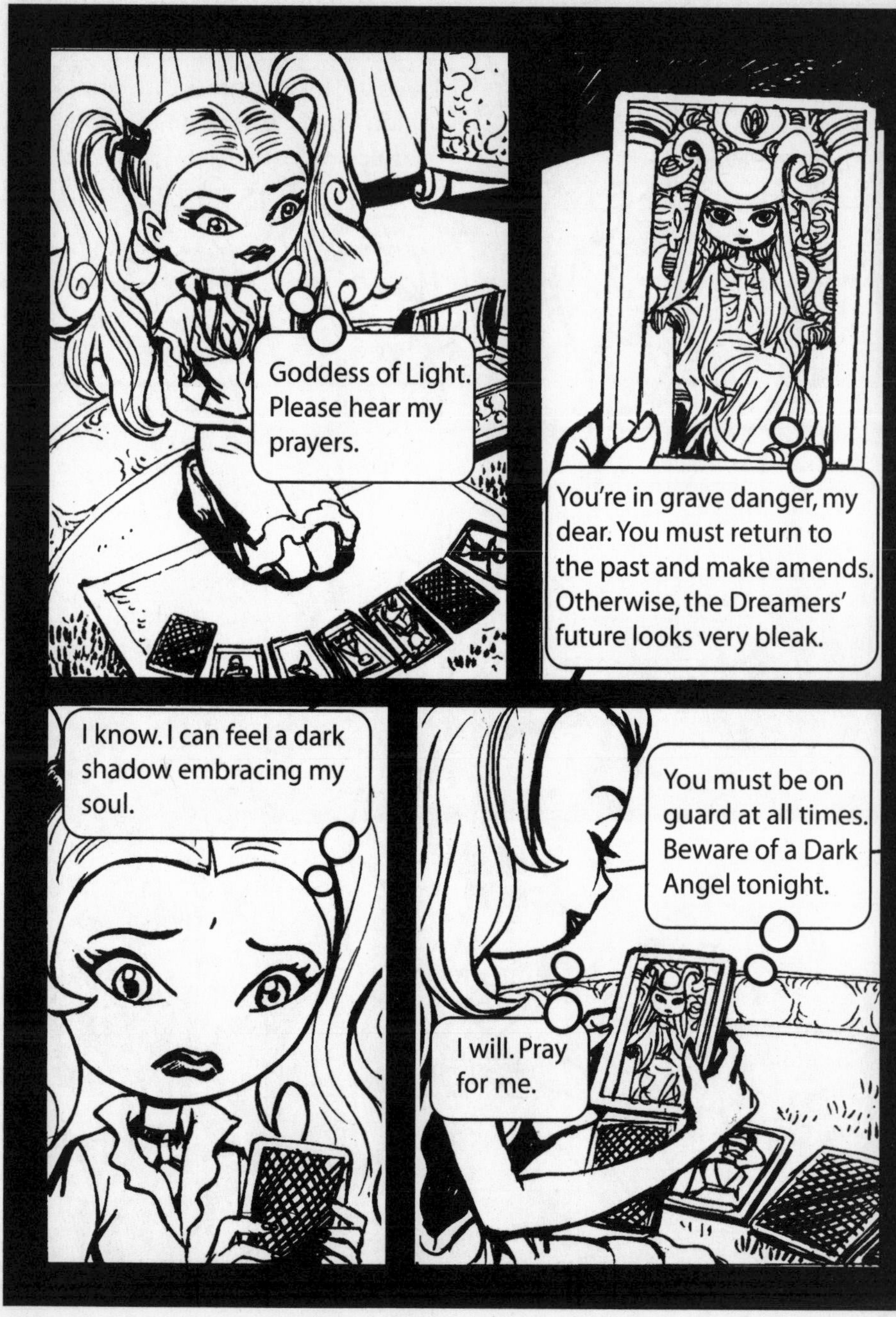
Goddess of Light. Please hear my prayers.
You're in grave danger, my dear. You must return to the past and make amends. Otherwise, the Dreamers' future looks very bleak.
I know. I can feel a dark shadow embracing my soul.
You must be on guard at all times. Beware of a Dark Angel tonight.
I will. Pray for me.

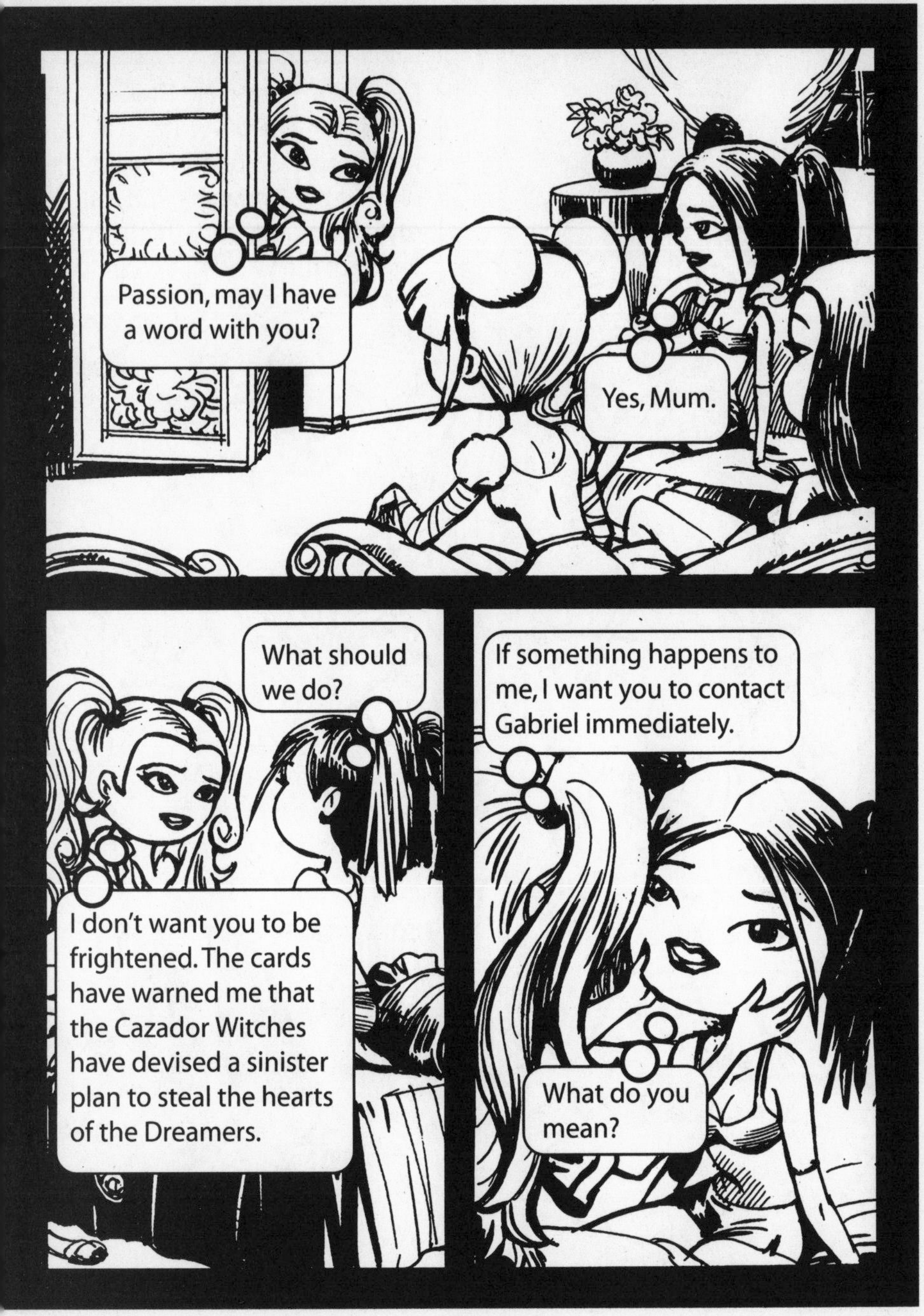
Passion, may I have a word with you?
Yes, Mum.
What should we do?
I don't want you to be frightened. The cards have warned me that the Cazador Witches have devised a sinister plan to steal the hearts of the Dreamers.
If something happens to me, I want you to contact Gabriel immediately.
What do you mean?

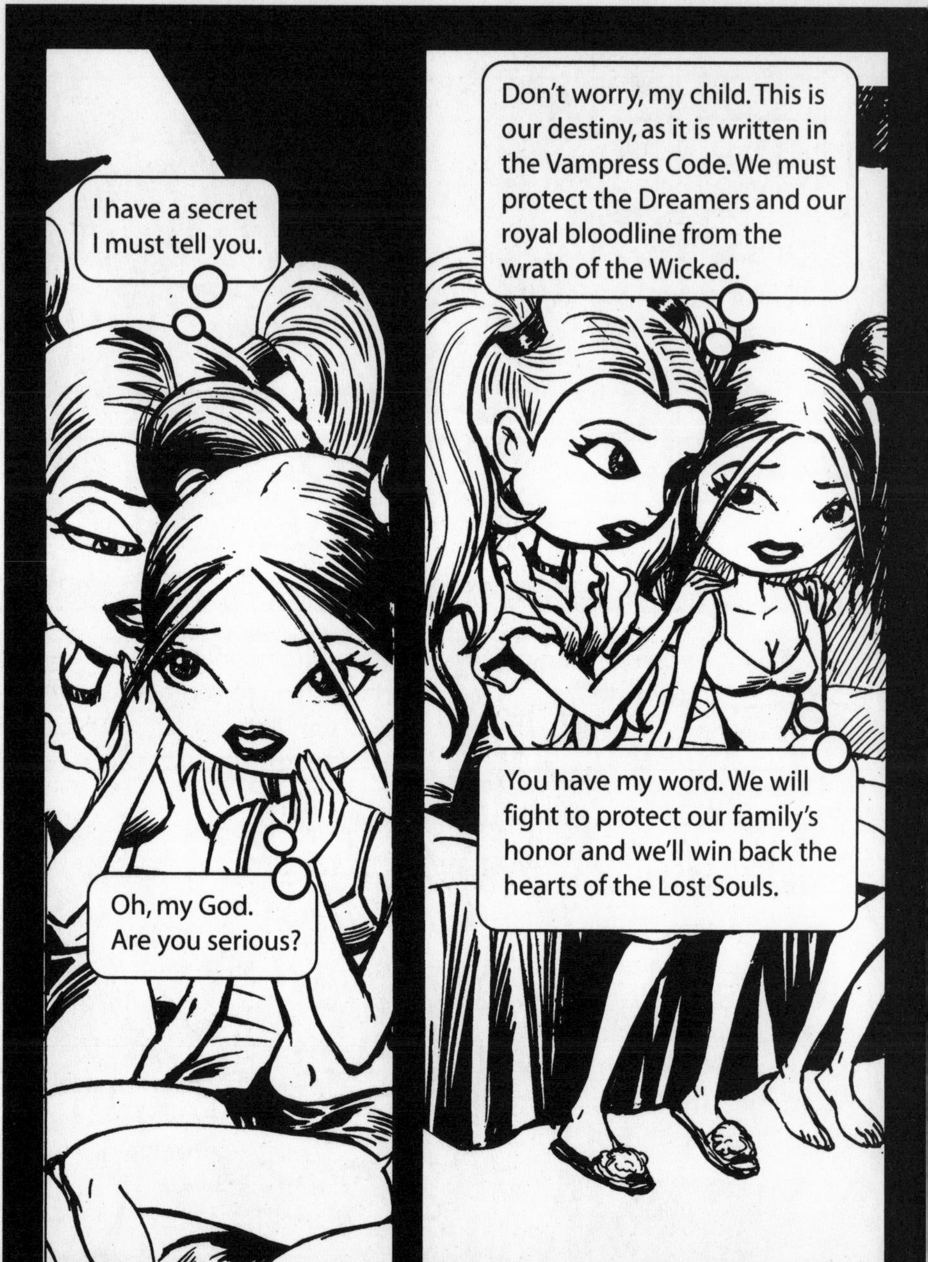
I have a secret I must tell you.
Oh, my God. Are you serious?
Don't worry, my child. This is our destiny, as it is written in the Vampress Code. We must protect the Dreamers and our royal bloodline from the wrath of the Wicked.
You have my word. We will fight to protect our family's honor and we'll win back the hearts of the Lost Souls.

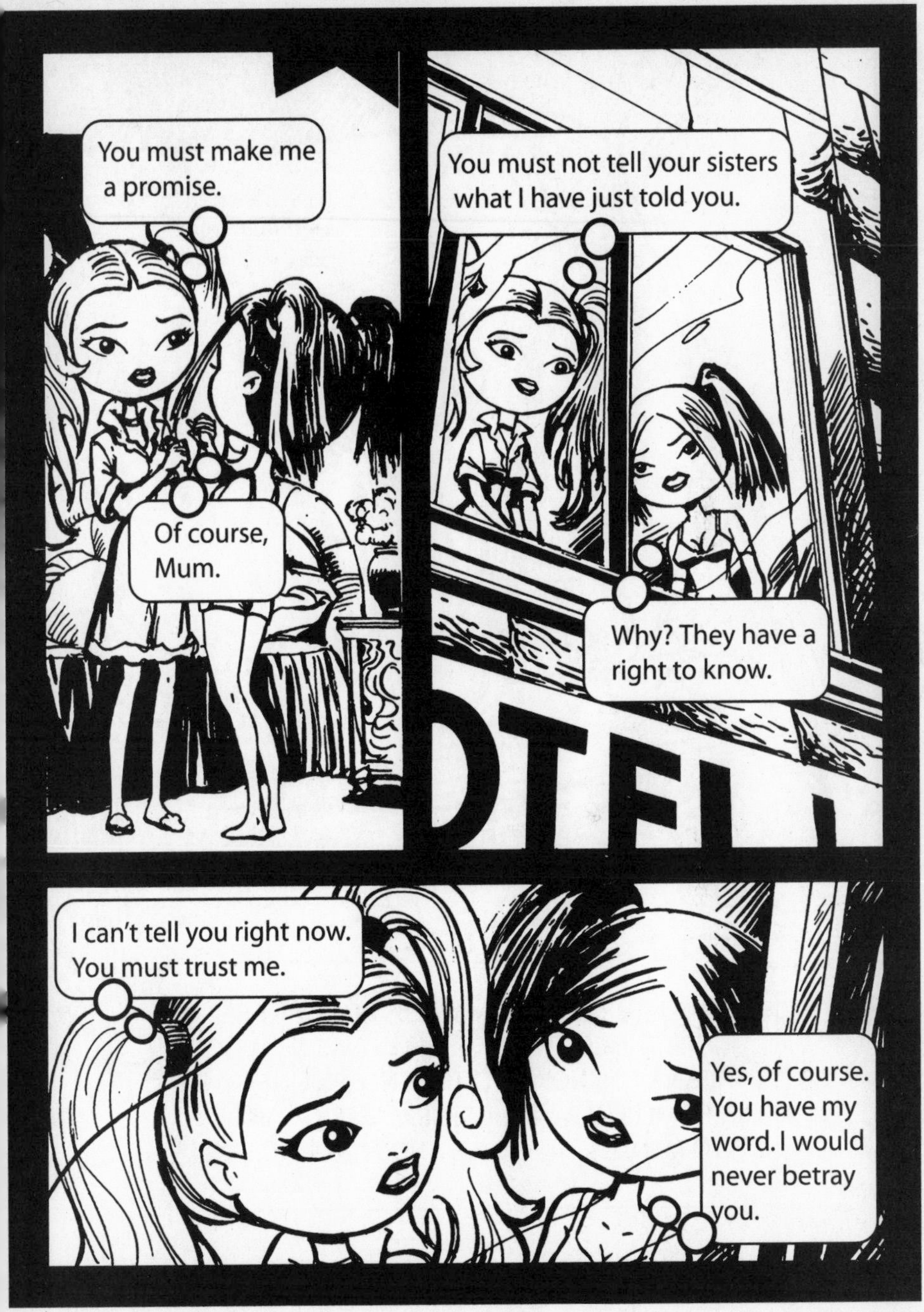
You must make me a promise.
Of course, Mum.
You must not tell your sisters what I have just told you.
Why? They have a right to know.
I can't tell you right now. You must trust me.
Yes, of course. You have my word. I would never betray you.

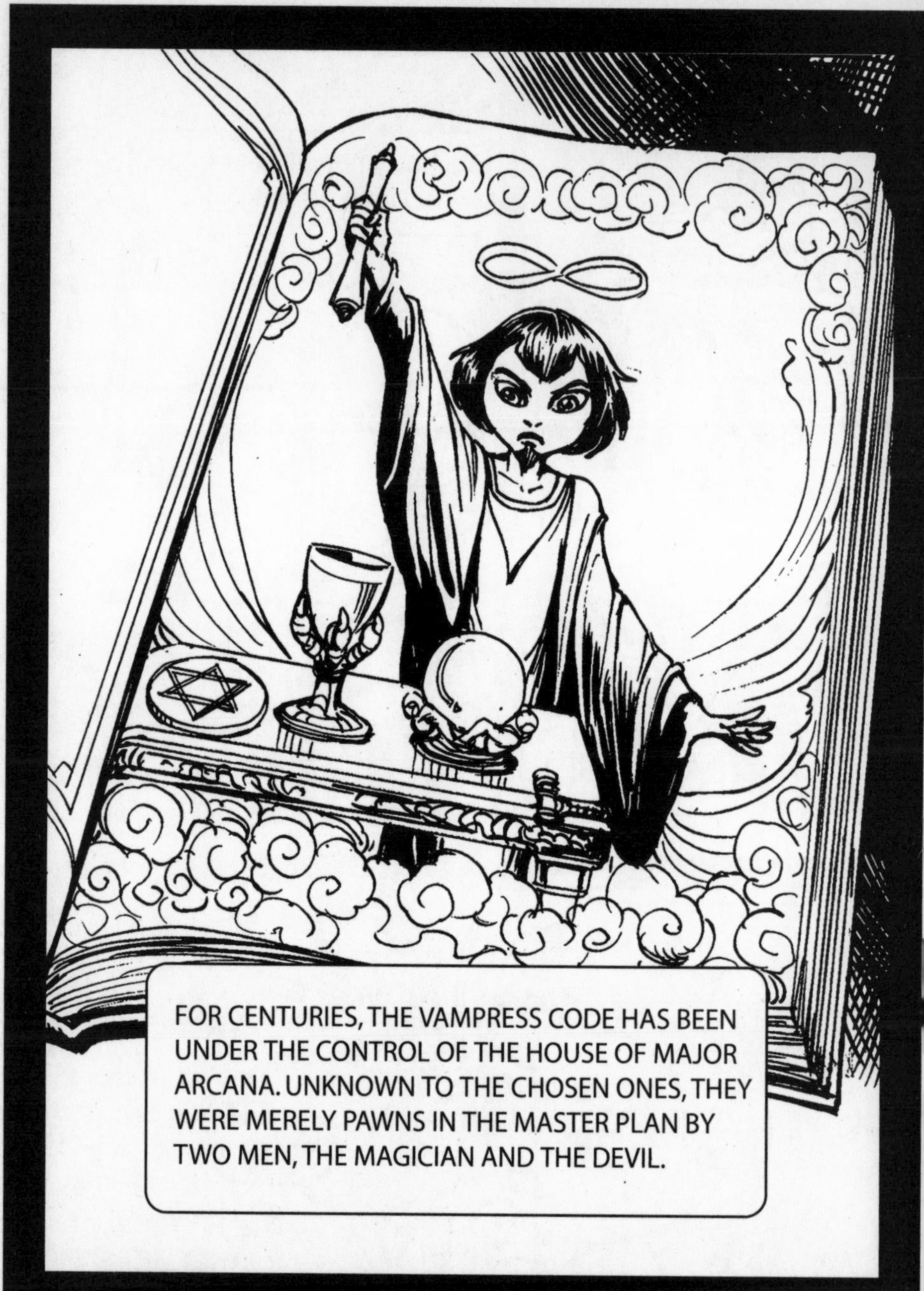
FOR CENTURIES, THE VAMPRESS CODE HAS BEEN UNDER THE CONTROL OF THE HOUSE OF MAJOR ARCANA. UNKNOWN TO THE CHOSEN ONES, THEY WERE MERELY PAWNS IN THE MASTER PLAN BY TWO MEN, THE MAGICIAN AND THE DEVIL.

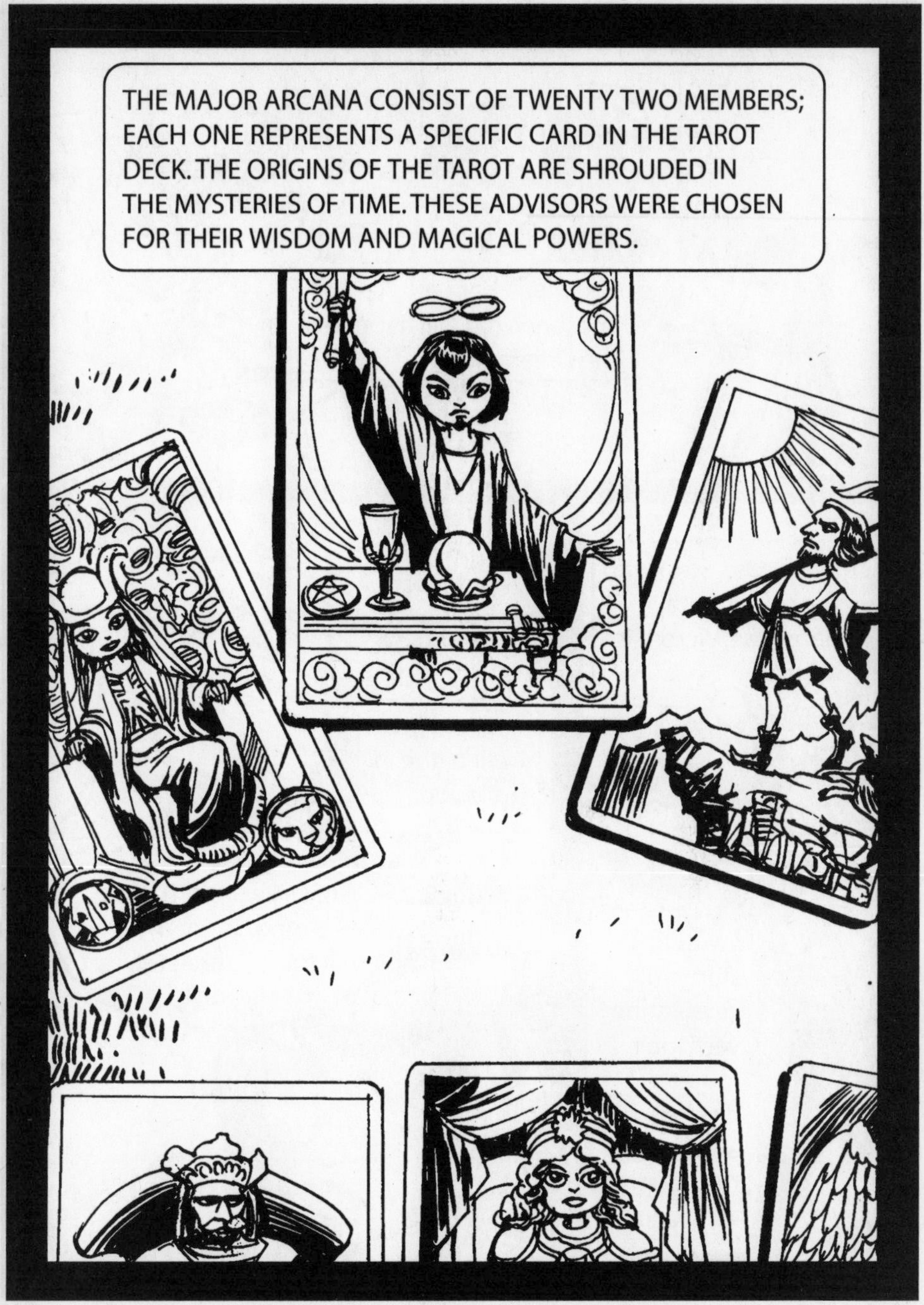
THE MAJOR ARCANA CONSIST OF TWENTY TWO MEMBERS; EACH ONE REPRESENTS A SPECIFIC CARD IN THE TAROT DECK. THE ORIGINS OF THE TAROT ARE SHROUDED IN THE MYSTERIES OF TIME. THESE ADVISORS WERE CHOSEN FOR THEIR WISDOM AND MAGICAL POWERS.

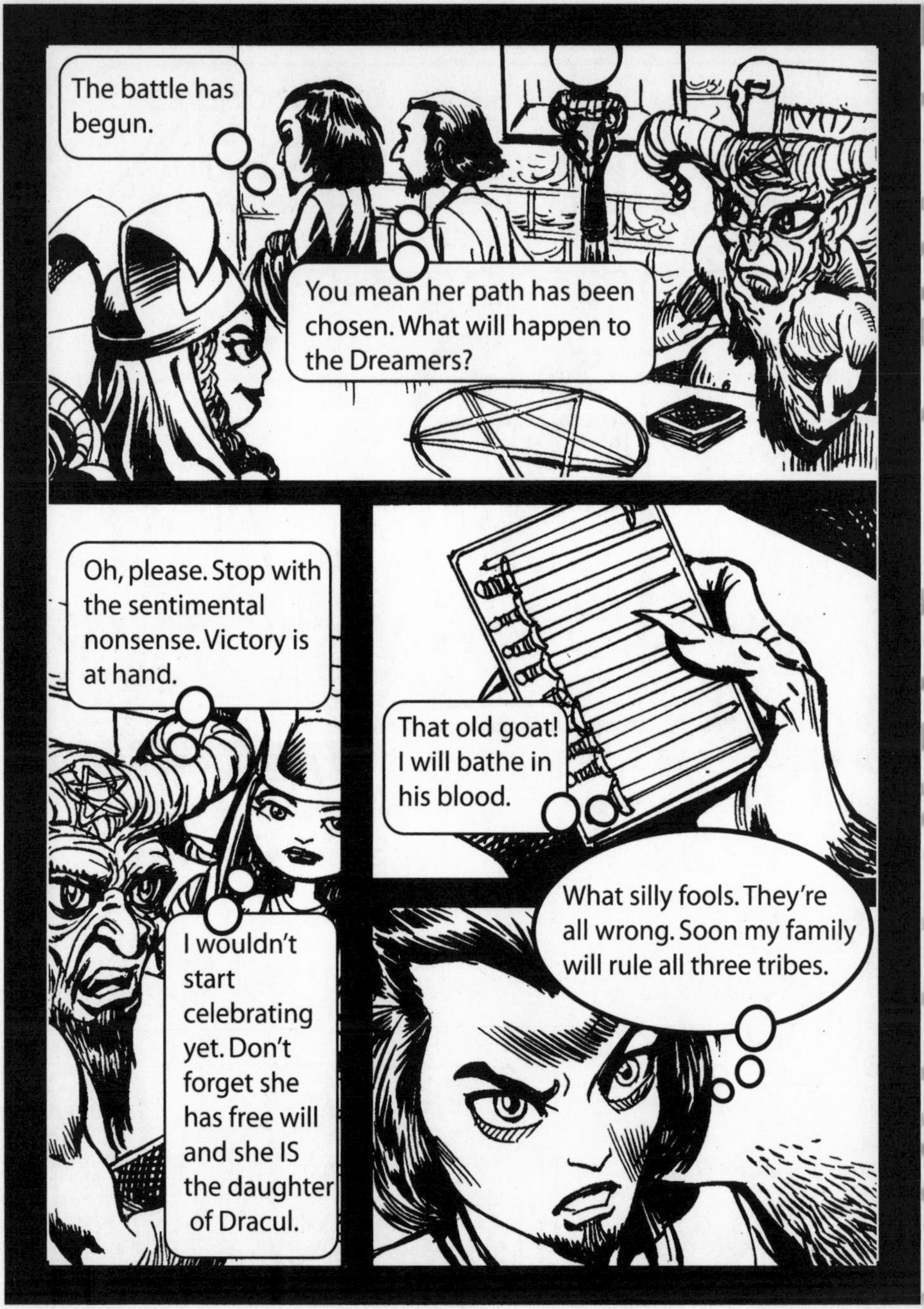
The battle has begun.
You mean her path has been chosen. What will happen to the Dreamers?
Oh, please. Stop with the sentimental nonsense. Victory is at hand.
I wouldn't start celebrating yet. Don't forget she has free will and she IS the daughter of Dracul.
That old goat! I will bathe in his blood.
What silly fools. They're all wrong. Soon my family will rule all three tribes.

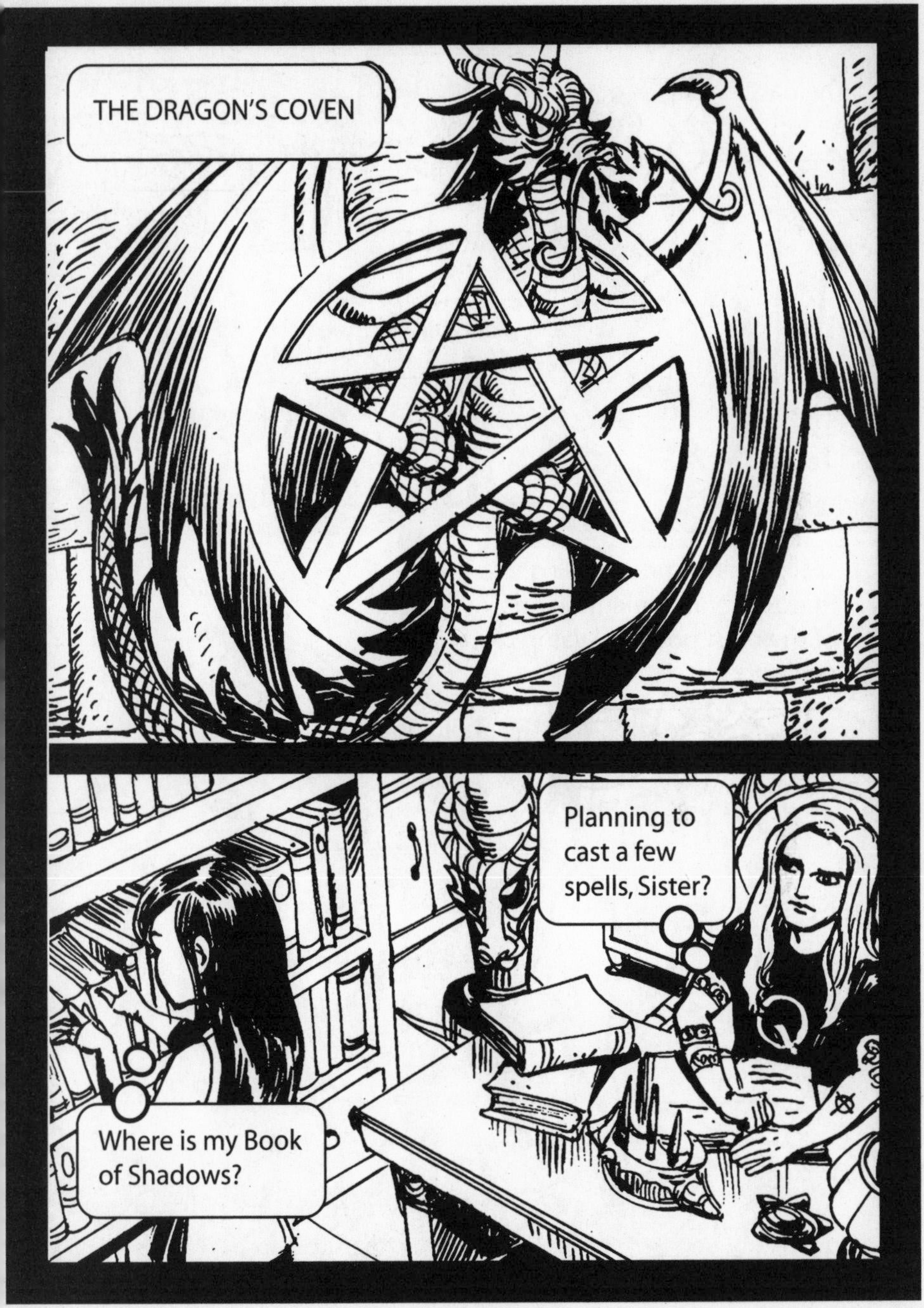
THE DRAGON'S COVEN
Where is my Book of Shadows?
Planning to cast a few spells, Sister?

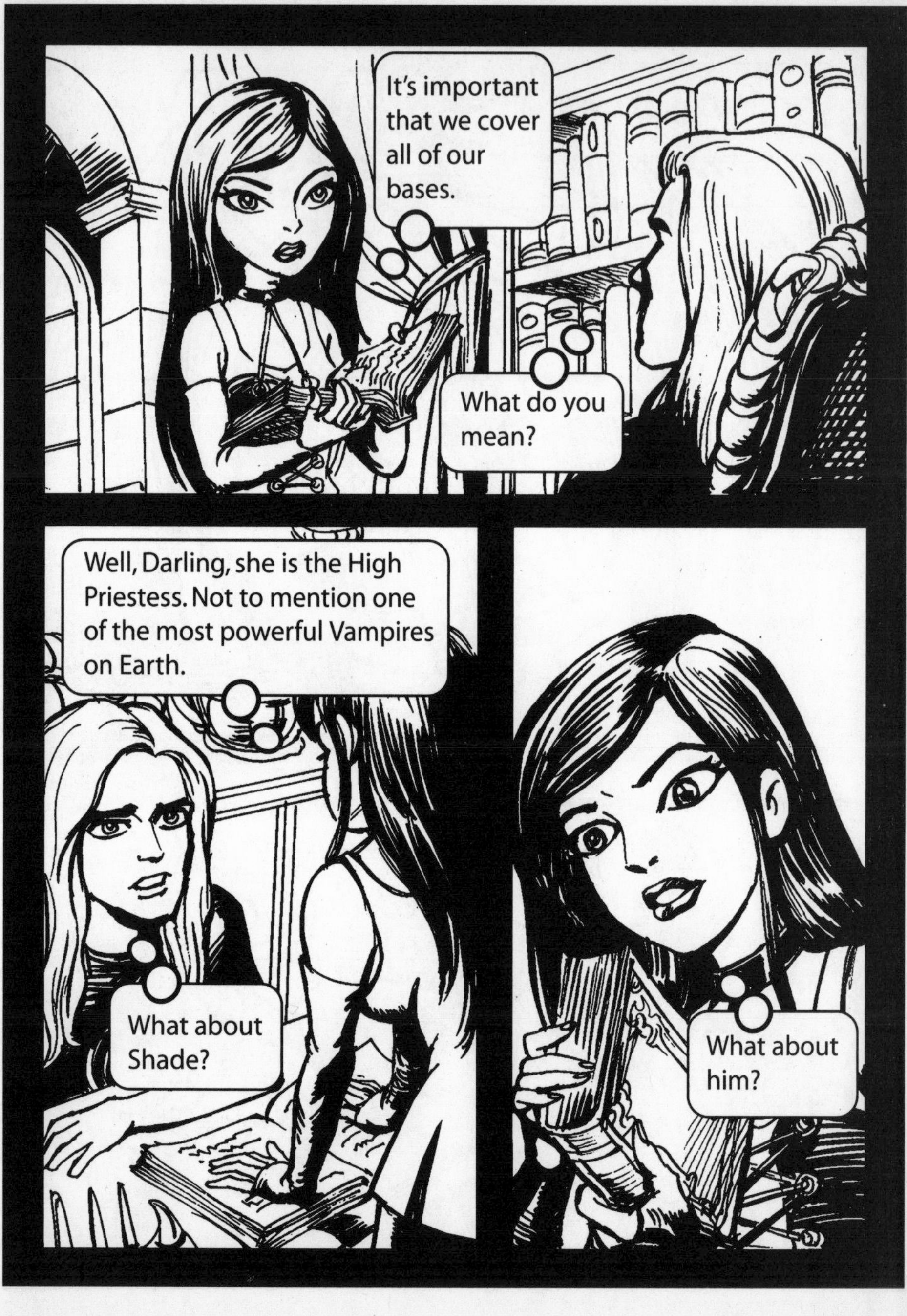
It's important that we cover all of our bases.
What do you mean?
Well, Darling, she is the High Priestess. Not to mention one of the most powerful Vampires on Earth.
What about Shade?
What about him?

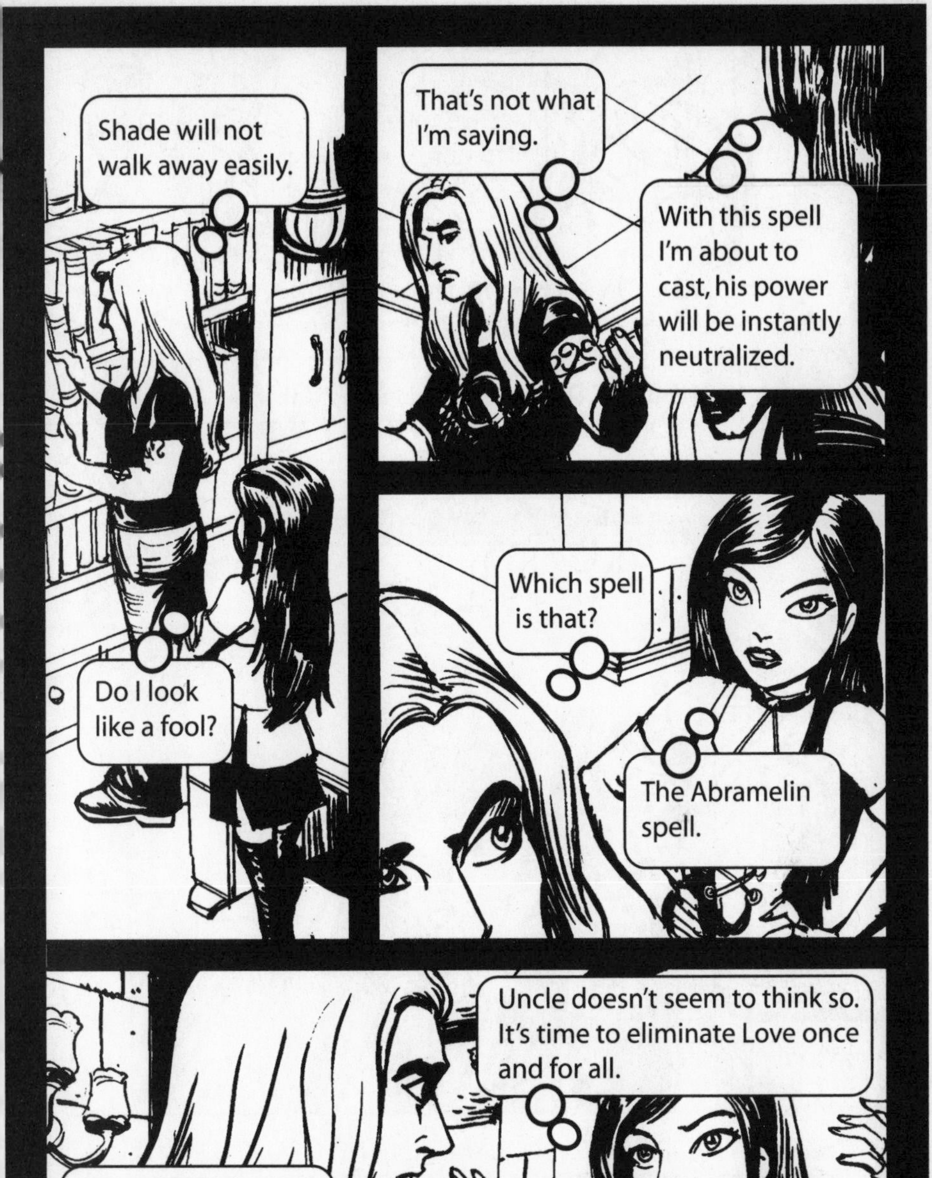
Shade will not walk away easily.
Do I look like a fool?
That's not what I'm saying.
With this spell I'm about to cast, his power will be instantly neutralized.
Which spell is that?
The Abramelin spell.
Are you serious? Isn't that a bit drastic?
Uncle doesn't seem to think so. It's time to eliminate Love once and for all.

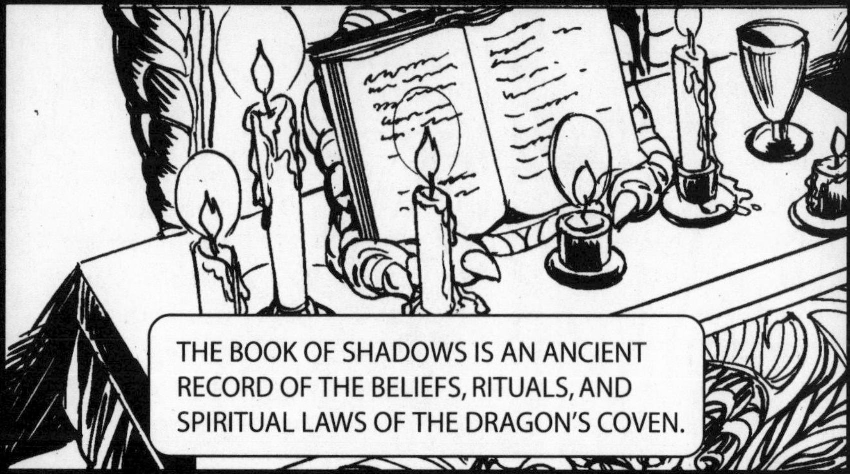
THE BOOK OF SHADOWS IS AN ANCIENT RECORD OF THE BELIEFS, RITUALS, AND SPIRITUAL LAWS OF THE DRAGON'S COVEN.
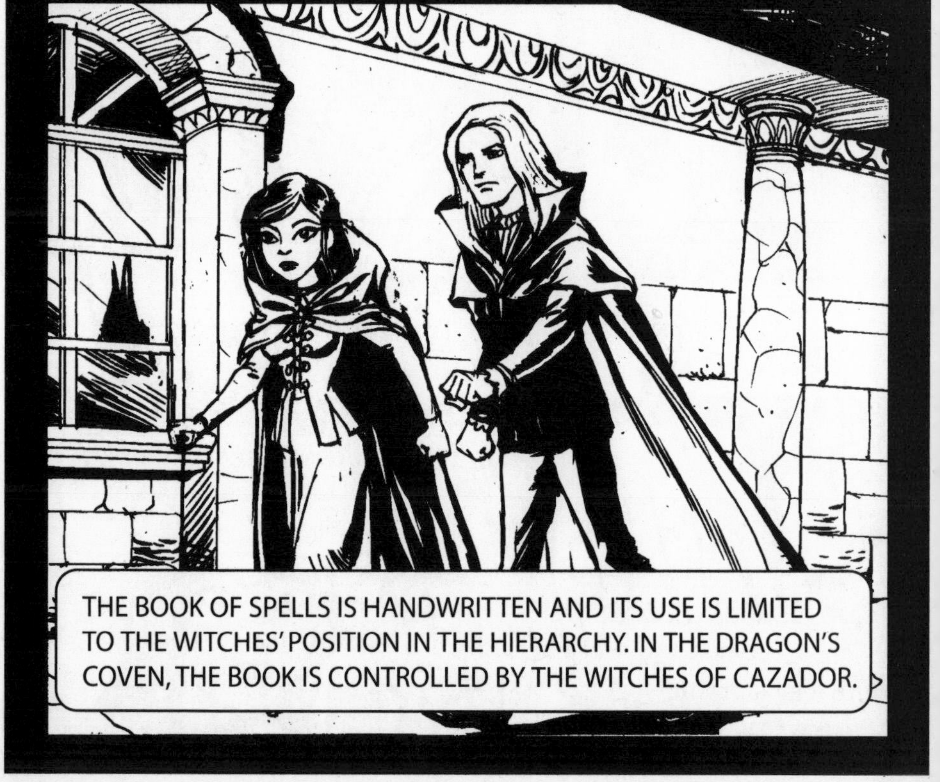
THE BOOK OF SPELLS IS HANDWRITTEN AND ITS USE IS LIMITED TO THE WITCHES' POSITION IN THE HIERARCHY. IN THE DRAGON'S COVEN, THE BOOK IS CONTROLLED BY THE WITCHES OF CAZADOR.

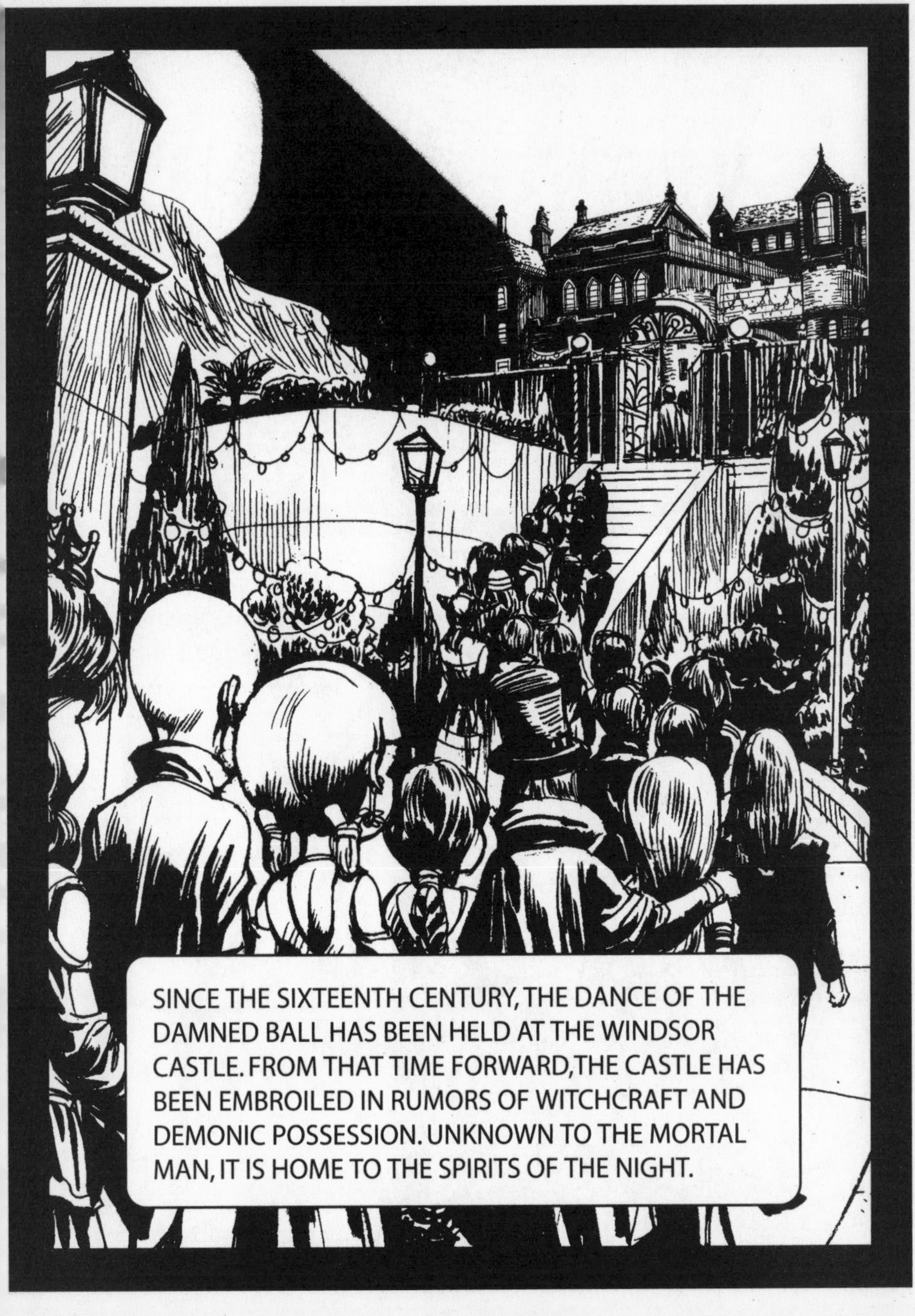
SINCE THE SIXTEENTH CENTURY, THE DANCE OF THE DAMNED BALL HAS BEEN HELD AT THE WINDSOR CASTLE. FROM THAT TIME FORWARD,THE CASTLE HAS BEEN EMBROILED IN RUMORS OF WITCHCRAFT AND DEMONIC POSSESSION. UNKNOWN TO THE MORTAL MAN, IT IS HOME TO THE SPIRITS OF THE NIGHT.

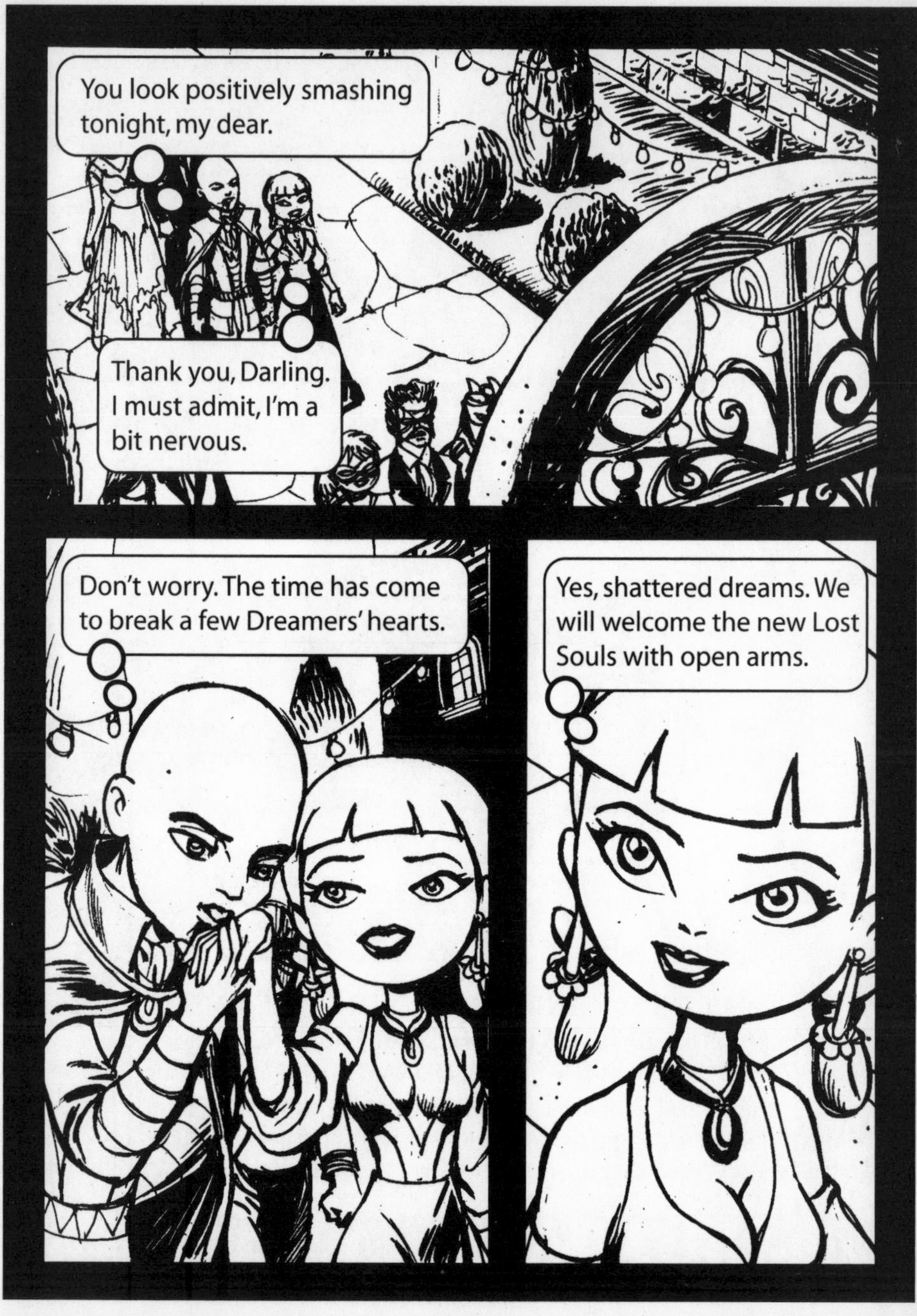
You look positively smashing tonight, my dear.
Thank you, Darling. I must admit, I'm a bit nervous.
Don't worry. The time has come to break a few Dreamers' hearts.
Yes, shattered dreams. We will welcome the new Lost Souls with open arms.

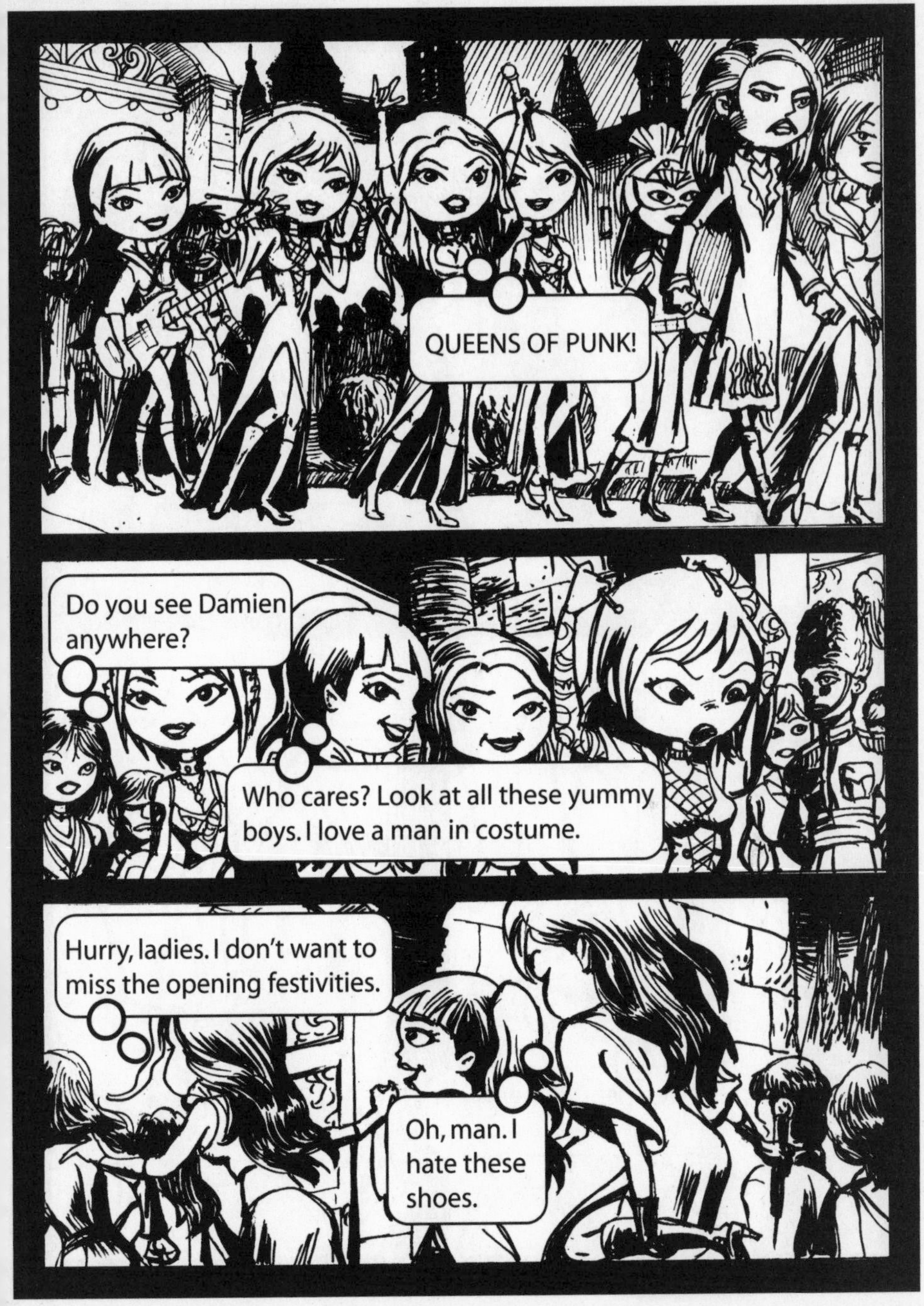
QUEENS OF PUNK!
Do you see Damien anywhere?
Who cares? Look at all these yummy boys. I love a man in costume.
Hurry, ladies. I don't want to miss the opening festivities.
Oh, man. I hate these shoes.

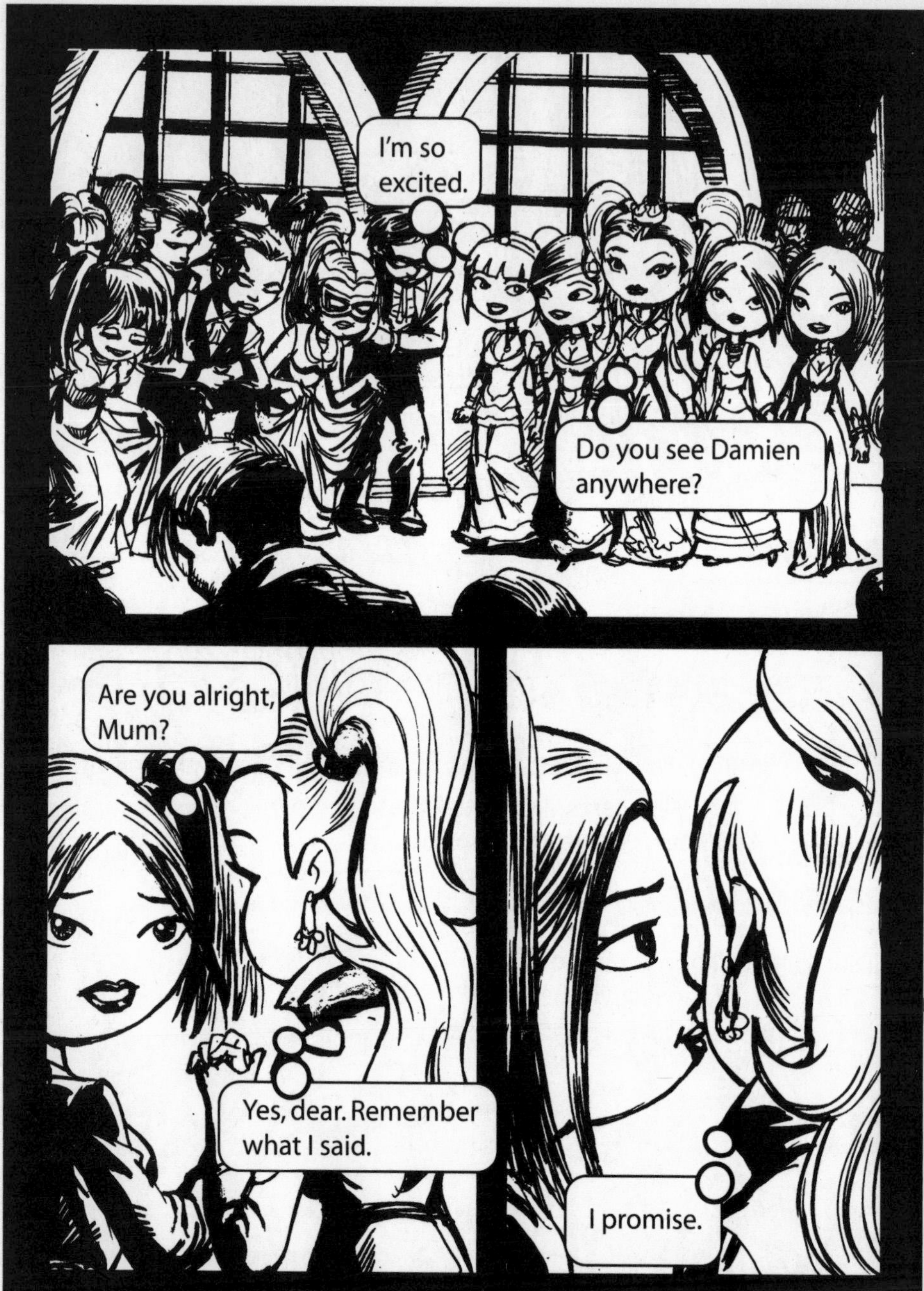
I'm so excited.
Do you see Damien anywhere?
Are you alright, Mum?
Yes, dear. Remember what I said.
I promise.

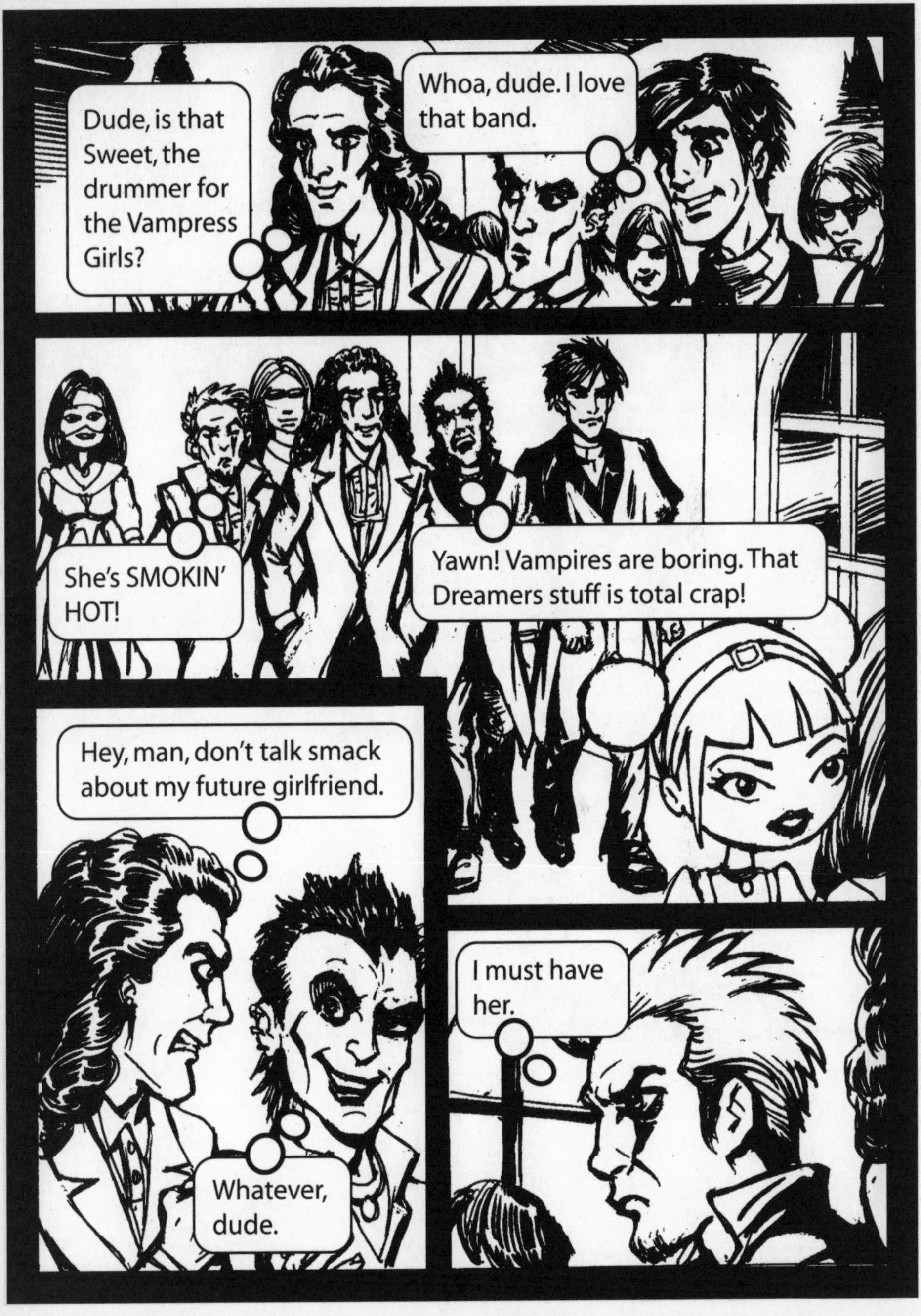
Dude, is that Sweet, the drummer for the Vampress Girls?
Whoa, dude. I love that band.
She's SMOKIN' HOT!
Yawn! Vampires are boring. That Dreamers stuff is total crap!
Hey, man, don't talk smack about my future girlfriend.
Whatever, dude.
I must have her.

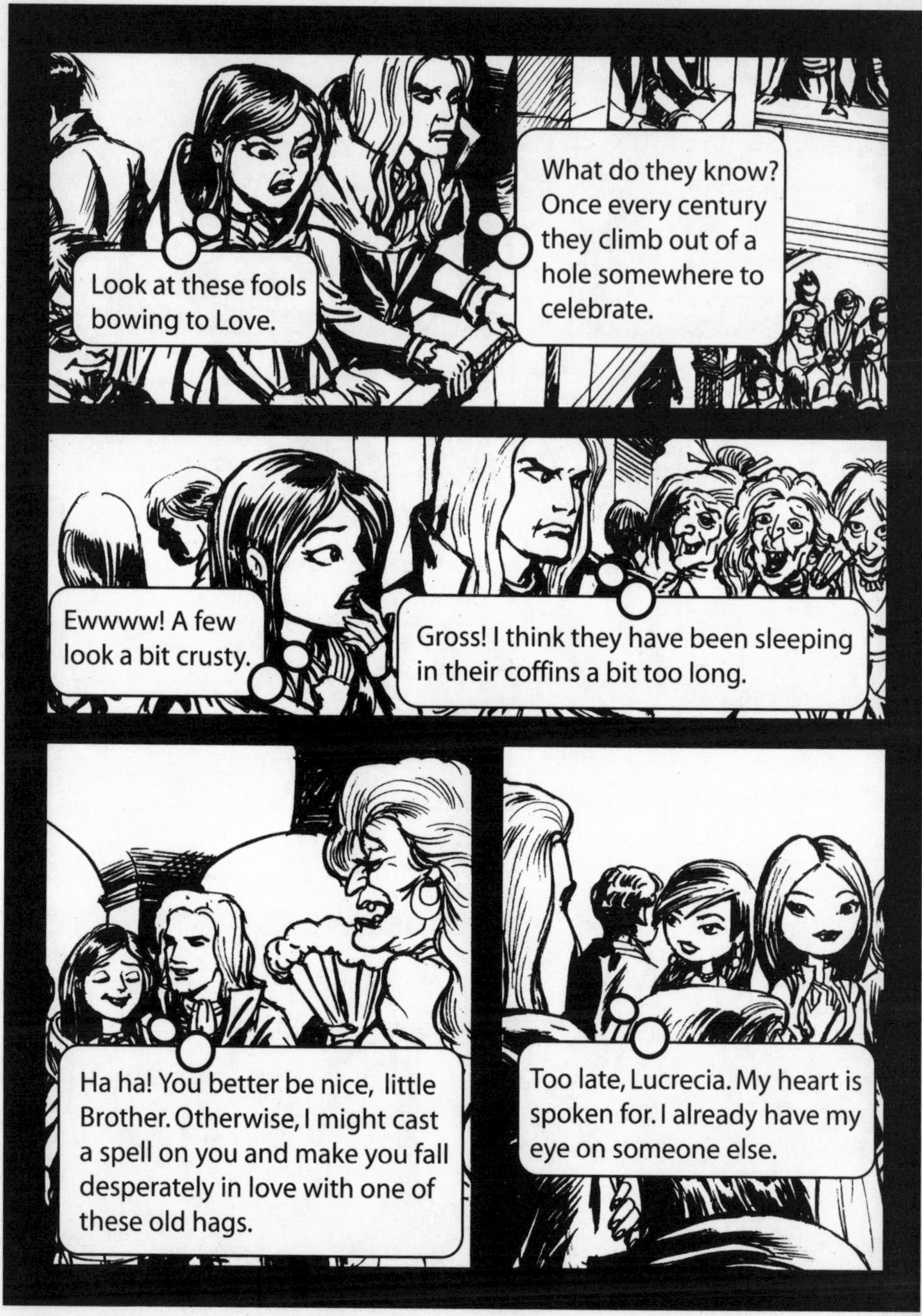
Look at these fools bowing to Love.
What do they know? Once every century they climb out of a hole somewhere to celebrate.
Ewwww! A few look a bit crusty.
Gross! I think they have been sleeping in their coffins a bit too long.
Ha ha! You better be nice, little Brother. Otherwise, I might cast a spell on you and make you fall desperately in love with one of these old hags.
Too late, Lucrecia. My heart is spoken for. I already have my eye on someone else.

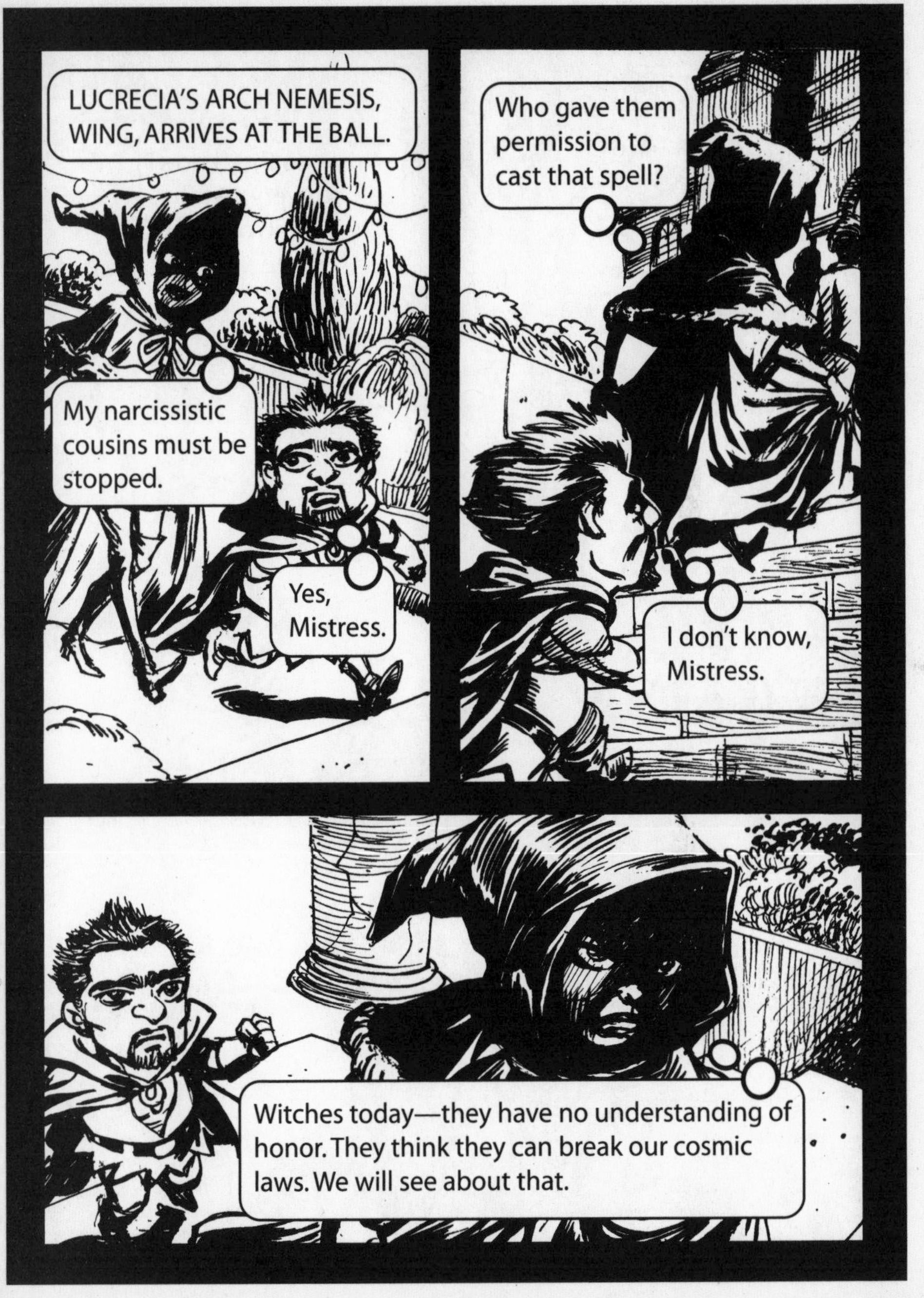
LUCRECIA'S ARCH NEMESIS, WING, ARRIVES AT THE BALL.
My narcissistic cousins must be stopped.
Yes, Mistress.
Who gave them permission to cast that spell?
I don't know, Mistress.
Witches today—they have no understanding of honor. They think they can break our cosmic laws. We will see about that.

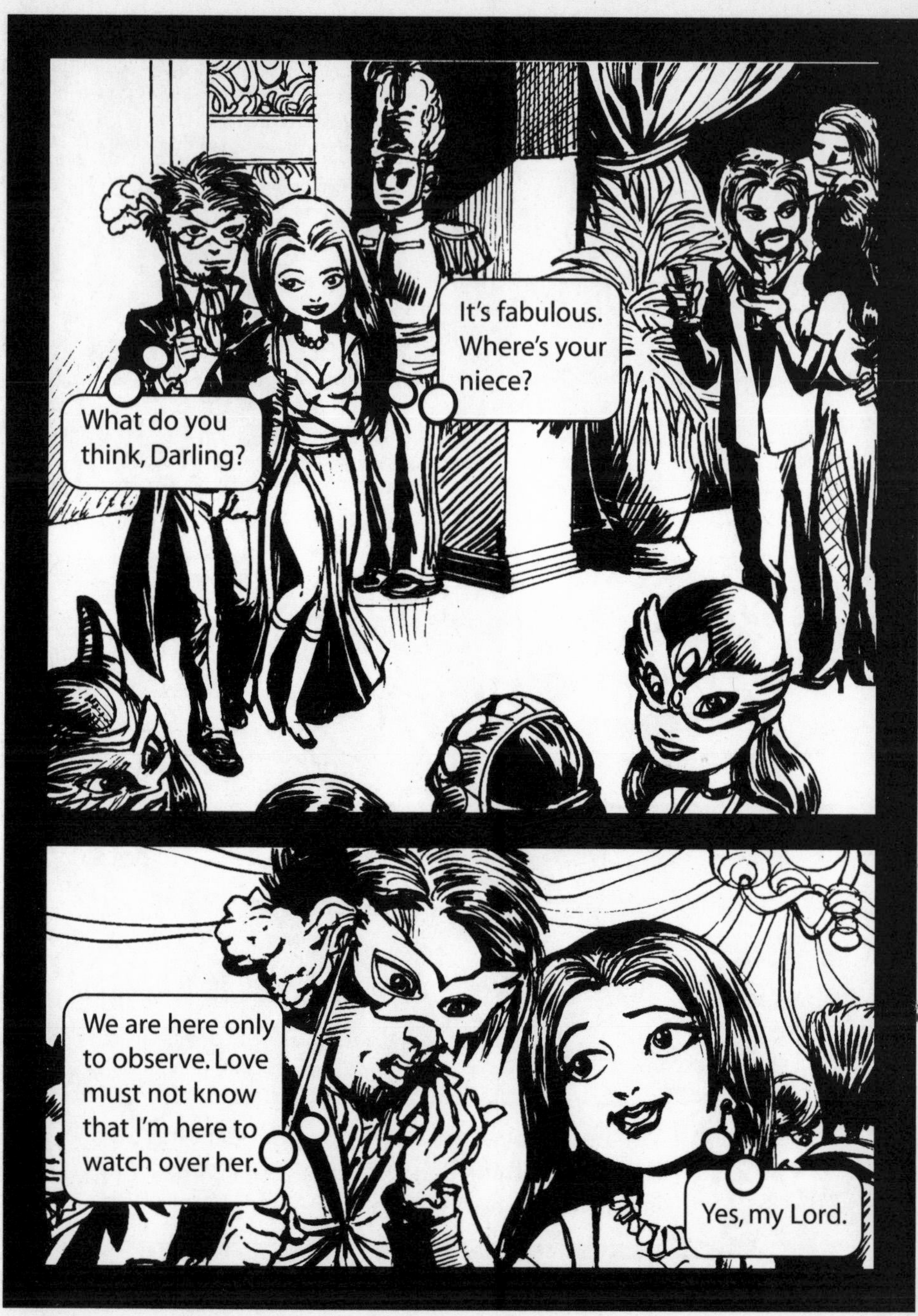
What do you think, Darling?
It's fabulous. Where's your niece?
We are here only to observe. Love must not know that I'm here to watch over her.
Yes, my Lord.

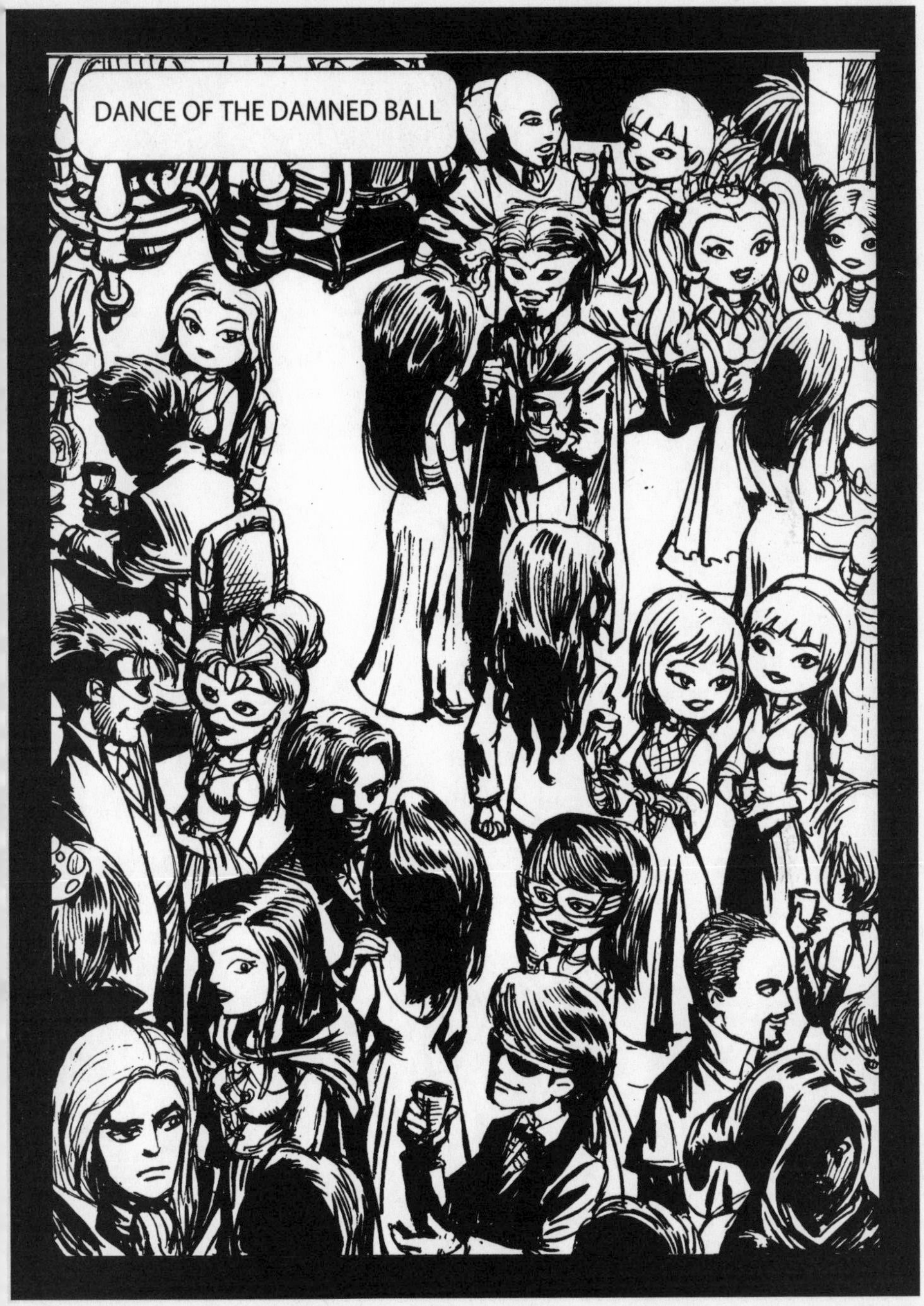
DANCE OF THE DAMNED BALL

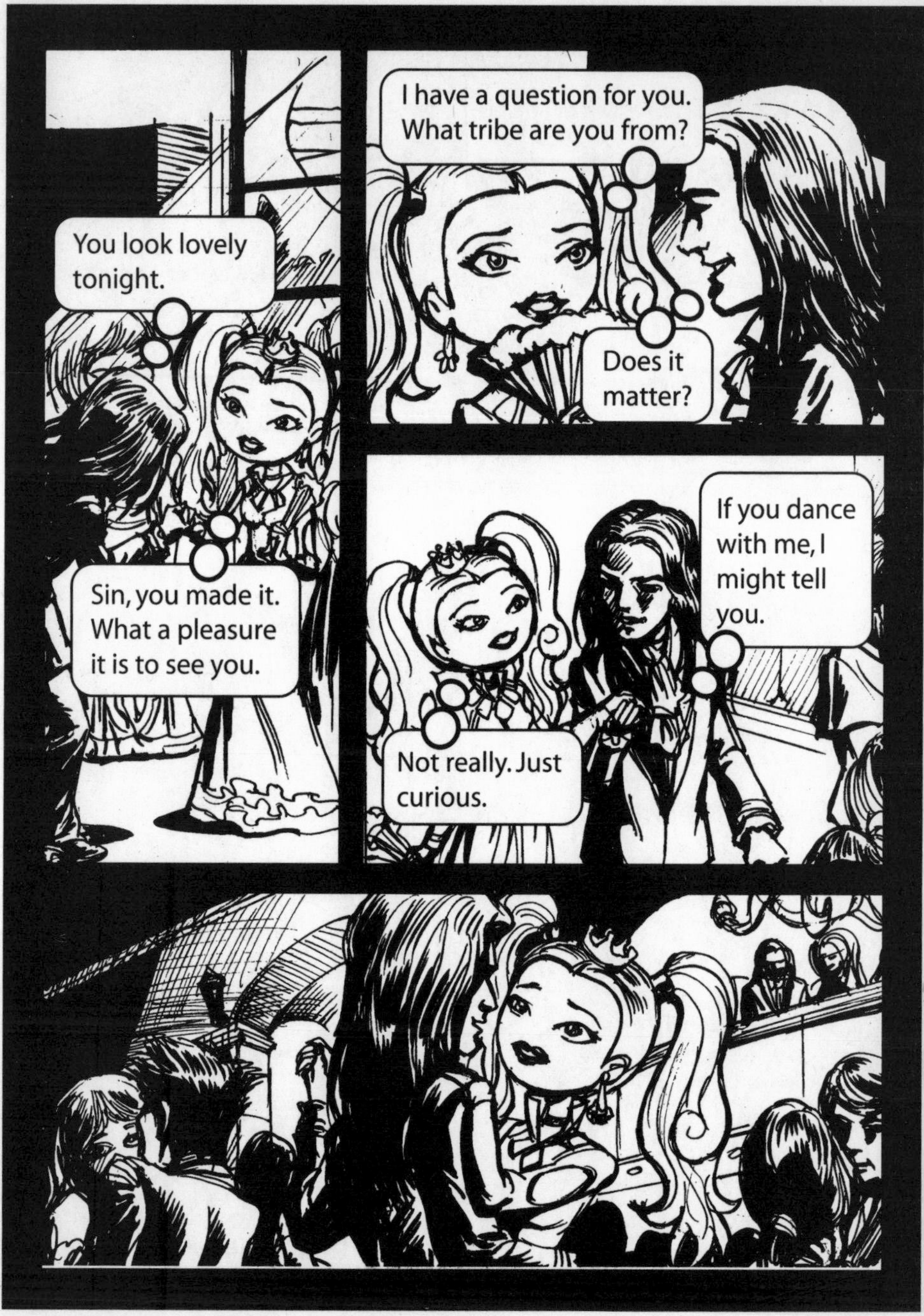
You look lovely tonight.
Sin, you made it. What a pleasure it is to see you.
I have a question for you. What tribe are you from?
Does it matter?
Not really. Just curious.
If you dance with me, I might tell you.

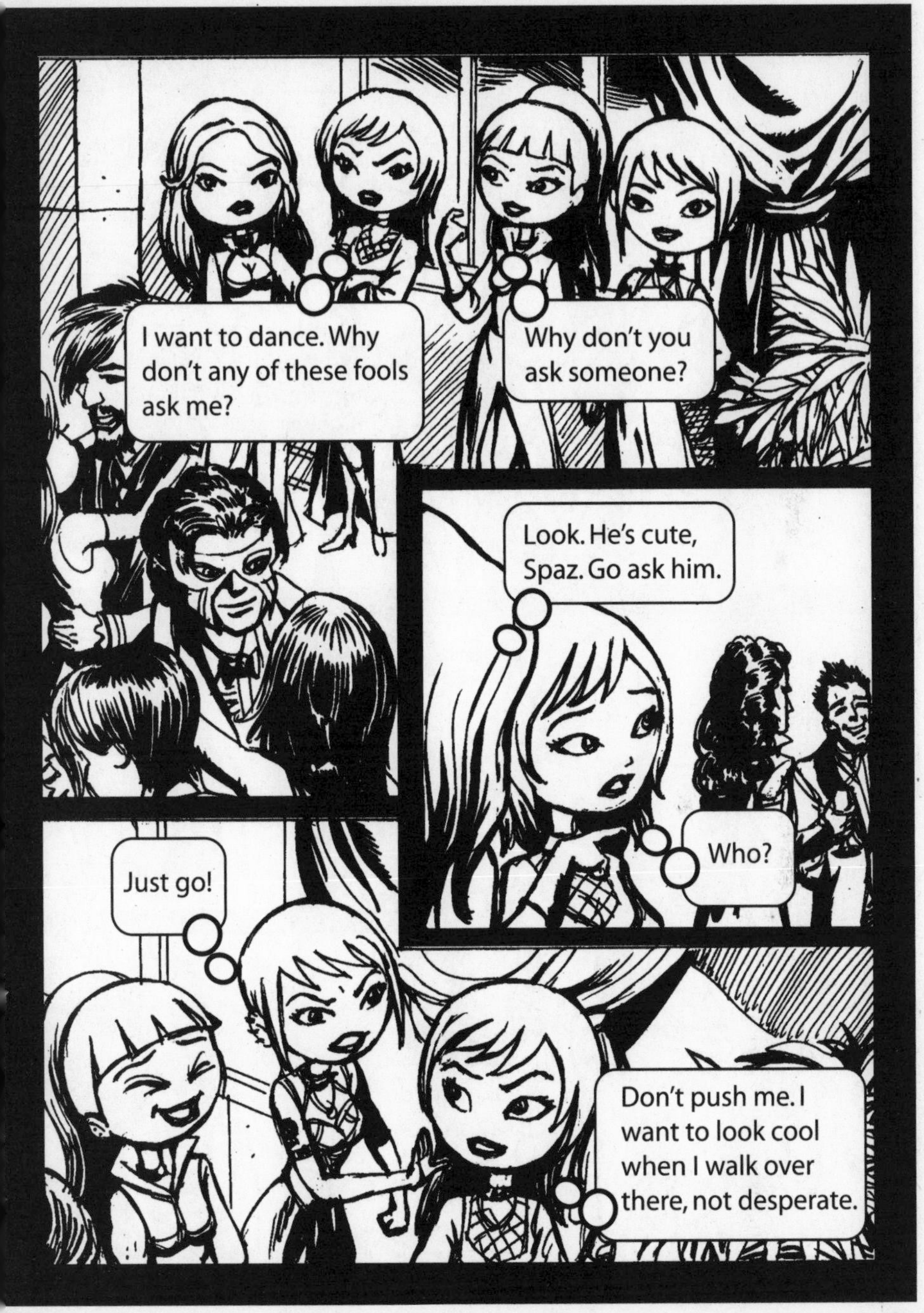
I want to dance. Why don't any of these fools ask me?
Why don't you ask someone?
Look. He's cute, Spaz. Go ask him.
Who?
Just go!
Don't push me. I want to look cool when I walk over there, not desperate.

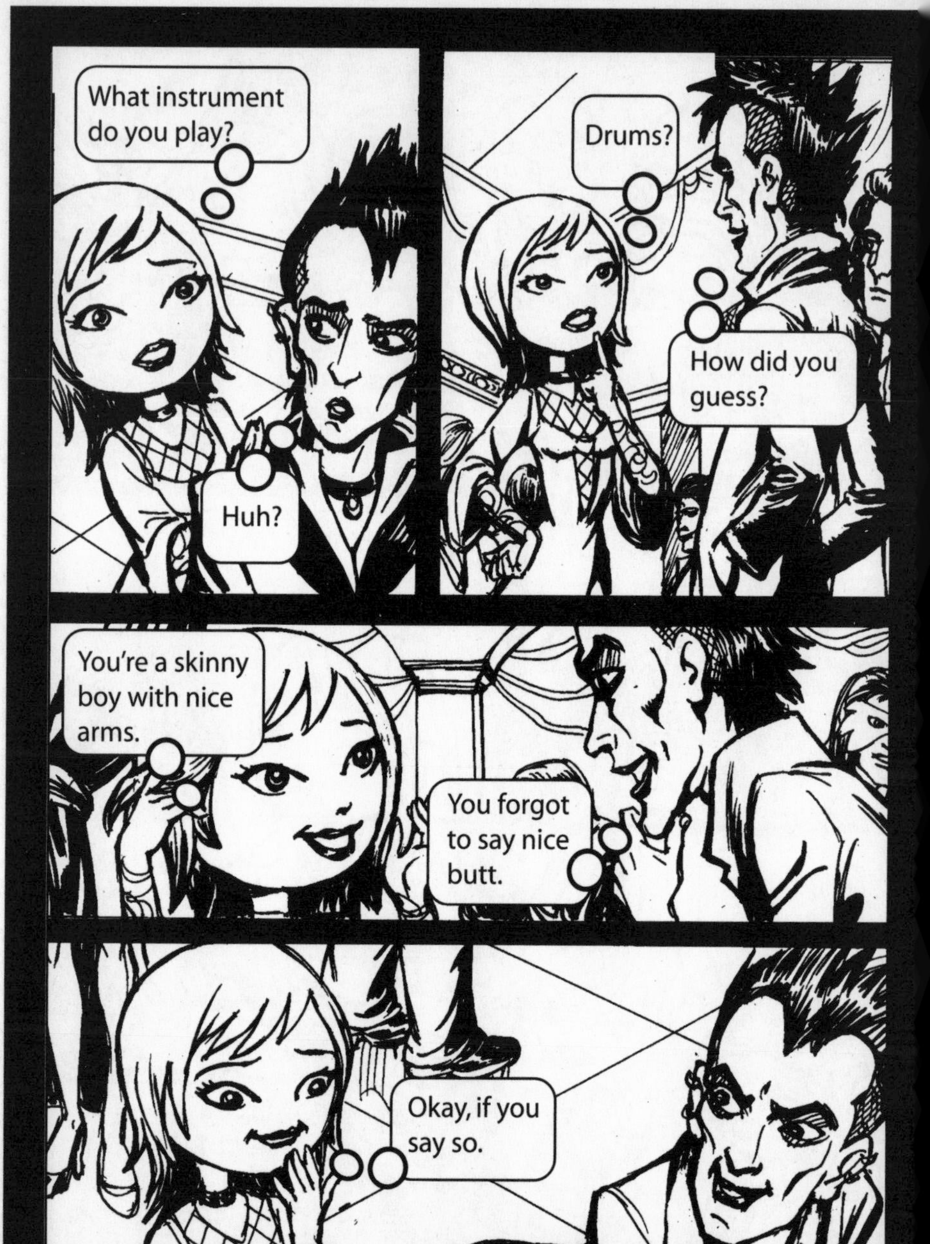
What instrument do you play?
Huh?
Drums?
How did you guess?
You're a skinny boy with nice arms.
You forgot to say nice butt.
Okay, if you say so.

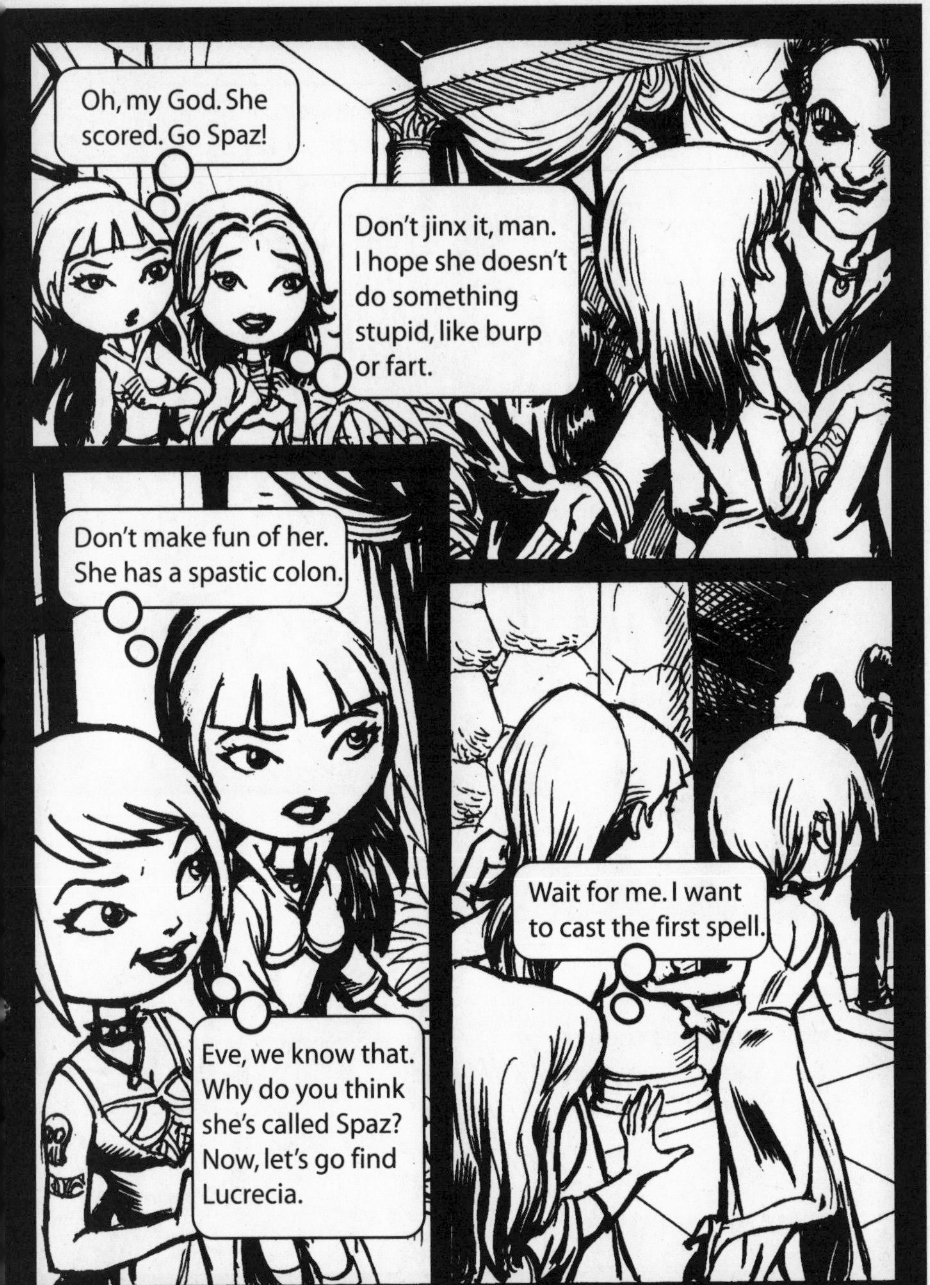
Oh, my God. She scored. Go Spaz!
Don't jinx it, man. I hope she doesn't do something stupid, like burp or fart.
Don't make fun of her. She has a spastic colon.
Eve, we know that. Why do you think she's called Spaz? Now, let's go find Lucrecia.
Wait for me. I want to cast the first spell.

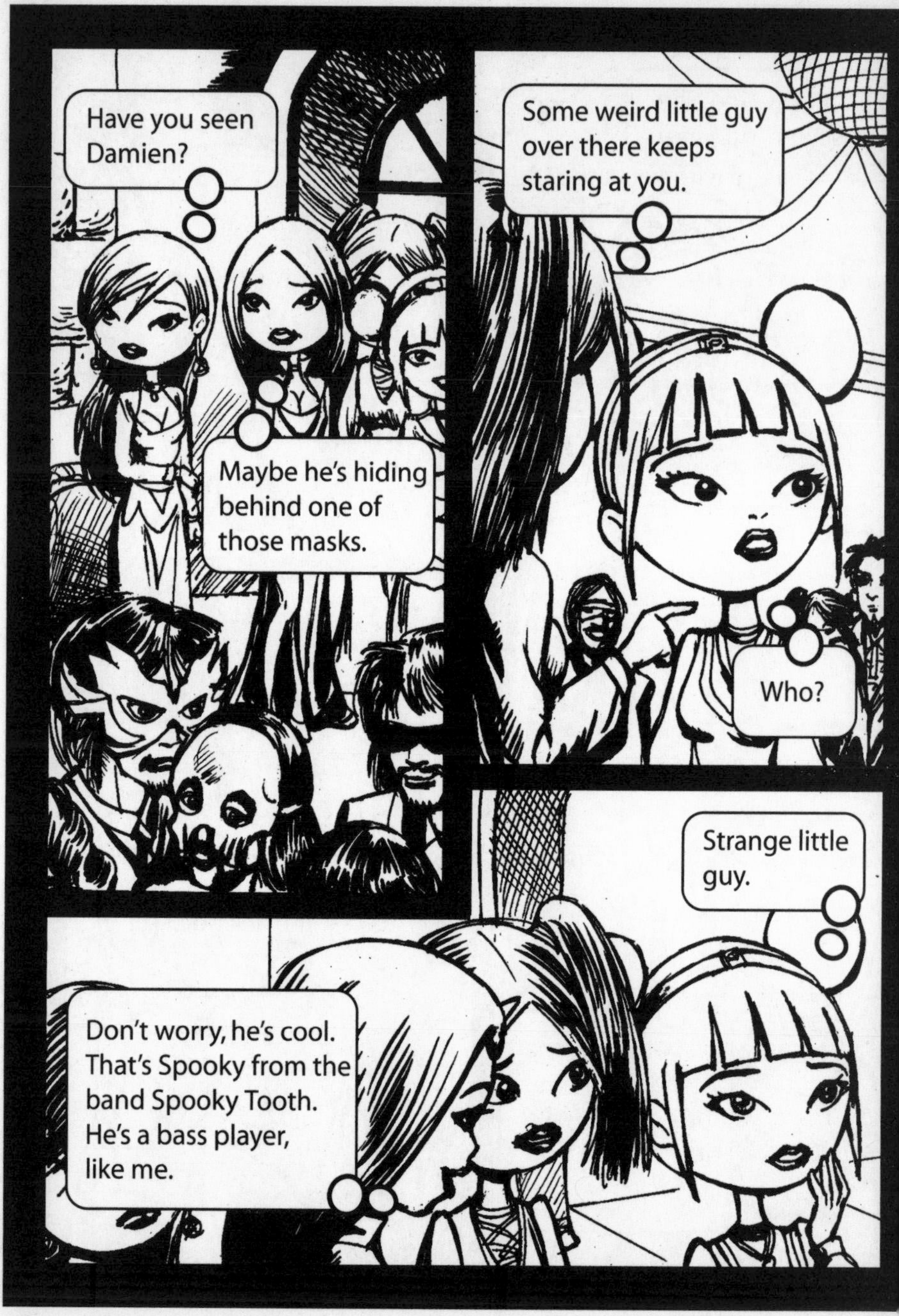
Have you seen Damien?
Maybe he's hiding behind one of those masks.
Some weird little guy over there keeps staring at you.
Who?
Strange little guy.
Don't worry, he's cool. That's Spooky from the band Spooky Tooth. He's a bass player, like me.

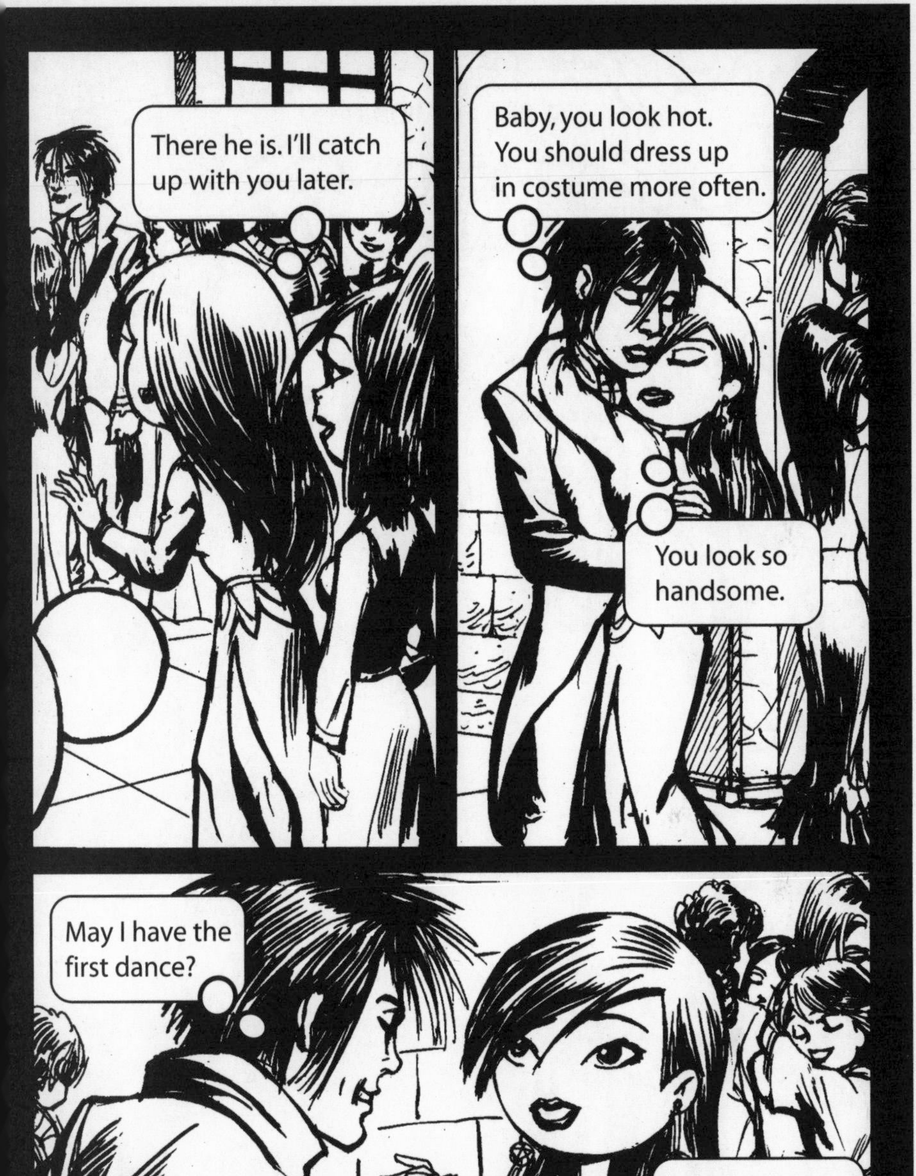
There he is. I'll catch up with you later.
Baby, you look hot. You should dress up in costume more often.
You look so handsome.
May I have the first dance?
I thought you would never ask.

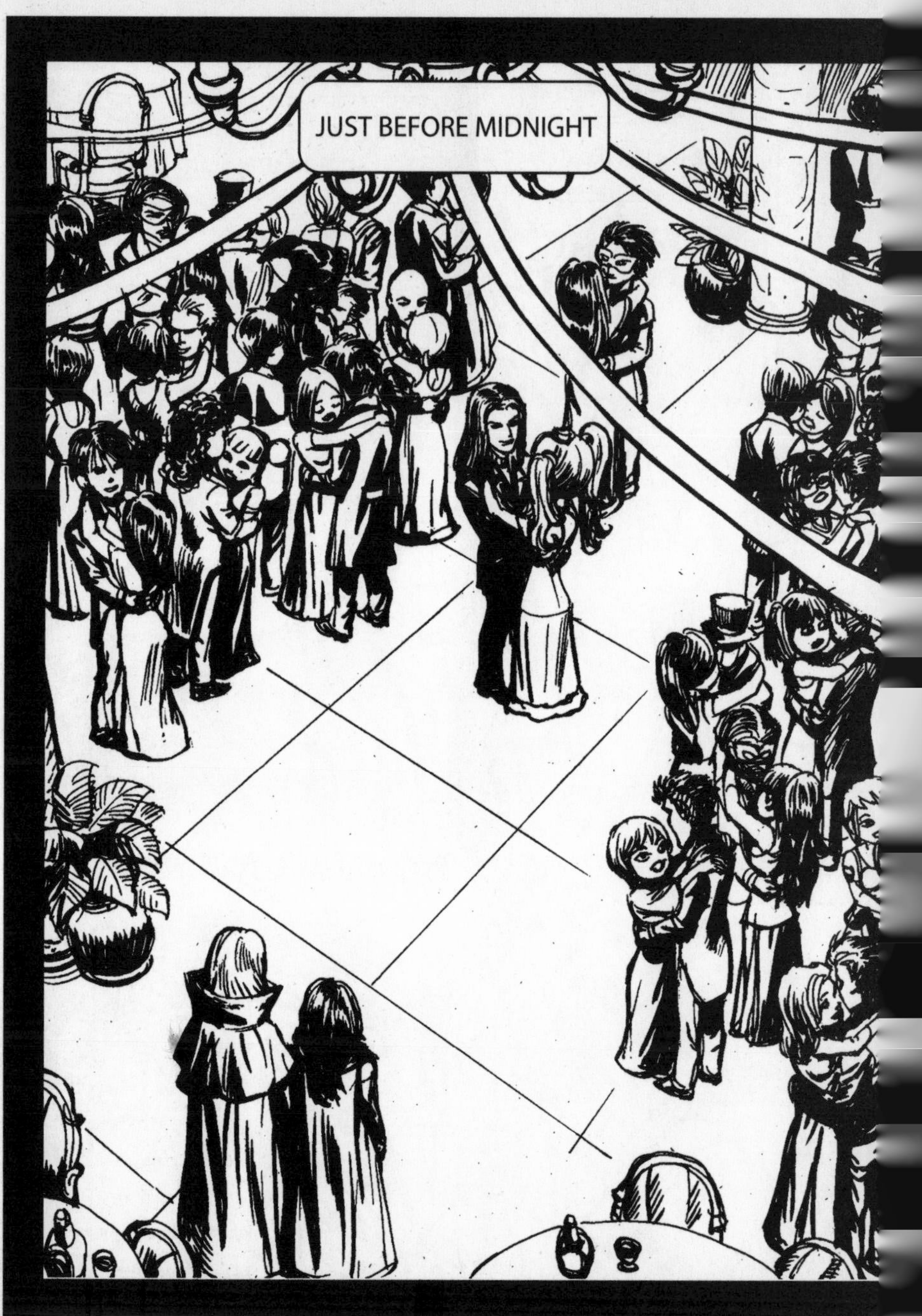
JUST BEFORE MIDNIGHT

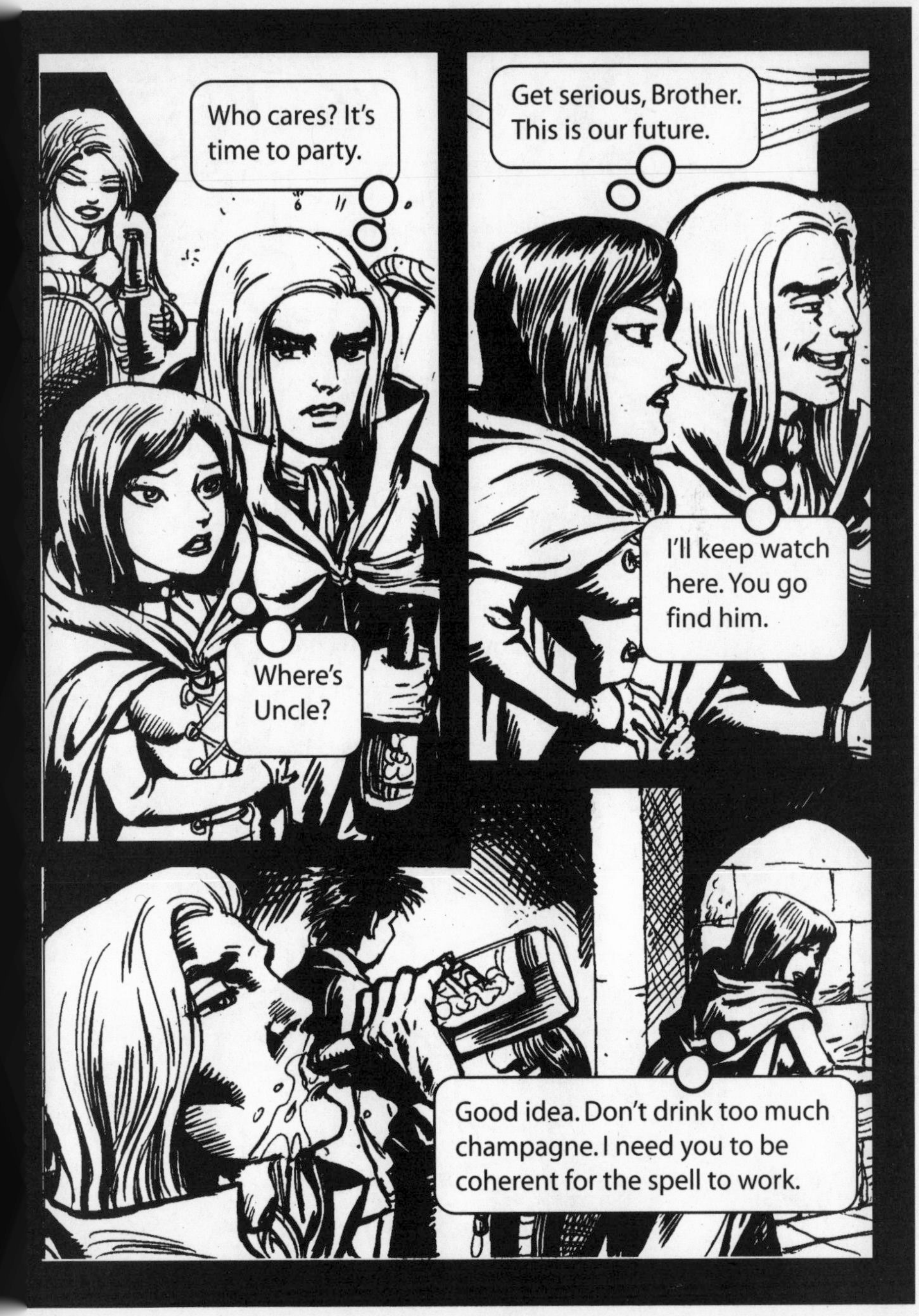
Who cares? It's time to party.
Where's Uncle?
Get serious, Brother. This is our future.
I'll keep watch here. You go find him.
Good idea. Don't drink too much champagne. I need you to be coherent for the spell to work.

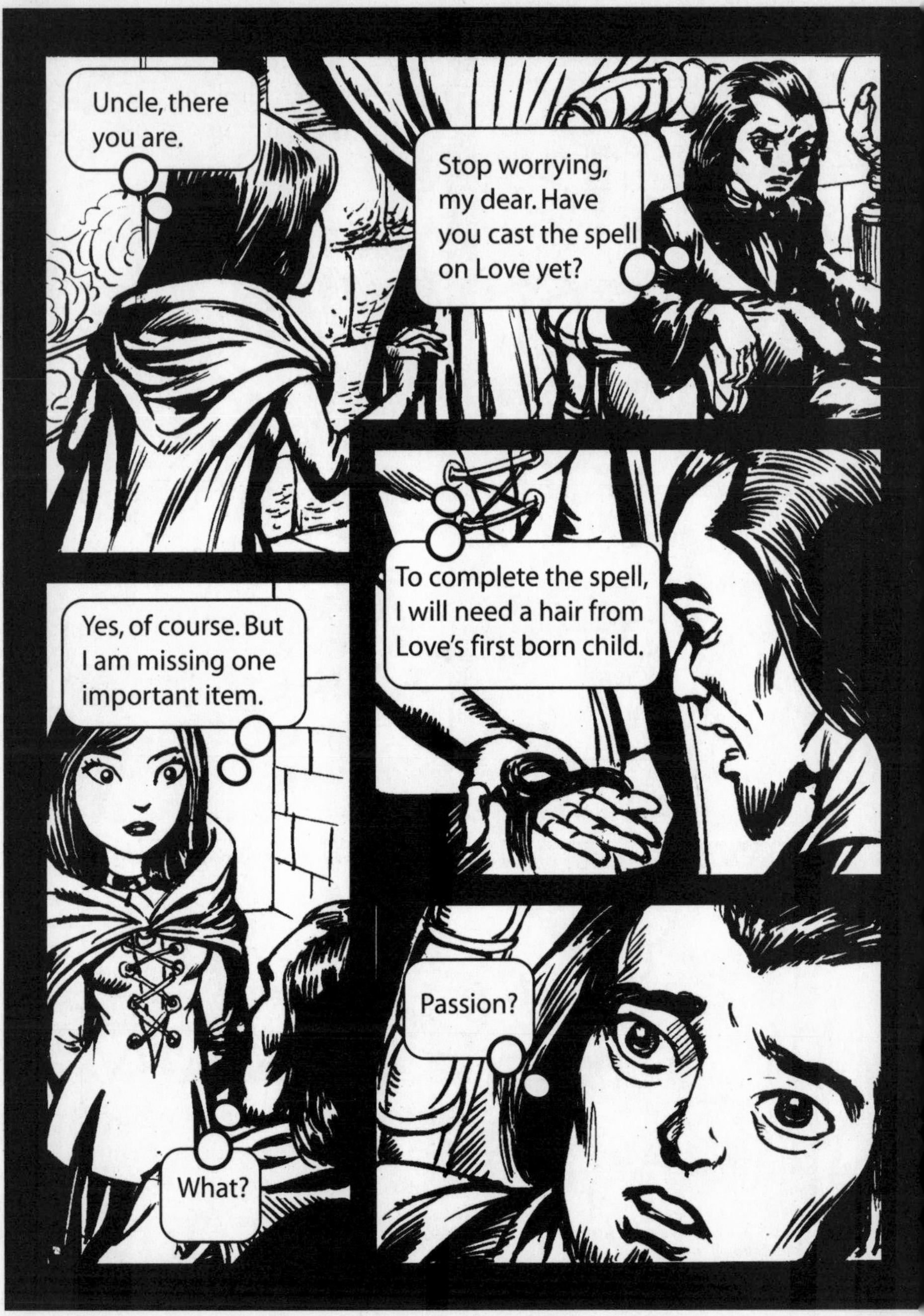
Uncle, there you are.
Stop worrying, my dear. Have you cast the spell on Love yet?
Yes, of course. But I am missing one important item.
What?
To complete the spell, I will need a hair from Love's first born child.
Passion?

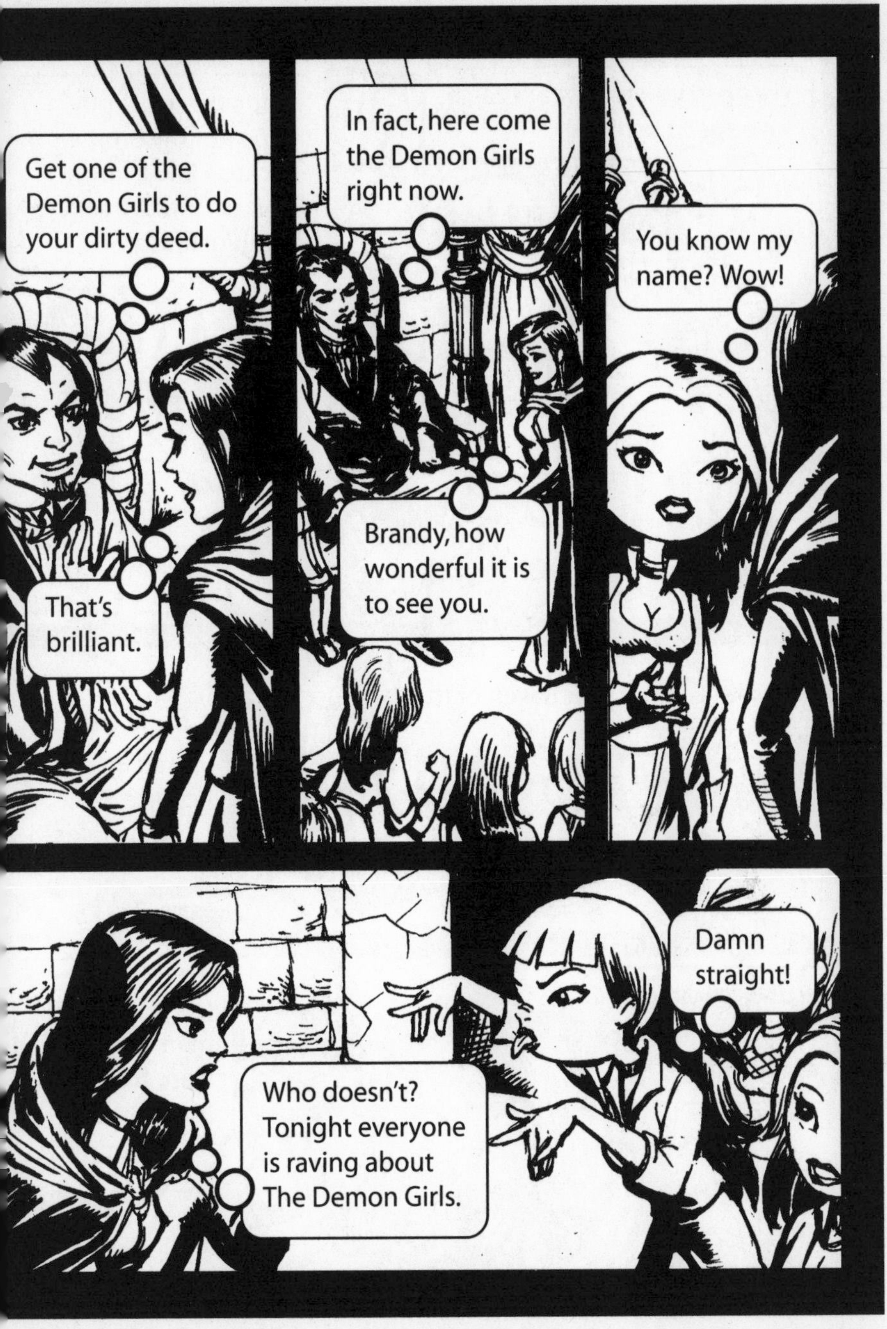
Get one of the Demon Girls to do your dirty deed.
That's brilliant.
In fact, here come the Demon Girls right now.
Brandy, how wonderful it is to see you.
You know my name? Wow!
Who doesn't? Tonight everyone is raving about The Demon Girls.
Damn straight!

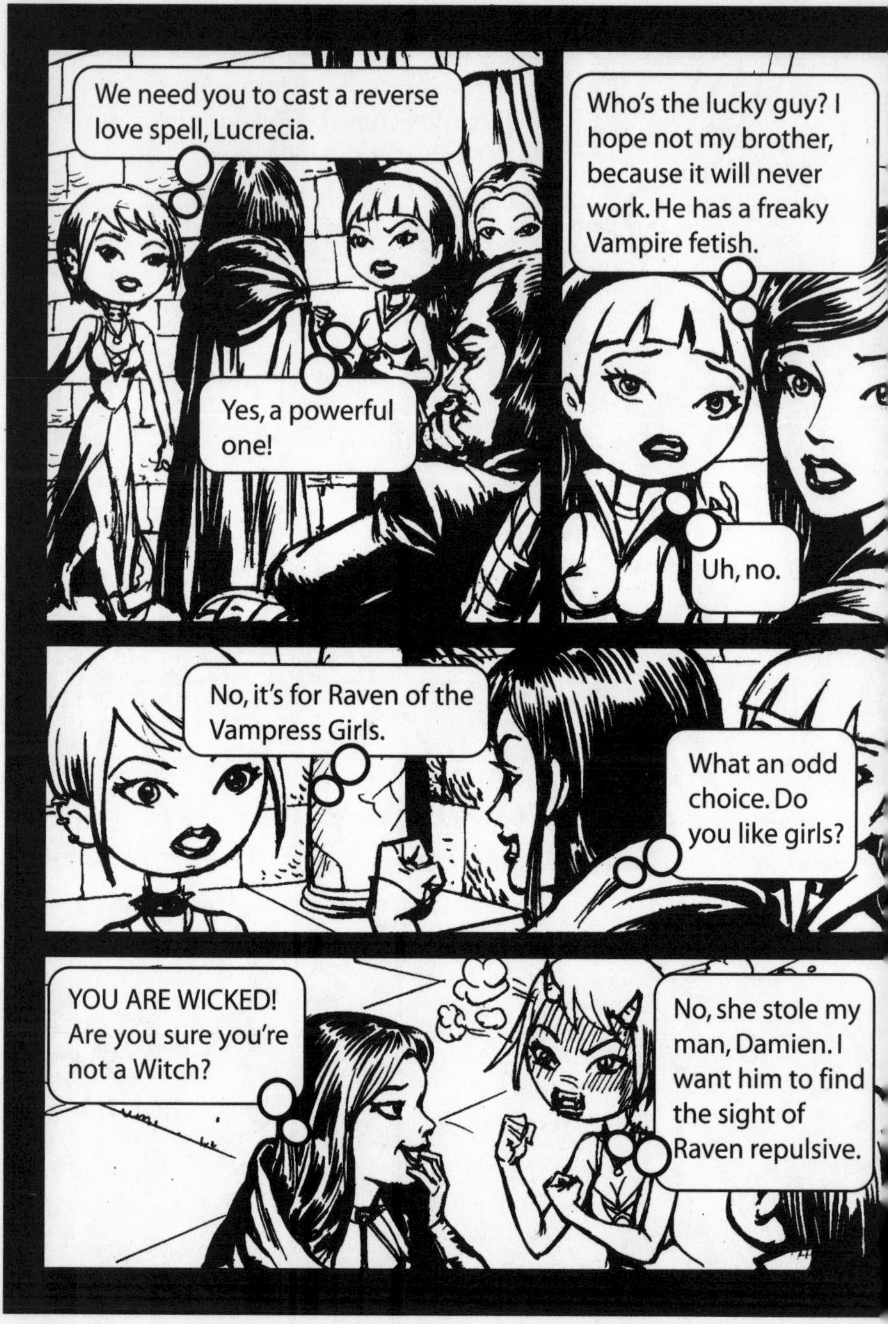
We need you to cast a reverse love spell, Lucrecia.
Yes, a powerful one!
Who's the lucky guy? I hope not my brother, because it will never work. He has a freaky Vampire fetish.
Uh, no.
No, it's for Raven of the Vampress Girls.
What an odd choice. Do you like girls?
YOU ARE WICKED! Are you sure you're not a Witch?
No, she stole my man, Damien. I want him to find the sight of Raven repulsive.

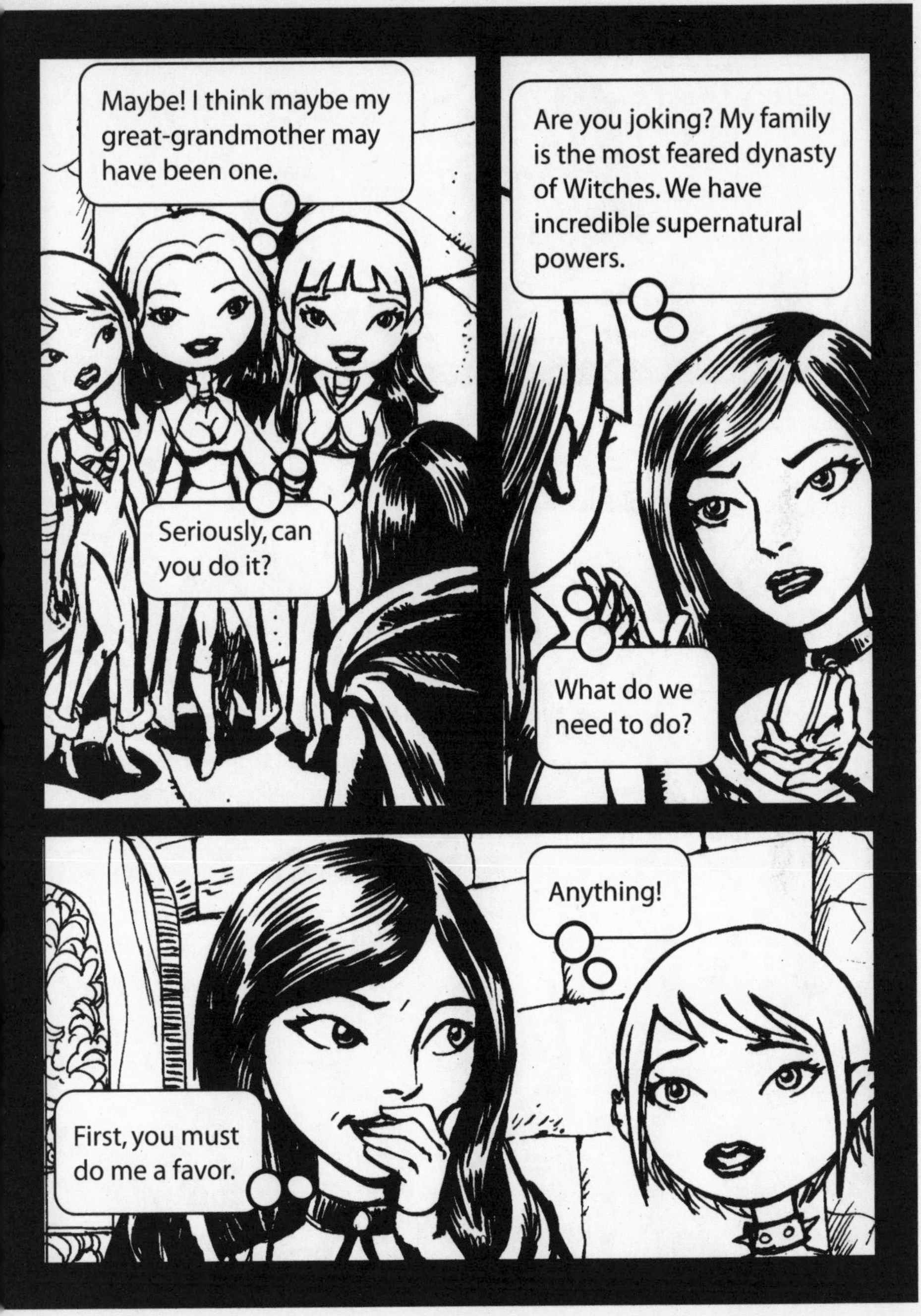
Maybe! I think maybe my great-grandmother may have been one.
Seriously, can you do it?
Are you joking? My family is the most feared dynasty of Witches. We have incredible supernatural powers.
What do we need to do?
Anything!
First, you must do me a favor.

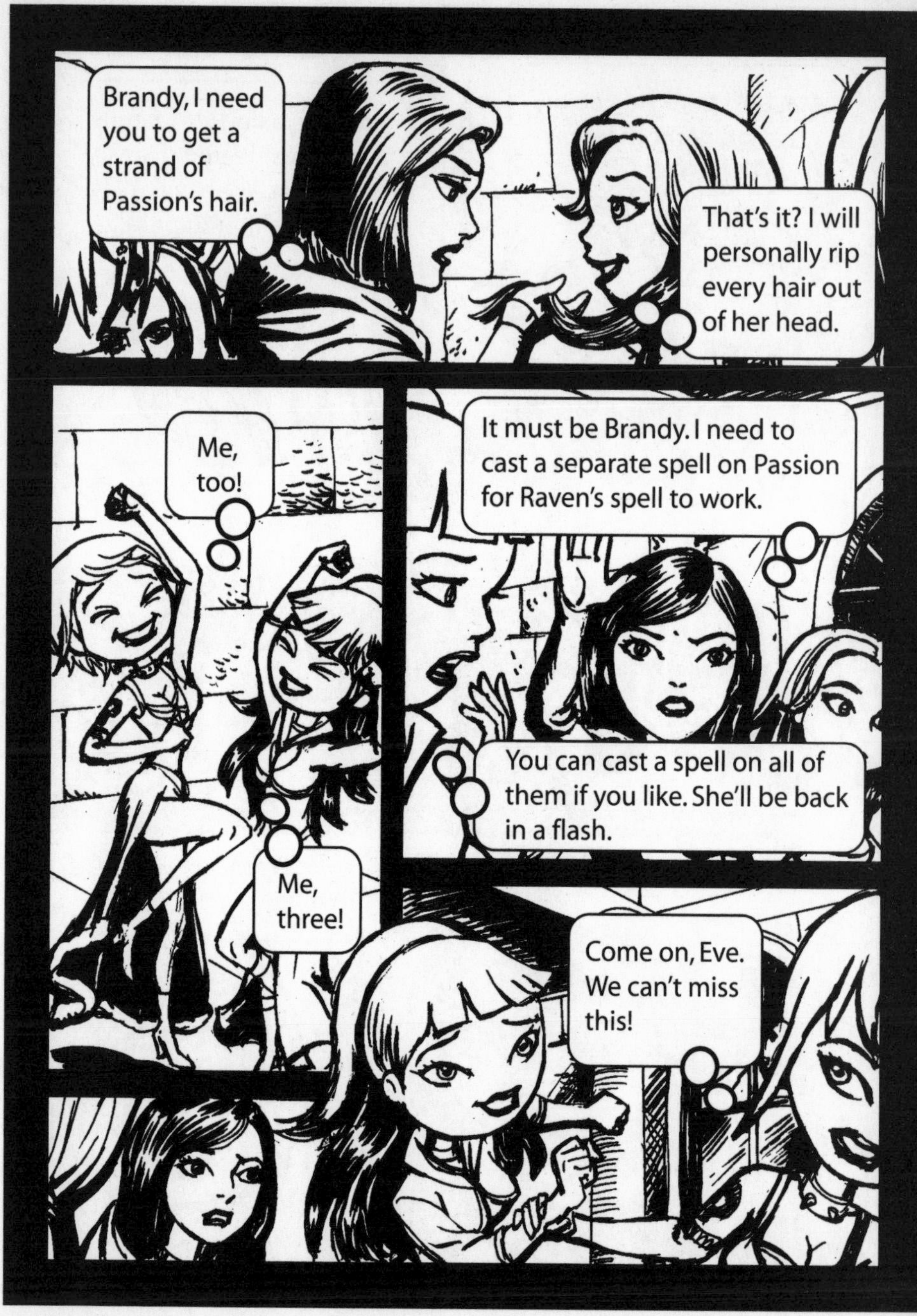
Brandy, I need you to get a strand of Passion's hair.
That's it? I will personally rip every hair out of her head.
Me, too!
Me, three!
It must be Brandy. I need to cast a separate spell on Passion for Raven's spell to work.
You can cast a spell on all of them if you like. She'll be back in a flash.
Come on, Eve. We can't miss this!

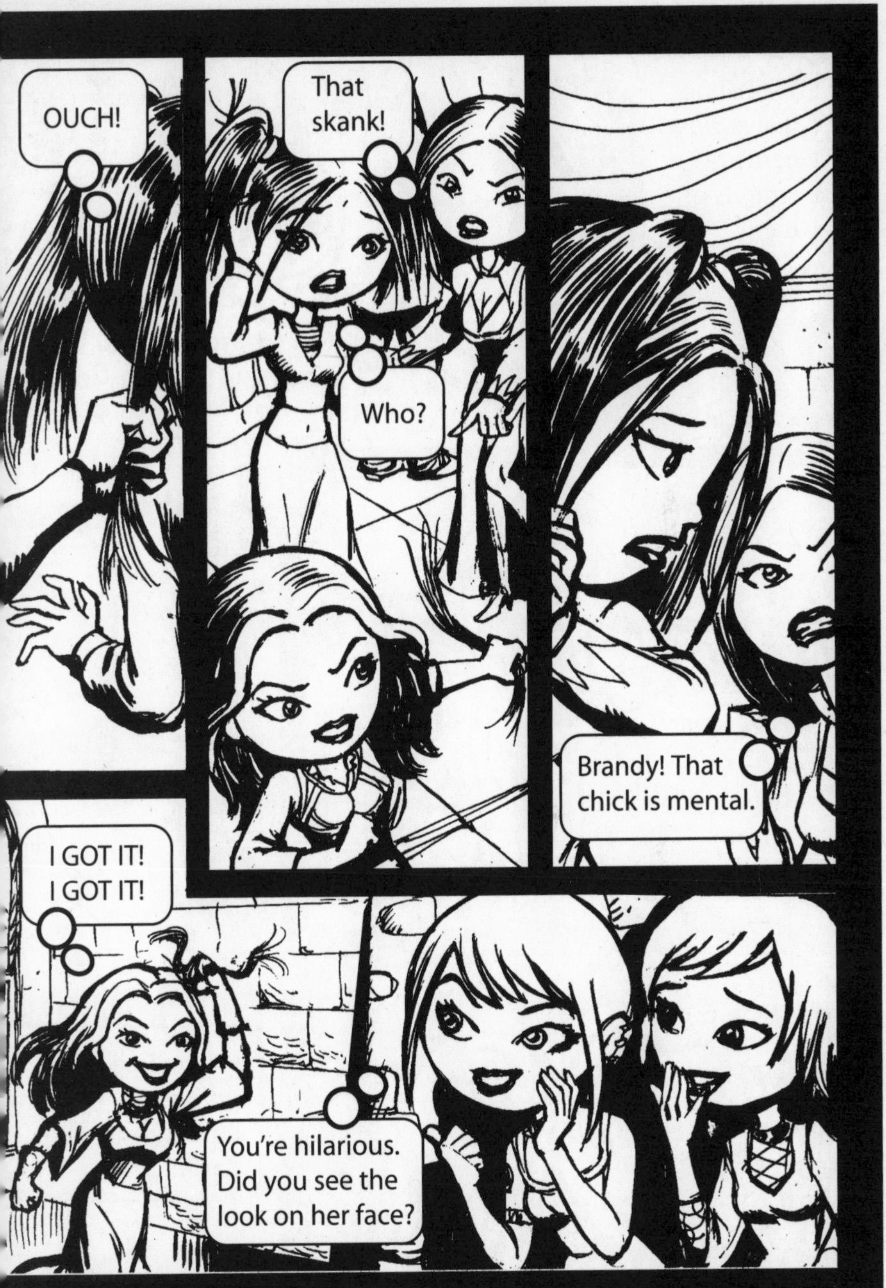
OUCH!
That skank!
Who?
Brandy! That chick is mental.
I GOT IT! I GOT IT!
You're hilarious. Did you see the look on her face?

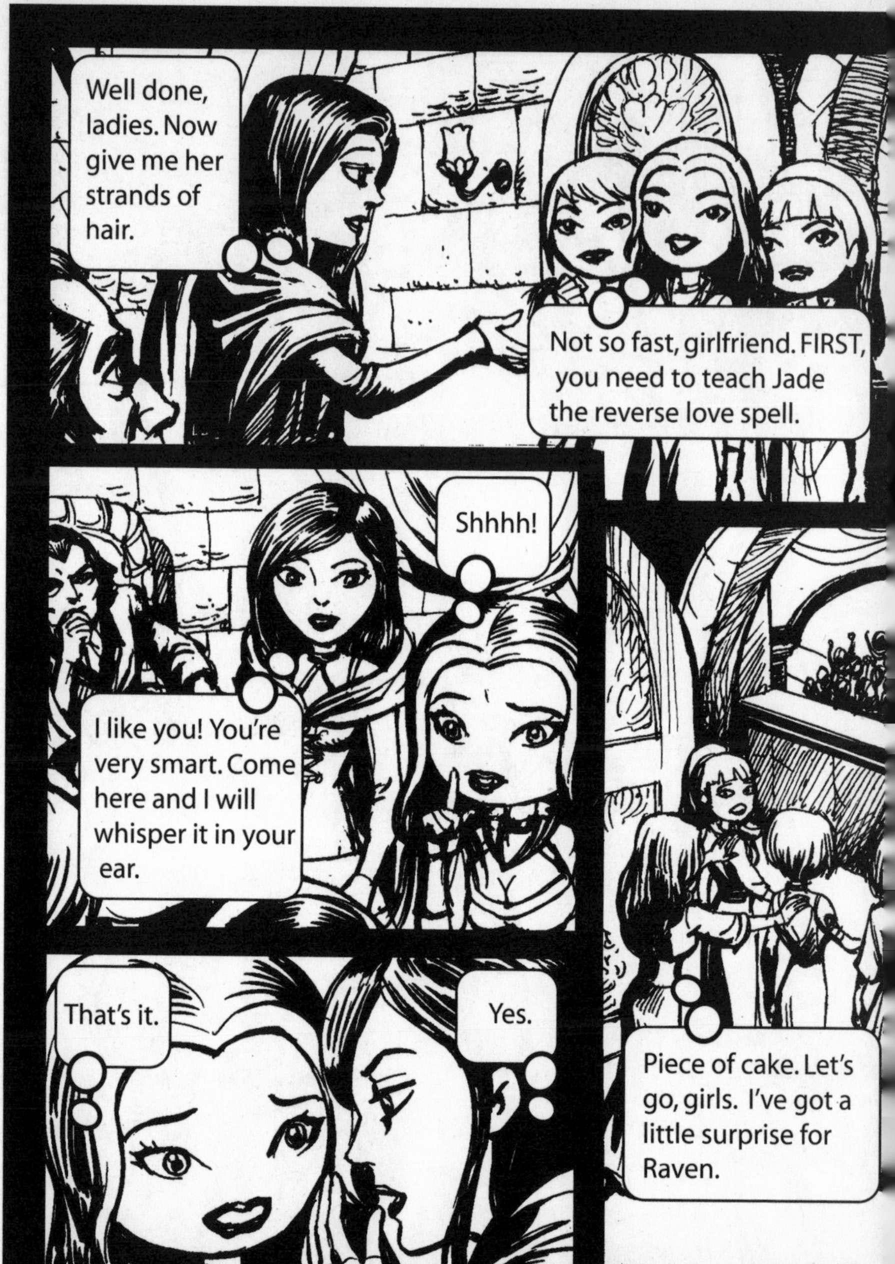
Well done, ladies. Now give me her strands of hair.
Not so fast, girlfriend. FIRST, you need to teach Jade the reverse love spell.
Shhhh!
I like you! You're very smart. Come here and I will whisper it in your ear.
That's it.
Yes.
Piece of cake. Let's go, girls. I've got a little surprise for Raven.

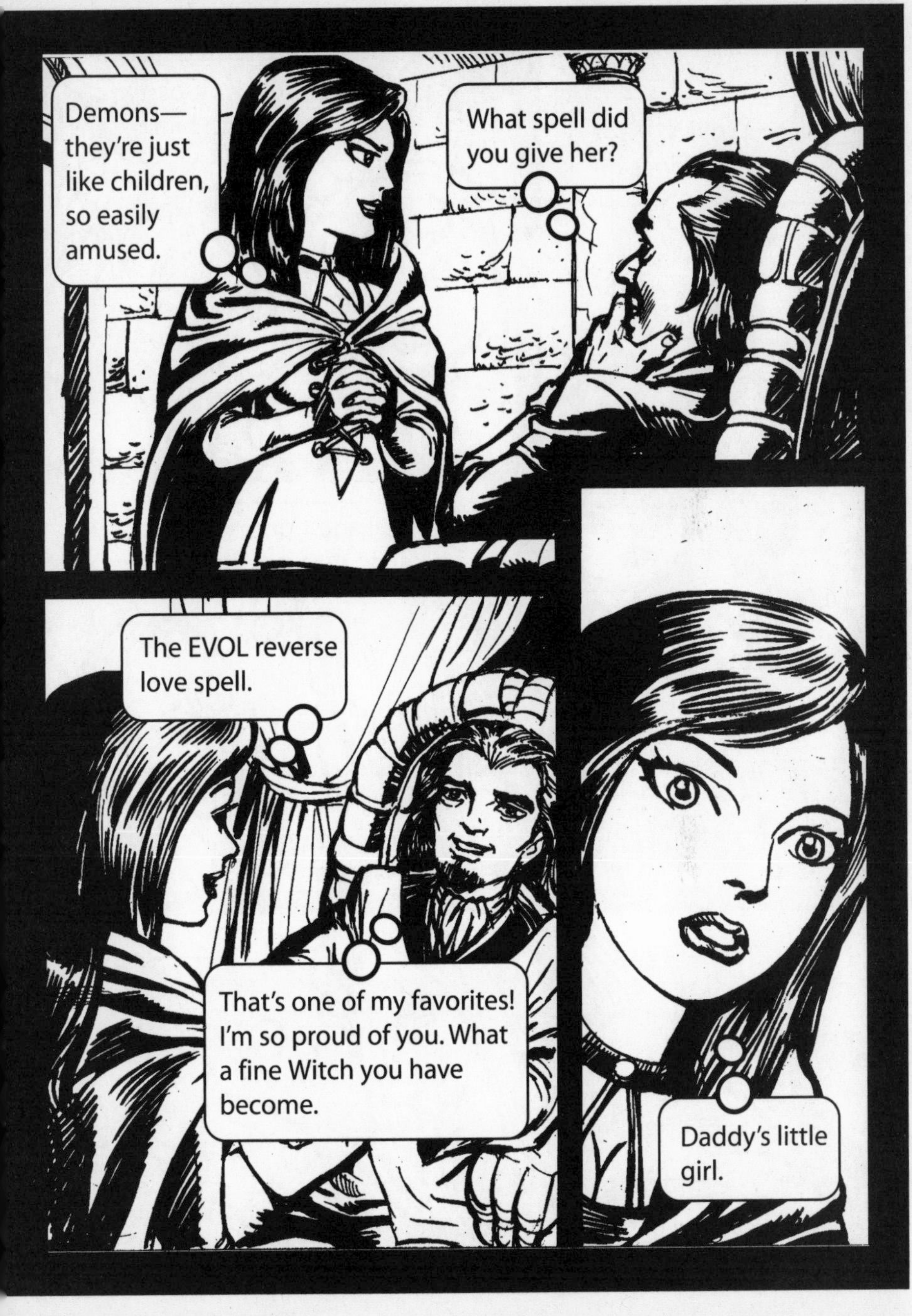
Demons—they're just like children, so easily amused.
What spell did you give her?
The EVOL reverse love spell.
That's one of my favorites! I'm so proud of you. What a fine Witch you have become.
Daddy's little girl.

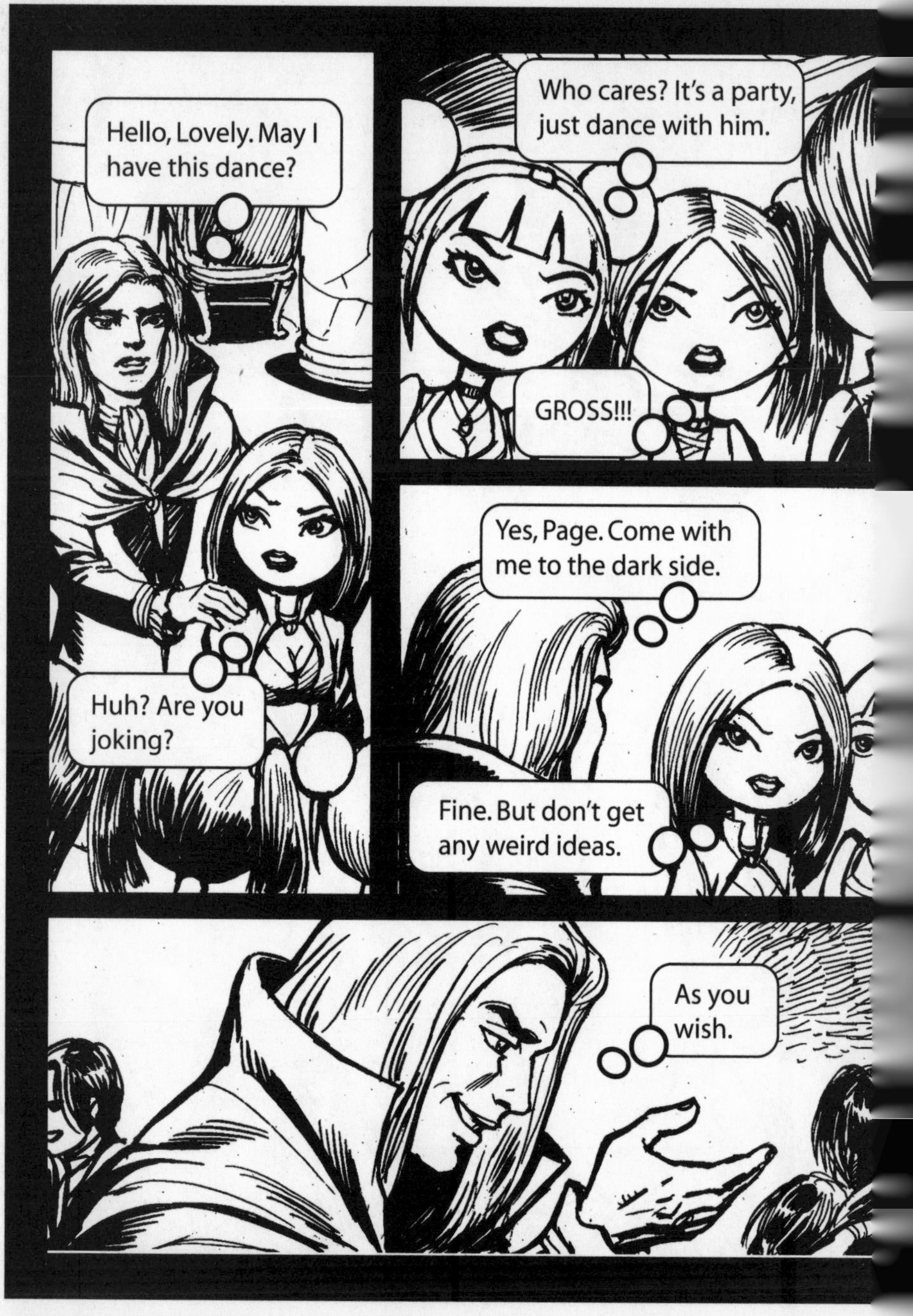
Hello, Lovely. May I have this dance?
Huh? Are you joking?
Who cares? It's a party, just dance with him.
GROSS!!!
Yes, Page. Come with me to the dark side.
Fine. But don't get any weird ideas.
As you wish.

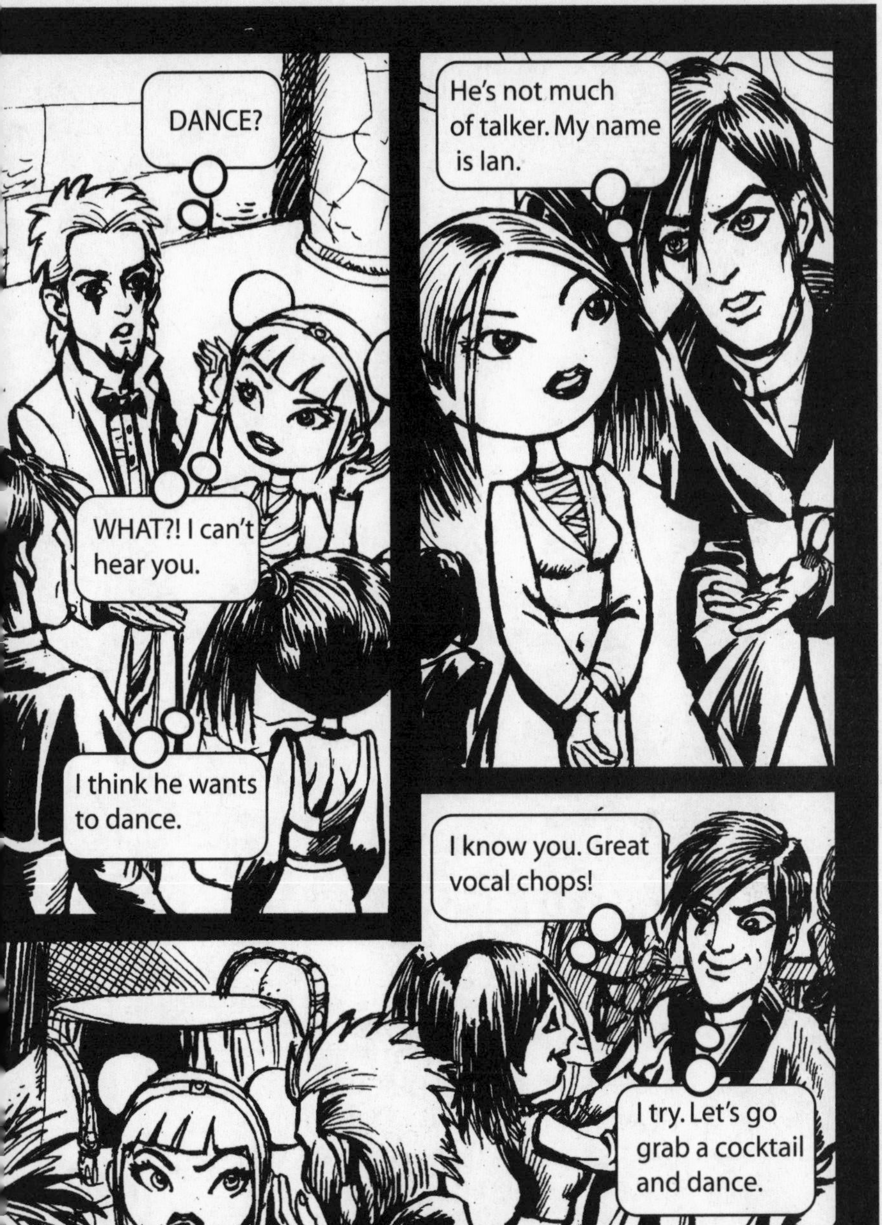
DANCE?
WHAT?! I can't hear you.
I think he wants to dance.
He's not much of talker. My name is Ian.
I know you. Great vocal chops!
I try. Let's go grab a cocktail and dance.

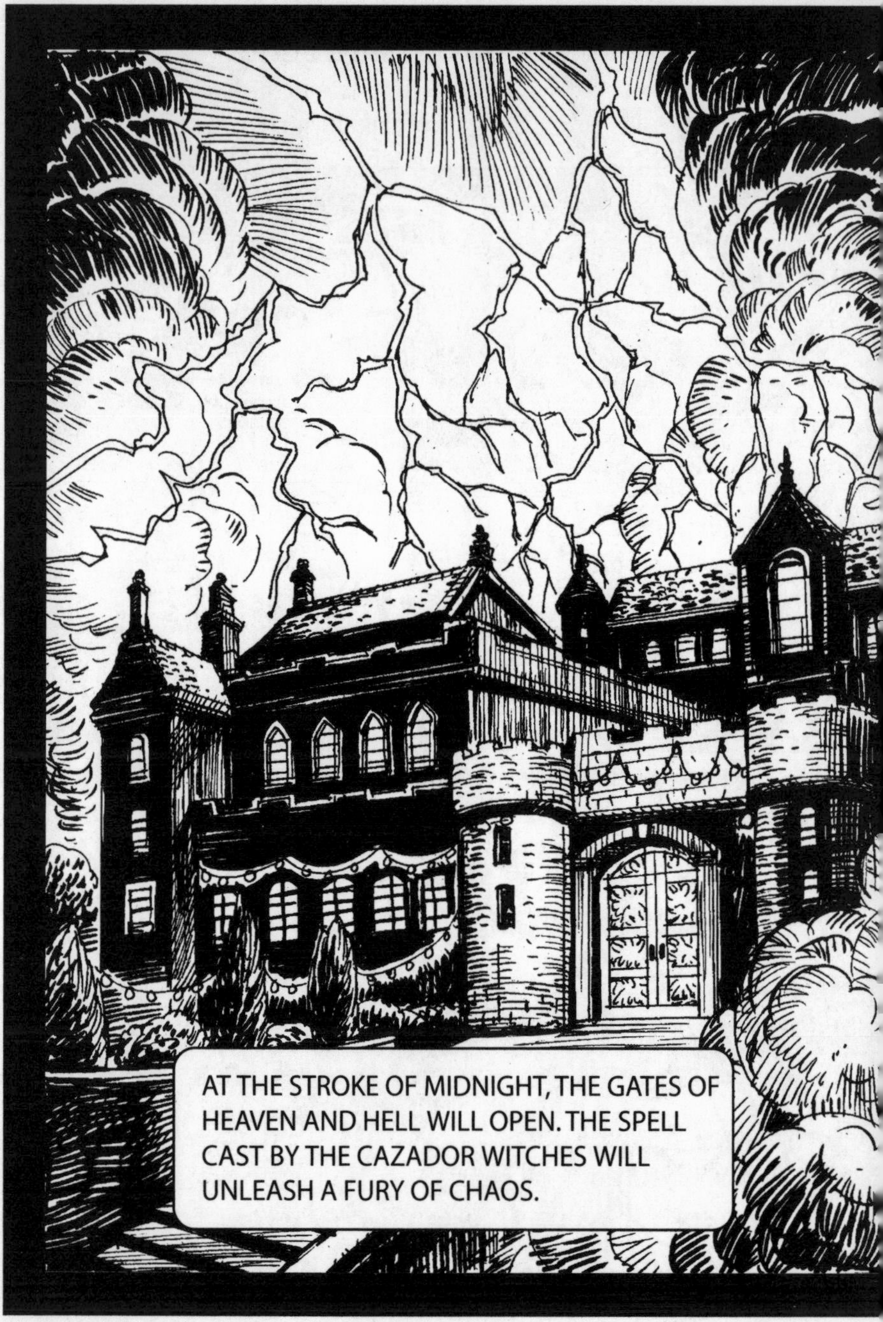
AT THE STROKE OF MIDNIGHT, THE GATES OF HEAVEN AND HELL WILL OPEN. THE SPELL CAST BY THE CAZADOR WITCHES WILL UNLEASH A FURY OF CHAOS.

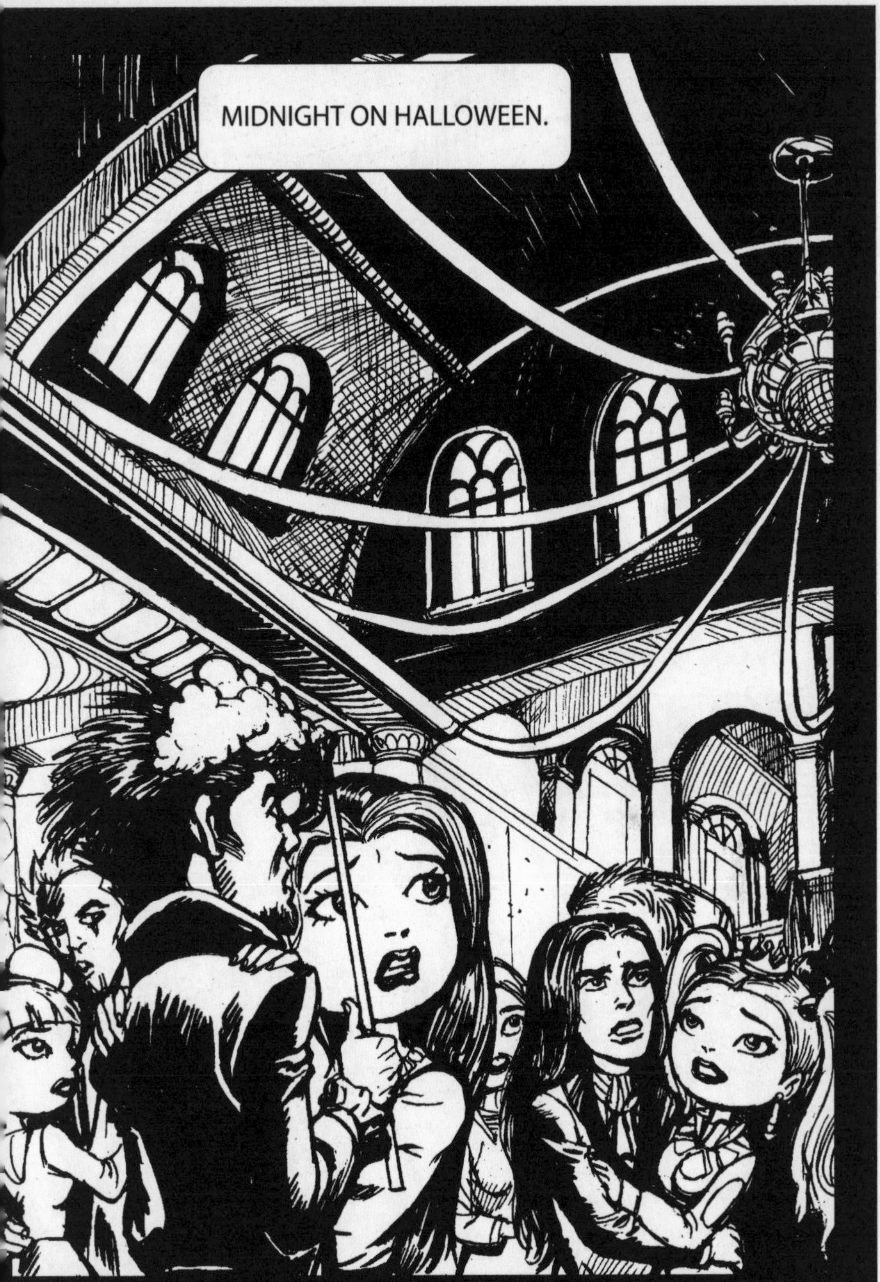
MIDNIGHT ON HALLOWEEN.

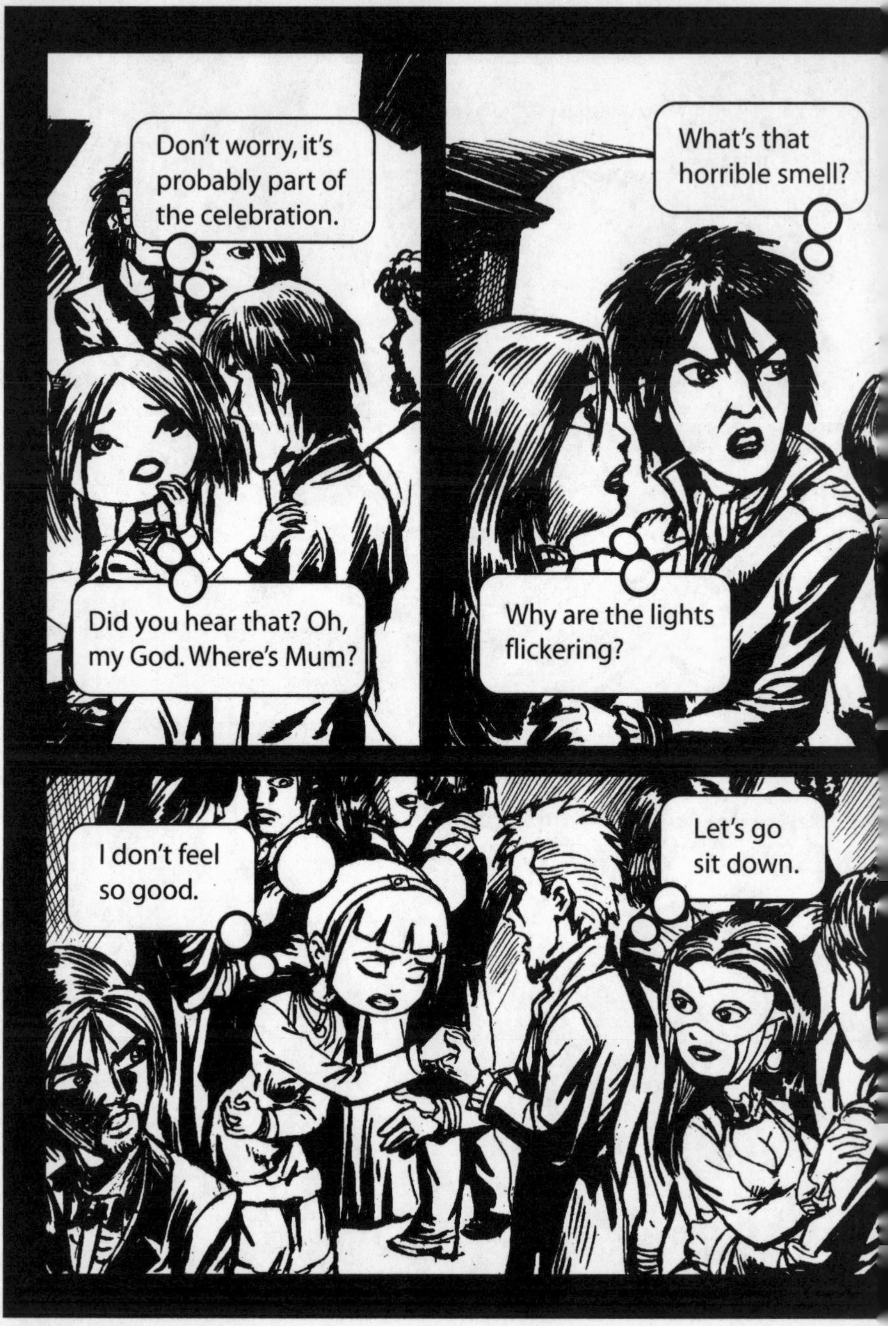
Don't worry, it's probably part of the celebration.
Did you hear that? Oh, my God. Where's Mum?
What's that horrible smell?
Why are the lights flickering?
I don't feel so good.
Let's go sit down.

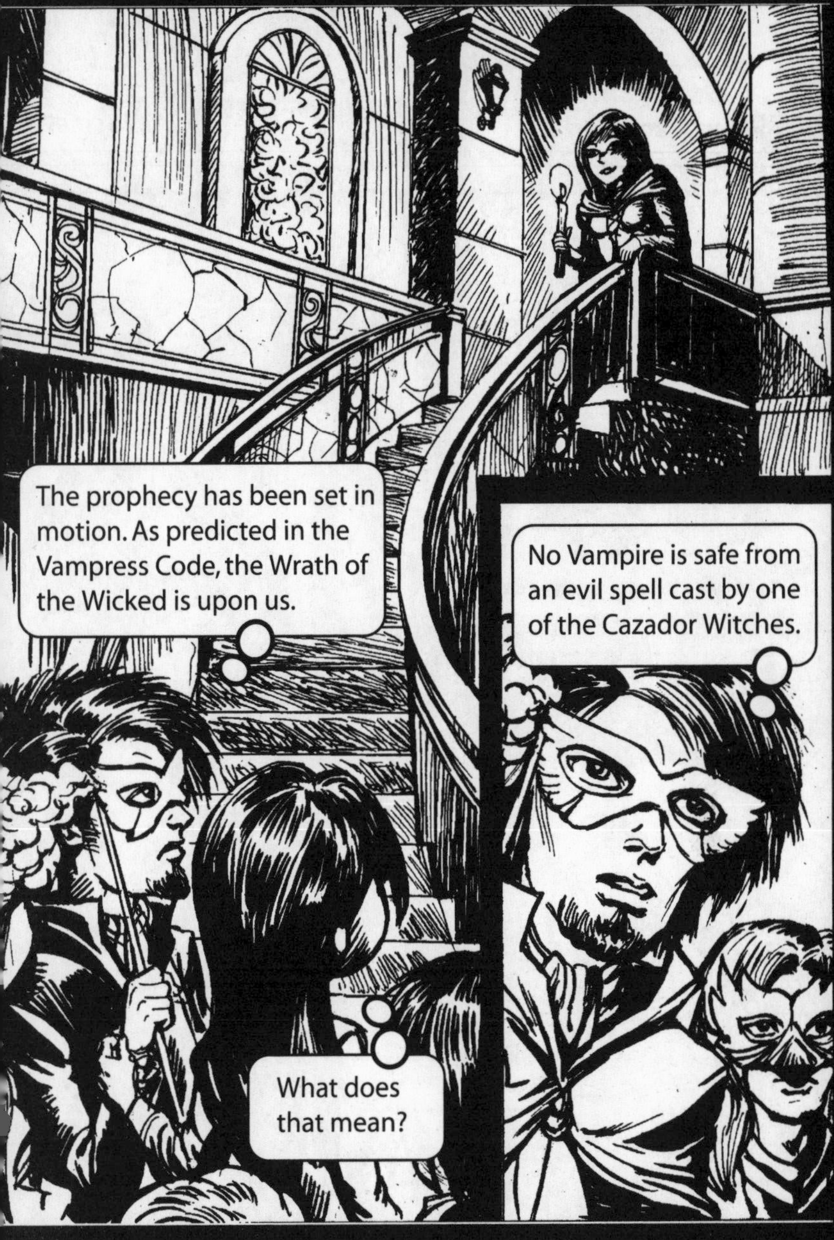
The prophecy has been set in motion. As predicted in the Vampress Code, the Wrath of the Wicked is upon us.
What does that mean?
No Vampire is safe from an evil spell cast by one of the Cazador Witches.

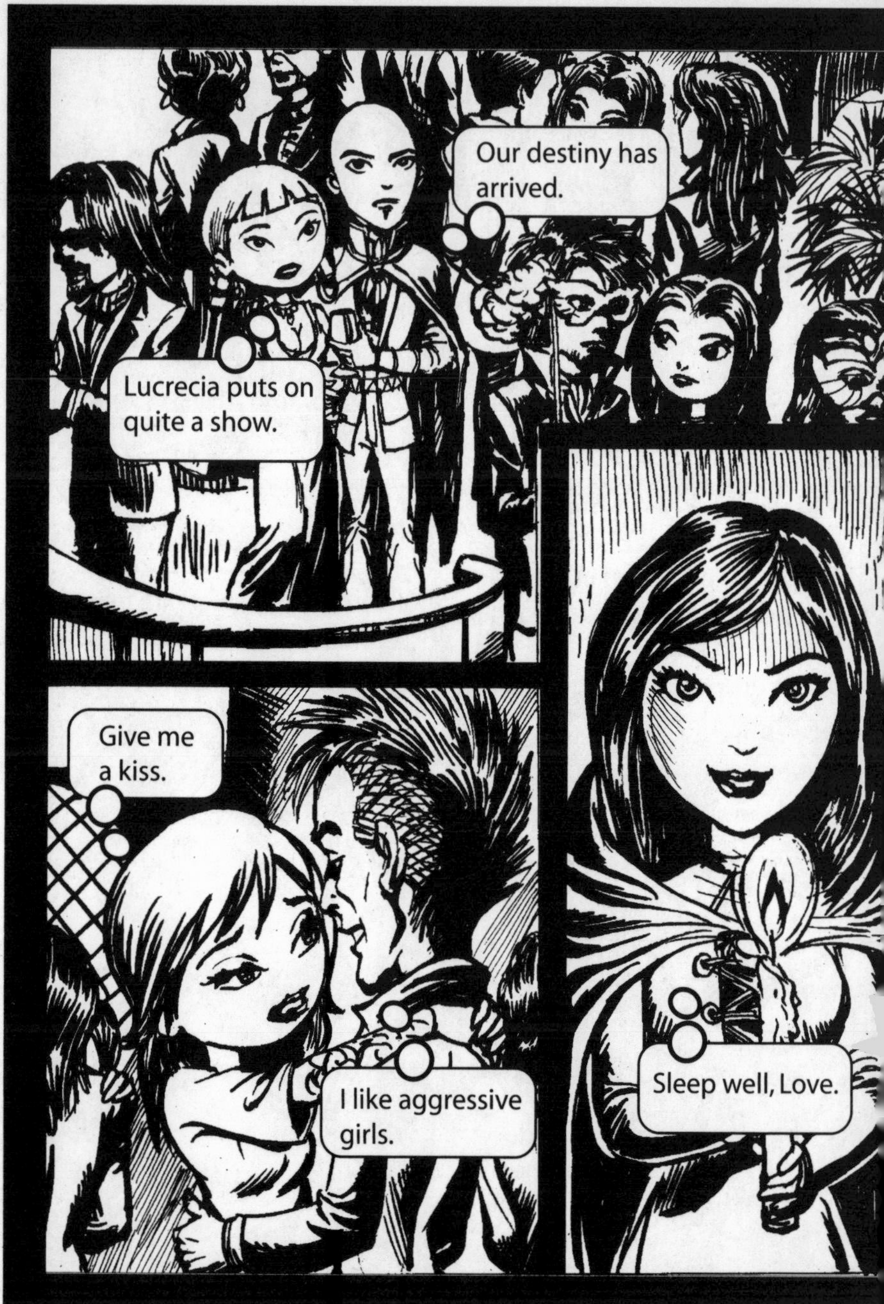
Our destiny has arrived.
Lucrecia puts on quite a show.
Give me a kiss.
I like aggressive girls.
Sleep well, Love.

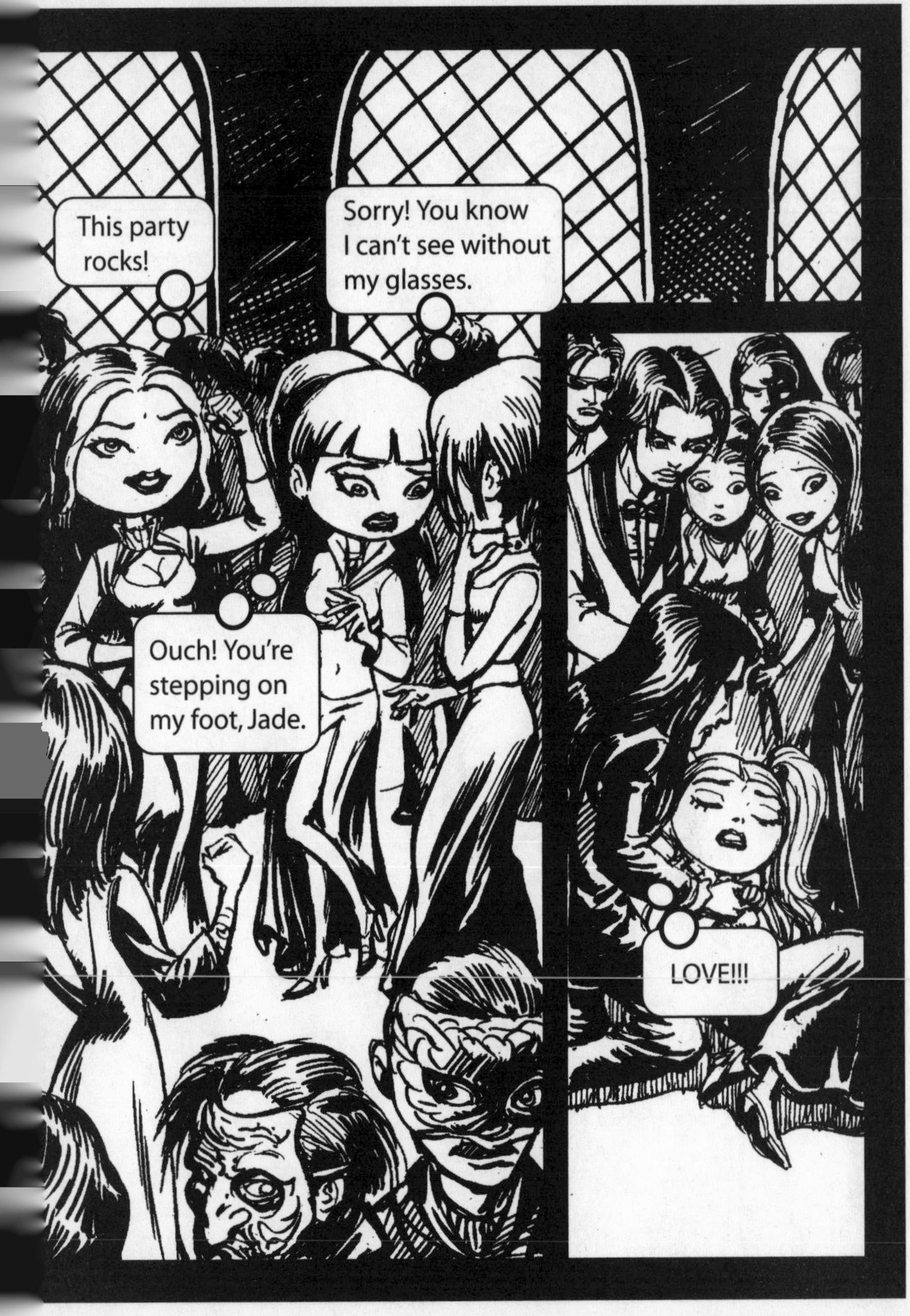
This party rocks!
Sorry! You know I can't see without my glasses.
Ouch! You're stepping on my foot, Jade.
LOVE!!!

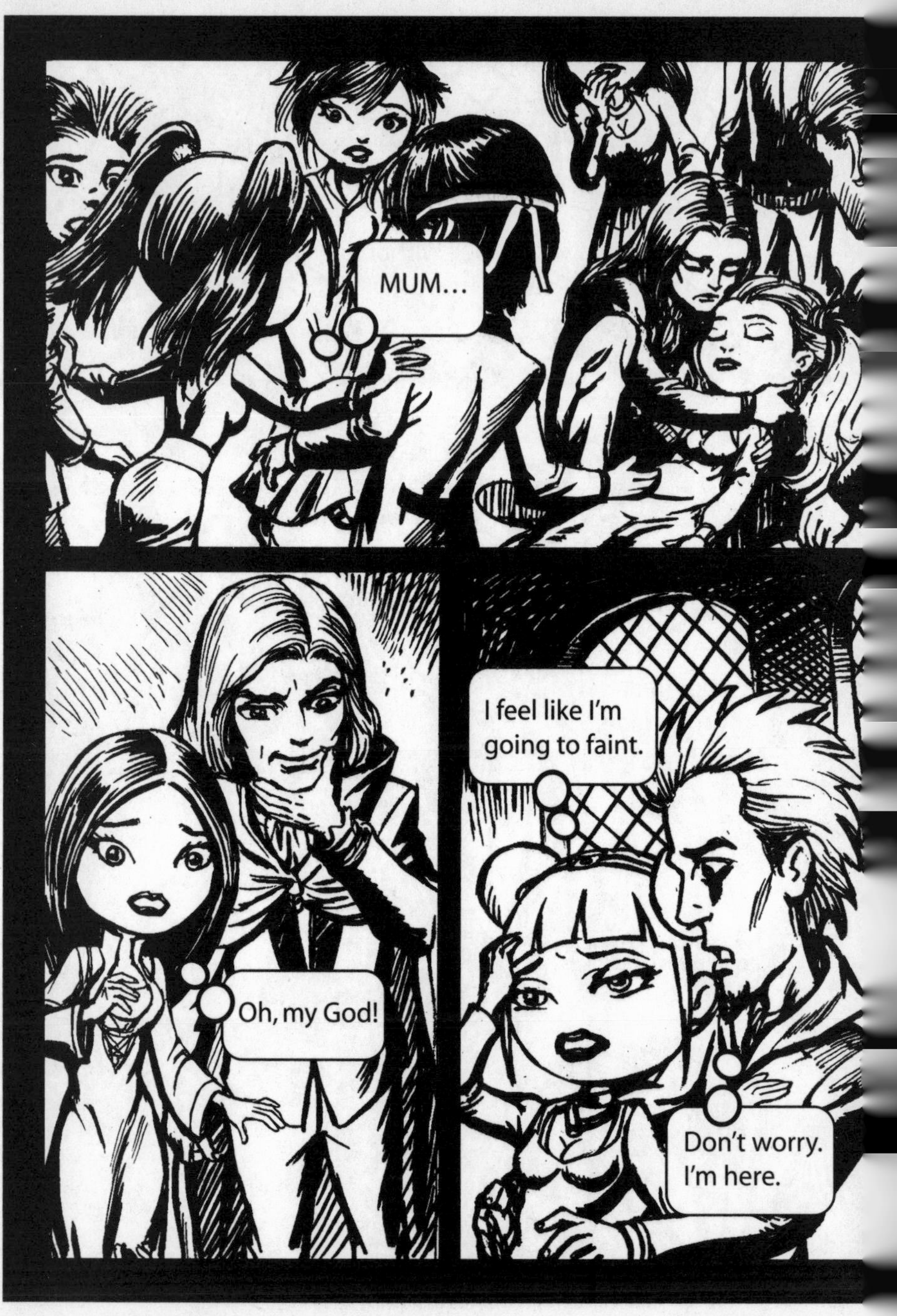
MUM...
Oh, my God!
I feel like I'm going to faint.
Don't worry. I'm here.

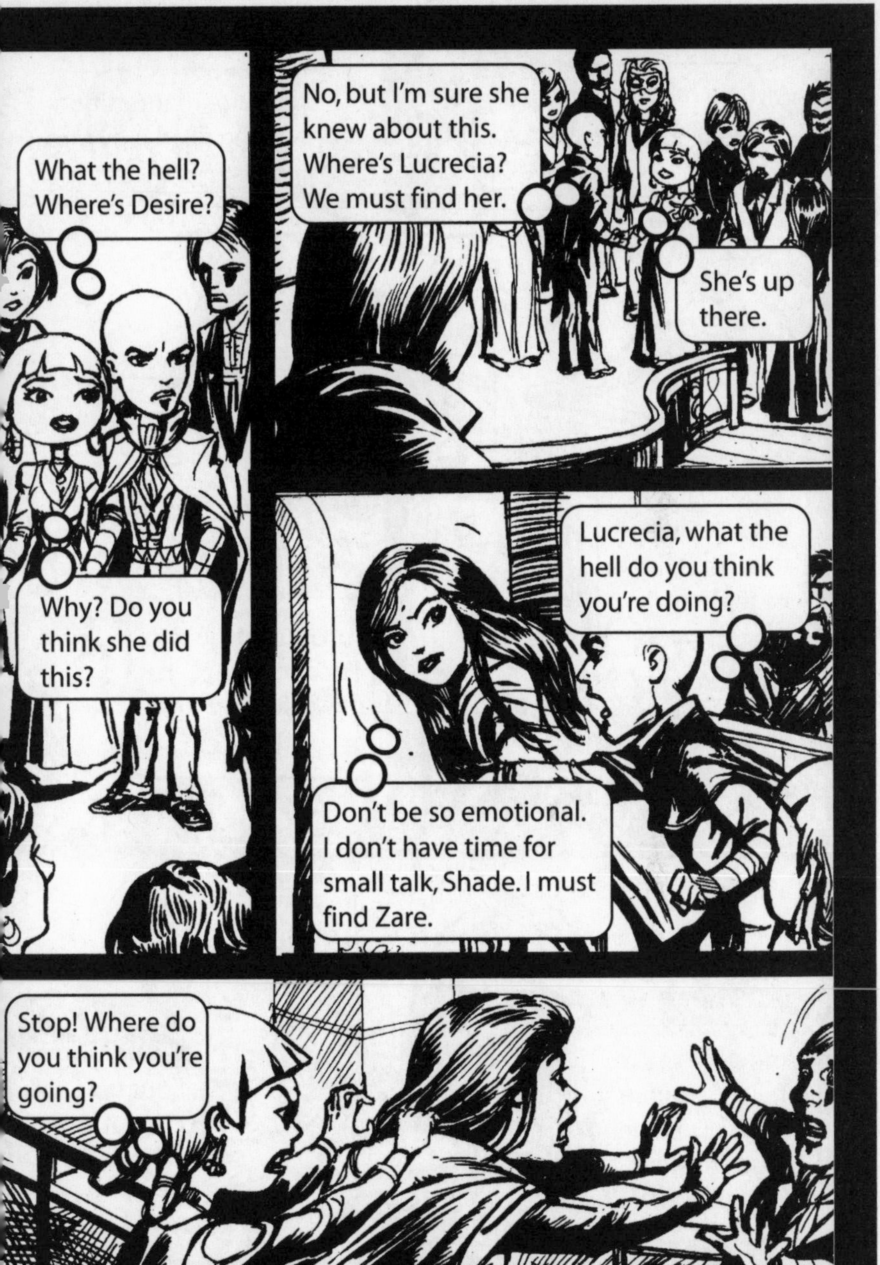
What the hell? Where's Desire?
Why? Do you think she did this?
No, but I'm sure she knew about this. Where's Lucrecia? We must find her.
She's up there.
Lucrecia, what the hell do you think you're doing?
Don't be so emotional. I don't have time for small talk, Shade. I must find Zare.
Stop! Where do you think you're going?

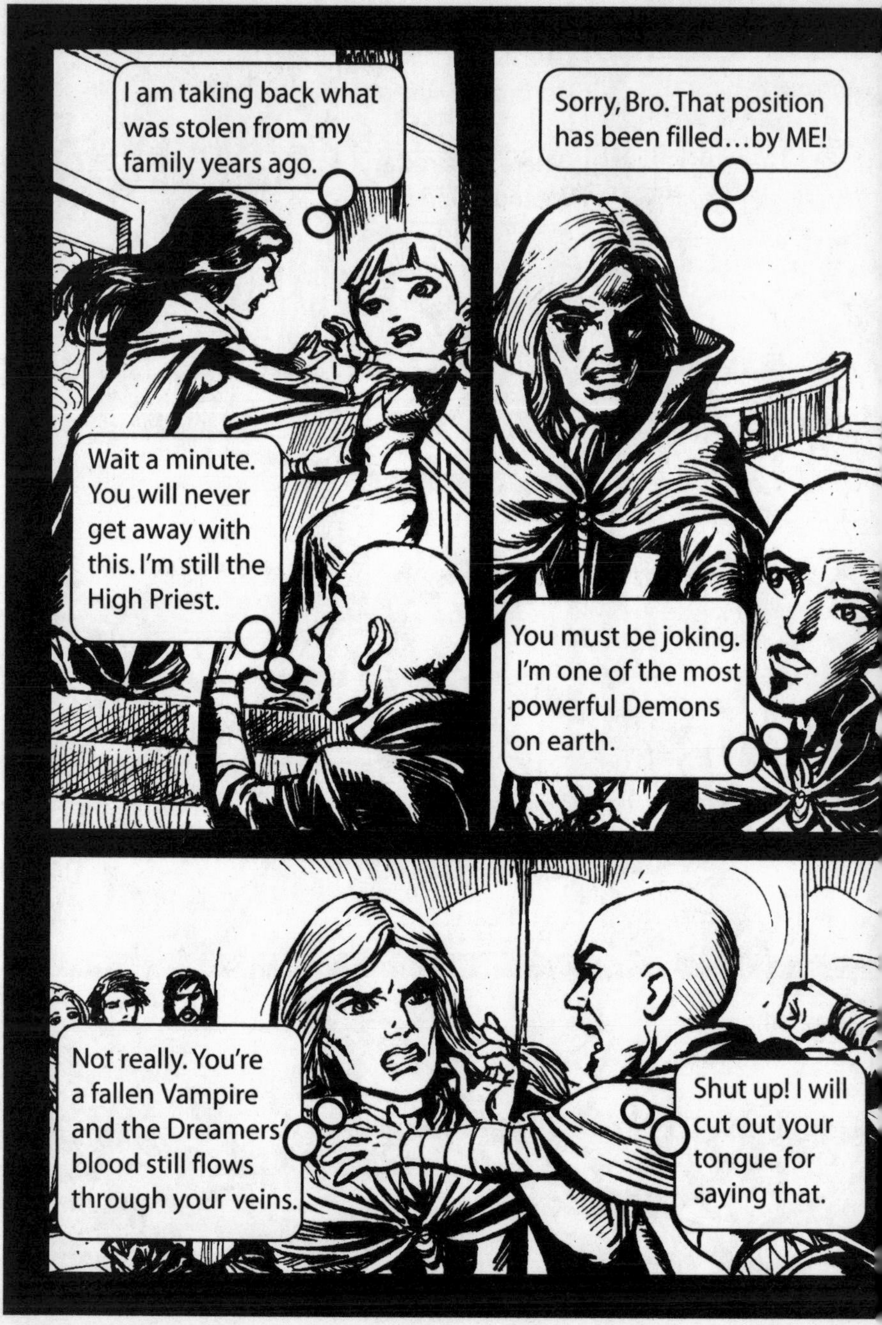
I am taking back what was stolen from my family years ago.
Wait a minute. You will never get away with this. I'm still the High Priest.
Sorry, Bro. That position has been filled…by ME!
You must be joking. I'm one of the most powerful Demons on earth.
Not really. You're a fallen Vampire and the Dreamers' blood still flows through your veins.
Shut up! I will cut out your tongue for saying that.

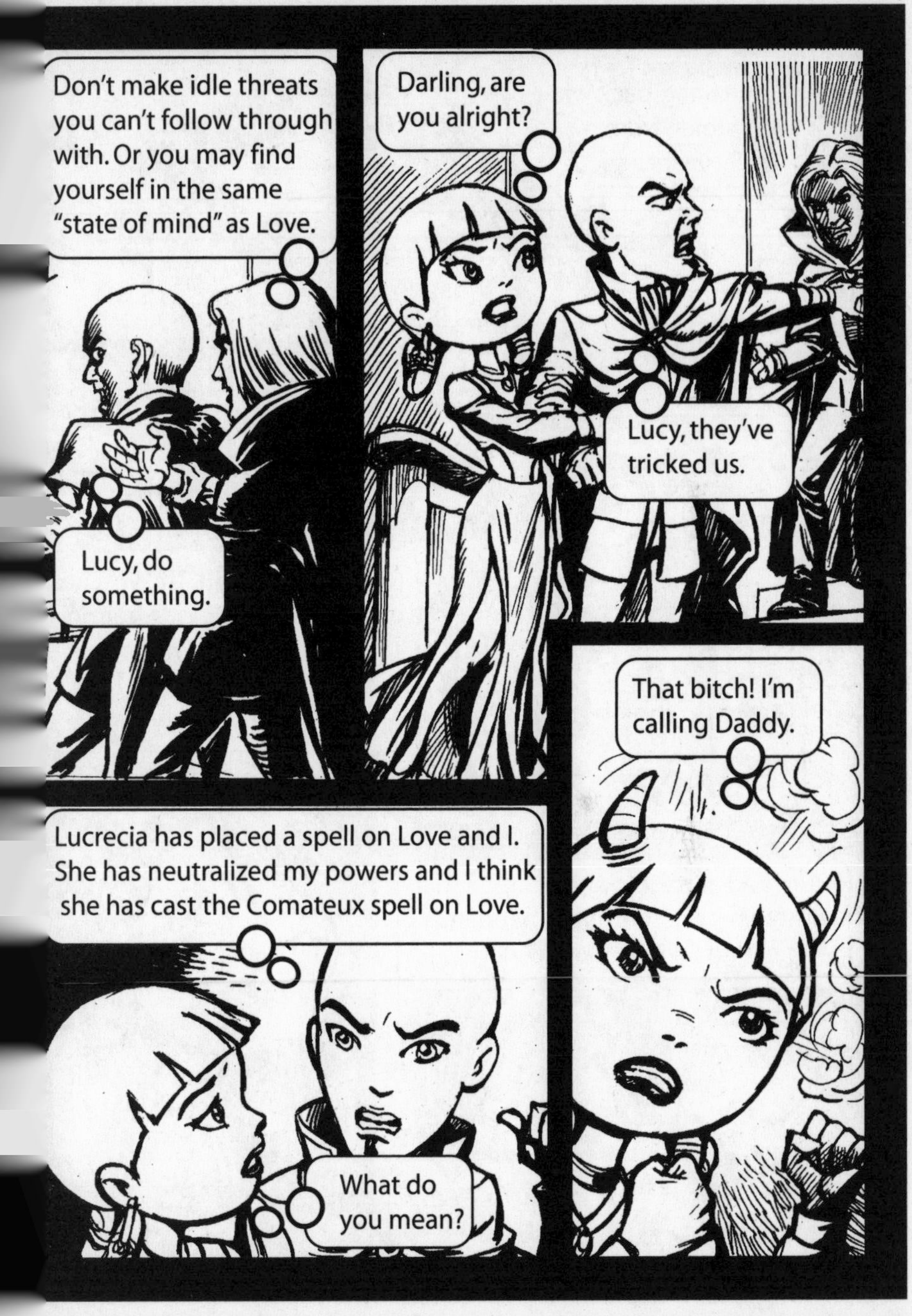
Don't make idle threats you can't follow through with. Or you may find yourself in the same "state of mind" as Love.
Lucy, do something.
Darling, are you alright?
Lucy, they've tricked us.
Lucrecia has placed a spell on Love and I. She has neutralized my powers and I think she has cast the Comateux spell on Love.
What do you mean?
That bitch! I'm calling Daddy.

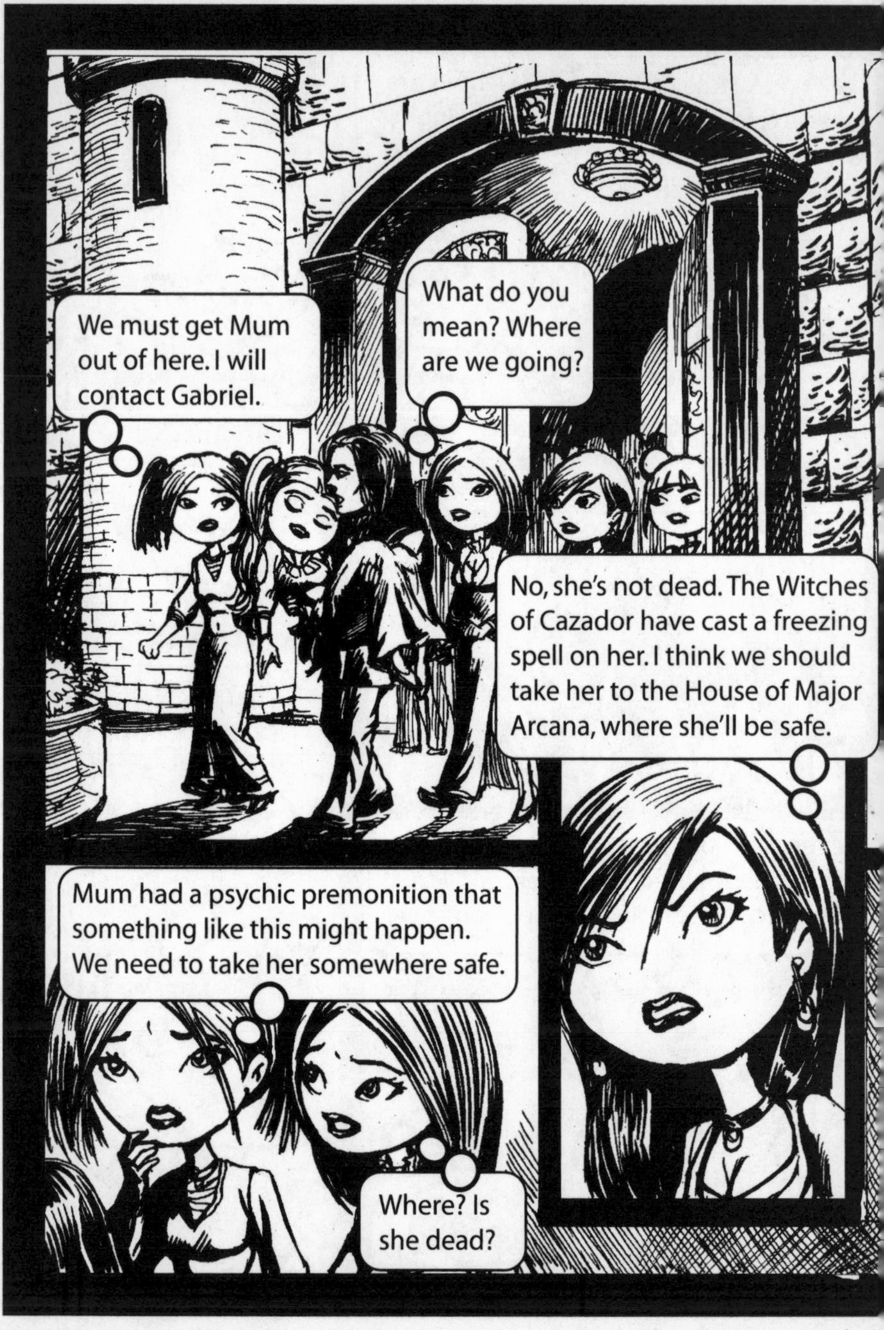

We must get Mum out of here. I will contact Gabriel.
What do you mean? Where are we going?
No, she's not dead. The Witches of Cazador have cast a freezing spell on her. I think we should take her to the House of Major Arcana, where she'll be safe.
Mum had a psychic premonition that something like this might happen. We need to take her somewhere safe.
Where? Is she dead?

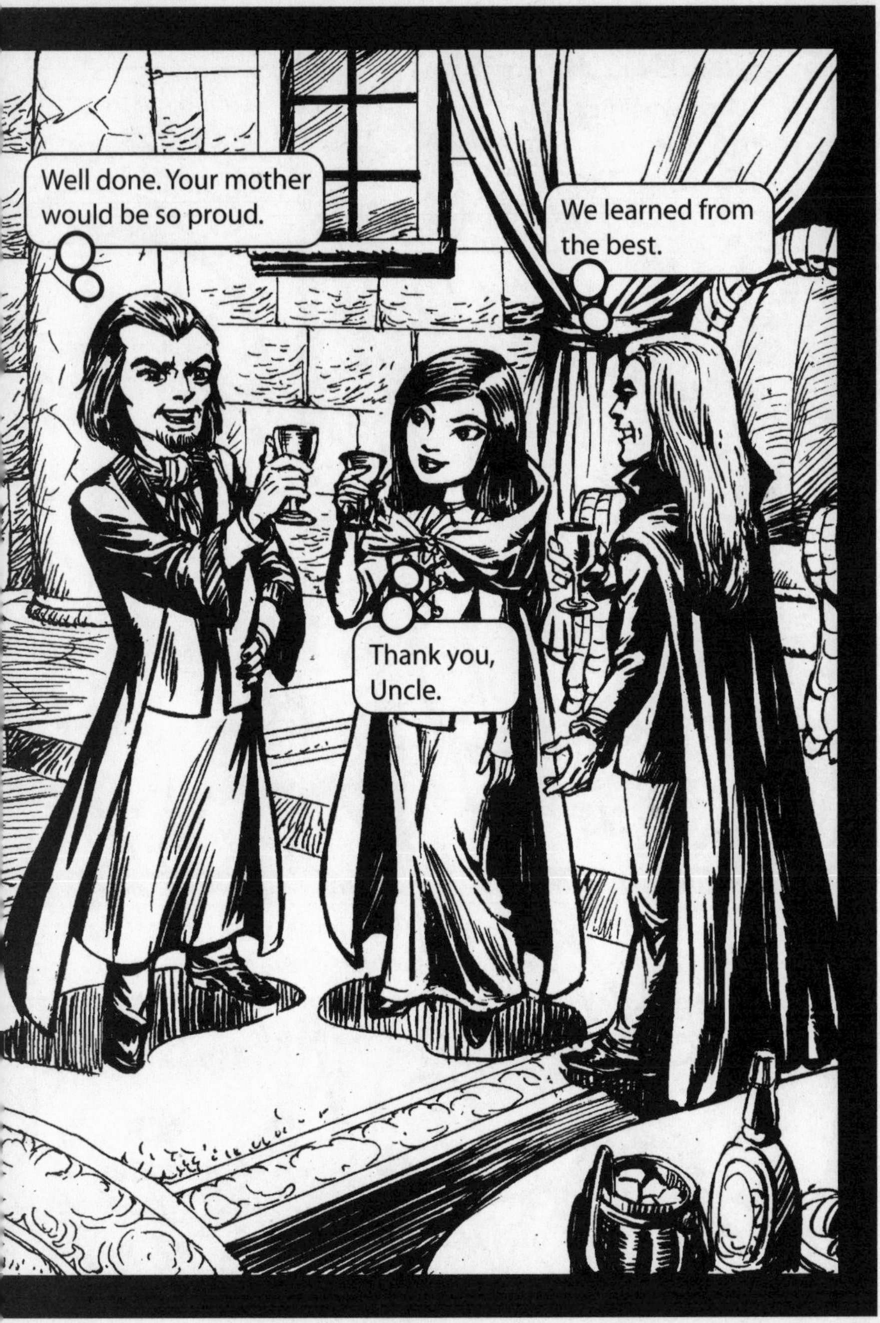
Well done. Your mother would be so proud.
We learned from the best.
Thank you, Uncle.

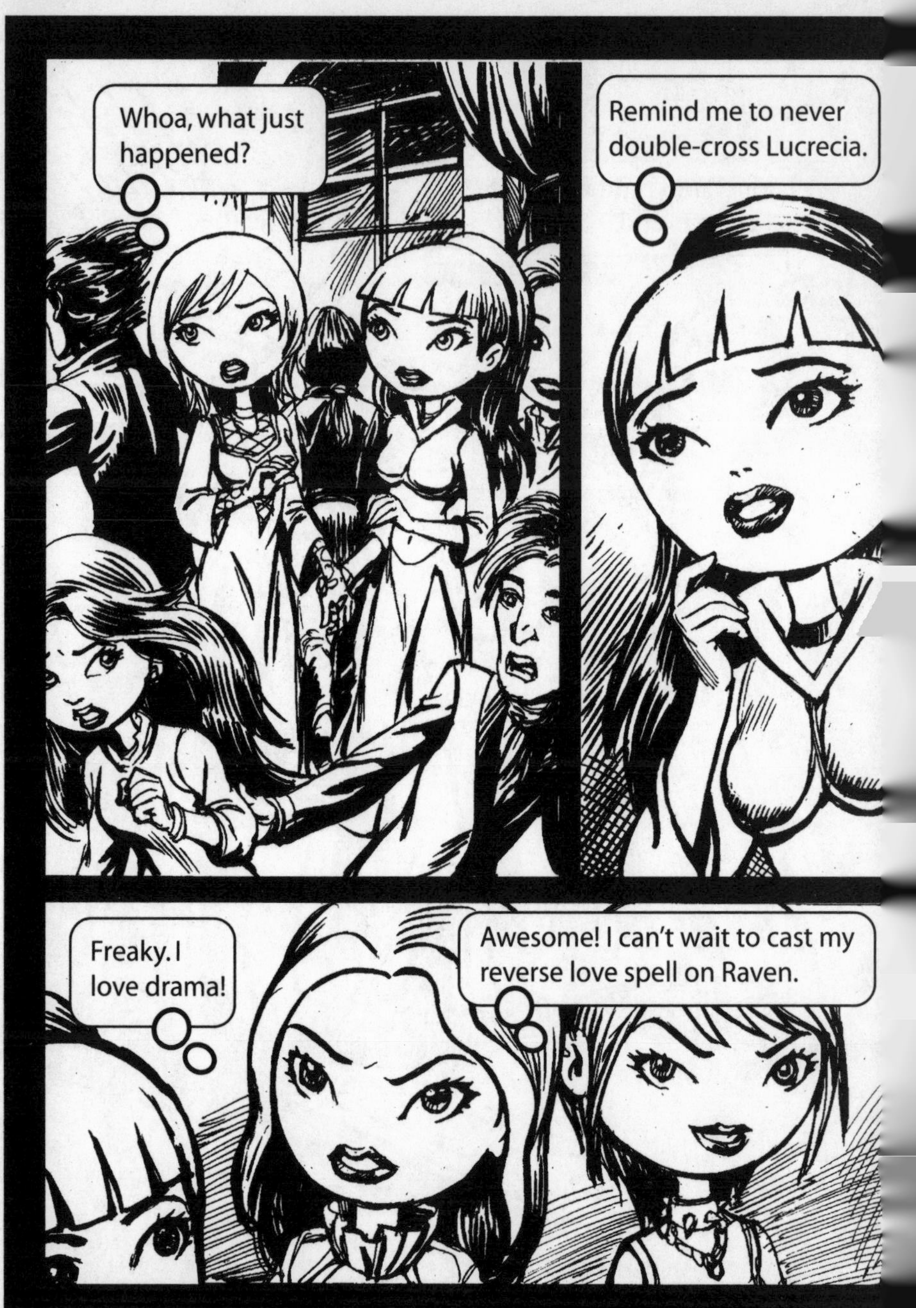
Whoa, what just happened?
Remind me to never double-cross Lucrecia.
Freaky. I love drama!
Awesome! I can't wait to cast my reverse love spell on Raven.

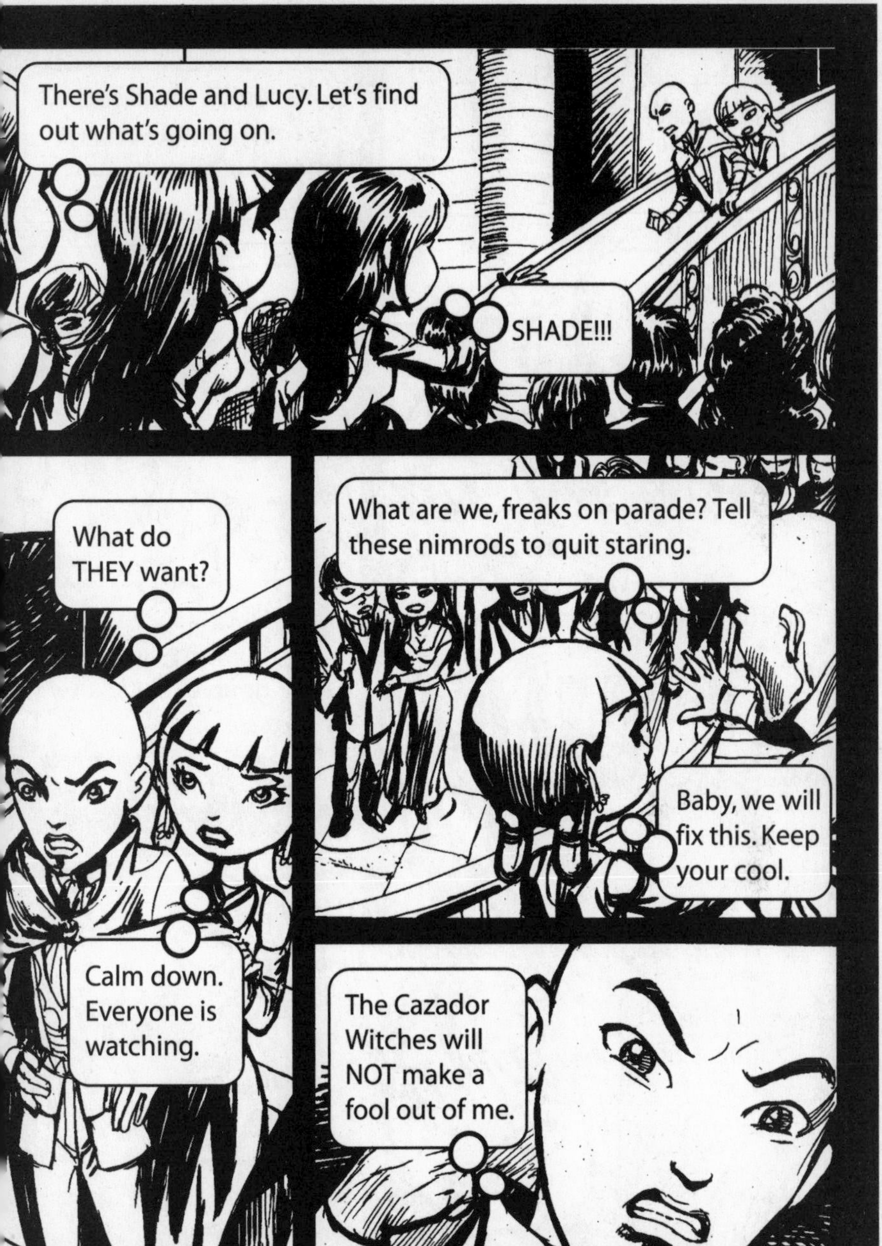
There's Shade and Lucy. Let's find out what's going on.
SHADE!!!
What do THEY want?
Calm down. Everyone is watching.
What are we, freaks on parade? Tell these nimrods to quit staring.
Baby, we will fix this. Keep your cool.
The Cazador Witches will NOT make a fool out of me.

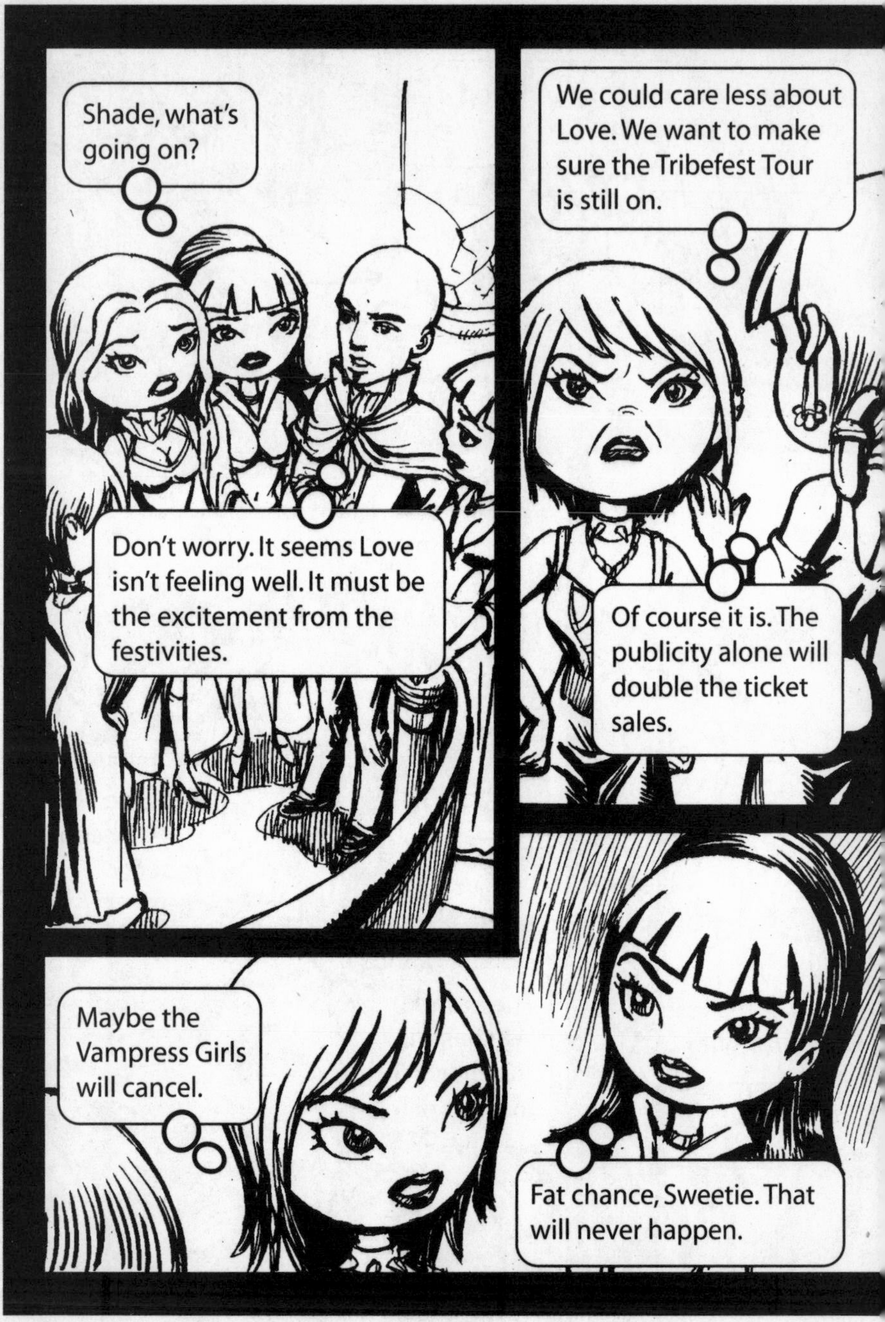

Shade, what's going on?
Don't worry. It seems Love isn't feeling well. It must be the excitement from the festivities.
We could care less about Love. We want to make sure the Tribefest Tour is still on.
Of course it is. The publicity alone will double the ticket sales.
Maybe the Vampress Girls will cancel.
Fat chance, Sweetie. That will never happen.

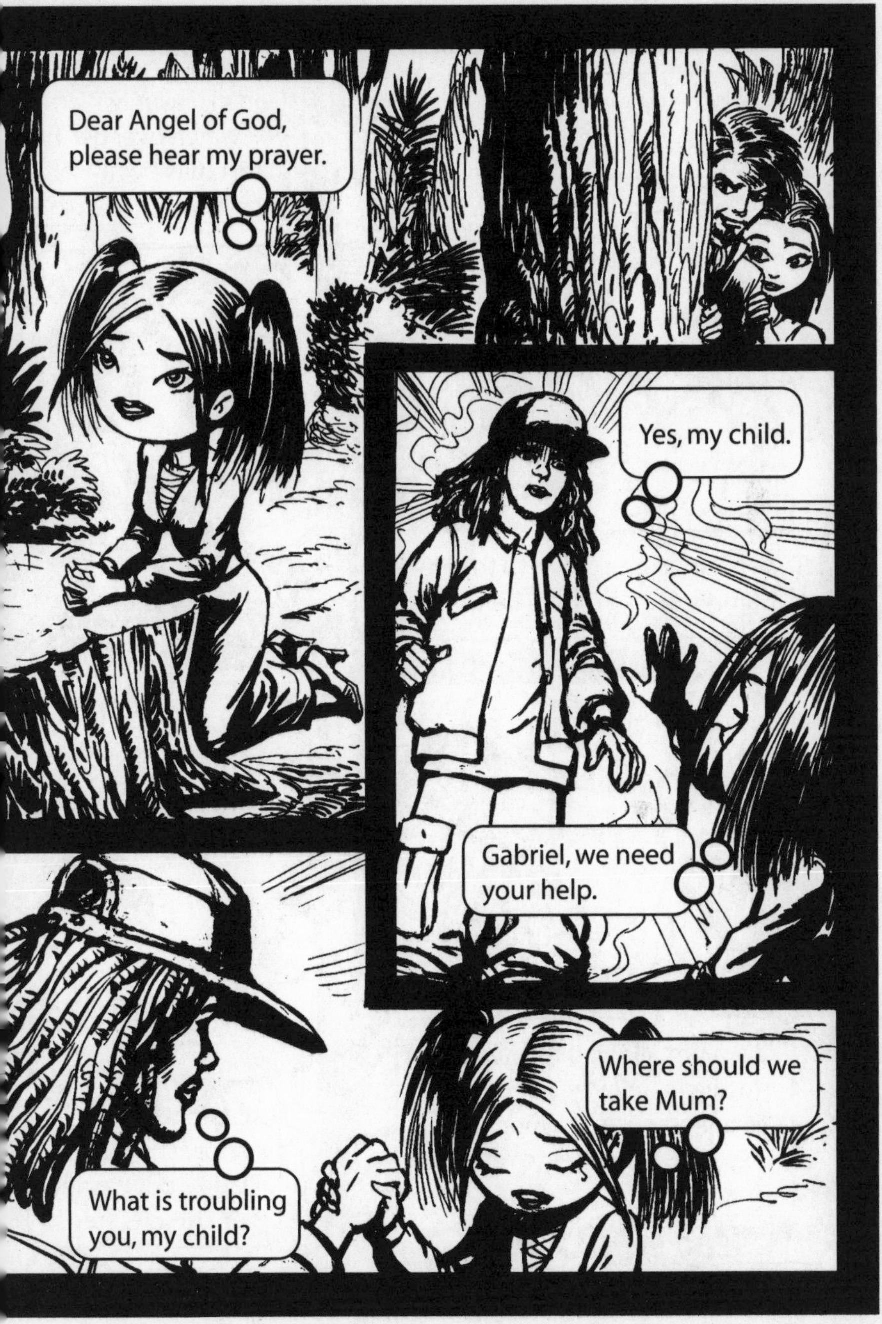

Dear Angel of God, please hear my prayer.
Yes, my child.
Gabriel, we need your help.
What is troubling you, my child?
Where should we take Mum?

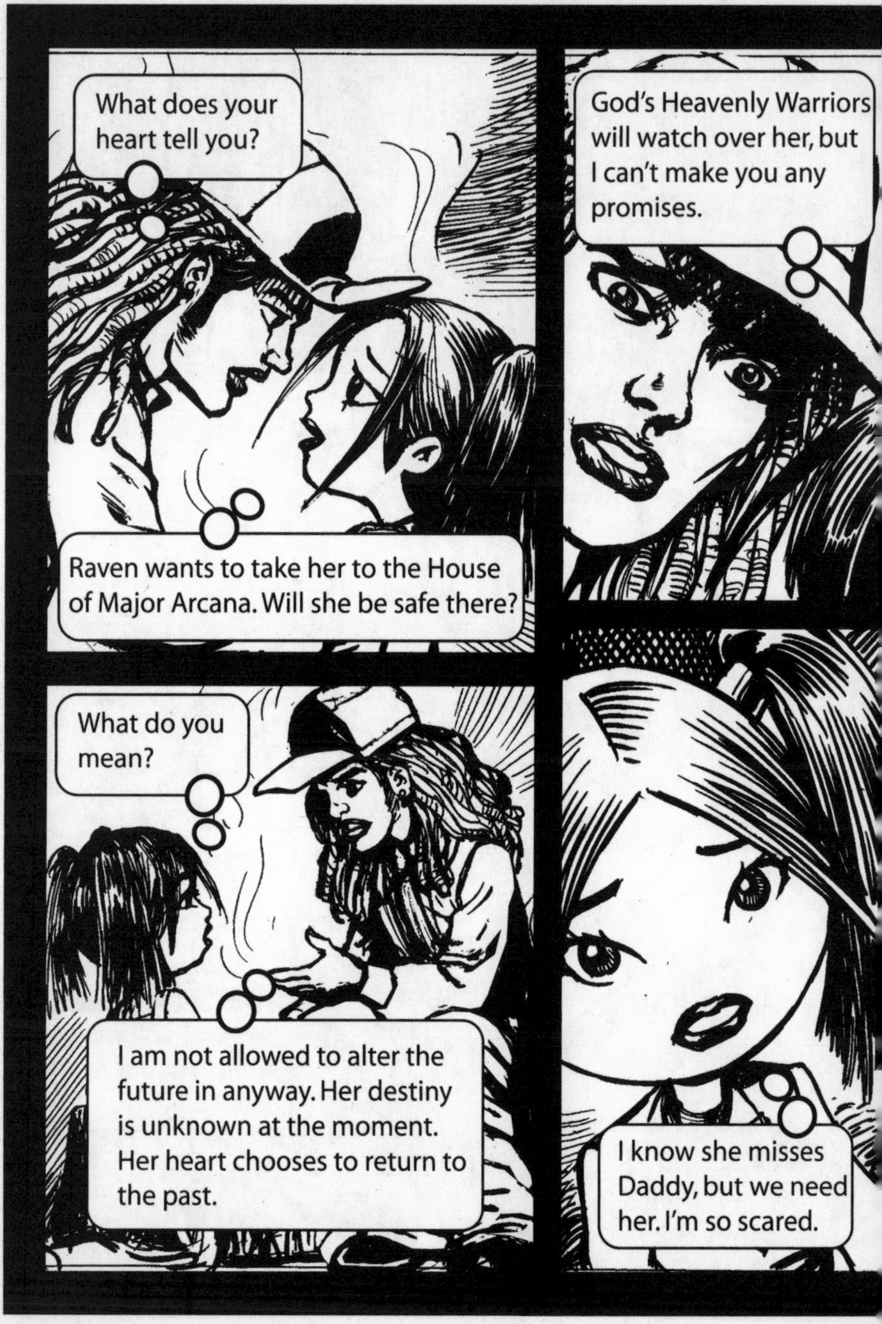
What does your heart tell you?
Raven wants to take her to the House of Major Arcana. Will she be safe there?
God's Heavenly Warriors will watch over her, but I can't make you any promises.
What do you mean?
I am not allowed to alter the future in anyway. Her destiny is unknown at the moment. Her heart chooses to return to the past.
I know she misses Daddy, but we need her. I'm so scared.

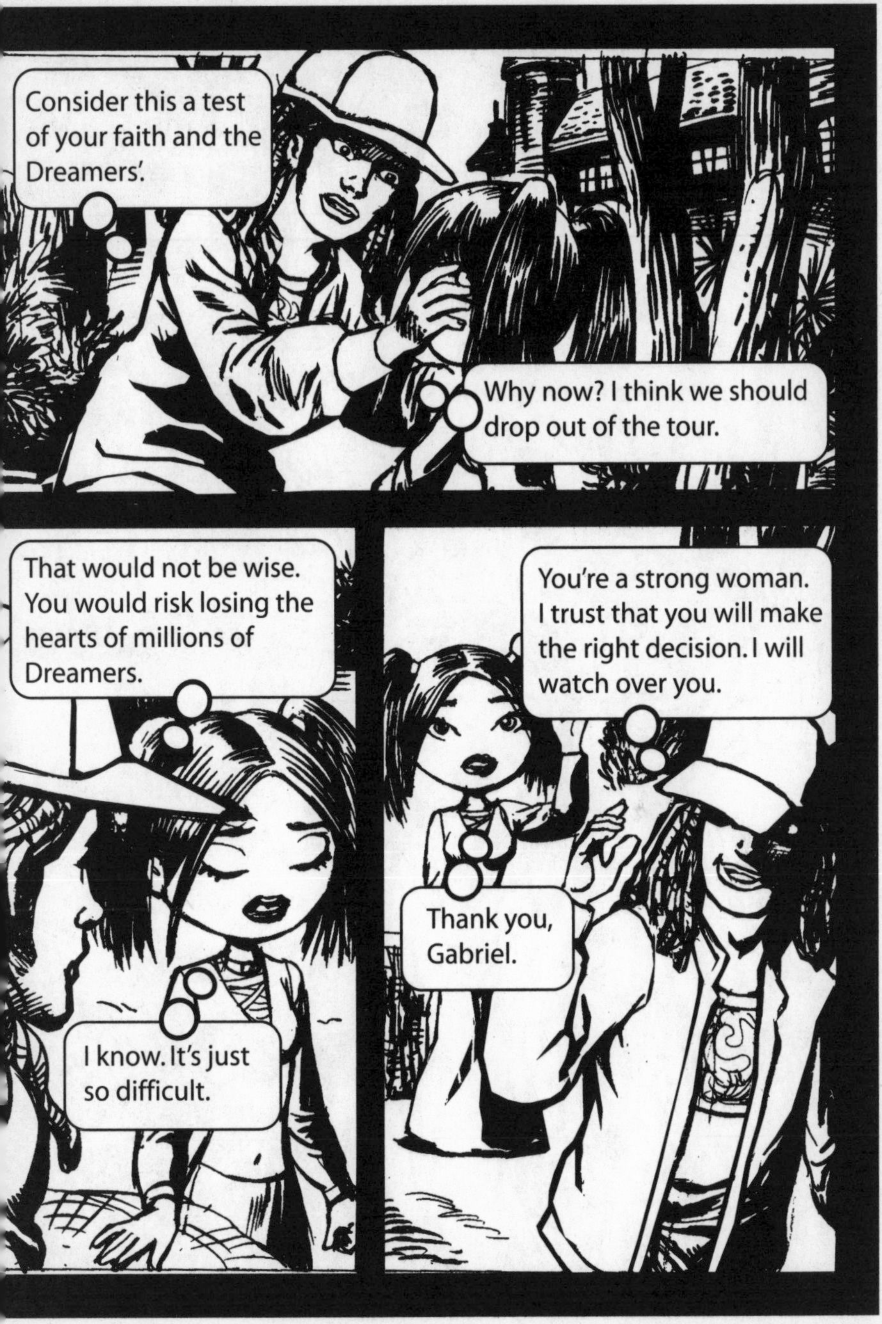
Consider this a test of your faith and the Dreamers'.
Why now? I think we should drop out of the tour.
That would not be wise. You would risk losing the hearts of millions of Dreamers.
I know. It's just so difficult.
You're a strong woman. I trust that you will make the right decision. I will watch over you.
Thank you, Gabriel.

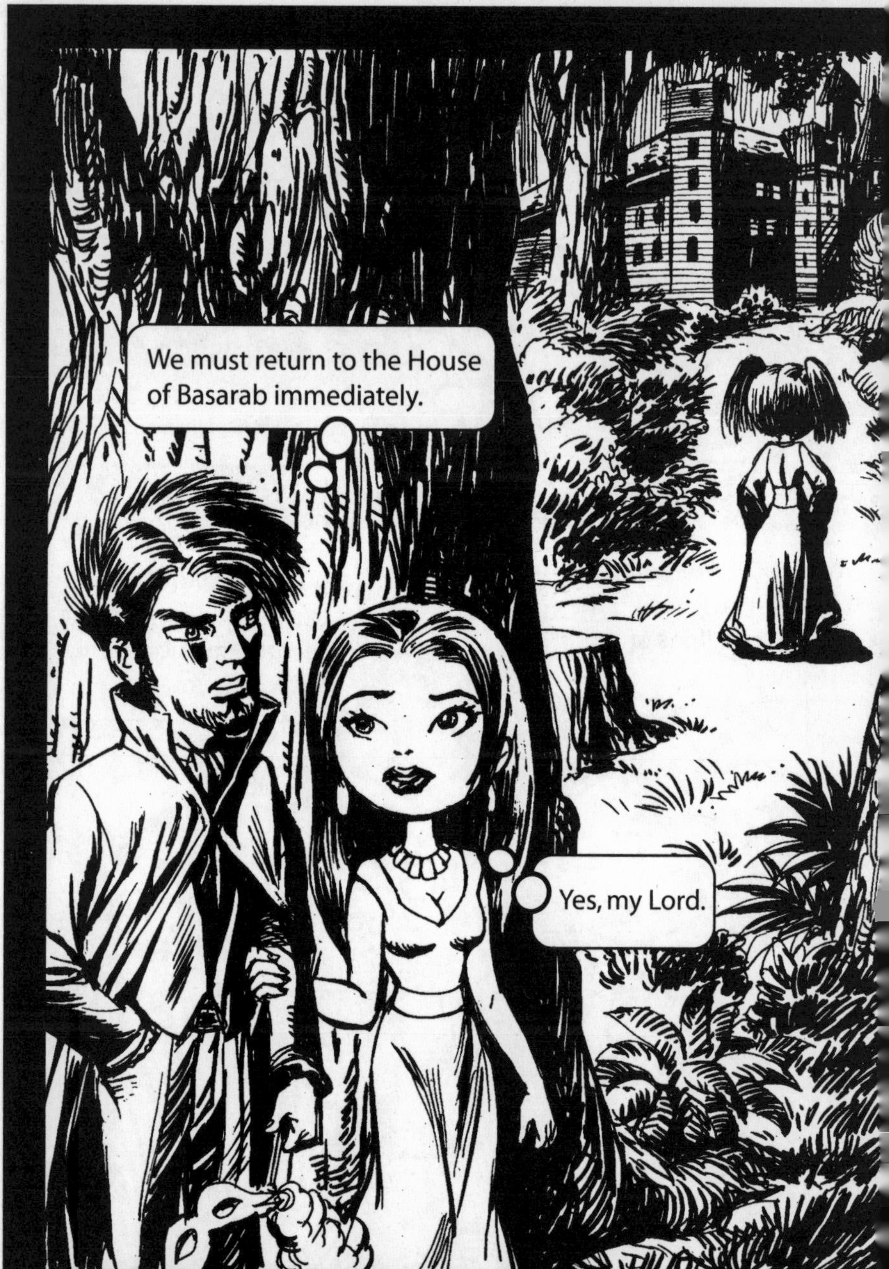
We must return to the House of Basarab immediately.
Yes, my Lord.

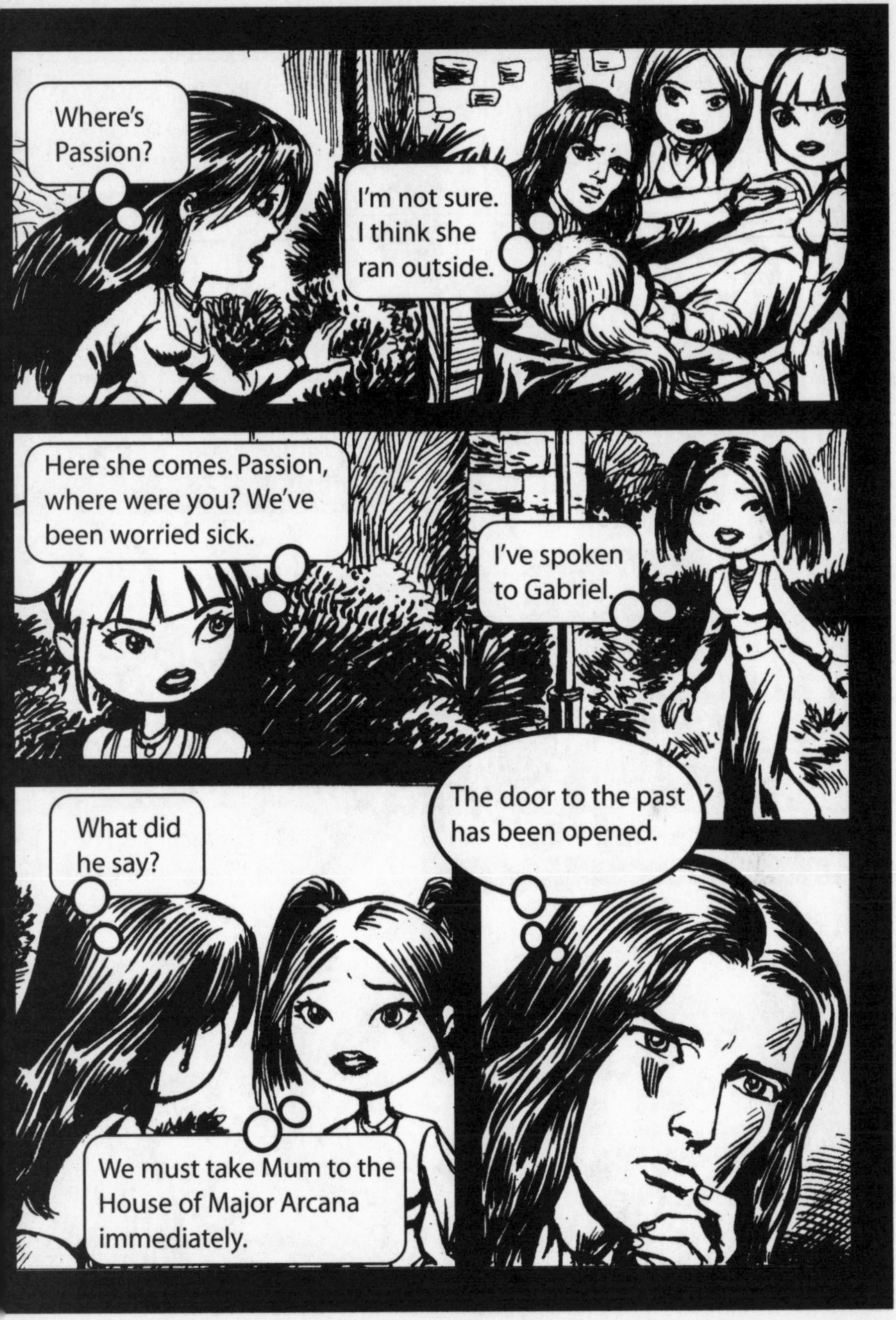
Where's Passion?
I'm not sure. I think she ran outside.
Here she comes. Passion, where were you? We've been worried sick.
I've spoken to Gabriel.
What did he say?
We must take Mum to the House of Major Arcana immediately.
The door to the past has been opened.

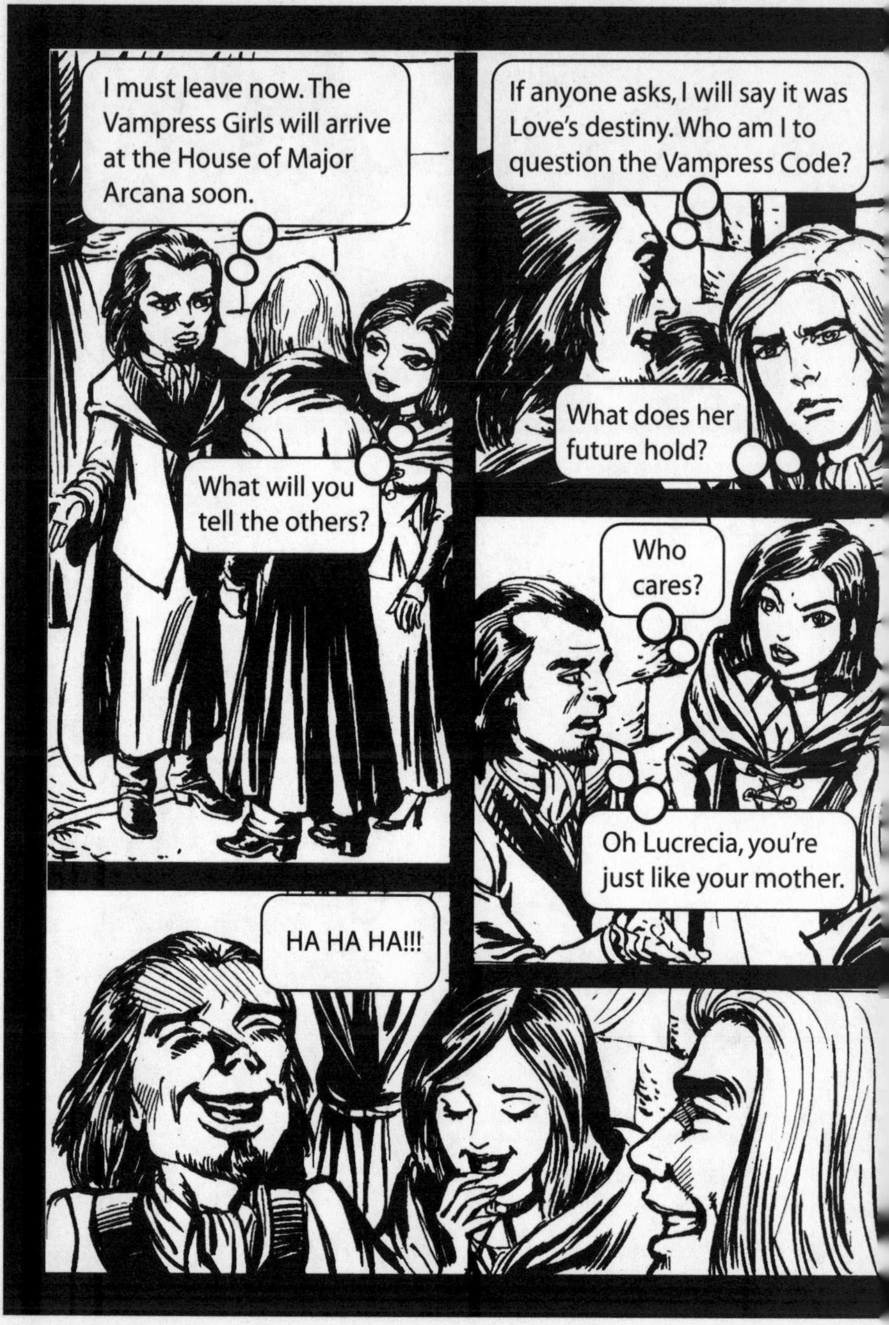
I must leave now. The Vampress Girls will arrive at the House of Major Arcana soon.
What will you tell the others?
If anyone asks, I will say it was Love's destiny. Who am I to question the Vampress Code?
What does her future hold?
Who cares?
Oh Lucrecia, you're just like your mother.
HA HA HA!!!

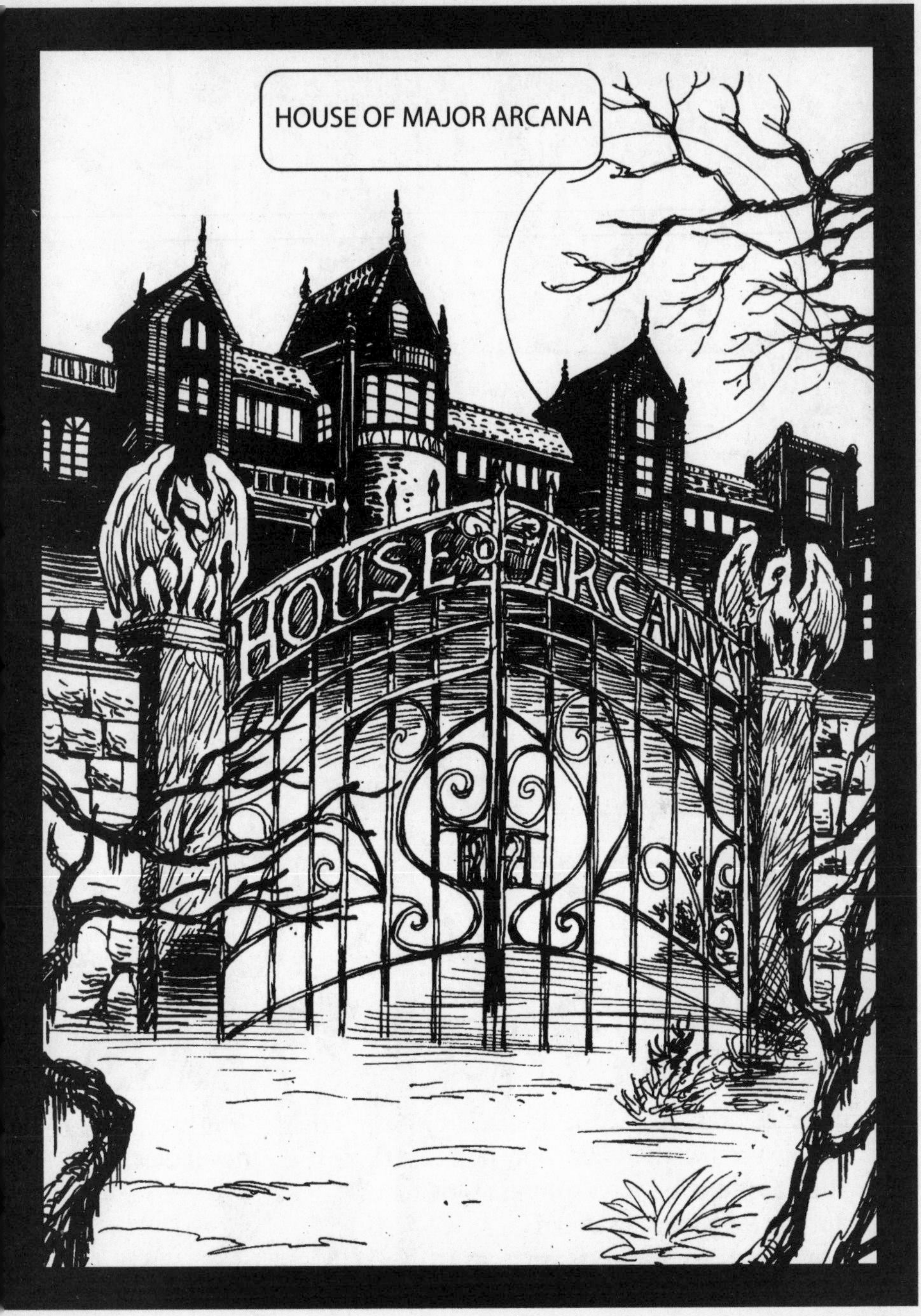
HOUSE OF MAJOR ARCANA
HOUSE of ARCANA

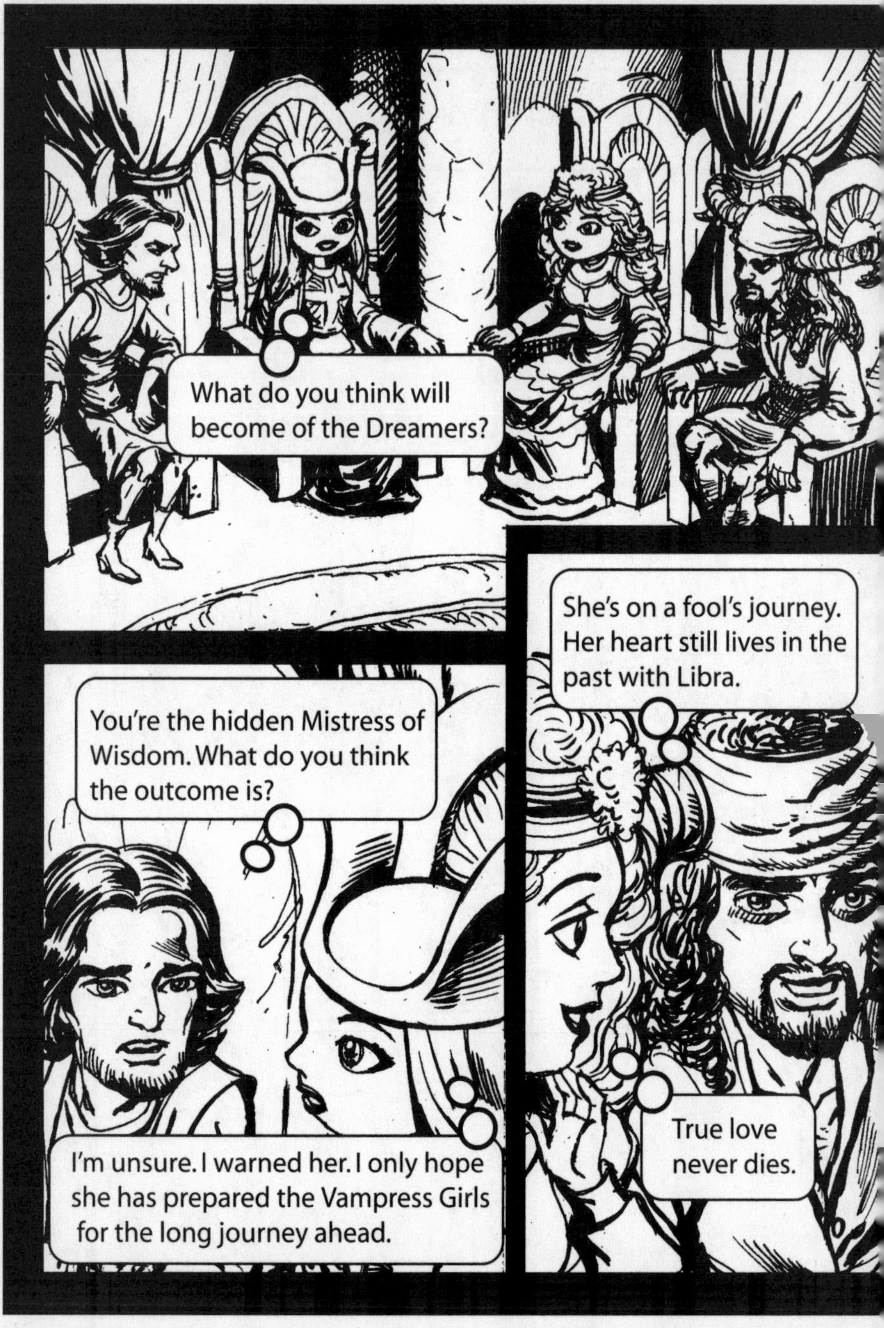
What do you think will become of the Dreamers?
She's on a fool's journey. Her heart still lives in the past with Libra.
You're the hidden Mistress of Wisdom. What do you think the outcome is?
I'm unsure. I warned her. I only hope she has prepared the Vampress Girls for the long journey ahead.
True love never dies.

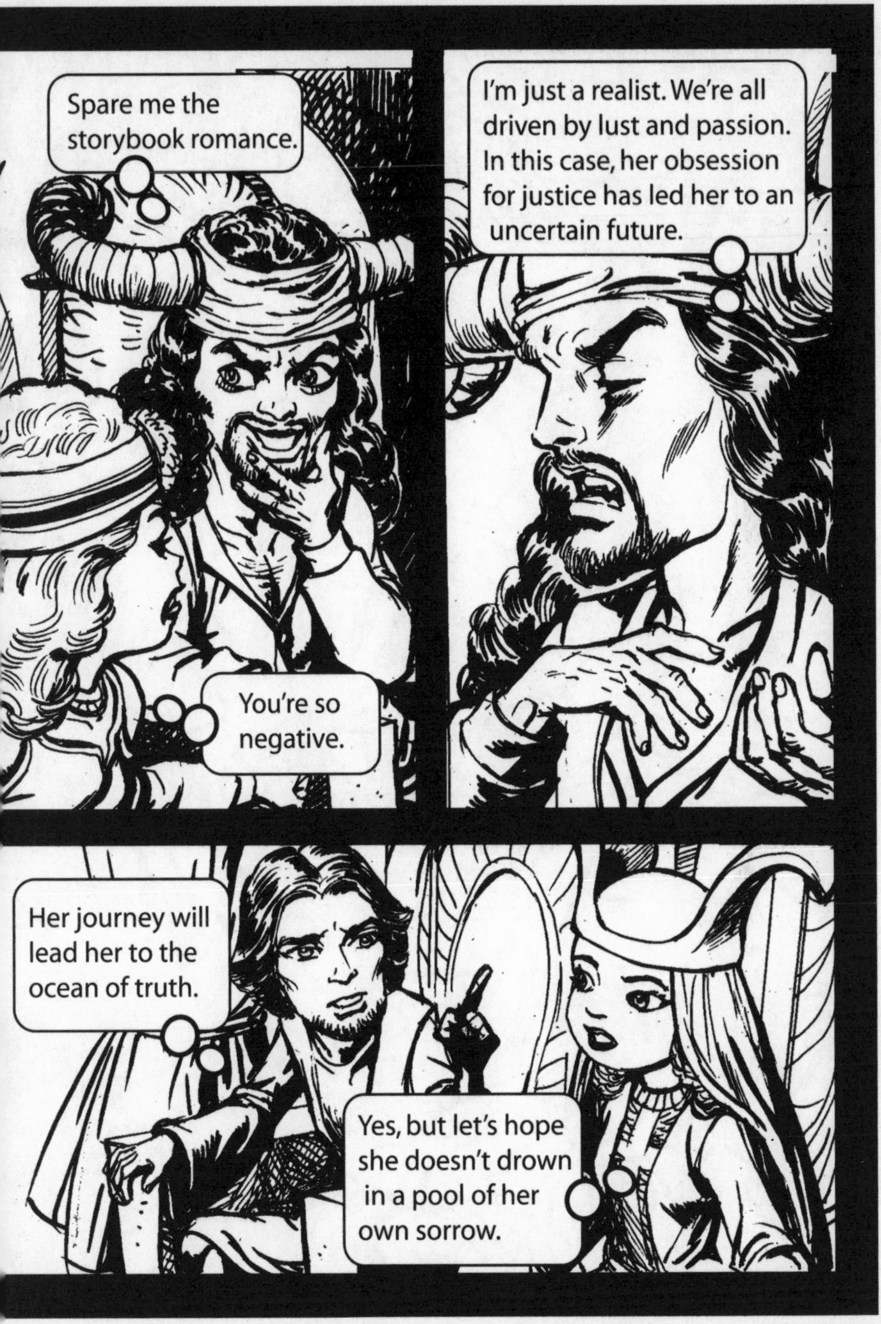
Spare me the storybook romance.
You're so negative.
I'm just a realist. We're all driven by lust and passion. In this case, her obsession for justice has led her to an uncertain future.
Her journey will lead her to the ocean of truth.
Yes, but let's hope she doesn't drown in a pool of her own sorrow.

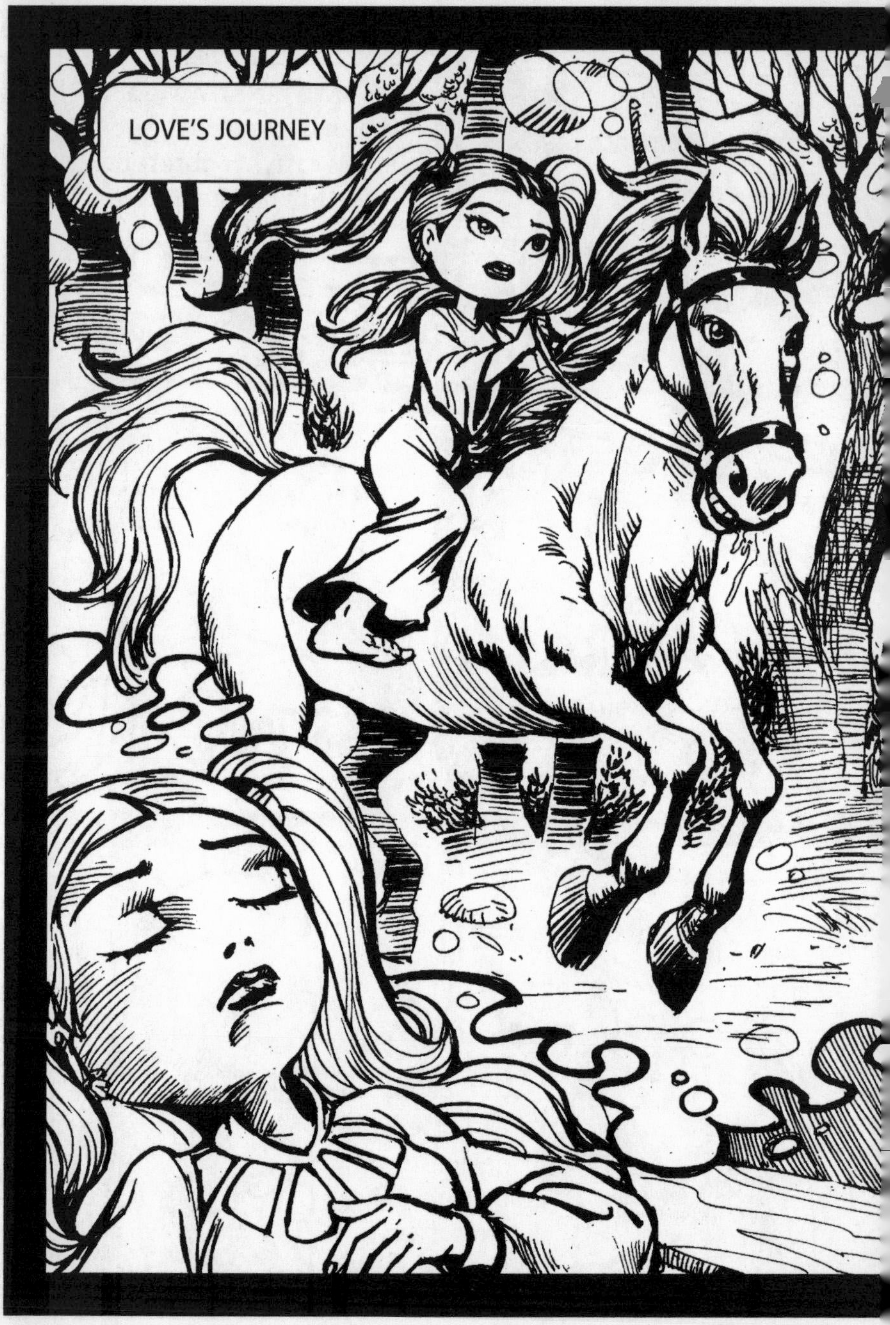
LOVE'S JOURNEY

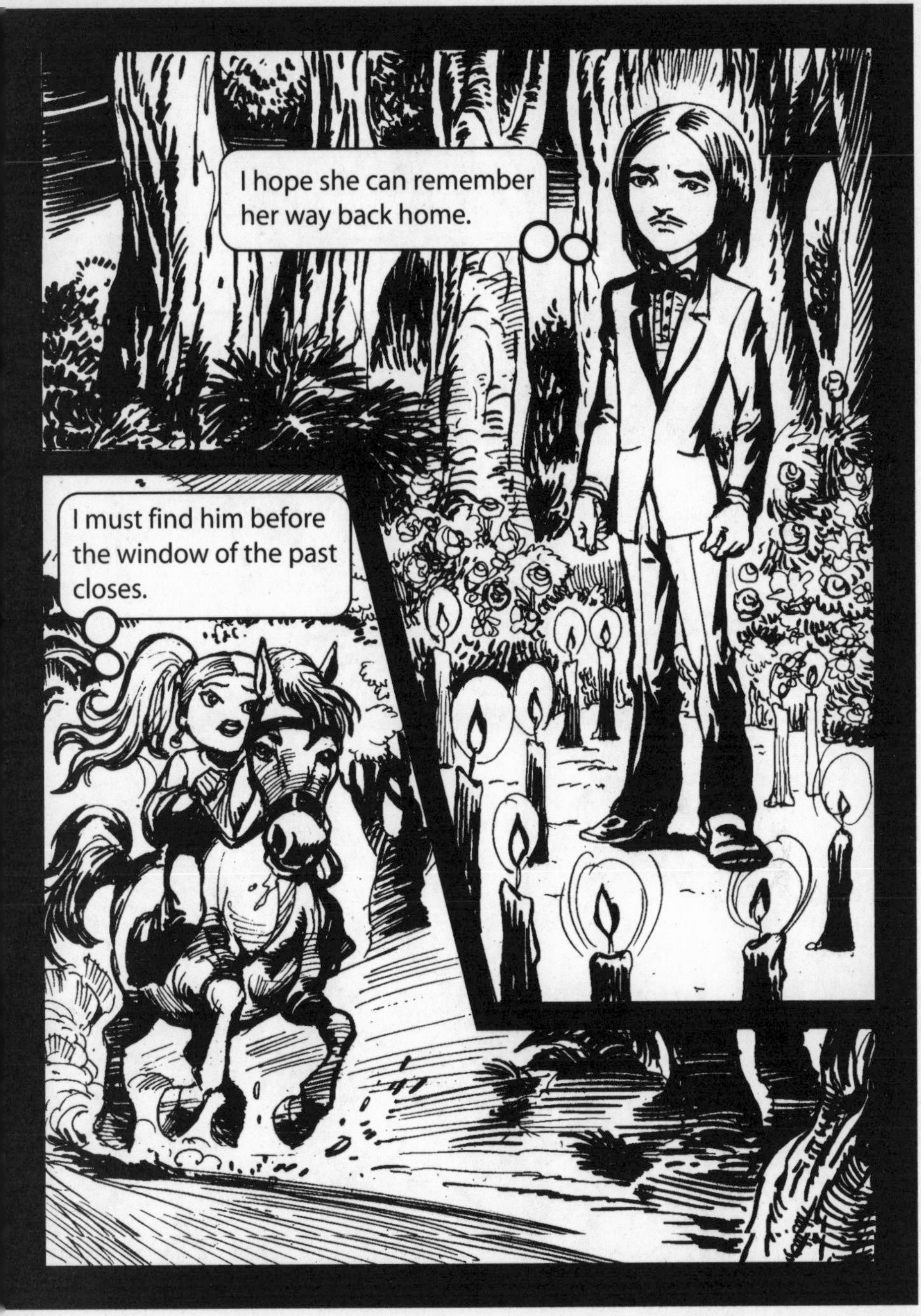
I hope she can remember her way back home.
I must find him before the window of the past closes.

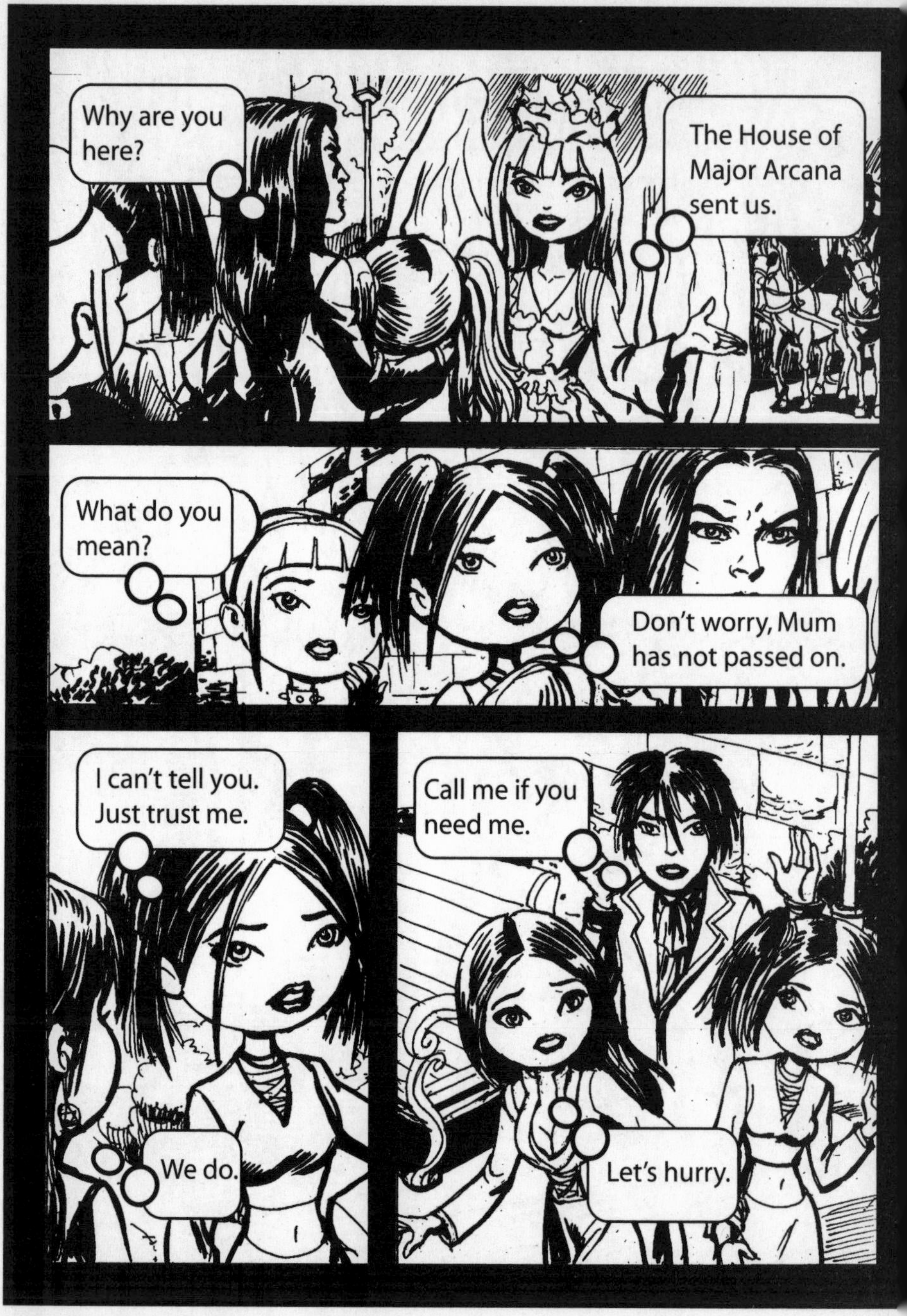
Why are you here?
The House of Major Arcana sent us.
What do you mean?
Don't worry, Mum has not passed on.
I can't tell you. Just trust me.
We do.
Call me if you need me.
Let's hurry.

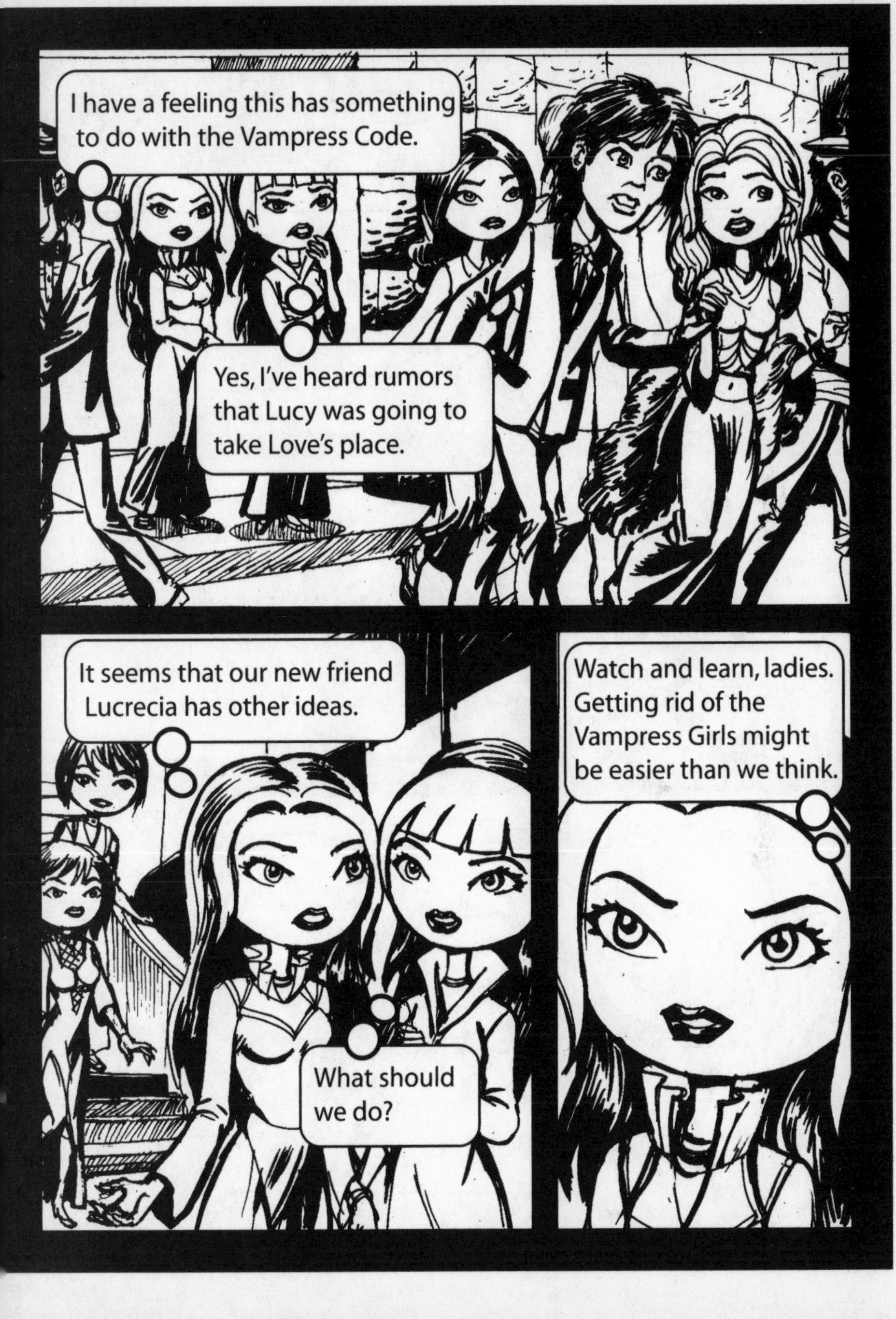
I have a feeling this has something to do with the Vampress Code.
Yes, I've heard rumors that Lucy was going to take Love's place.
It seems that our new friend Lucrecia has other ideas.
What should we do?
Watch and learn, ladies. Getting rid of the Vampress Girls might be easier than we think.

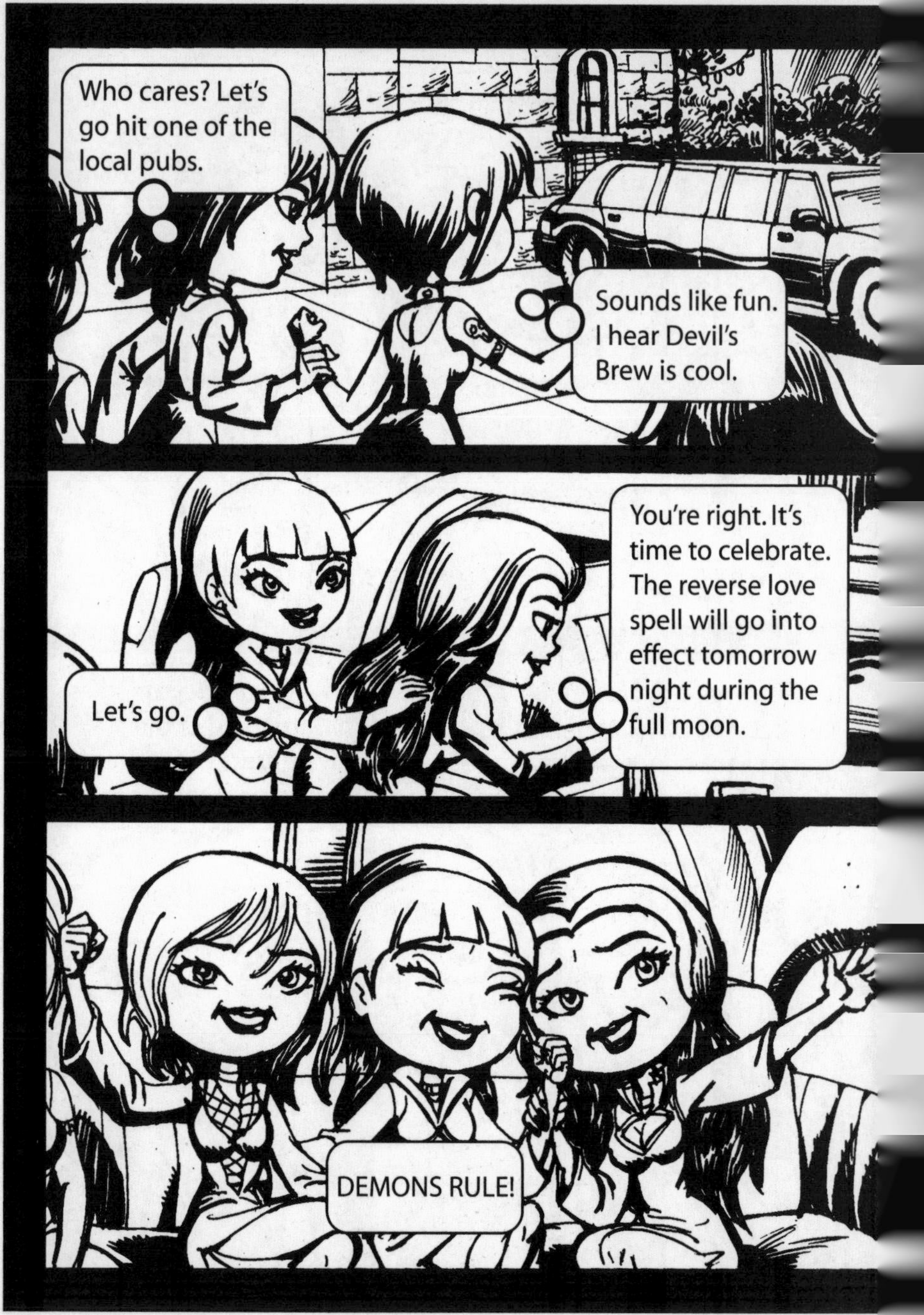
Who cares? Let's go hit one of the local pubs.
Sounds like fun. I hear Devil's Brew is cool.
Let's go.
You're right. It's time to celebrate. The reverse love spell will go into effect tomorrow night during the full moon.
DEMONS RULE!

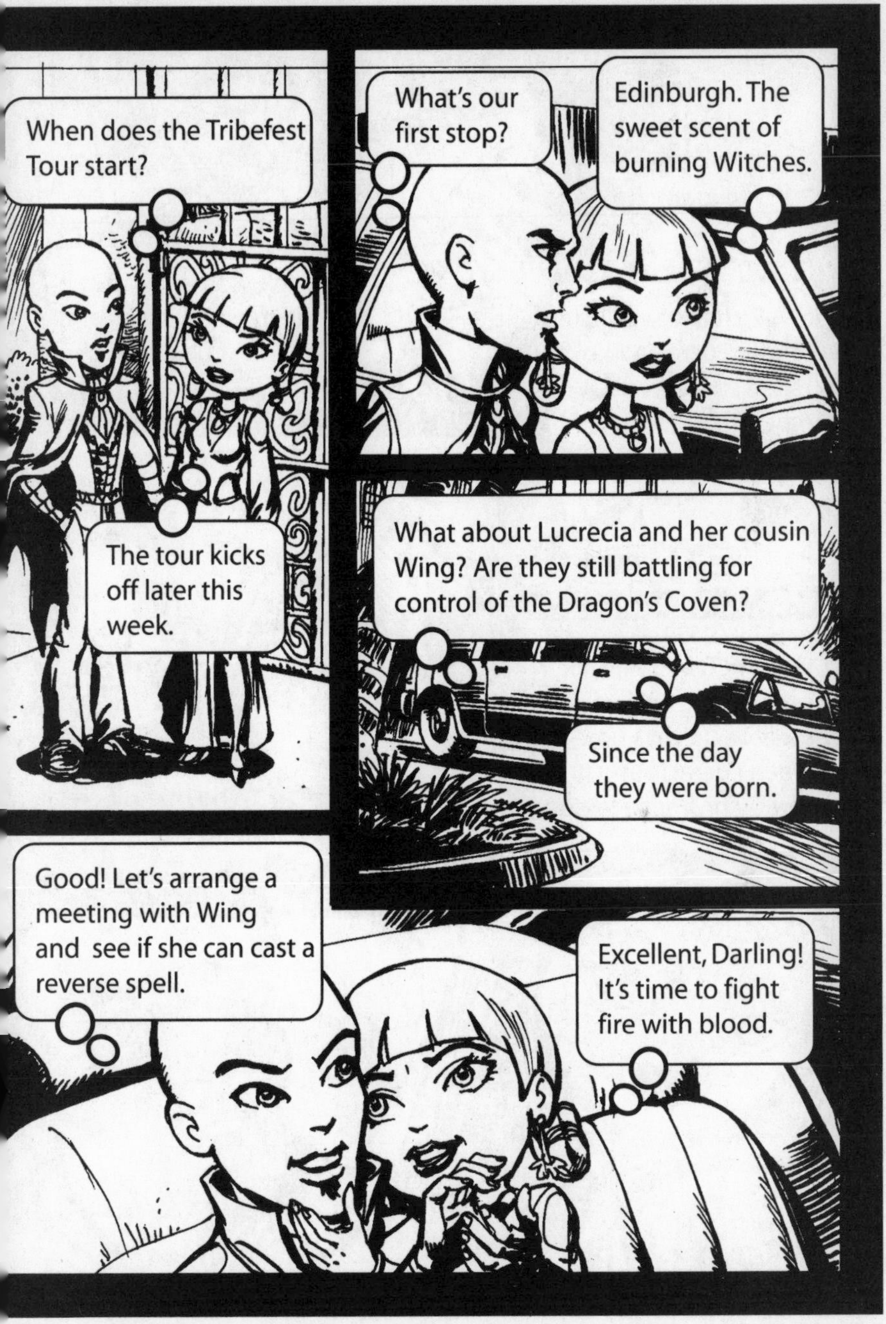
When does the Tribefest Tour start?
The tour kicks off later this week.
What's our first stop?
Edinburgh. The sweet scent of burning Witches.
What about Lucrecia and her cousin Wing? Are they still battling for control of the Dragon's Coven?
Since the day they were born.
Good! Let's arrange a meeting with Wing and see if she can cast a reverse spell.
Excellent, Darling! It's time to fight fire with blood.

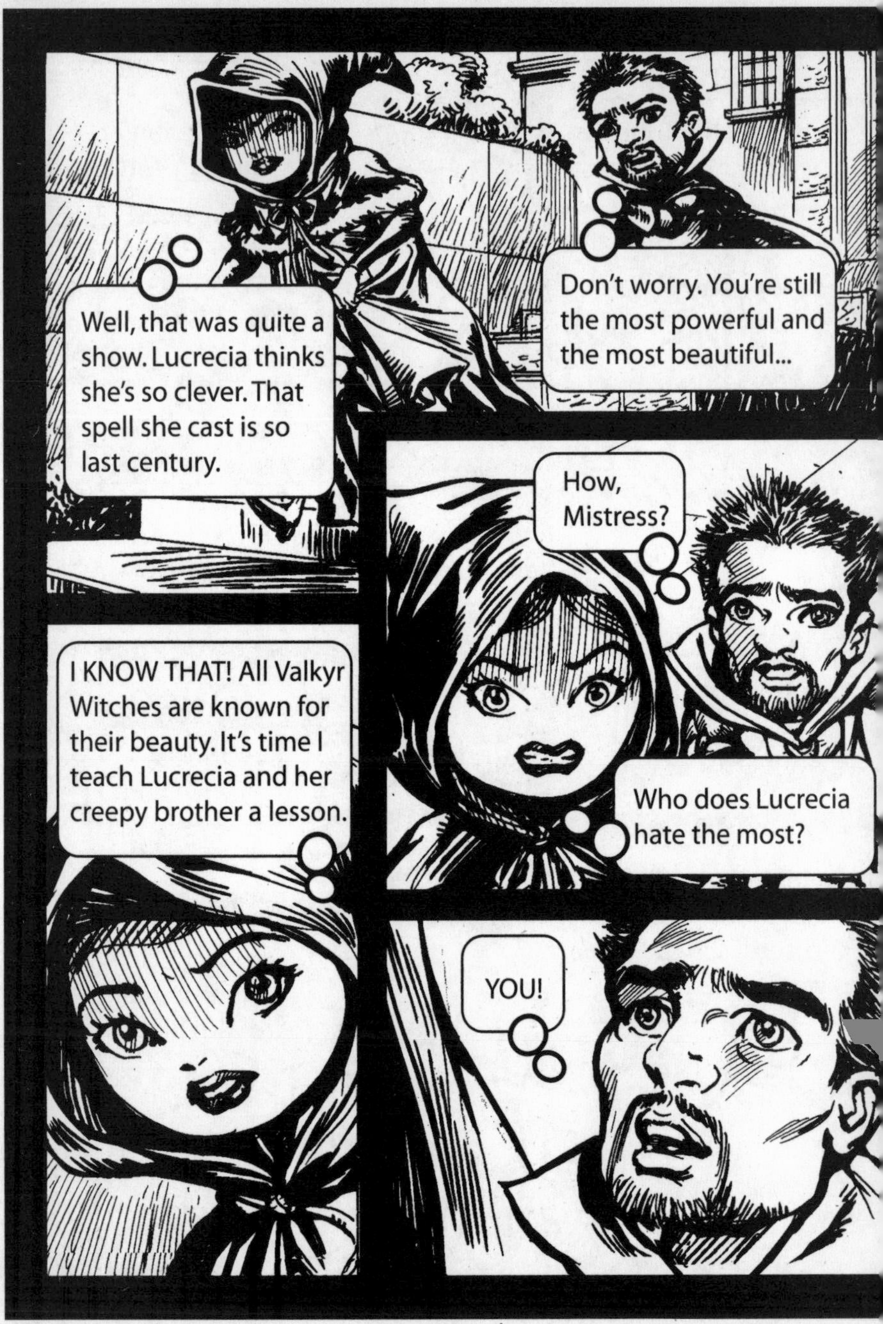
Well, that was quite a show. Lucrecia thinks she's so clever. That spell she cast is so last century.
Don't worry. You're still the most powerful and the most beautiful...
I KNOW THAT! All Valkyr Witches are known for their beauty. It's time I teach Lucrecia and her creepy brother a lesson.
How, Mistress?
Who does Lucrecia hate the most?
YOU!

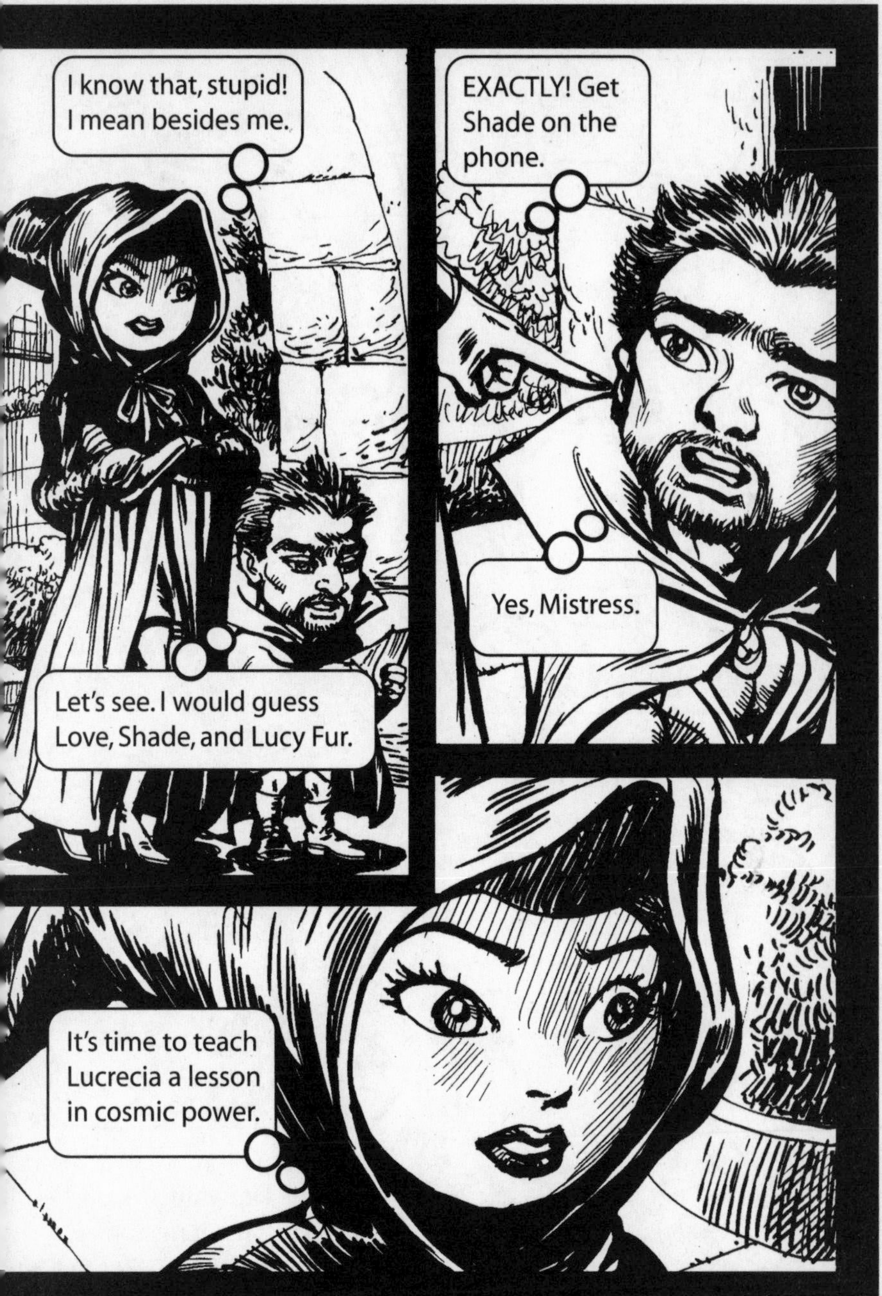
I know that, stupid! I mean besides me.
Let's see. I would guess Love, Shade, and Lucy Fur.
EXACTLY! Get Shade on the phone.
Yes, Mistress.
It's time to teach Lucrecia a lesson in cosmic power.

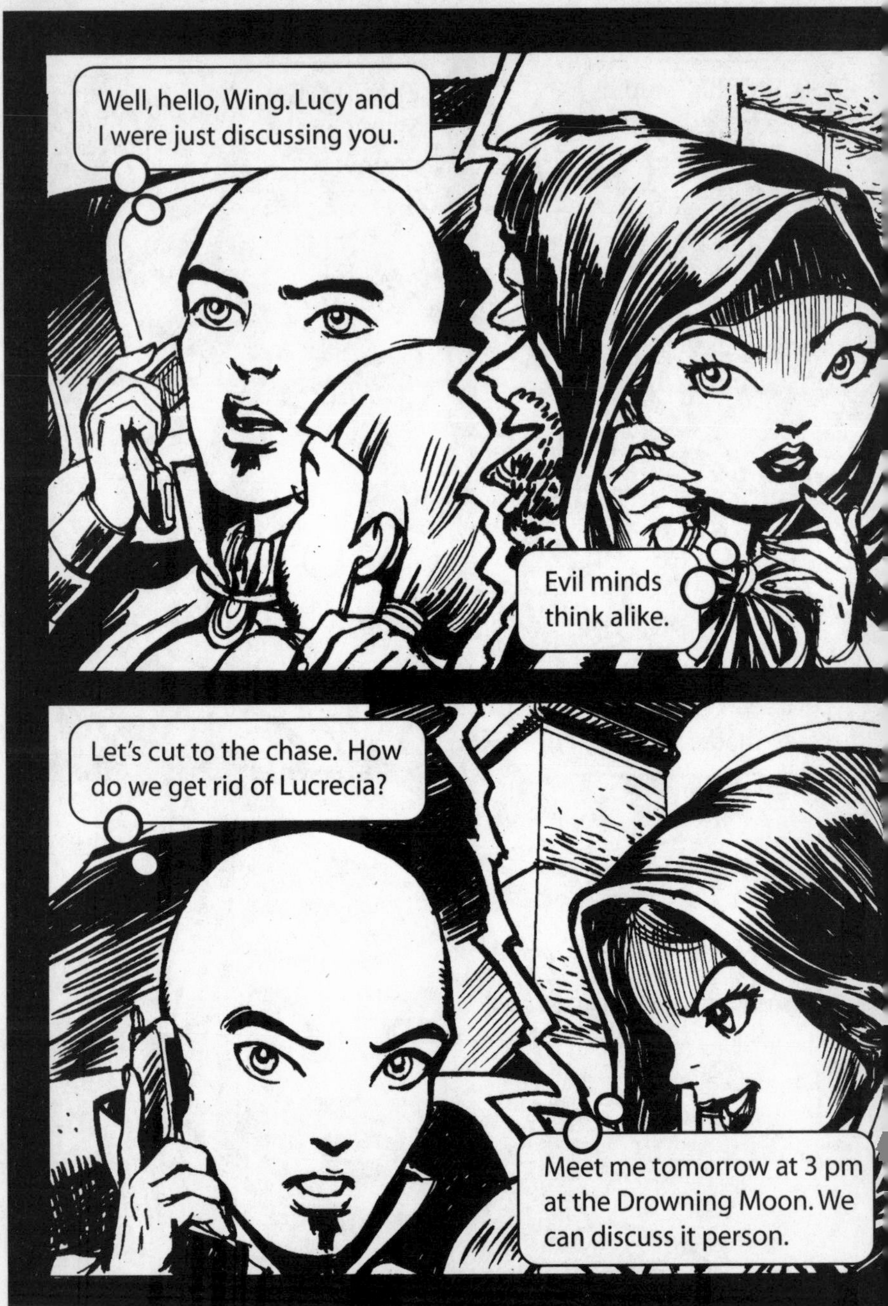
Well, hello, Wing. Lucy and I were just discussing you.
Evil minds think alike.
Let's cut to the chase. How do we get rid of Lucrecia?
Meet me tomorrow at 3 pm at the Drowning Moon. We can discuss it person.

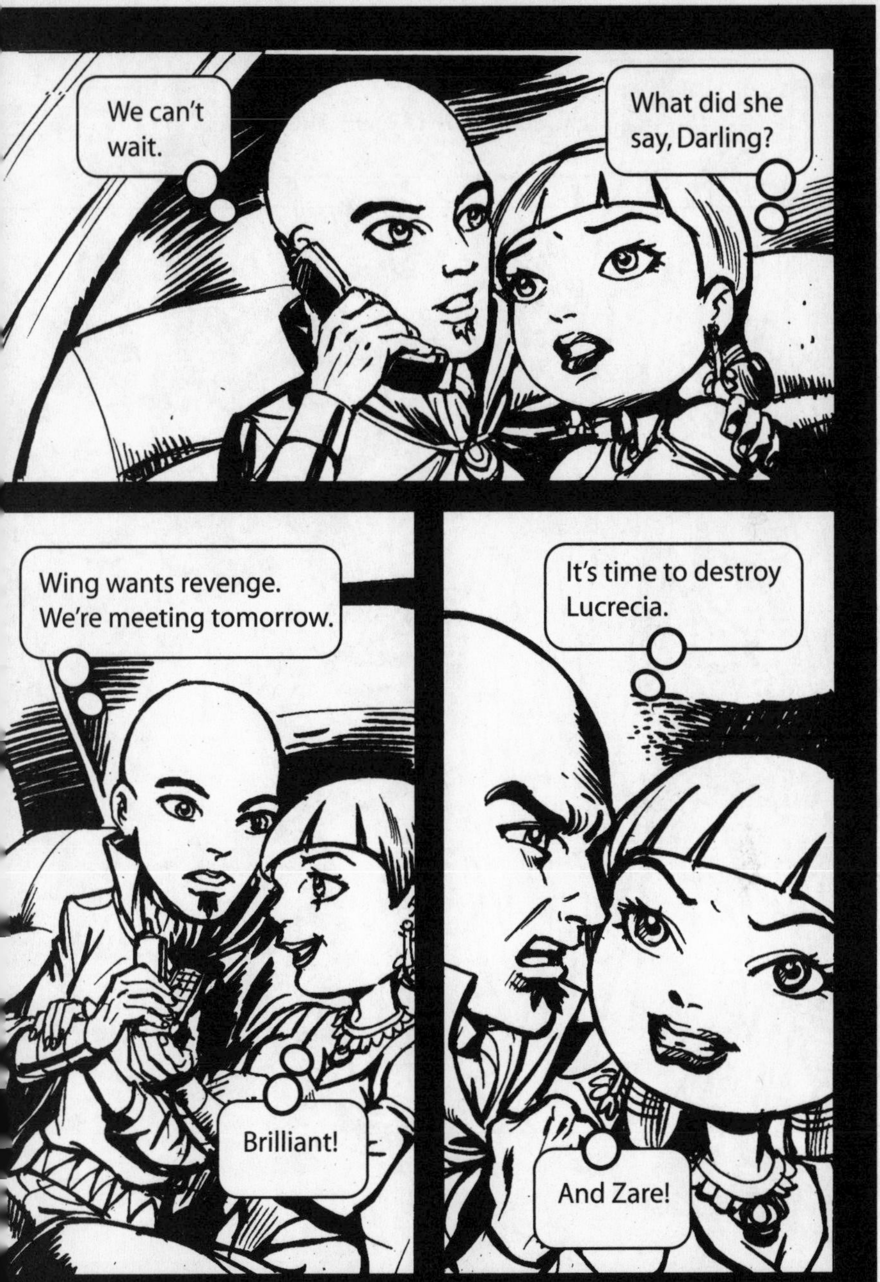
We can't wait.
What did she say, Darling?
Wing wants revenge. We're meeting tomorrow.
Brilliant!
It's time to destroy Lucrecia.
And Zare!

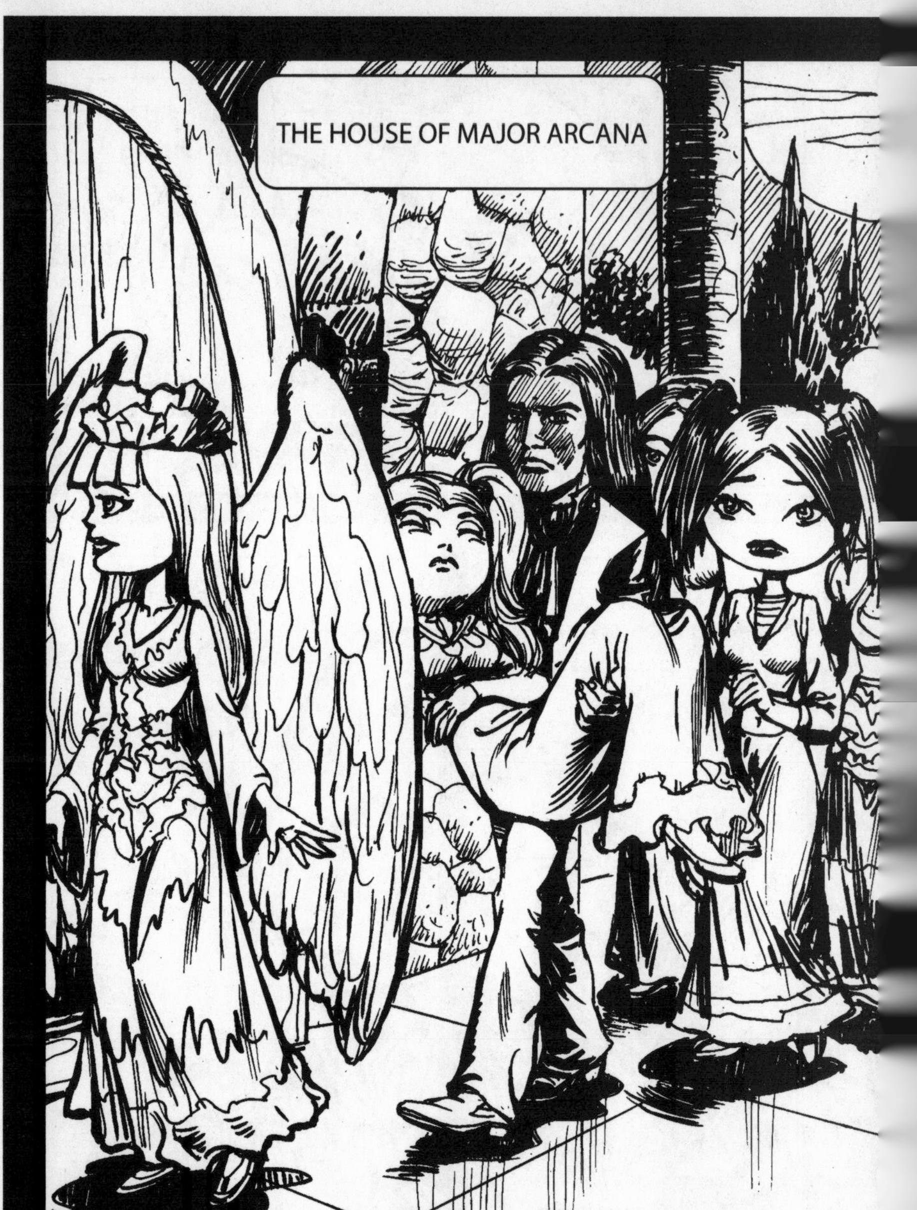
THE HOUSE OF MAJOR ARCANA

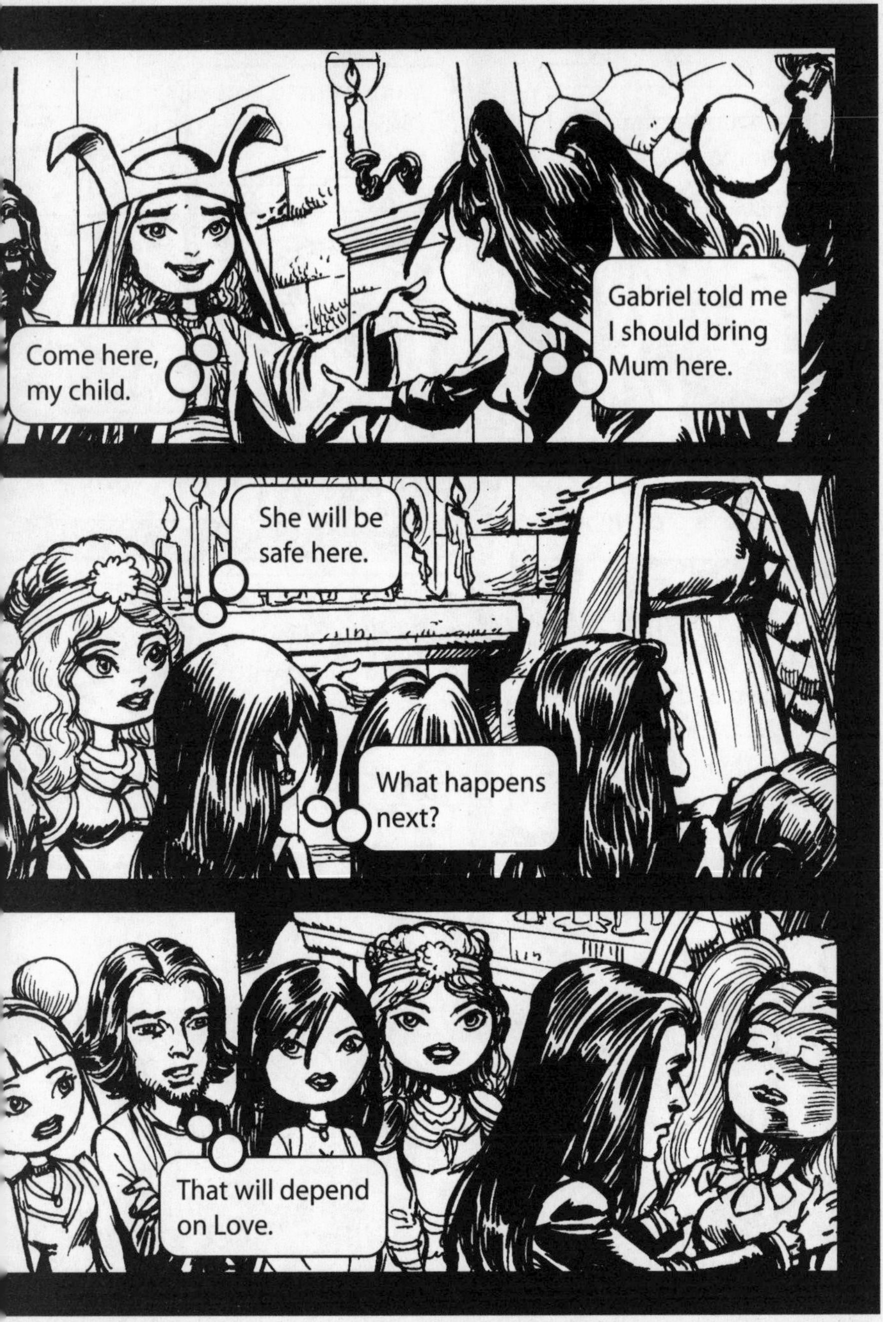
Come here, my child.
Gabriel told me I should bring Mum here.
She will be safe here.
What happens next?
That will depend on Love.

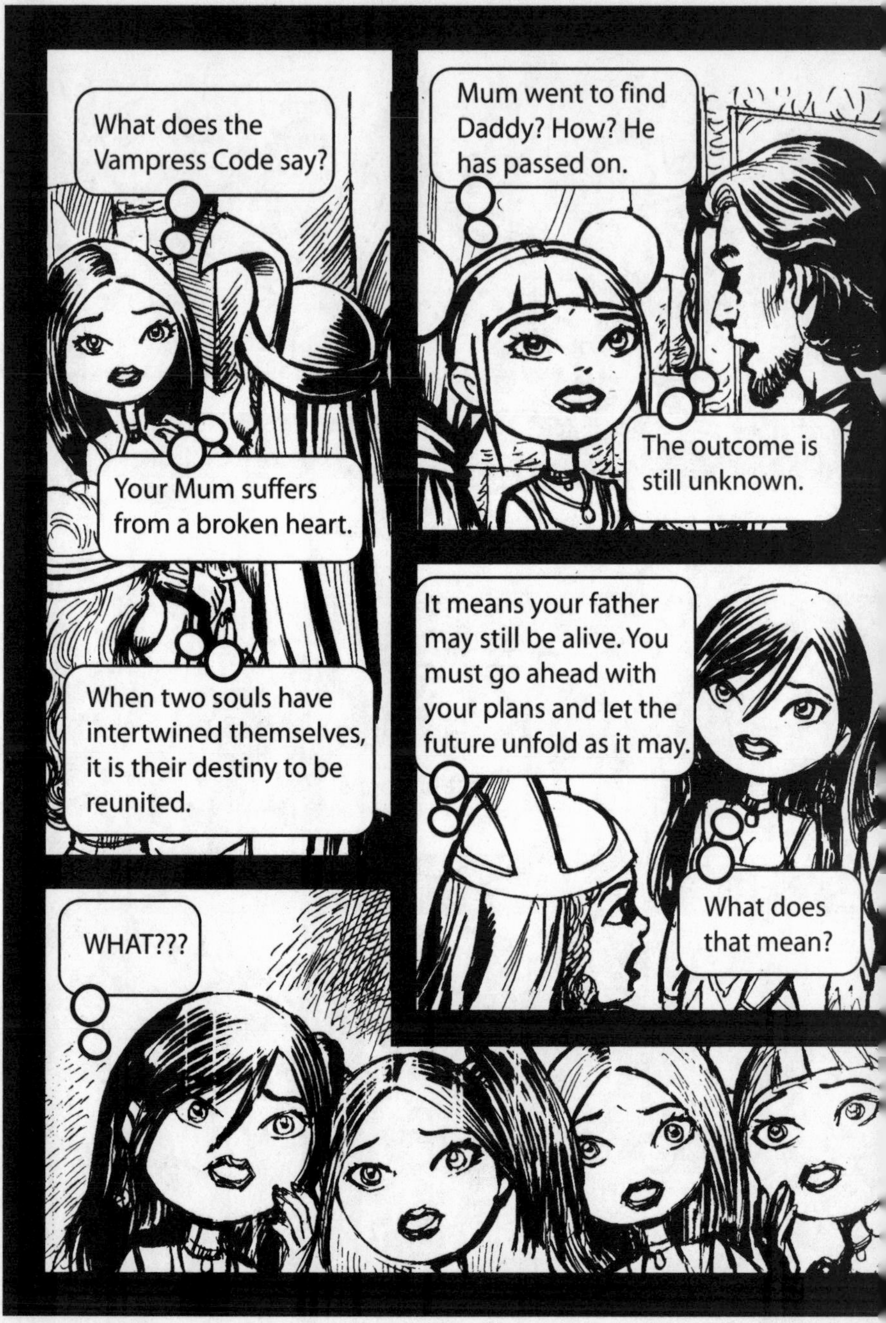
What does the Vampress Code say?
Your Mum suffers from a broken heart.
When two souls have intertwined themselves, it is their destiny to be reunited.
Mum went to find Daddy? How? He has passed on.
The outcome is still unknown.
What does that mean?
It means your father may still be alive. You must go ahead with your plans and let the future unfold as it may.
WHAT???

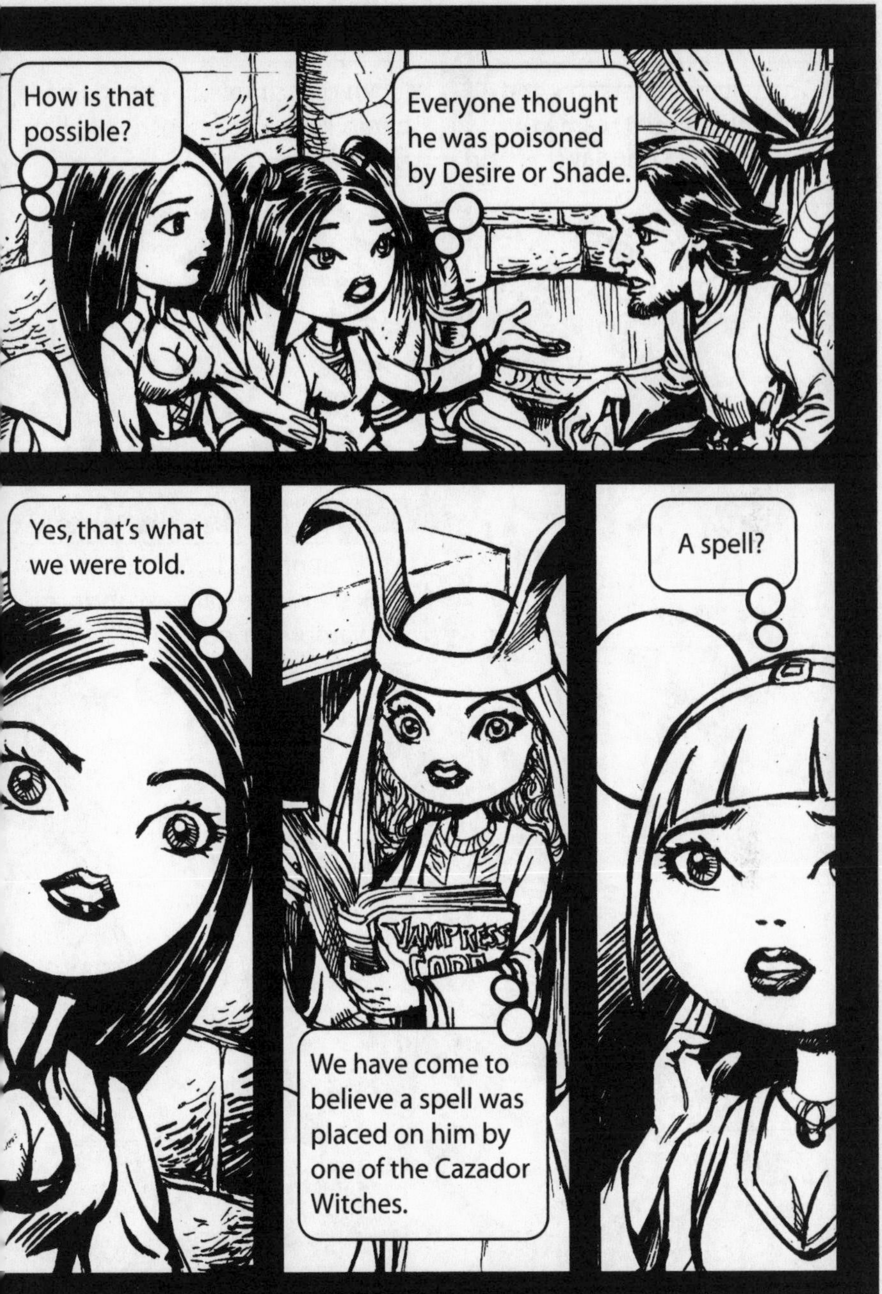
How is that possible?
Everyone thought he was poisoned by Desire or Shade.
Yes, that's what we were told.
We have come to believe a spell was placed on him by one of the Cazador Witches.
A spell?

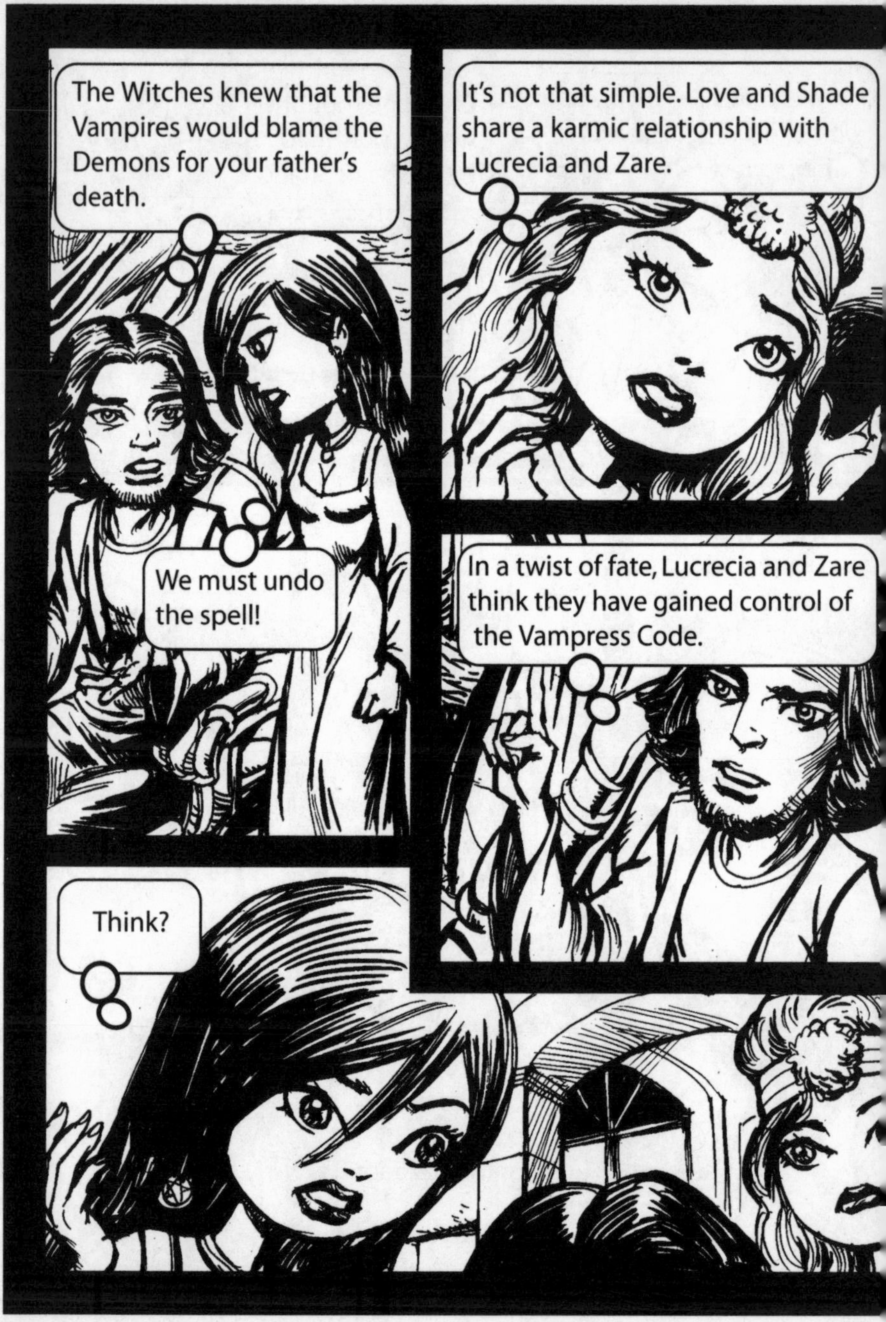
The Witches knew that the Vampires would blame the Demons for your father's death.
We must undo the spell!
It's not that simple. Love and Shade share a karmic relationship with Lucrecia and Zare.
In a twist of fate, Lucrecia and Zare think they have gained control of the Vampress Code.
Think?

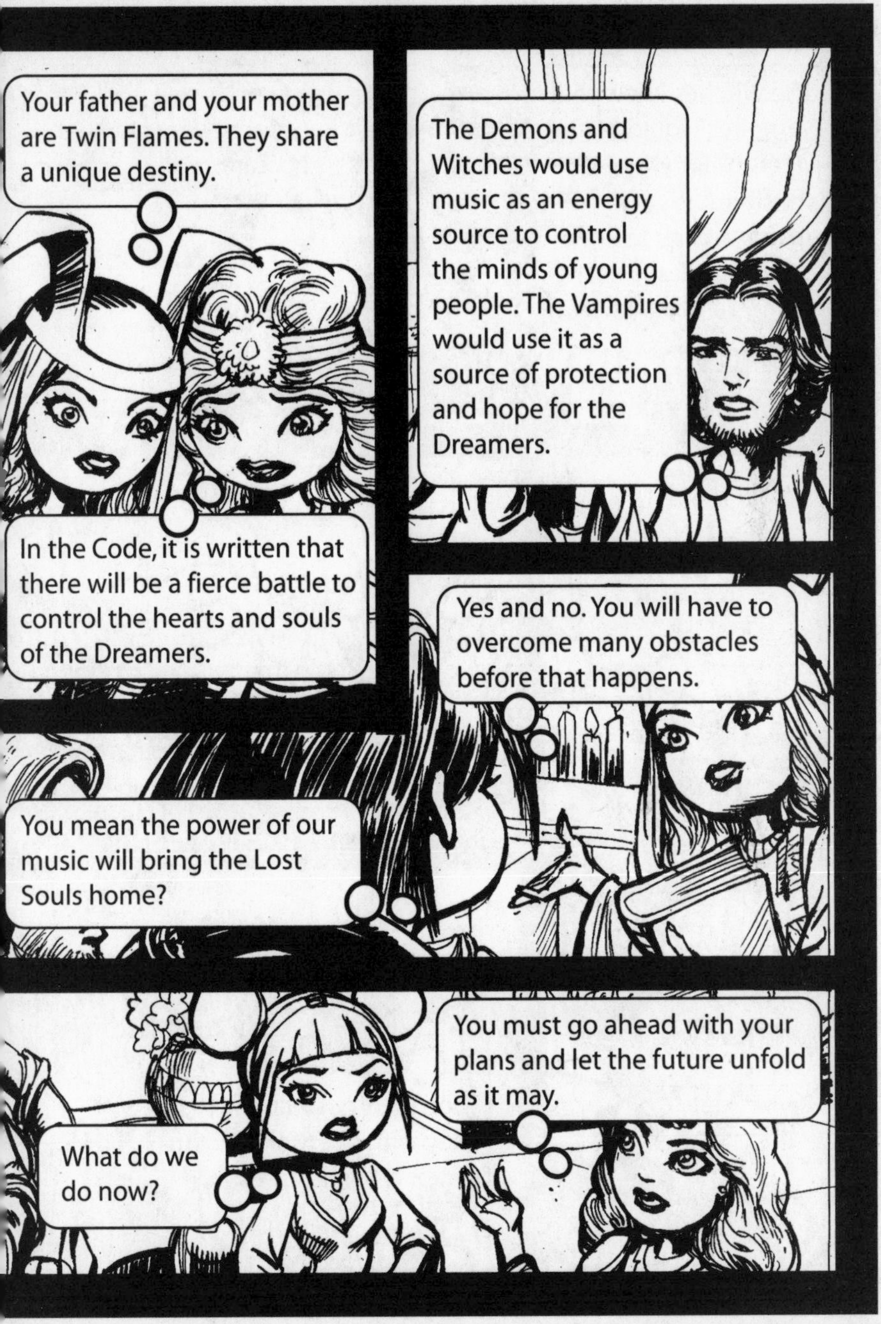
Your father and your mother are Twin Flames. They share a unique destiny.
The Demons and Witches would use music as an energy source to control the minds of young people. The Vampires would use it as a source of protection and hope for the Dreamers.
In the Code, it is written that there will be a fierce battle to control the hearts and souls of the Dreamers.
Yes and no. You will have to overcome many obstacles before that happens.
You mean the power of our music will bring the Lost Souls home?
What do we do now?
You must go ahead with your plans and let the future unfold as it may.

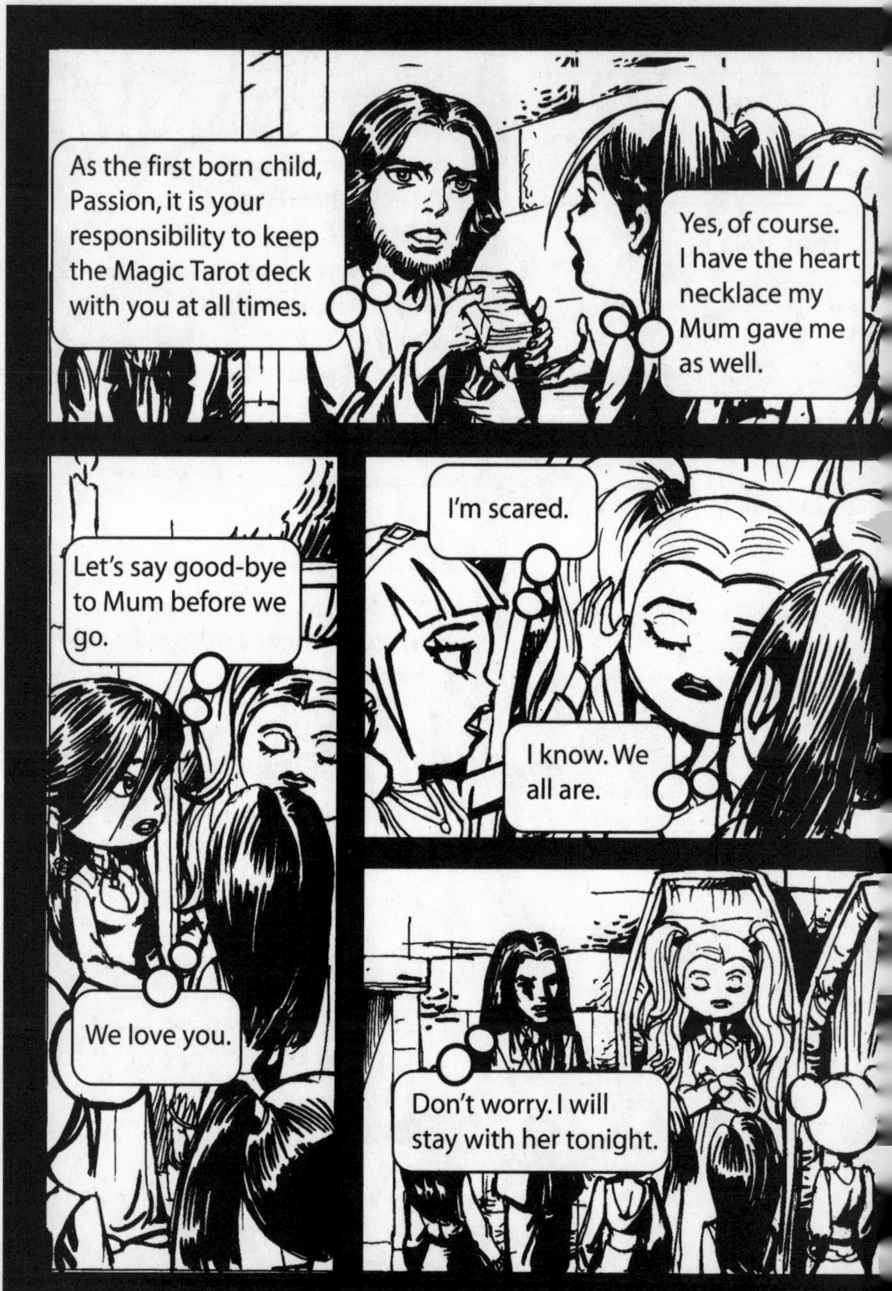
As the first born child, Passion, it is your responsibility to keep the Magic Tarot deck with you at all times.
Yes, of course. I have the heart necklace my Mum gave me as well.
Let's say good-bye to Mum before we go.
We love you.
I'm scared.
I know. We all are.
Don't worry. I will stay with her tonight.

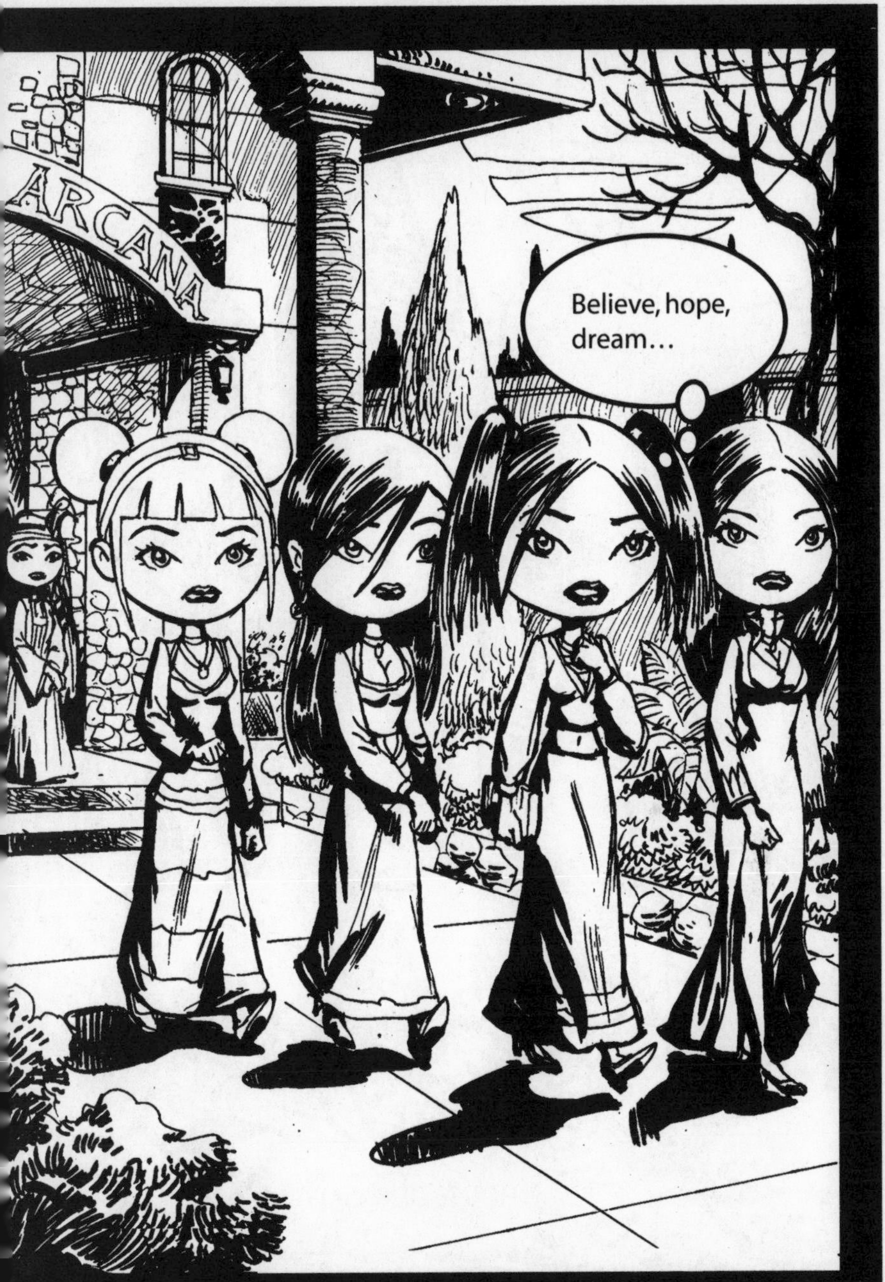
ARCANA
Believe, hope, dream…

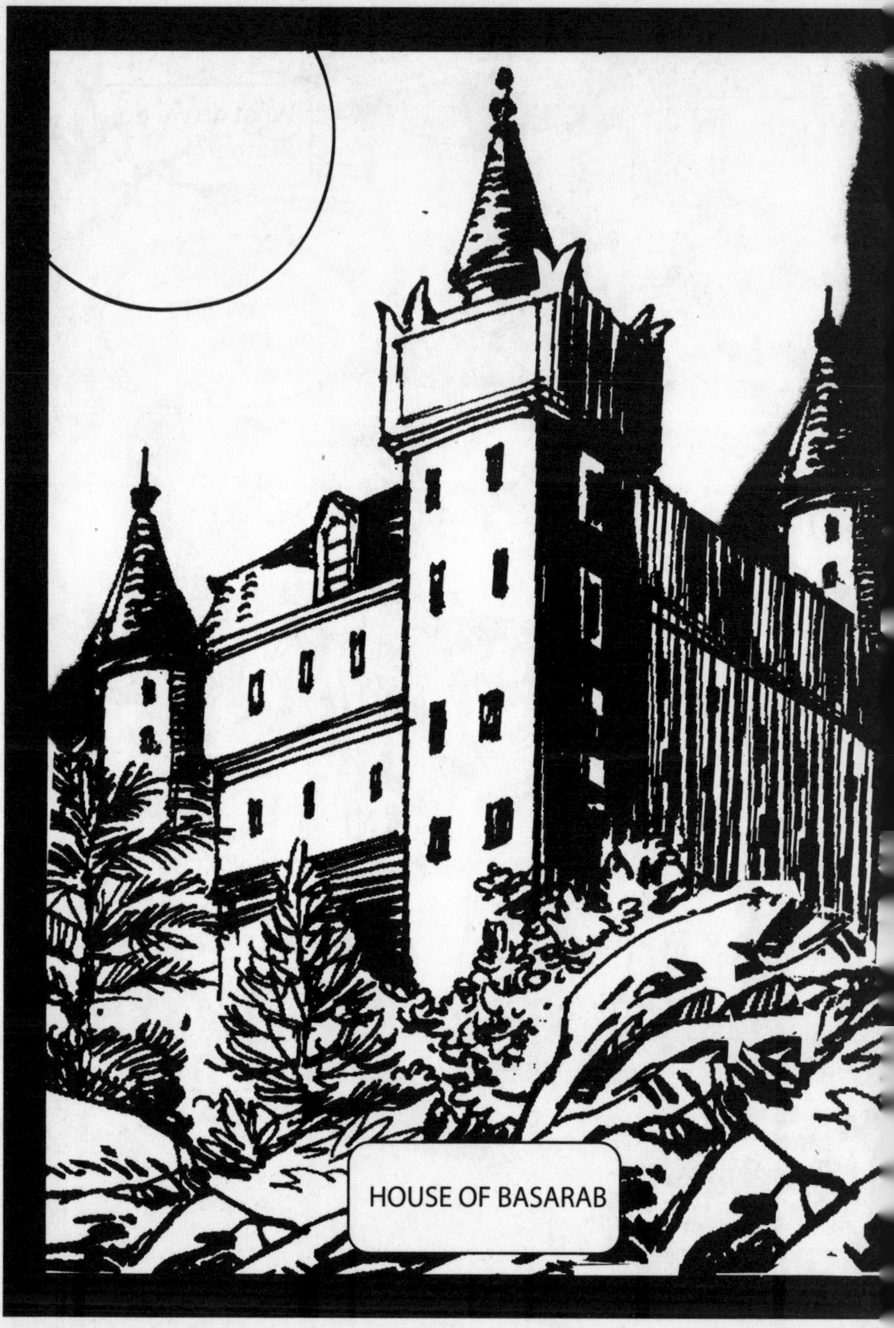
HOUSE OF BASARAB

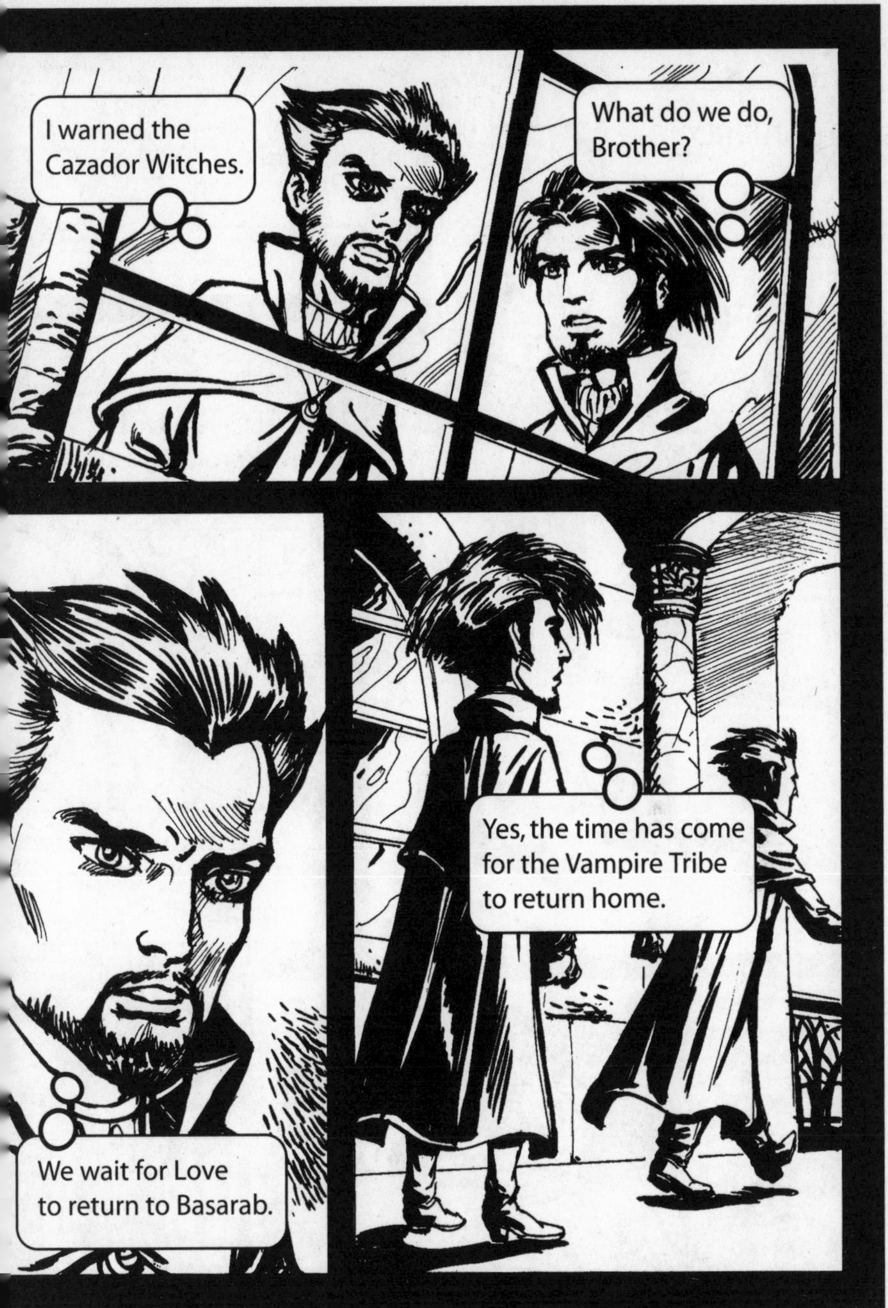
I warned the Cazador Witches.
What do we do, Brother?
We wait for Love to return to Basarab.
Yes, the time has come for the Vampire Tribe to return home.

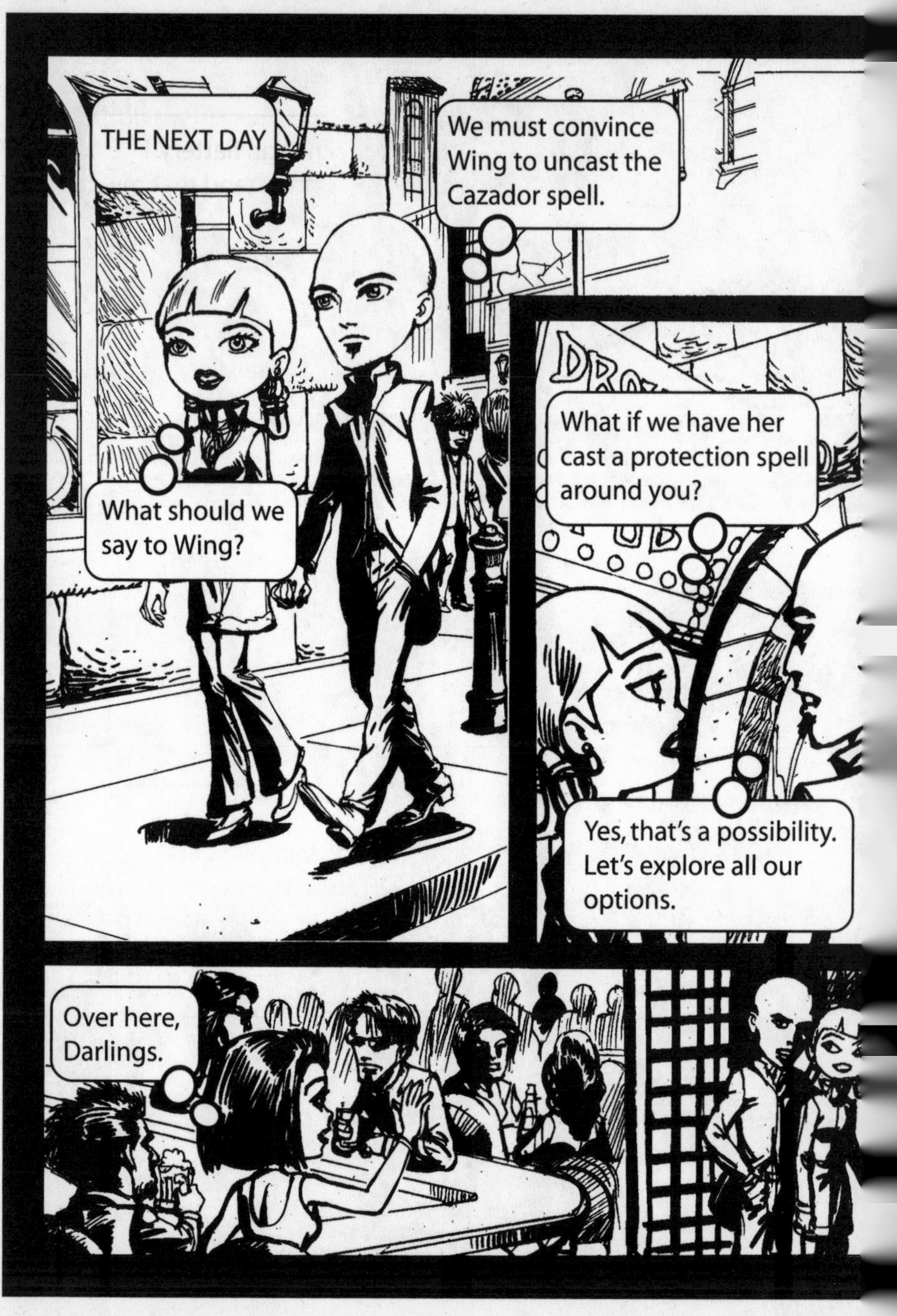
THE NEXT DAY
We must convince Wing to uncast the Cazador spell.
What should we say to Wing?
What if we have her cast a protection spell around you?
Yes, that's a possibility. Let's explore all our options.
Over here, Darlings.

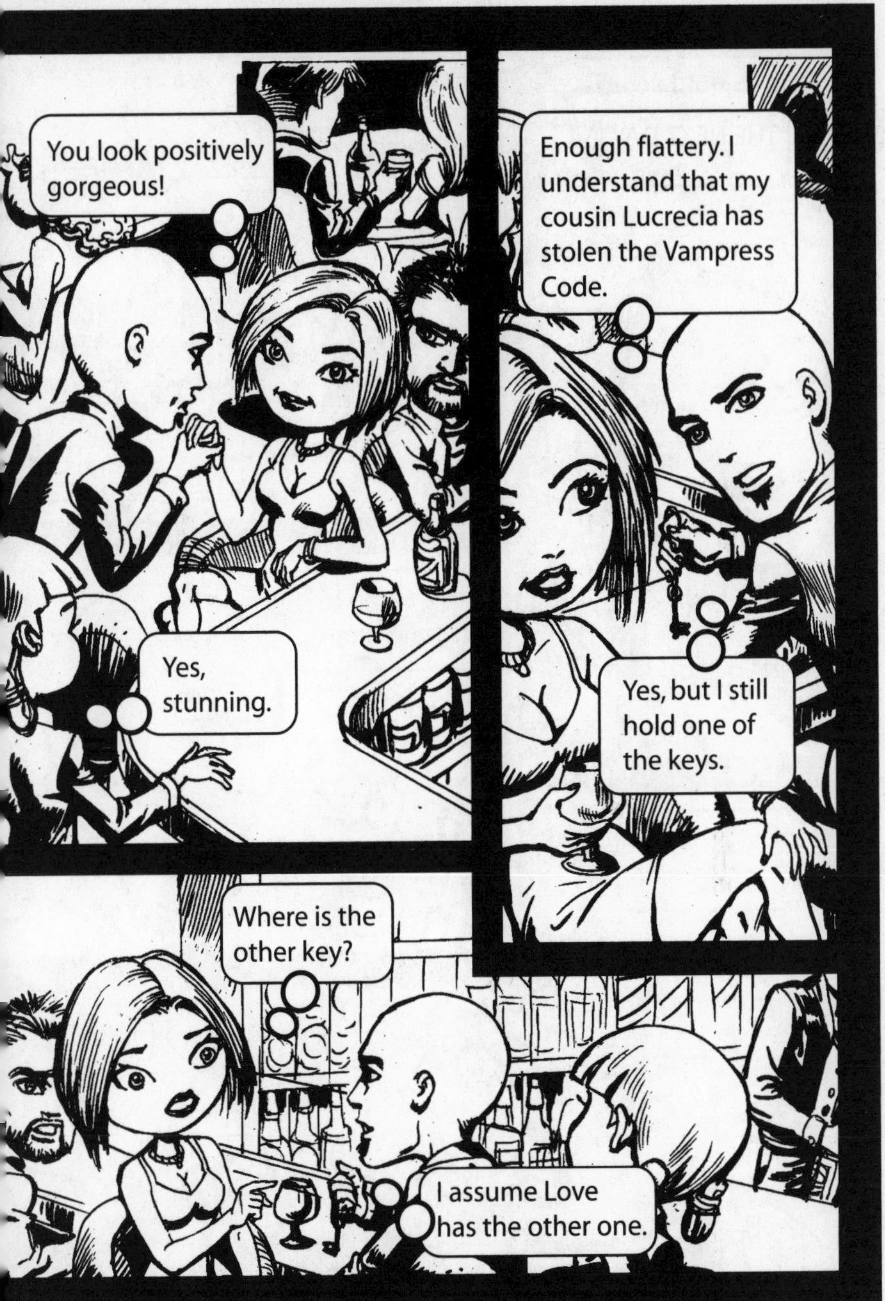
You look positively gorgeous!
Yes, stunning.
Enough flattery. I understand that my cousin Lucrecia has stolen the Vampress Code.
Yes, but I still hold one of the keys.
Where is the other key?
I assume Love has the other one.

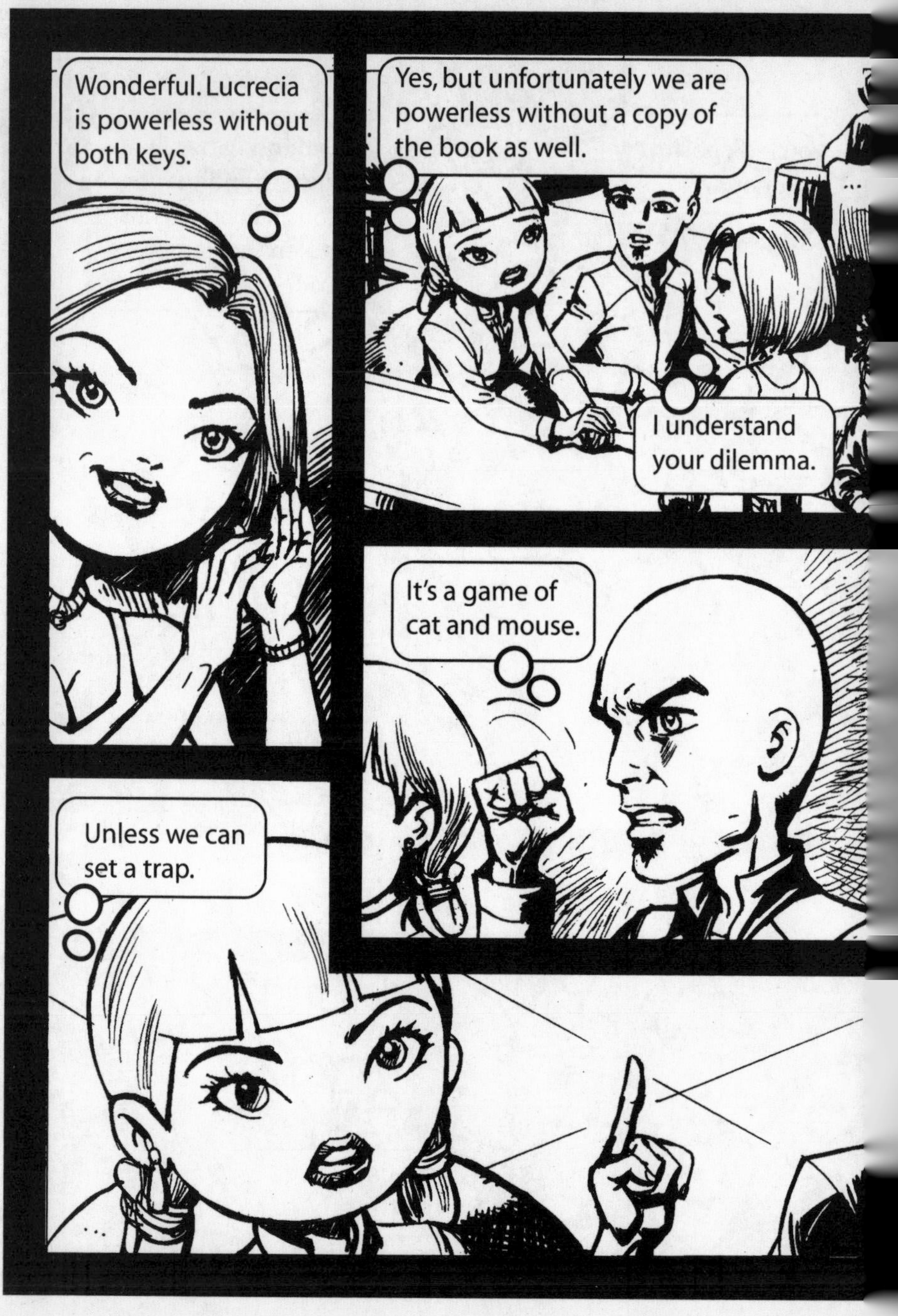

Wonderful. Lucrecia is powerless without both keys.
Yes, but unfortunately we are powerless without a copy of the book as well.
I understand your dilemma.
It's a game of cat and mouse.
Unless we can set a trap.

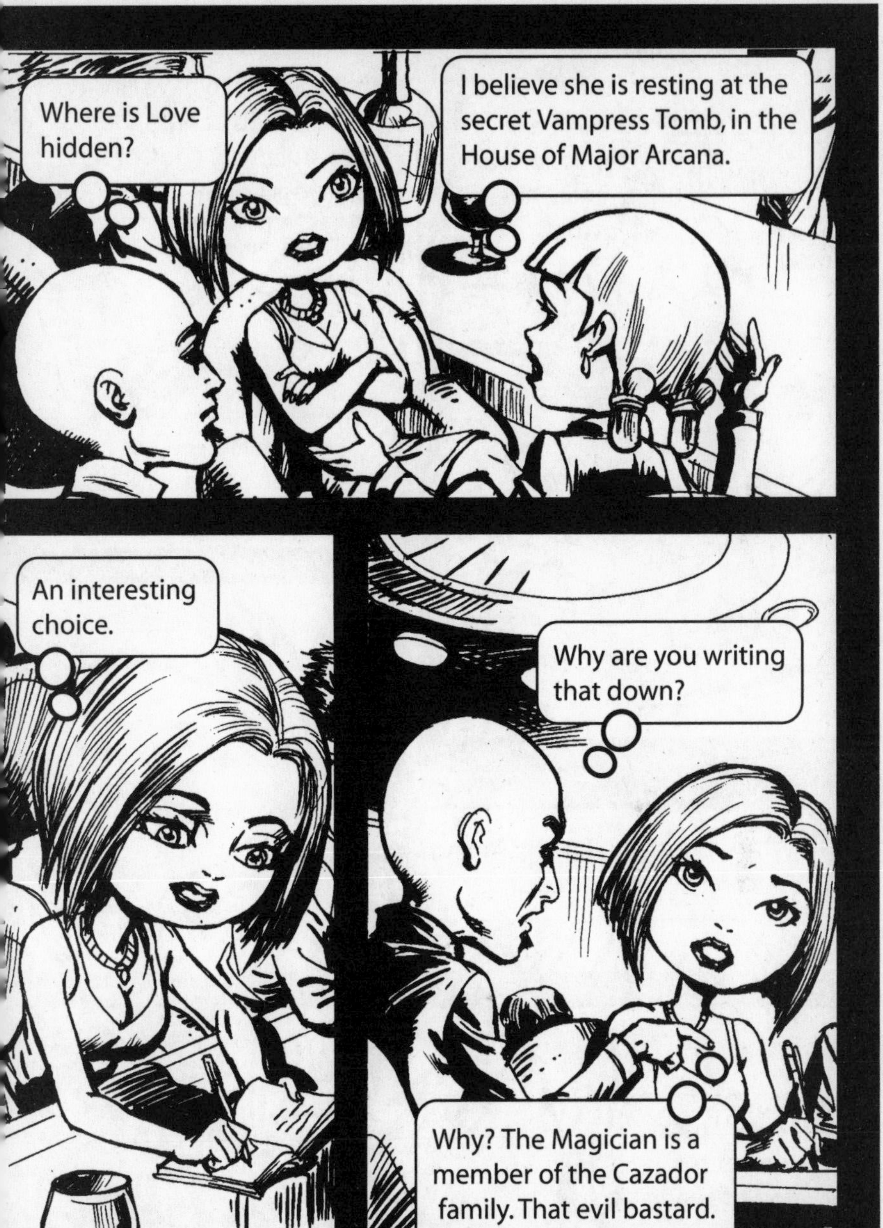

Where is Love hidden?
I believe she is resting at the secret Vampress Tomb, in the House of Major Arcana.
An interesting choice.
Why are you writing that down?
Why? The Magician is a member of the Cazador family. That evil bastard.

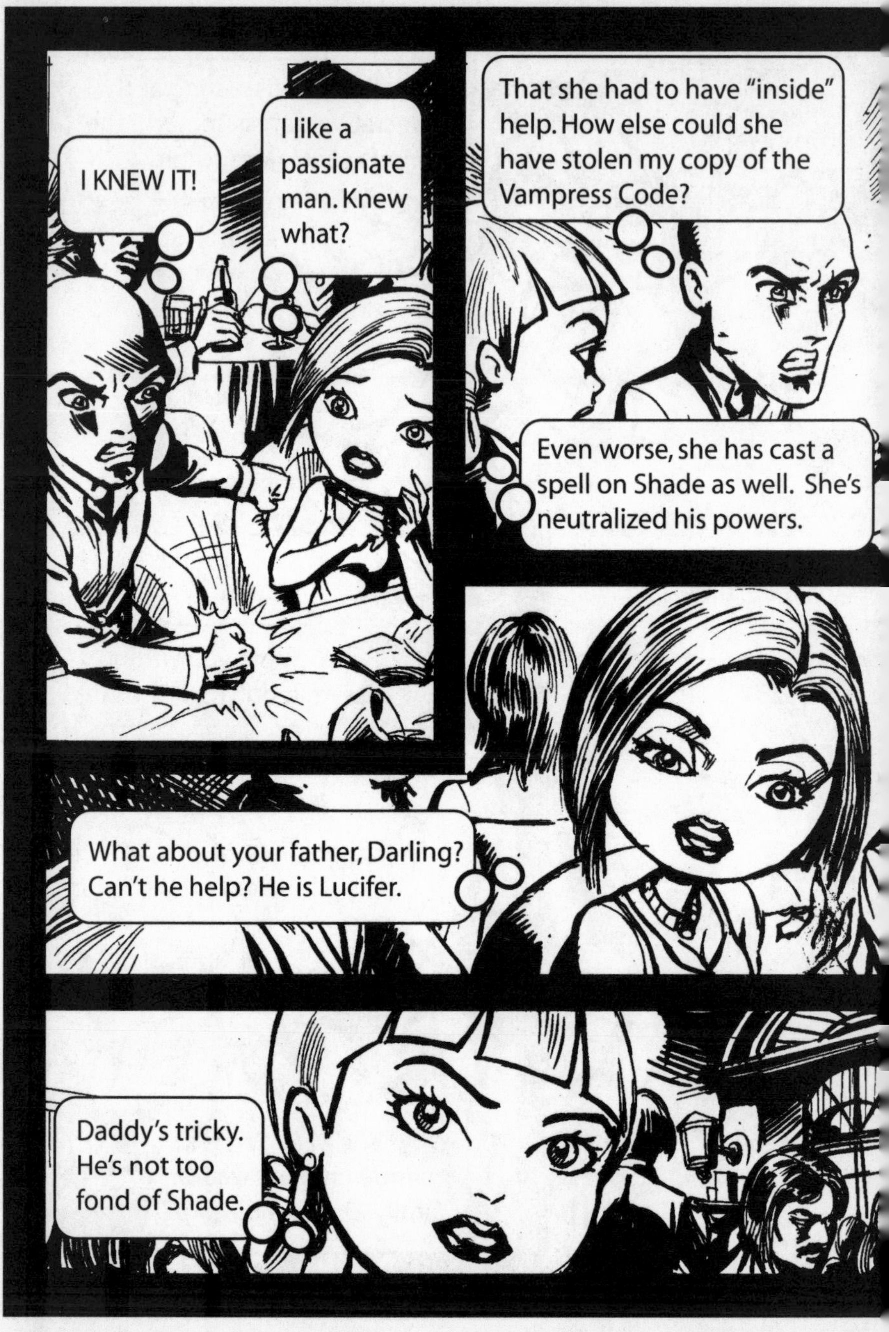
I KNEW IT!
I like a passionate man. Knew what?
That she had to have "inside" help. How else could she have stolen my copy of the Vampress Code?
Even worse, she has cast a spell on Shade as well. She's neutralized his powers.
What about your father, Darling? Can't he help? He is Lucifer.
Daddy's tricky. He's not too fond of Shade.

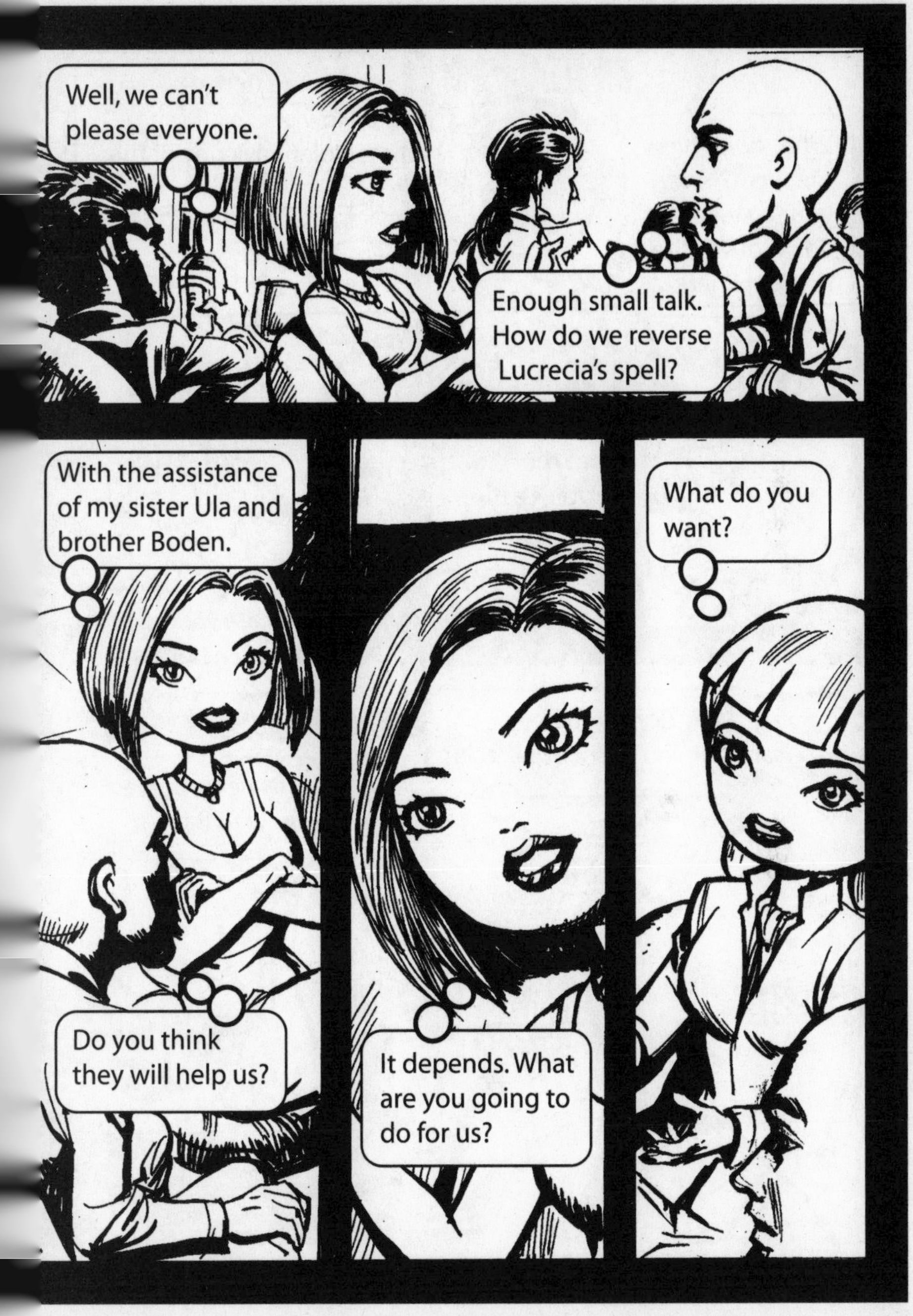
Well, we can't please everyone.
Enough small talk. How do we reverse Lucrecia's spell?
With the assistance of my sister Ula and brother Boden.
Do you think they will help us?
It depends. What are you going to do for us?
What do you want?

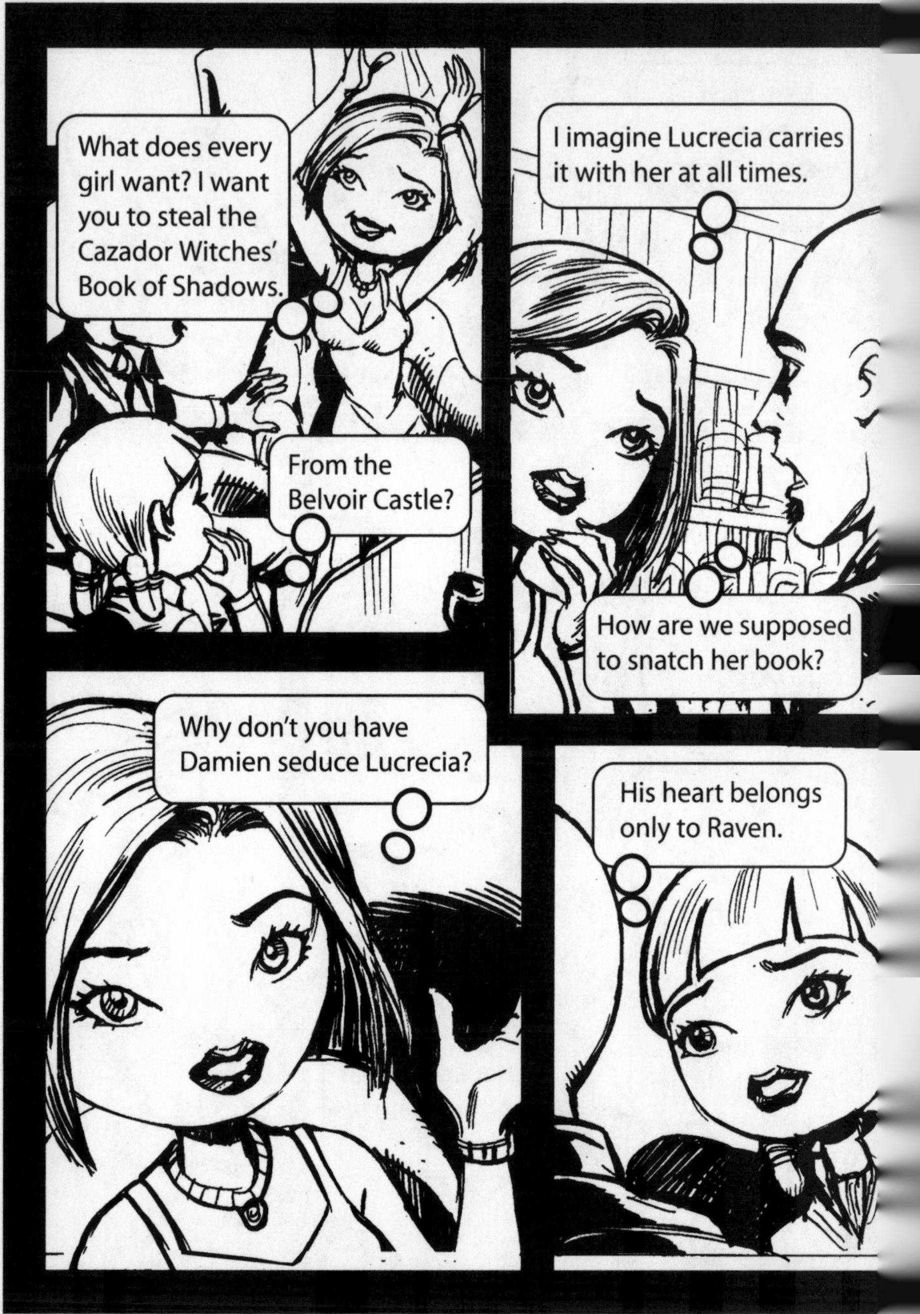

What does every girl want? I want you to steal the Cazador Witches' Book of Shadows.
From the Belvoir Castle?
I imagine Lucrecia carries it with her at all times.
How are we supposed to snatch her book?
Why don't you have Damien seduce Lucrecia?
His heart belongs only to Raven.

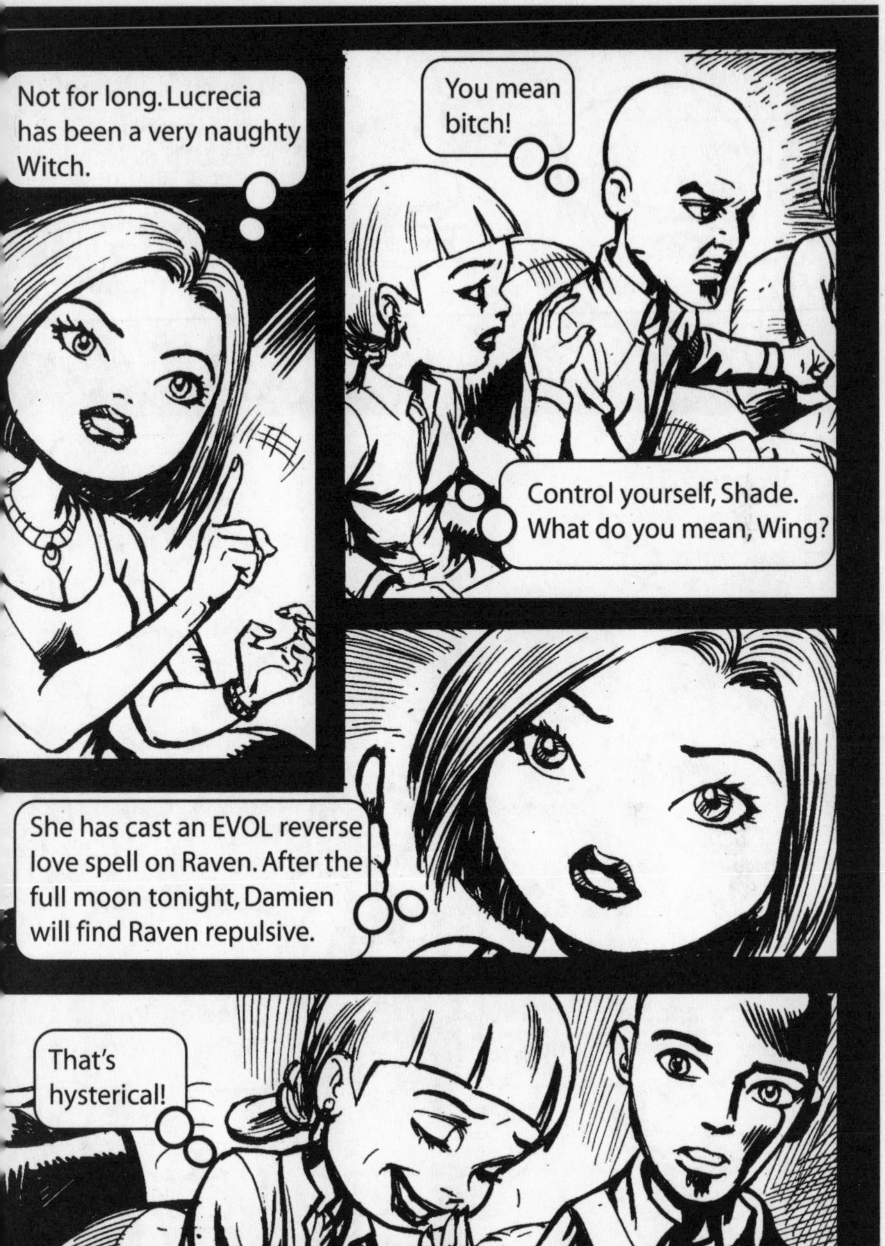
Not for long. Lucrecia has been a very naughty Witch.
You mean bitch!
Control yourself, Shade. What do you mean, Wing?
She has cast an EVOL reverse love spell on Raven. After the full moon tonight, Damien will find Raven repulsive.
That's hysterical!

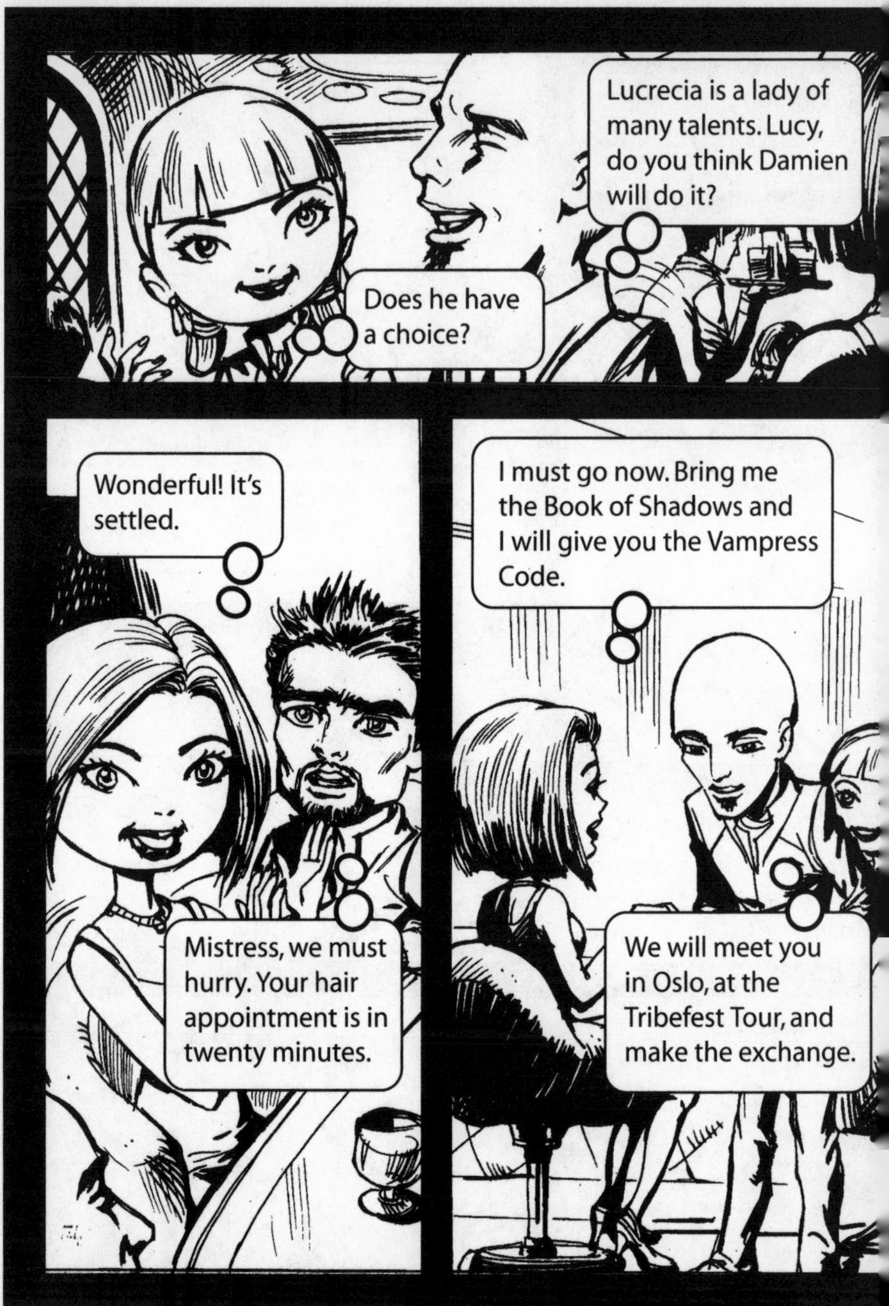
Lucrecia is a lady of many talents. Lucy, do you think Damien will do it?
Does he have a choice?
Wonderful! It's settled.
Mistress, we must hurry. Your hair appointment is in twenty minutes.
I must go now. Bring me the Book of Shadows and I will give you the Vampress Code.
We will meet you in Oslo, at the Tribefest Tour, and make the exchange.

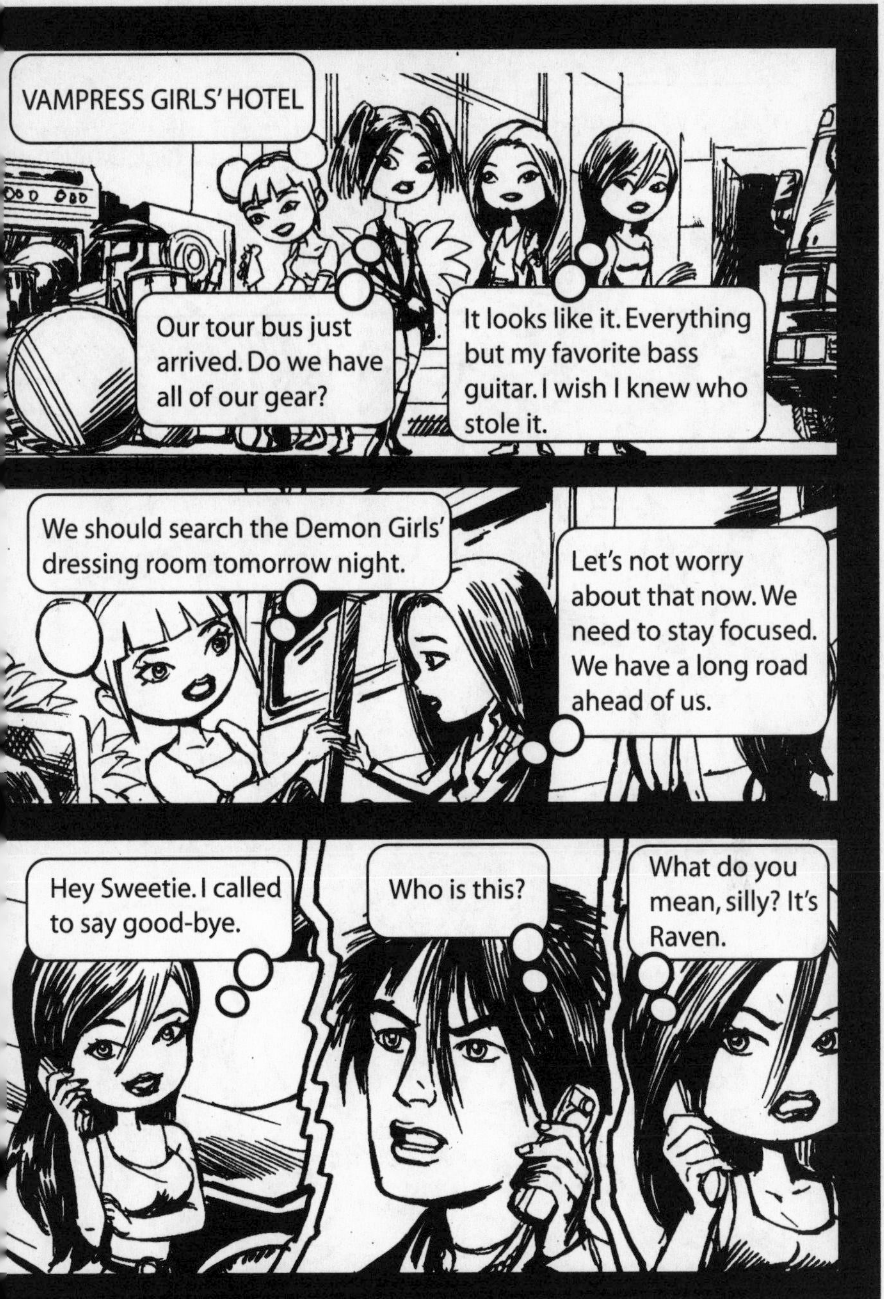
VAMPRESS GIRLS' HOTEL
Our tour bus just arrived. Do we have all of our gear?
It looks like it. Everything but my favorite bass guitar. I wish I knew who stole it.
We should search the Demon Girls' dressing room tomorrow night.
Let's not worry about that now. We need to stay focused. We have a long road ahead of us.
Hey Sweetie. I called to say good-bye.
Who is this?
What do you mean, silly? It's Raven.

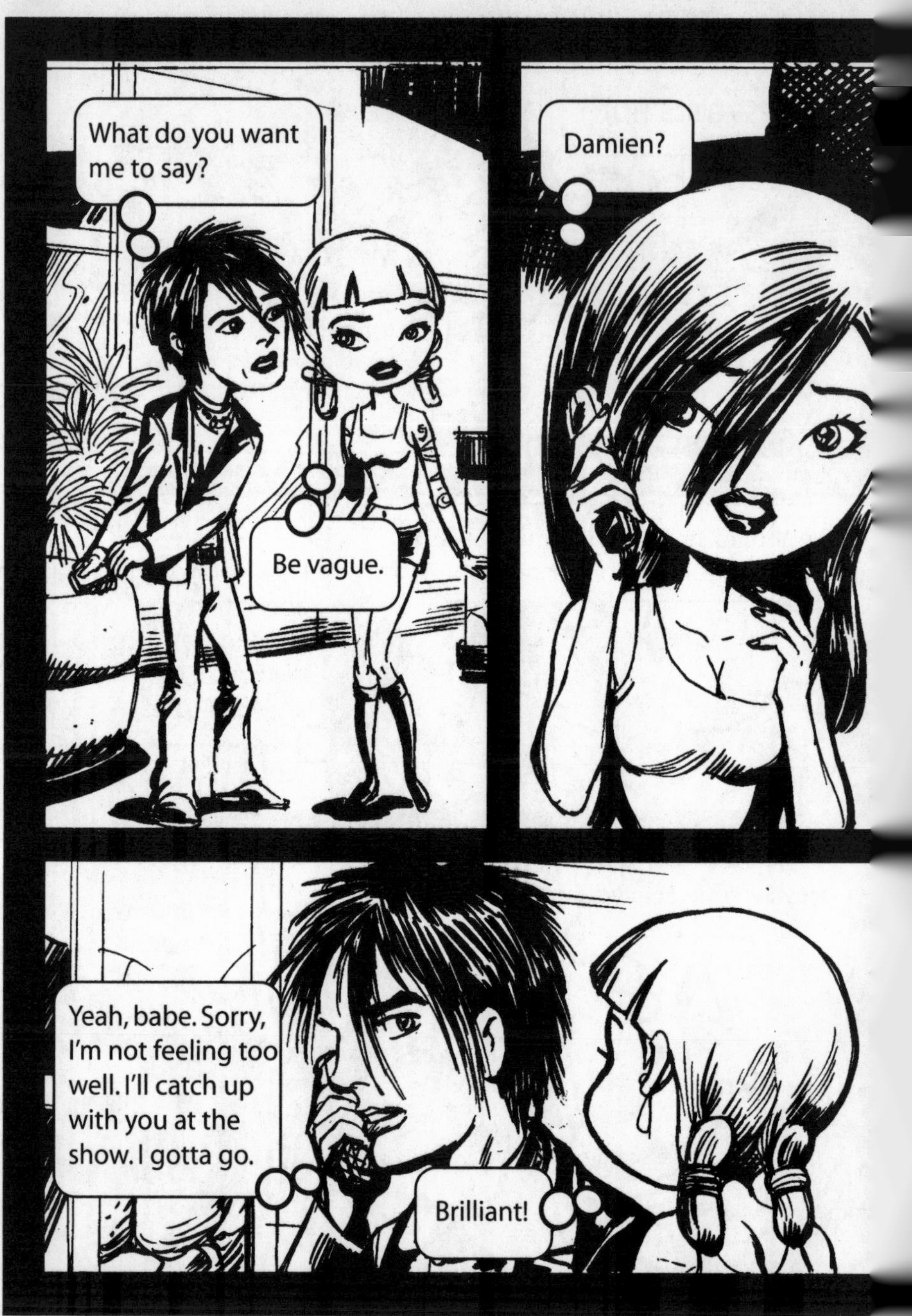
What do you want me to say?
Be vague.
Damien?
Yeah, babe. Sorry, I'm not feeling too well. I'll catch up with you at the show. I gotta go.
Brilliant!

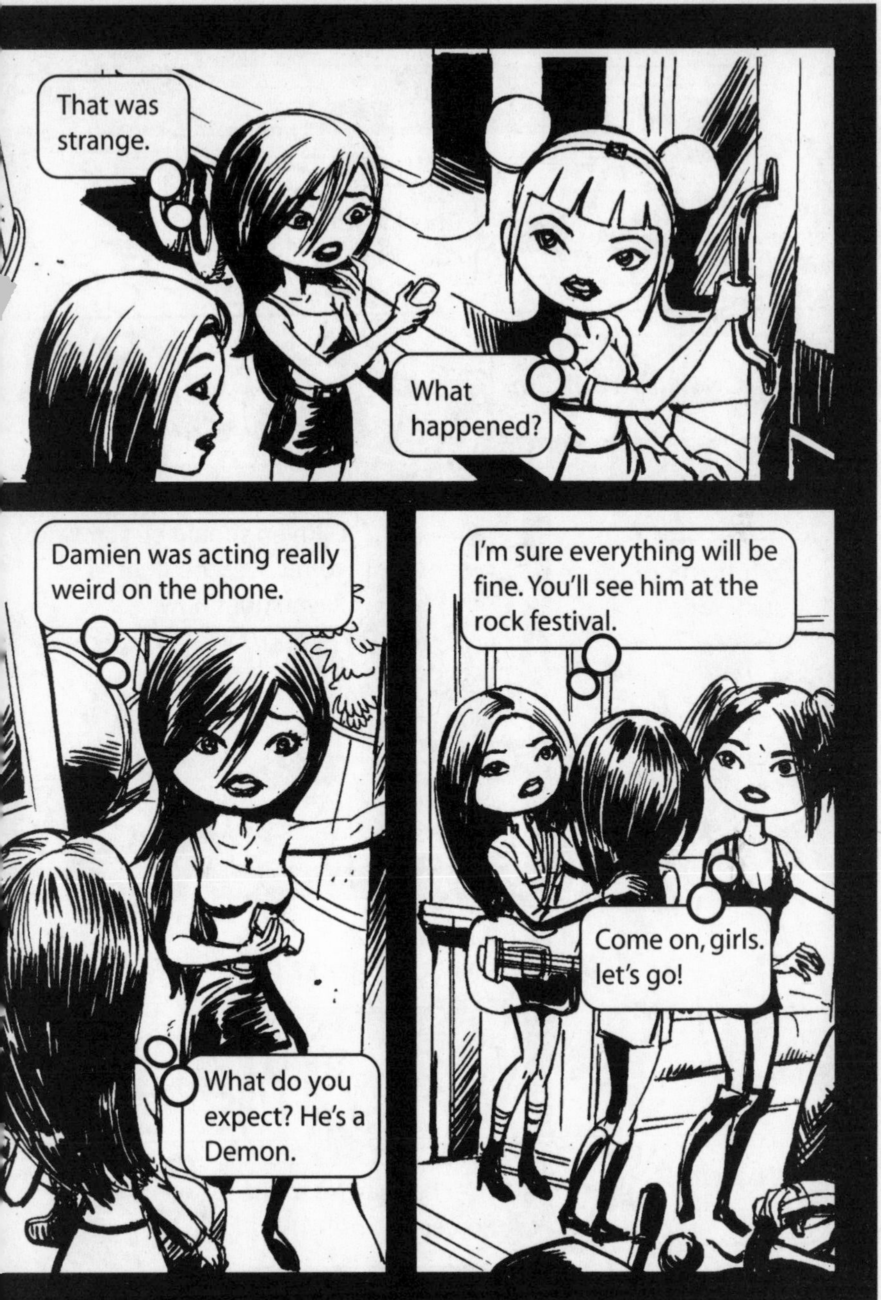
That was strange.
What happened?
Damien was acting really weird on the phone.
What do you expect? He's a Demon.
I'm sure everything will be fine. You'll see him at the rock festival.
Come on, girls. let's go!

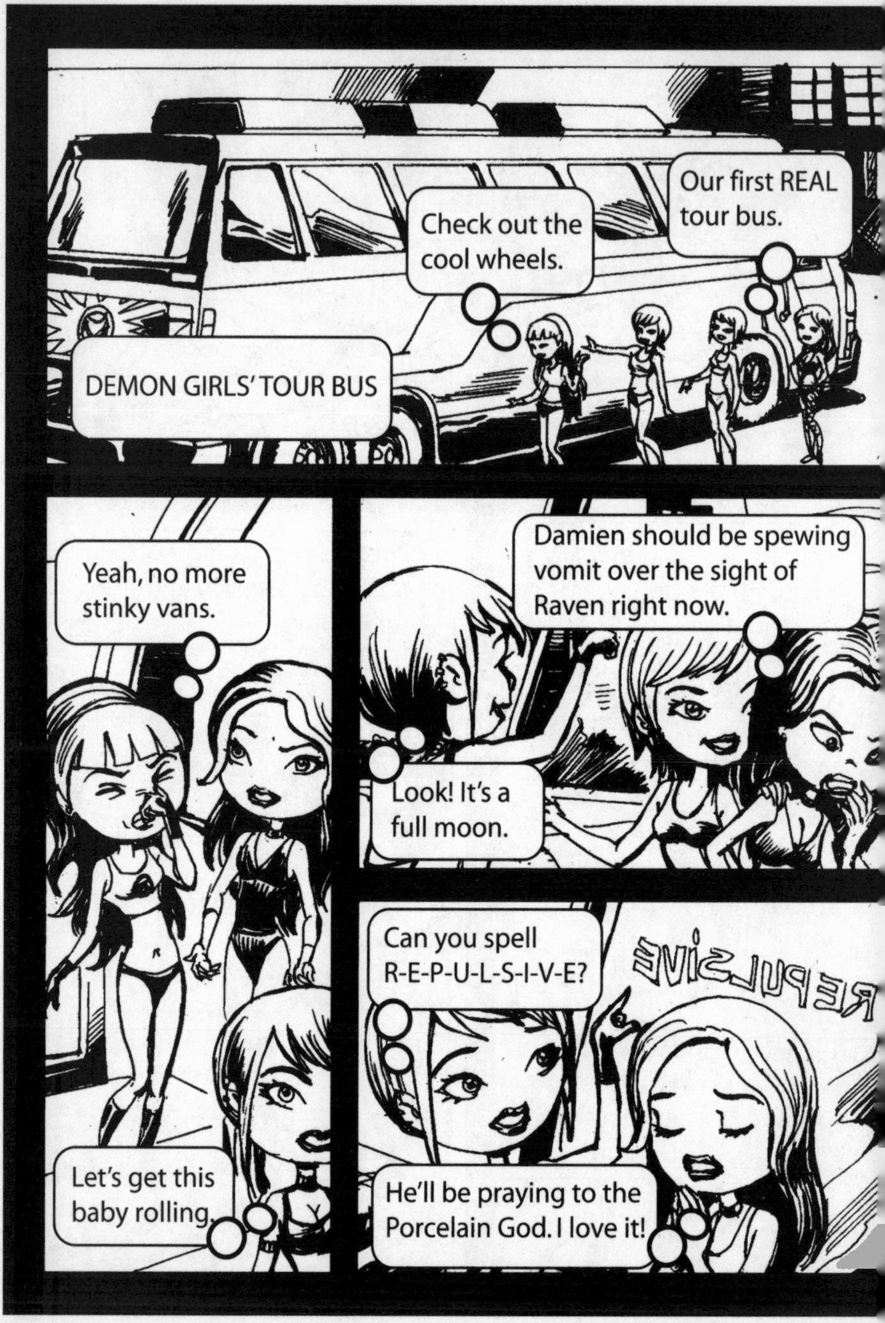
DEMON GIRLS' TOUR BUS
Check out the cool wheels.
Our first REAL tour bus.
Yeah, no more stinky vans.
Let's get this baby rolling.
Damien should be spewing vomit over the sight of Raven right now.
Look! It's a full moon.
Can you spell R-E-P-U-L-S-I-V-E?
REPULSIVE
He'll be praying to the Porcelain God. I love it!

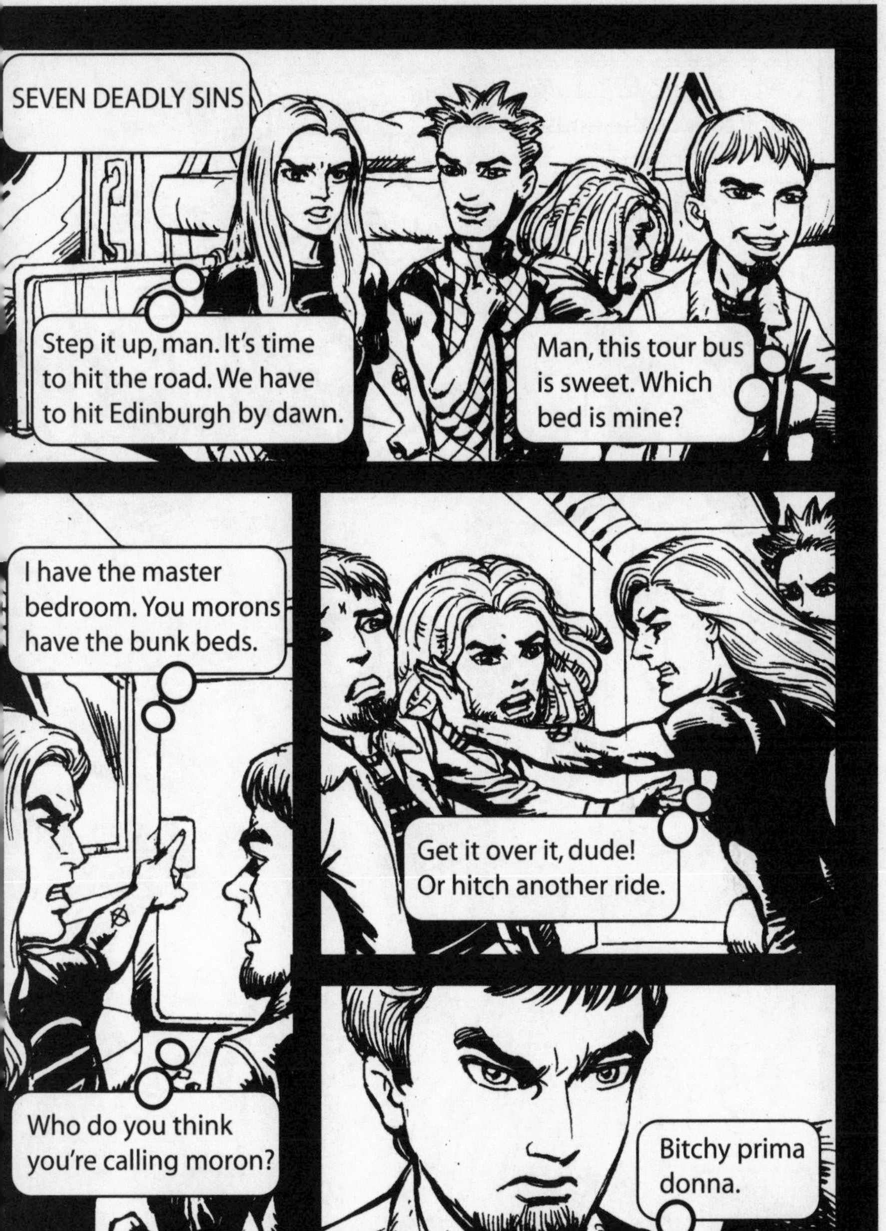
SEVEN DEADLY SINS
Step it up, man. It's time to hit the road. We have to hit Edinburgh by dawn.
Man, this tour bus is sweet. Which bed is mine?
I have the master bedroom. You morons have the bunk beds.
Who do you think you're calling moron?
Get it over it, dude! Or hitch another ride.
Bitchy prima donna.

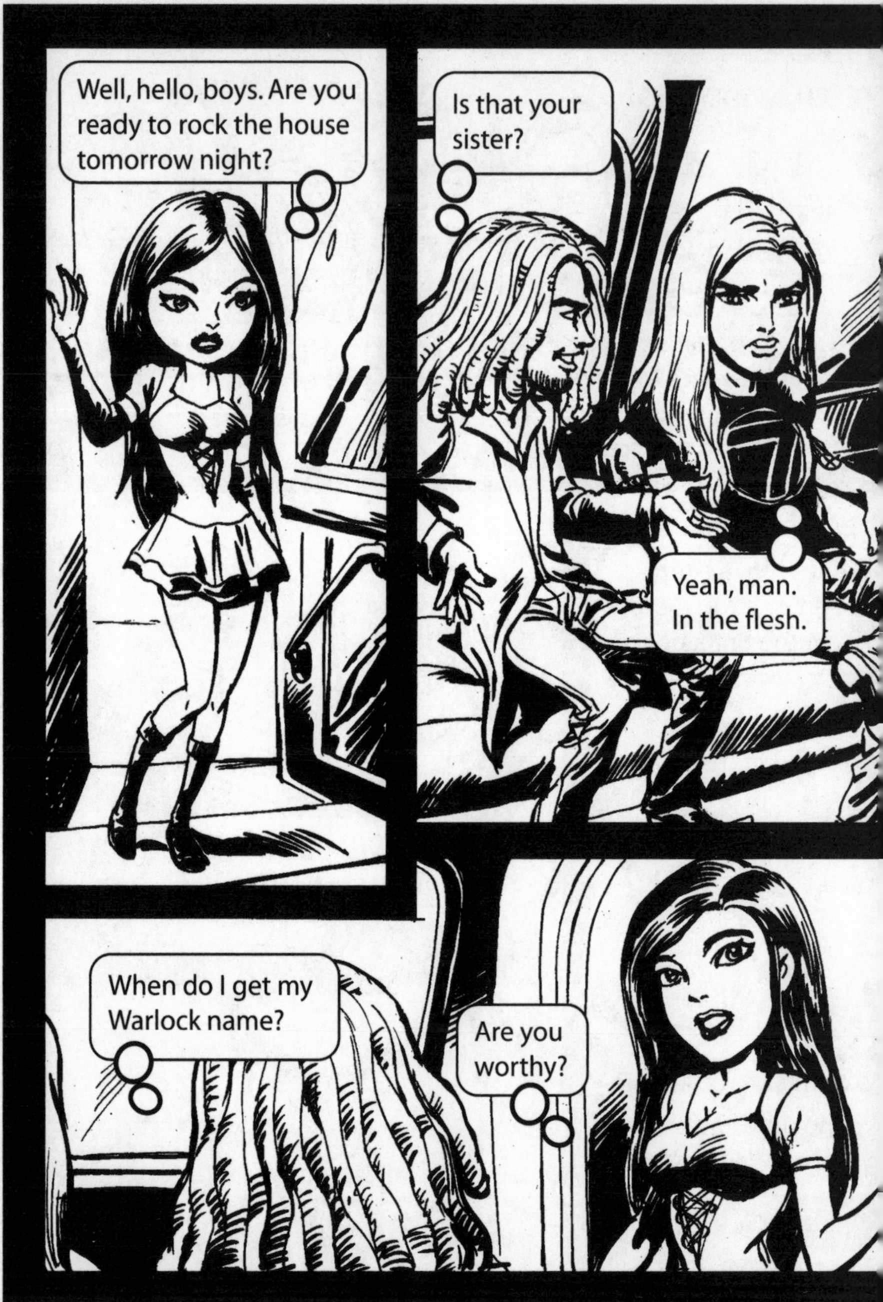

Well, hello, boys. Are you ready to rock the house tomorrow night?
Is that your sister?
Yeah, man. In the flesh.
When do I get my Warlock name?
Are you worthy?

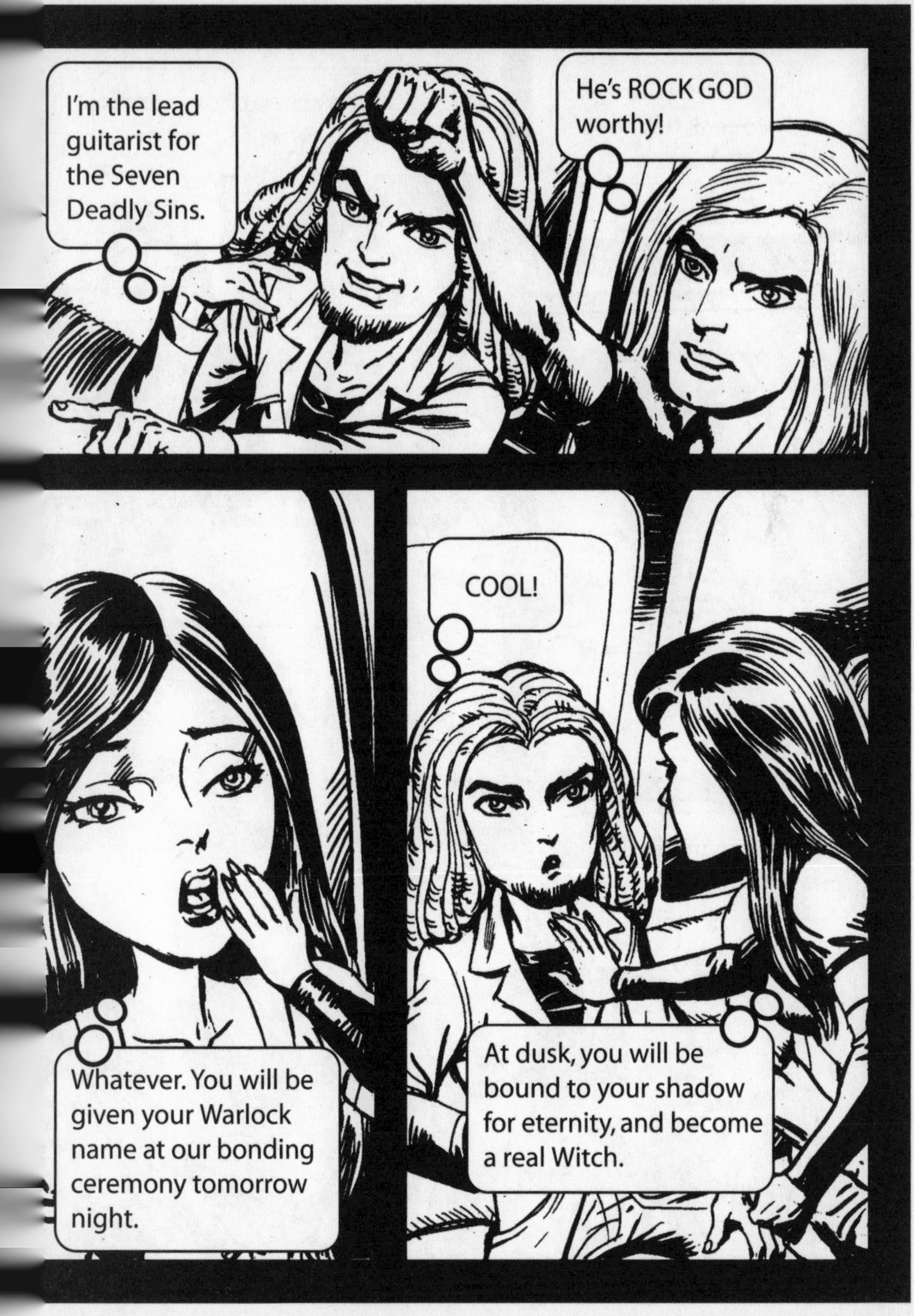

I'm the lead guitarist for the Seven Deadly Sins.
He's ROCK GOD worthy!
Whatever. You will be given your Warlock name at our bonding ceremony tomorrow night.
COOL!
At dusk, you will be bound to your shadow for eternity, and become a real Witch.

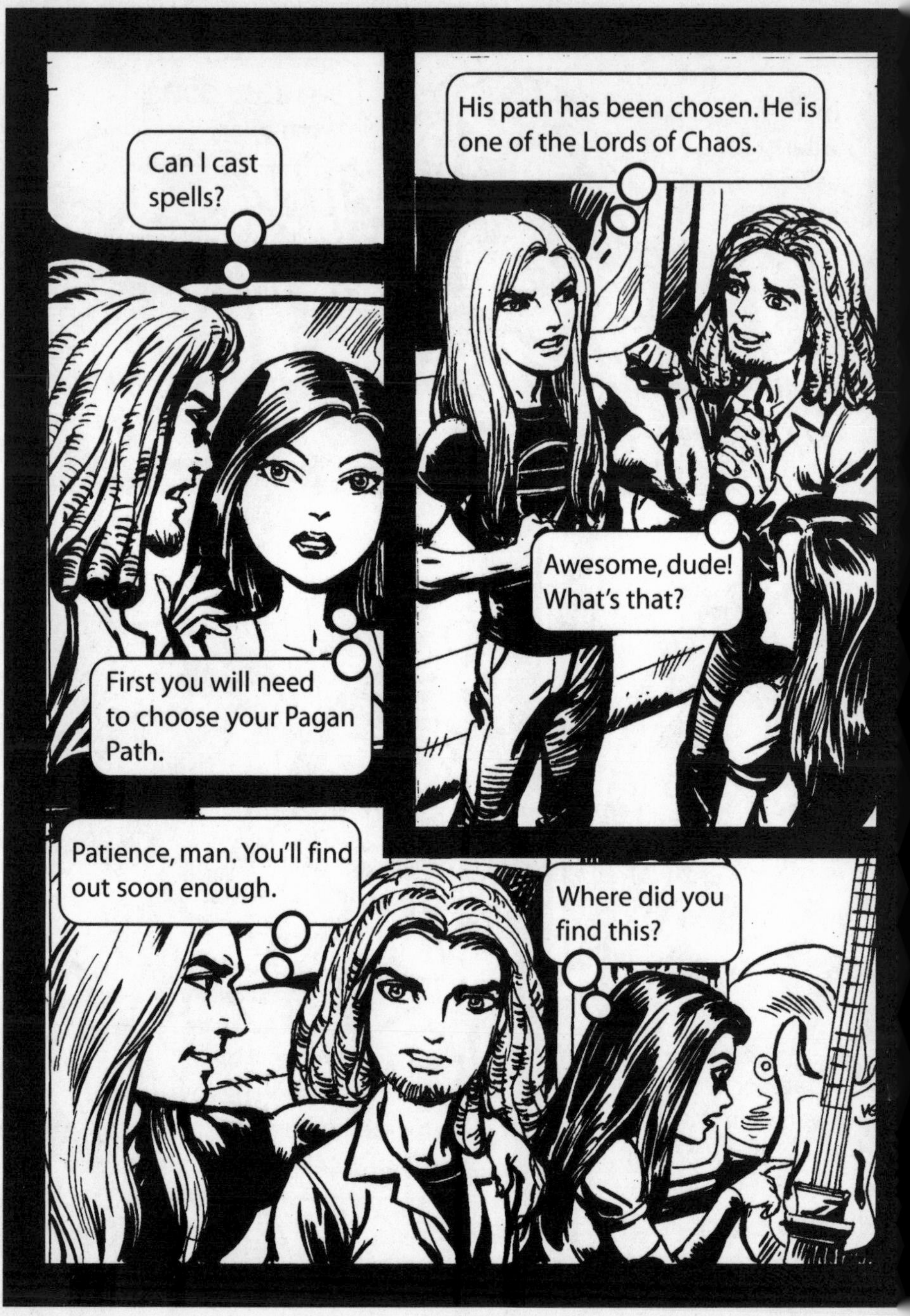
Can I cast spells?
First you will need to choose your Pagan Path.
His path has been chosen. He is one of the Lords of Chaos.
Awesome, dude! What's that?
Patience, man. You'll find out soon enough.
Where did you find this?

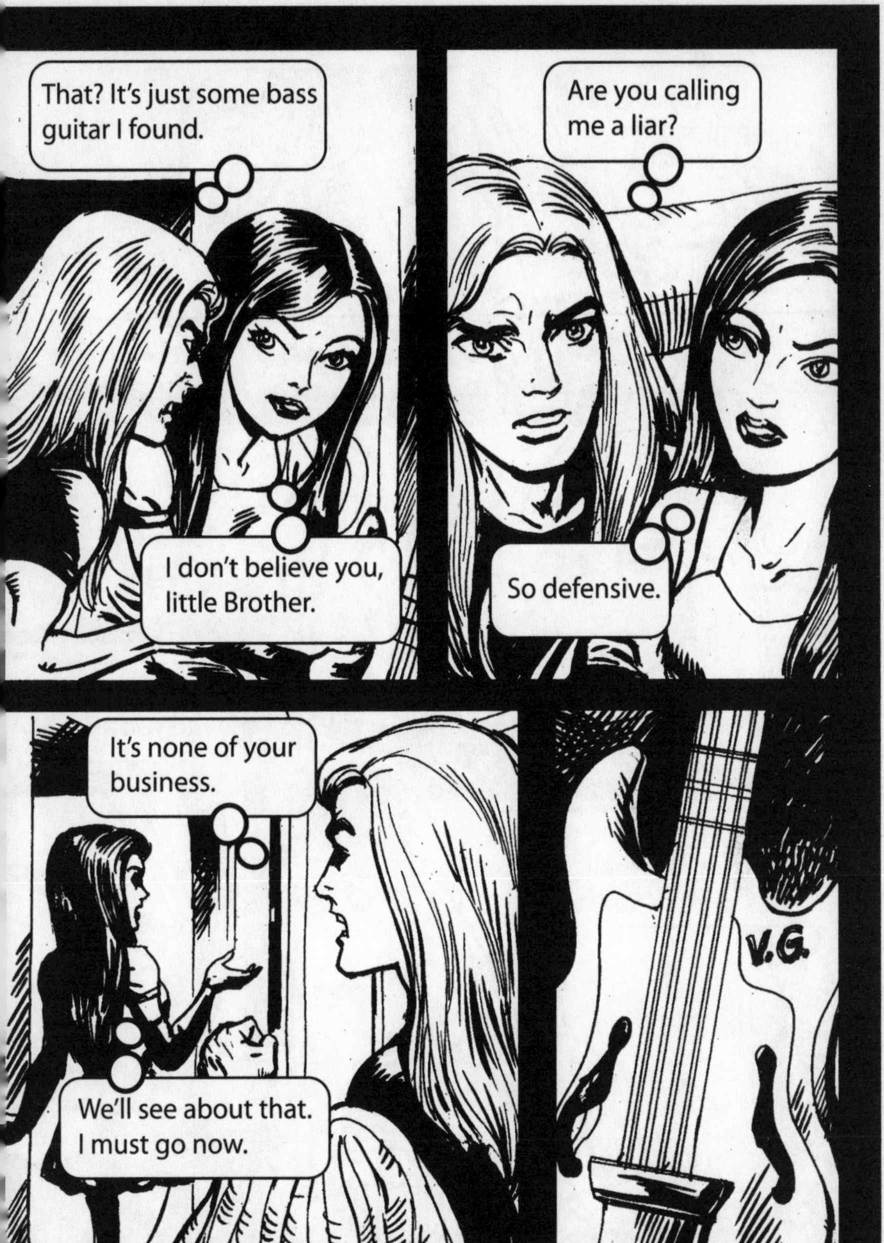
That? It's just some bass guitar I found.
I don't believe you, little Brother.
Are you calling me a liar?
So defensive.
It's none of your business.
We'll see about that. I must go now.
V.G.

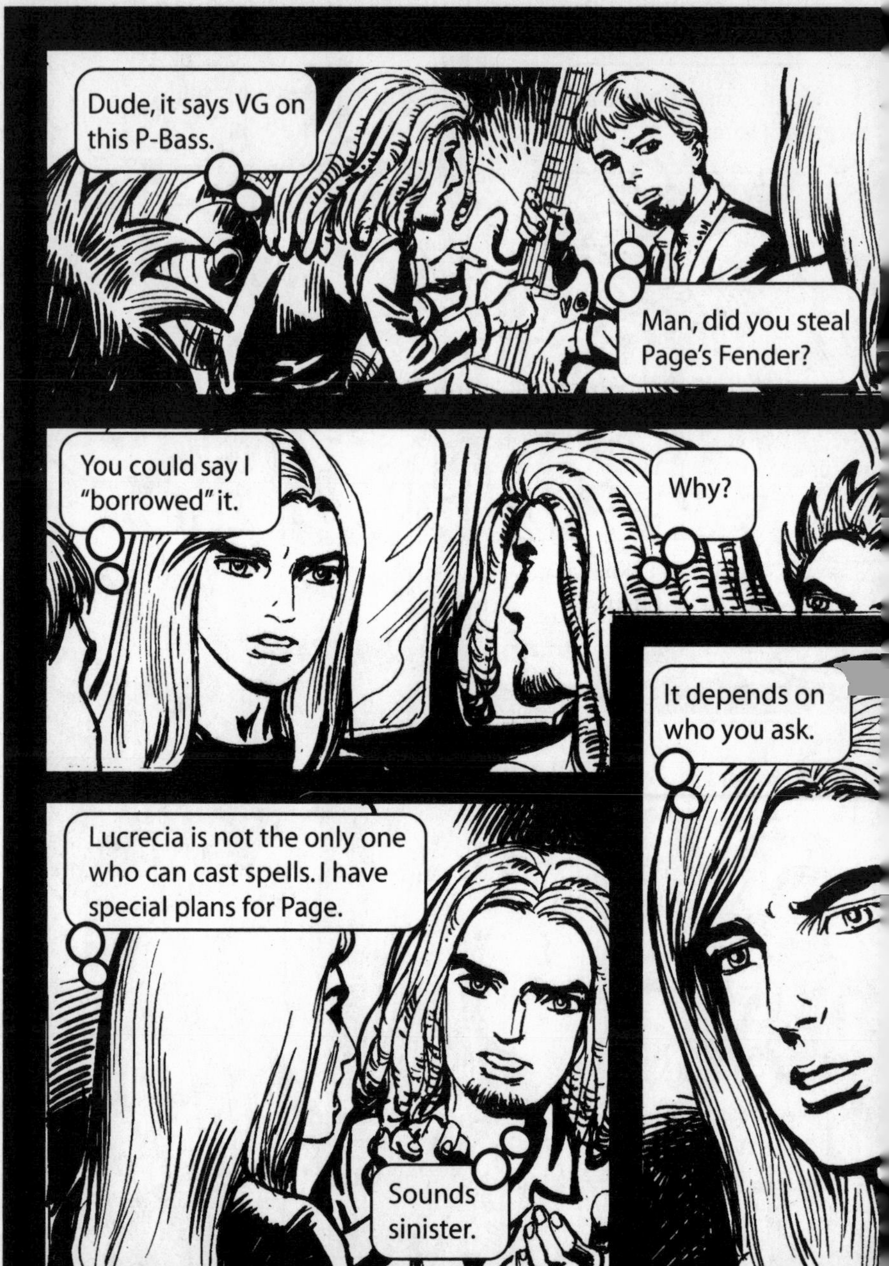

Dude, it says VG on this P-Bass.
Man, did you steal Page's Fender?
You could say I "borrowed" it.
Why?
It depends on who you ask.
Lucrecia is not the only one who can cast spells. I have special plans for Page.
Sounds sinister.

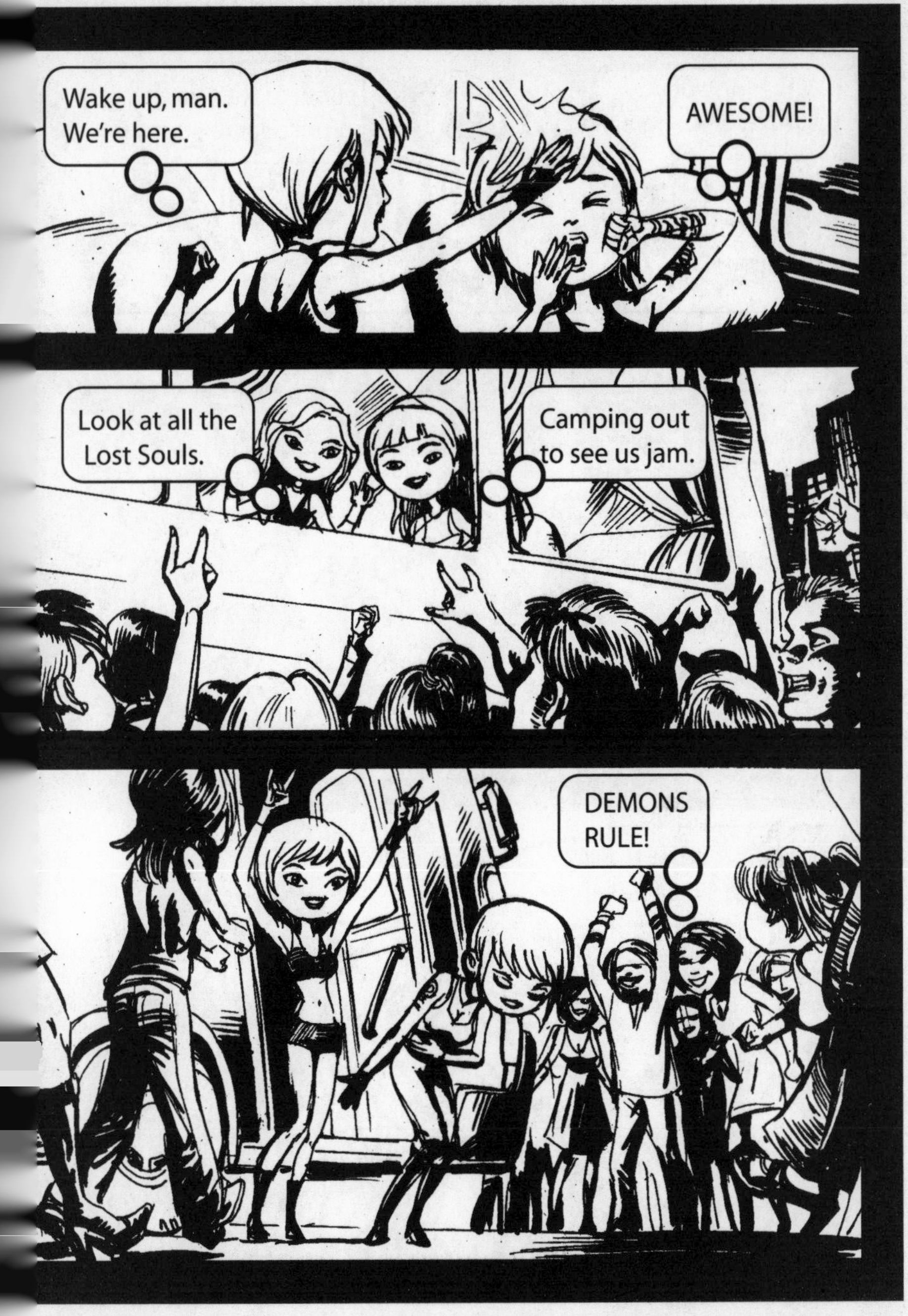
Wake up, man. We're here.
AWESOME!
Look at all the Lost Souls.
Camping out to see us jam.
DEMONS RULE!

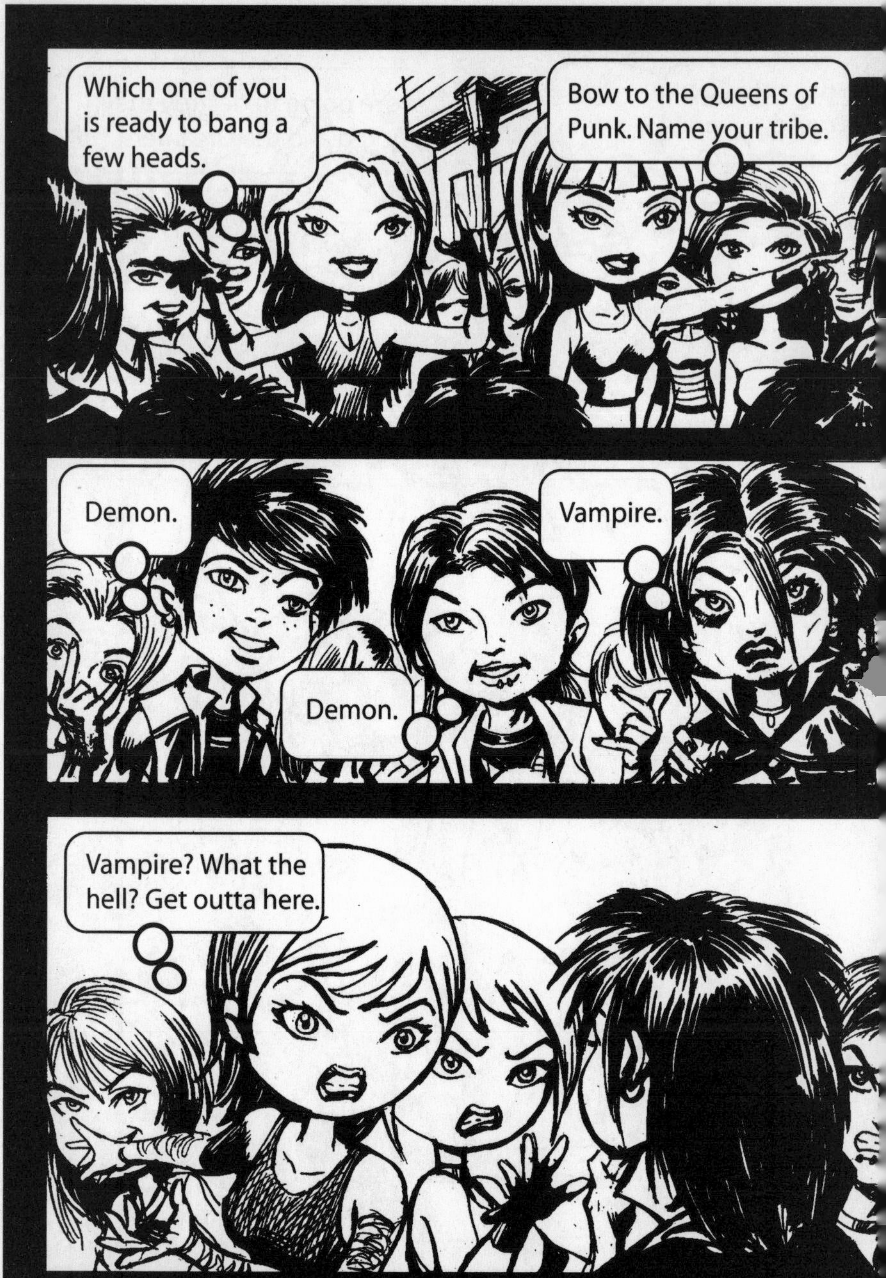
Which one of you is ready to bang a few heads.
Bow to the Queens of Punk. Name your tribe.
Demon.
Vampire.
Demon.
Vampire? What the hell? Get outta here.

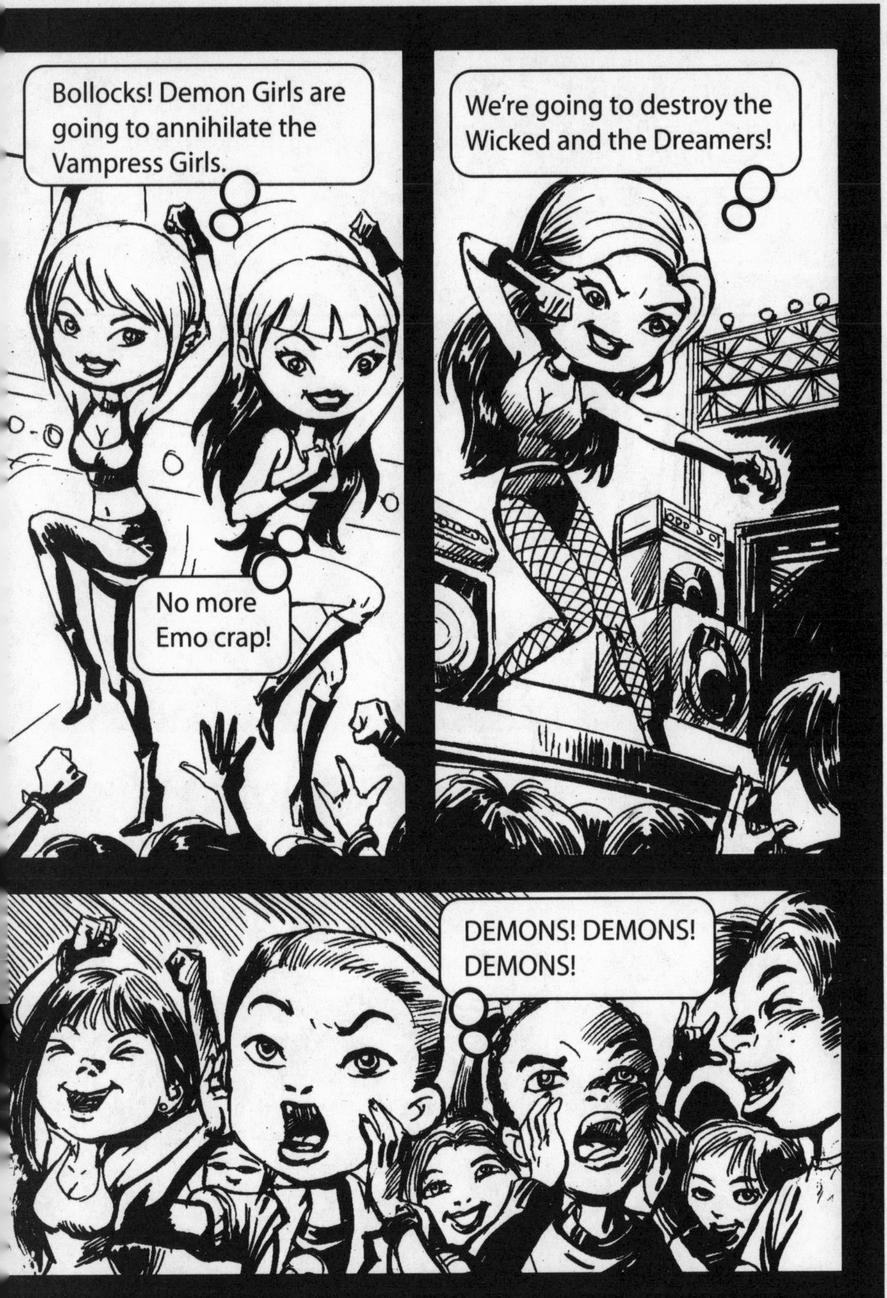
Bollocks! Demon Girls are going to annihilate the Vampress Girls.
No more Emo crap!
We're going to destroy the Wicked and the Dreamers!
DEMONS! DEMONS! DEMONS!

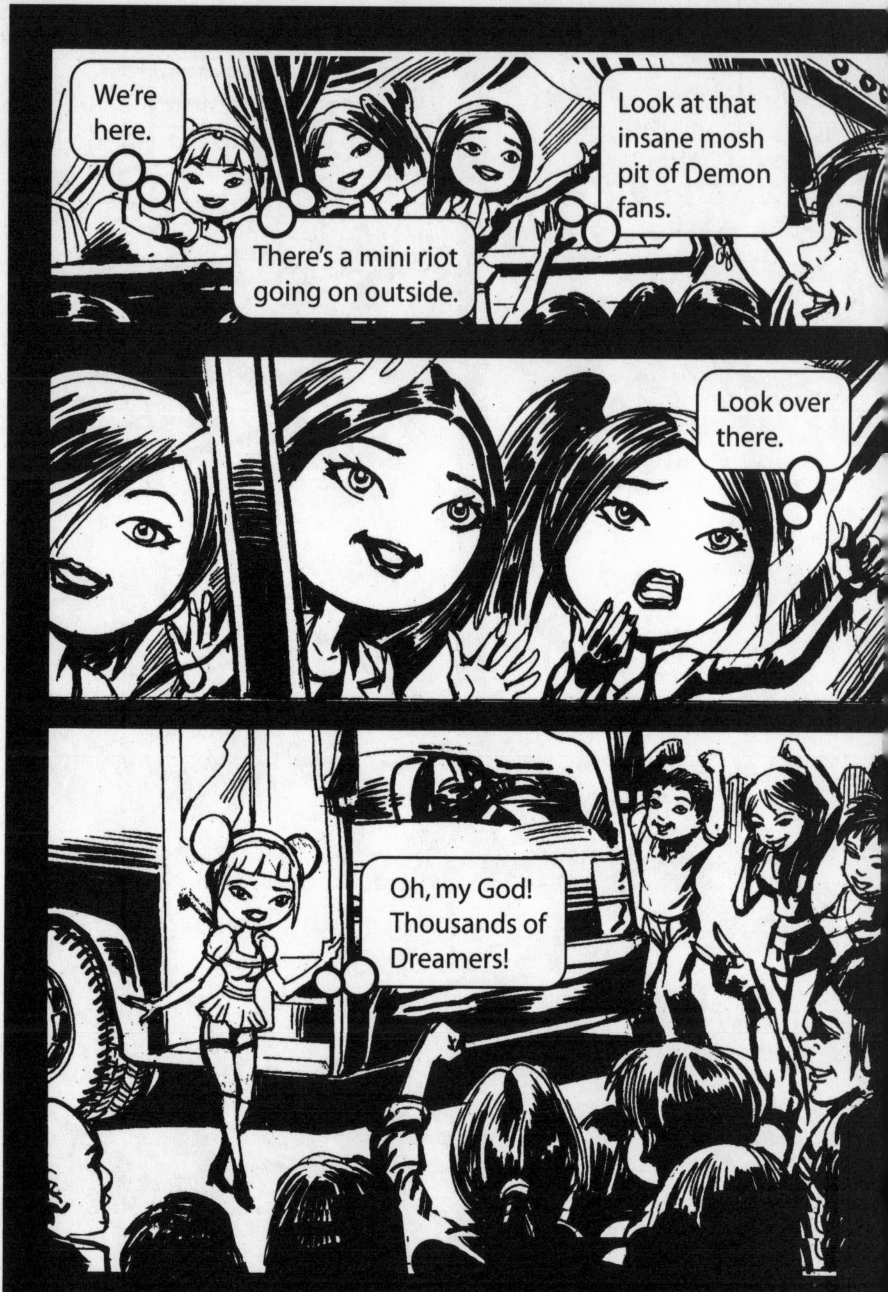
We're here.
There's a mini riot going on outside.
Look at that insane mosh pit of Demon fans.
Look over there.
Oh, my God! Thousands of Dreamers!

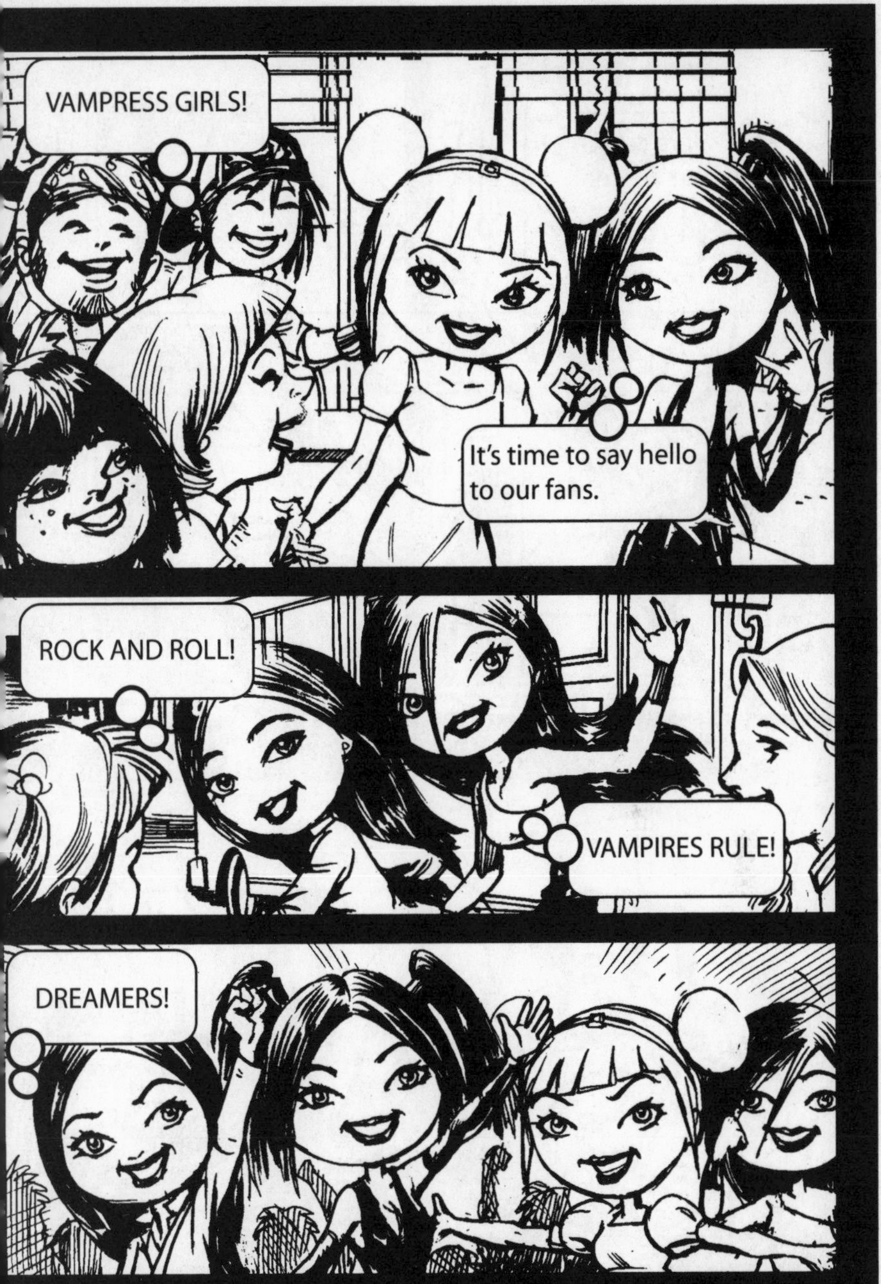
VAMPRESS GIRLS!
It's time to say hello to our fans.
ROCK AND ROLL!
VAMPIRES RULE!
DREAMERS!

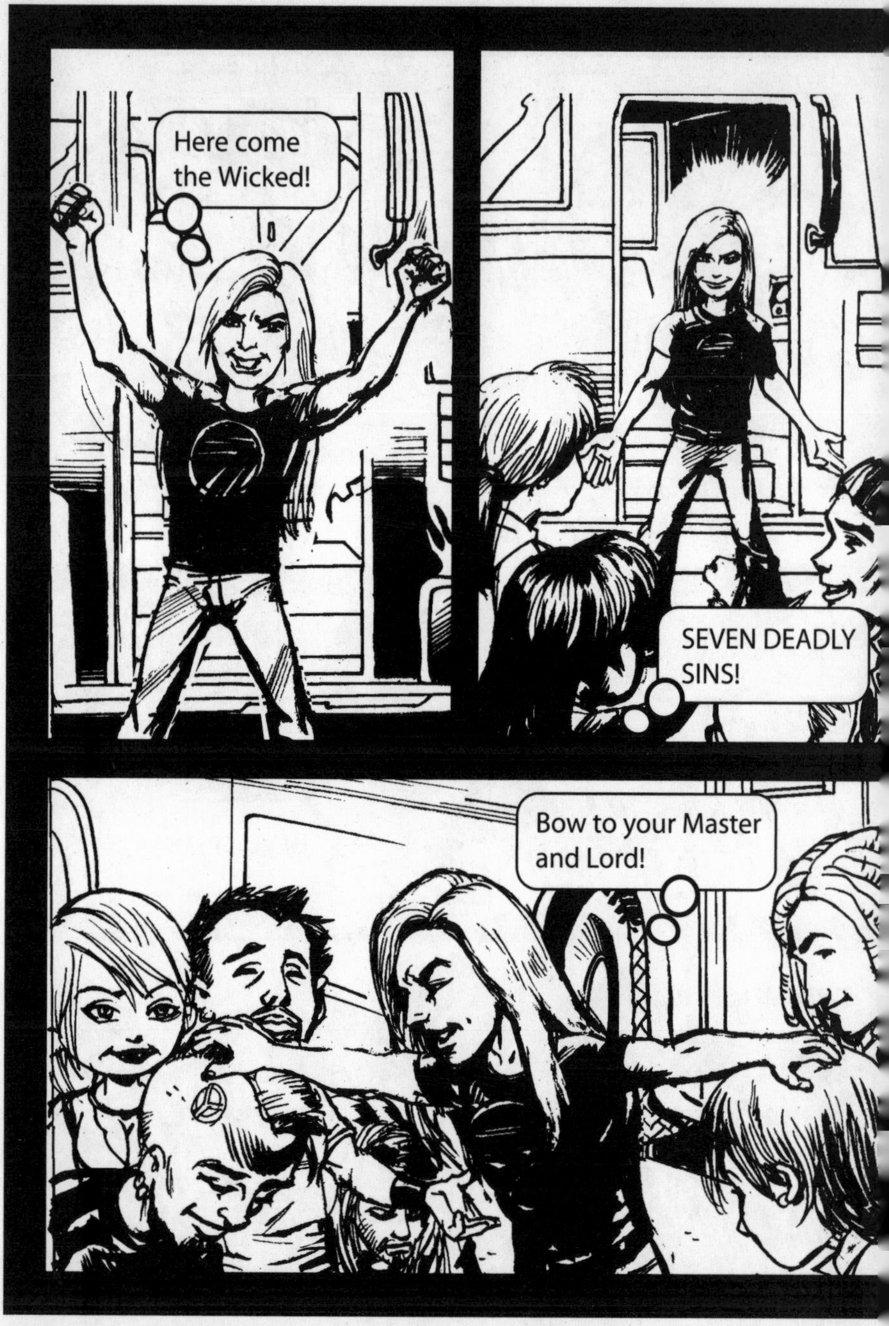
Here come the Wicked!
SEVEN DEADLY SINS!
Bow to your Master and Lord!

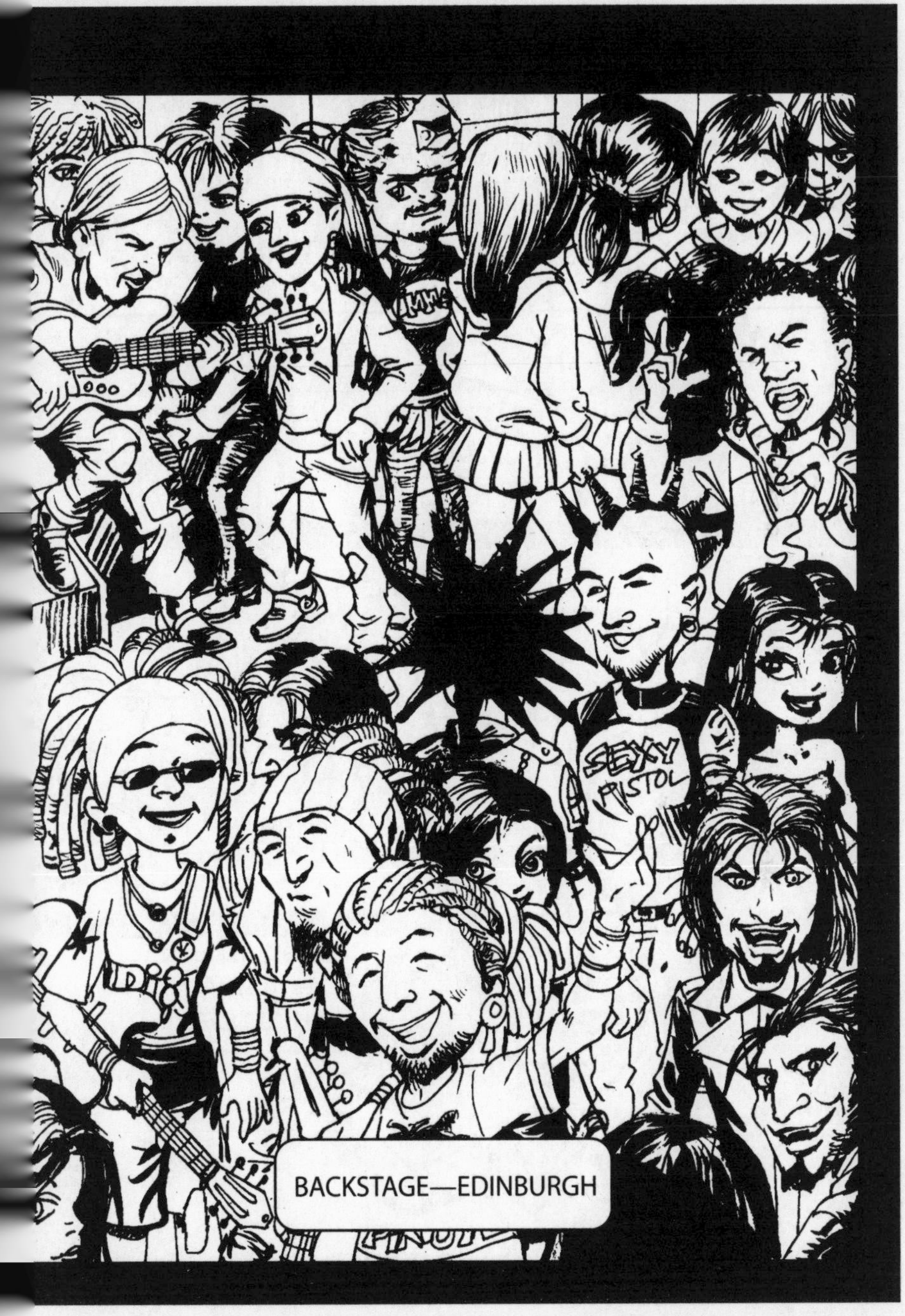
SEXY PISTOL
BACKSTAGE—EDINBURGH

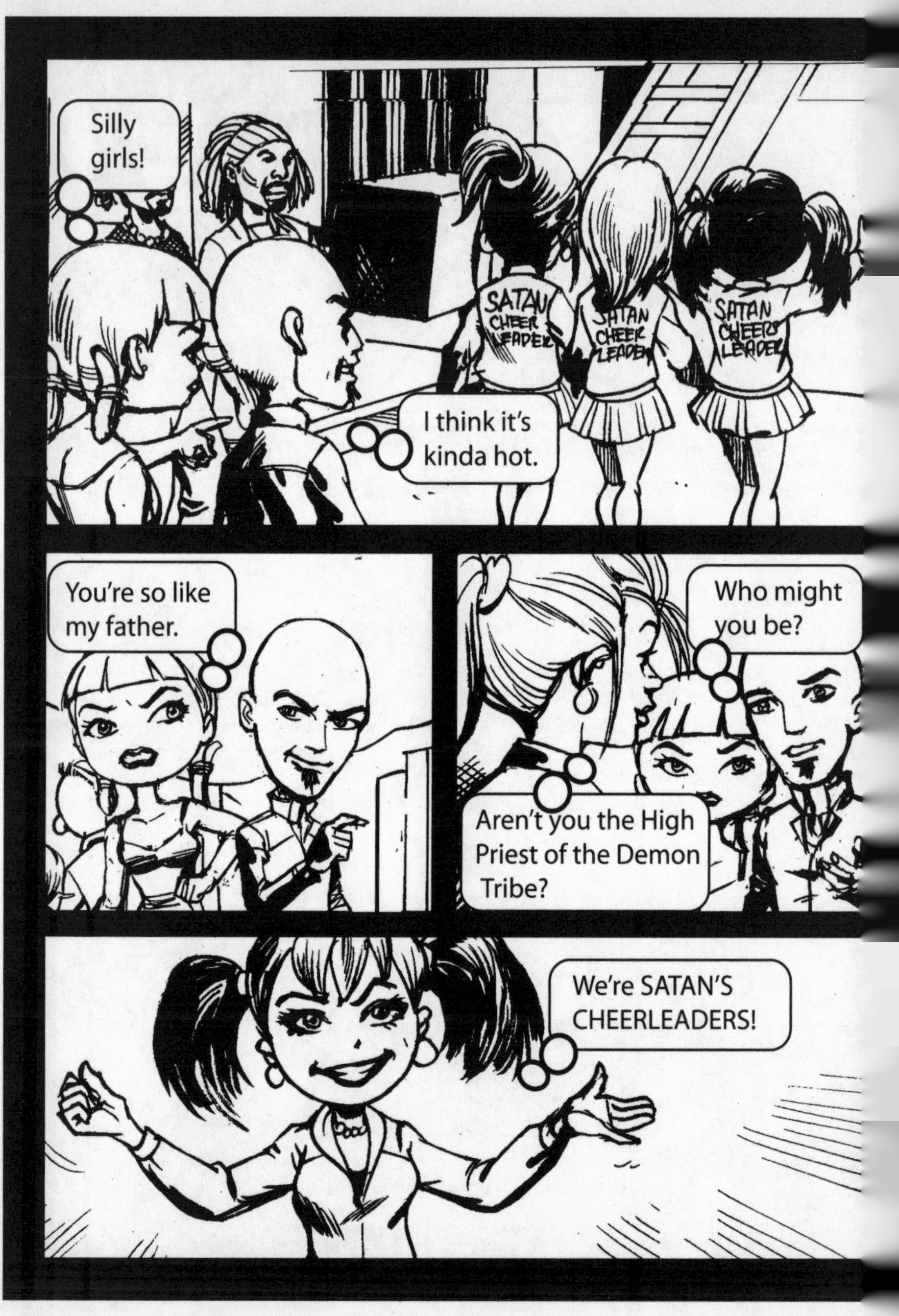
Silly girls!
SATAN CHEER LEADER
SATAN CHEER LEADER
SATAN CHEERS LEADER
I think it's kinda hot.
You're so like my father.
Who might you be?
Aren't you the High Priest of the Demon Tribe?
We're SATAN'S CHEERLEADERS!

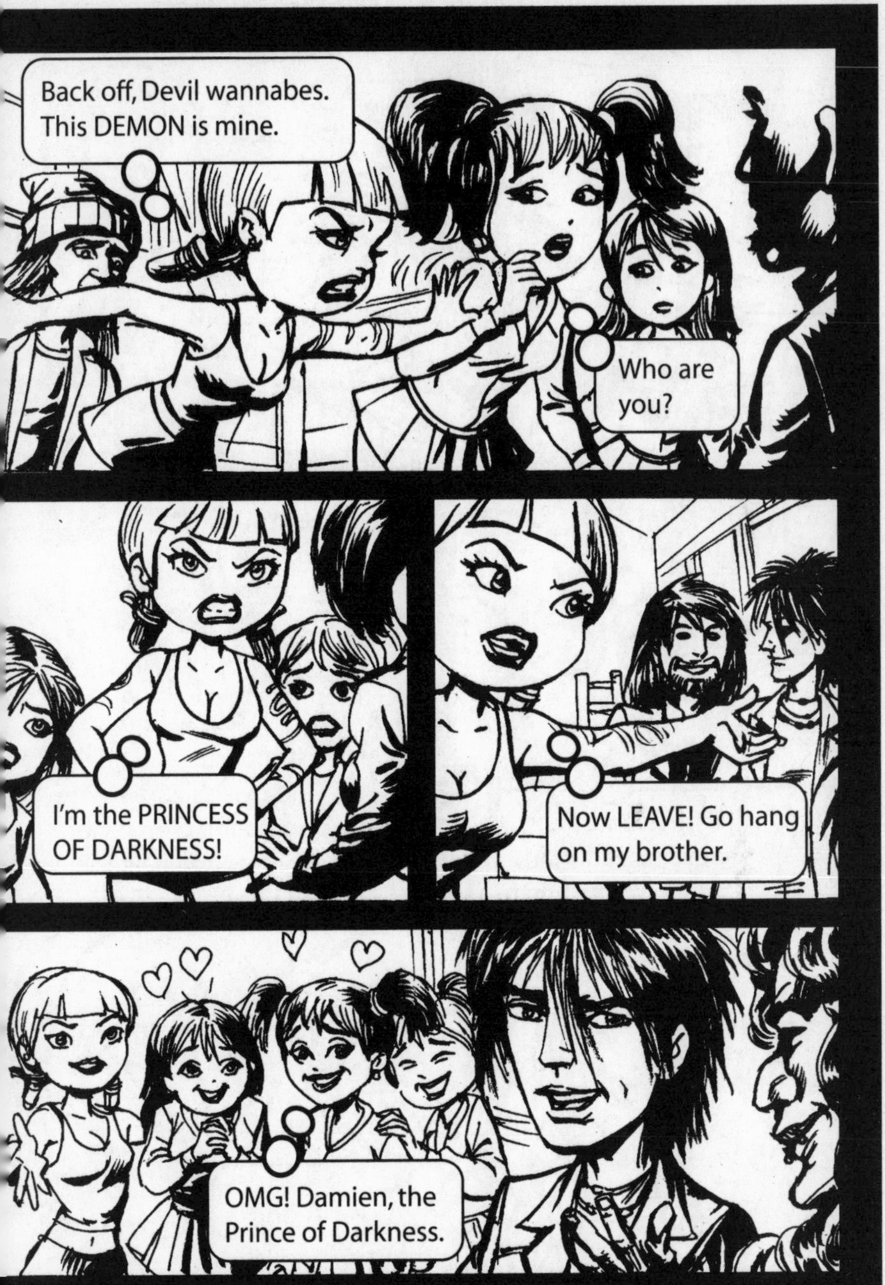
Back off, Devil wannabes. This DEMON is mine.
Who are you?
I'm the PRINCESS OF DARKNESS!
Now LEAVE! Go hang on my brother.
OMG! Damien, the Prince of Darkness.

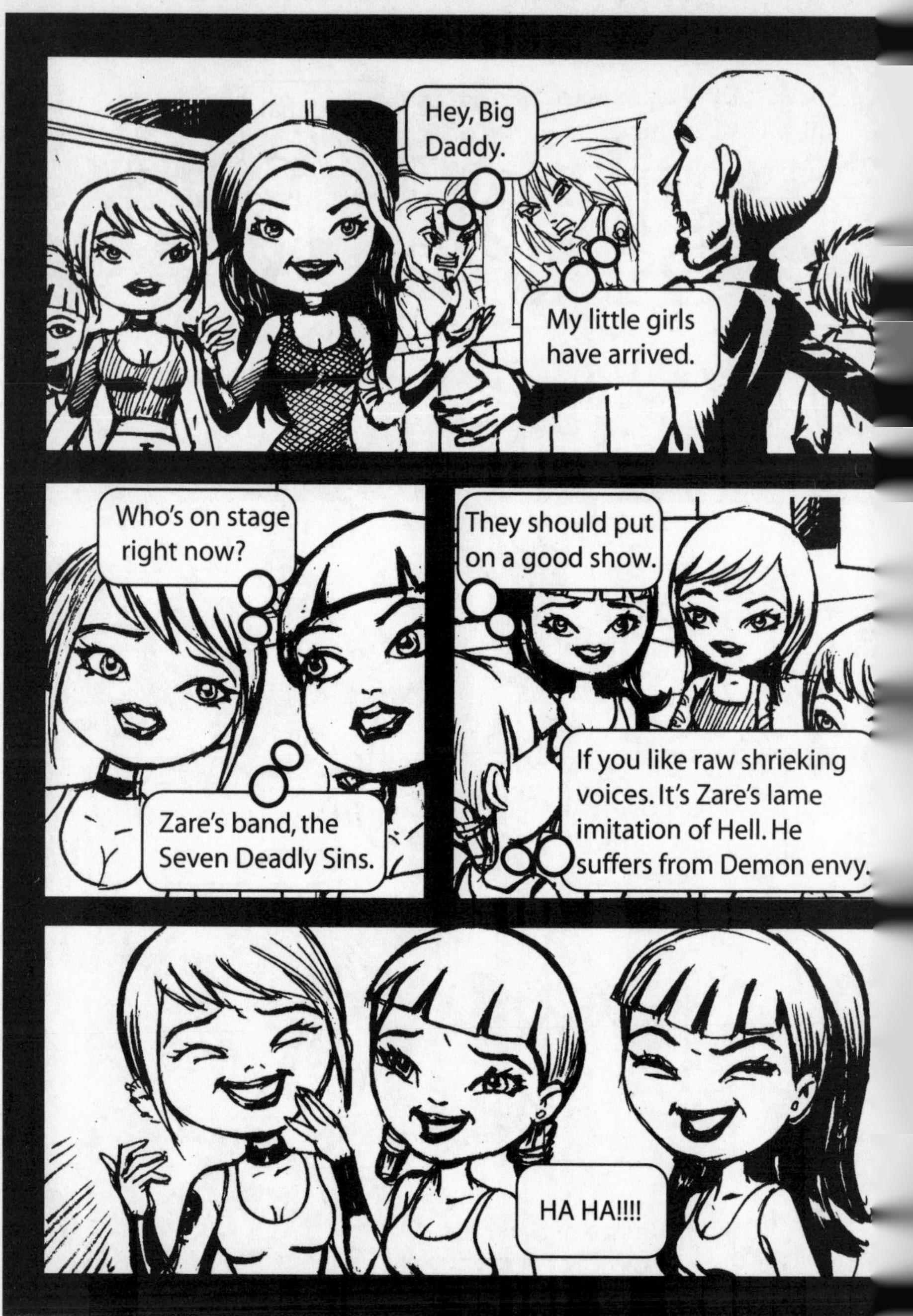
Hey, Big Daddy.
My little girls have arrived.
Who's on stage right now?
Zare's band, the Seven Deadly Sins.
They should put on a good show.
If you like raw shrieking voices. It's Zare's lame imitation of Hell. He suffers from Demon envy.
HA HA!!!!

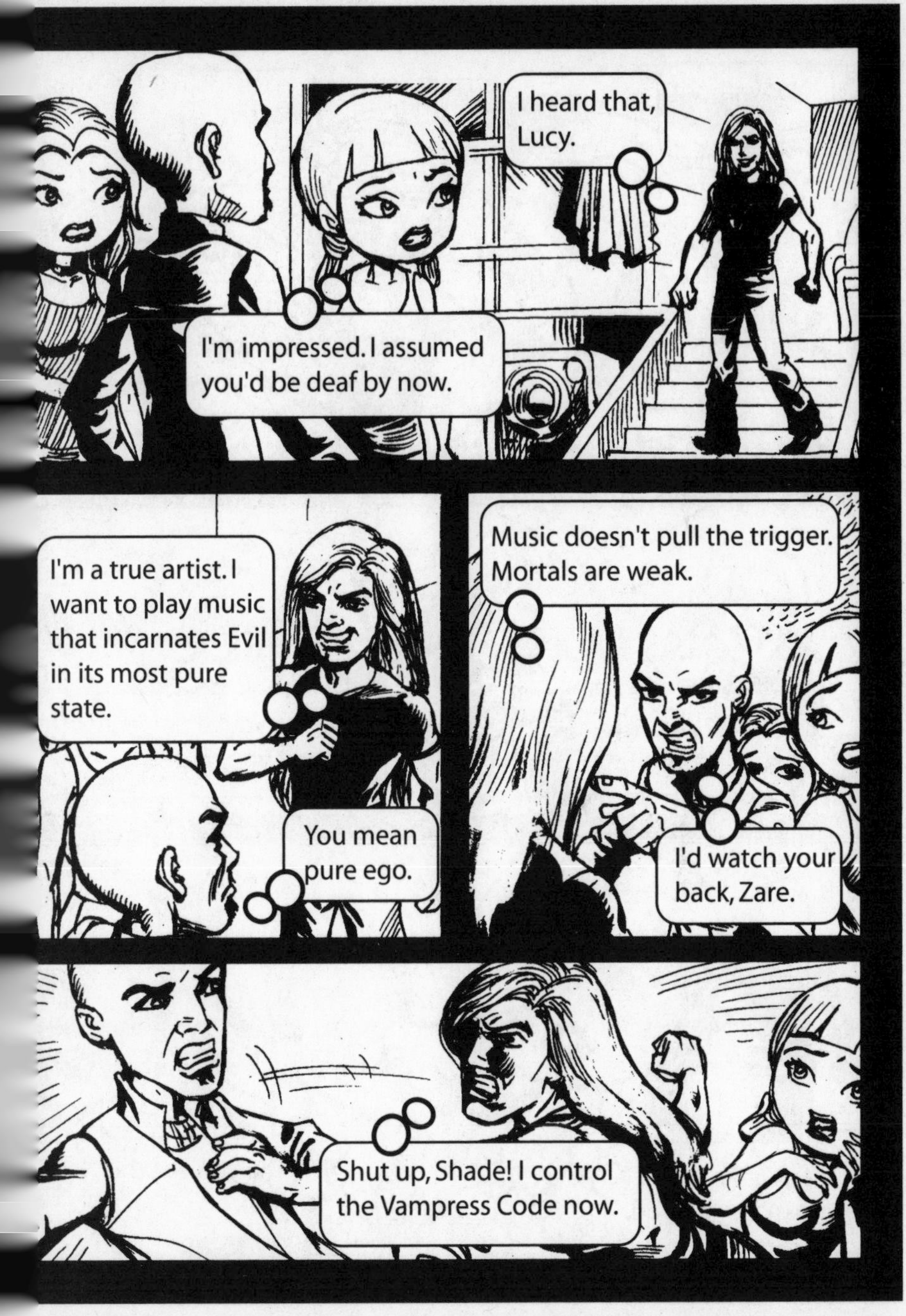
I heard that, Lucy.
I'm impressed. I assumed you'd be deaf by now.
I'm a true artist. I want to play music that incarnates Evil in its most pure state.
You mean pure ego.
Music doesn't pull the trigger. Mortals are weak.
I'd watch your back, Zare.
Shut up, Shade! I control the Vampress Code now.

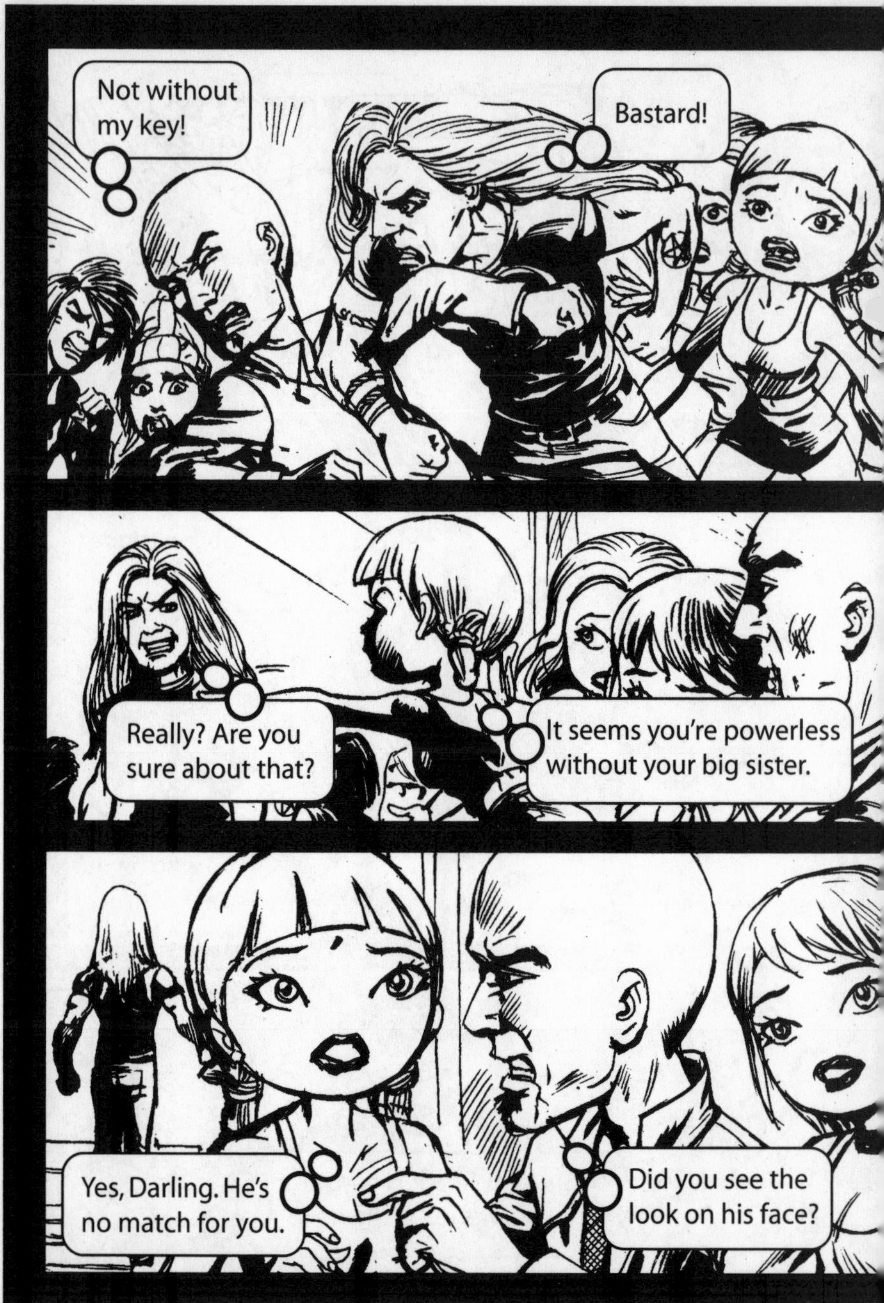
Not without my key!
Bastard!
Really? Are you sure about that?
It seems you're powerless without your big sister.
Yes, Darling. He's no match for you.
Did you see the look on his face?

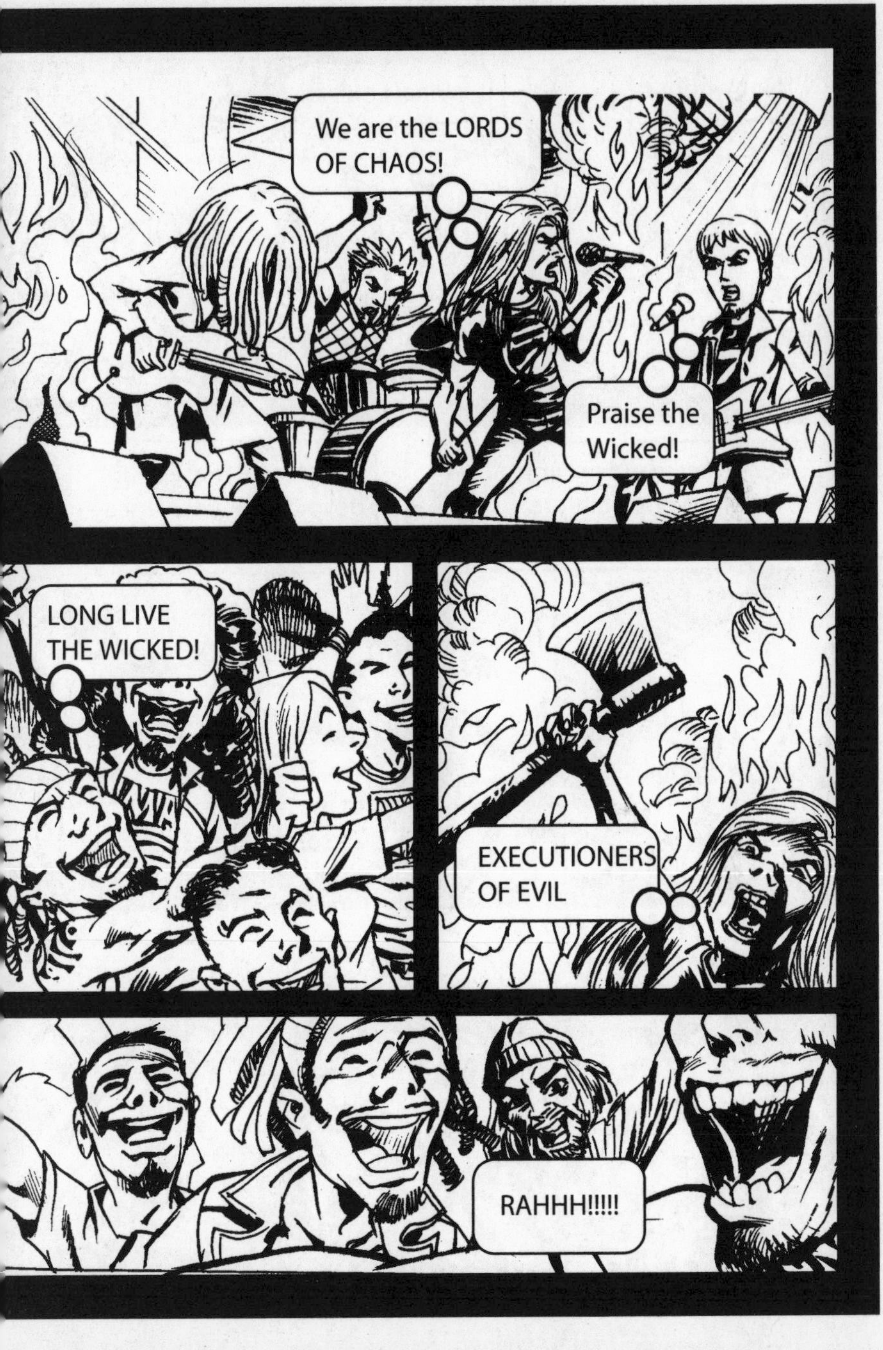
We are the LORDS OF CHAOS!
Praise the Wicked!
LONG LIVE THE WICKED!
EXECUTIONERS OF EVIL
RAHHH!!!!!

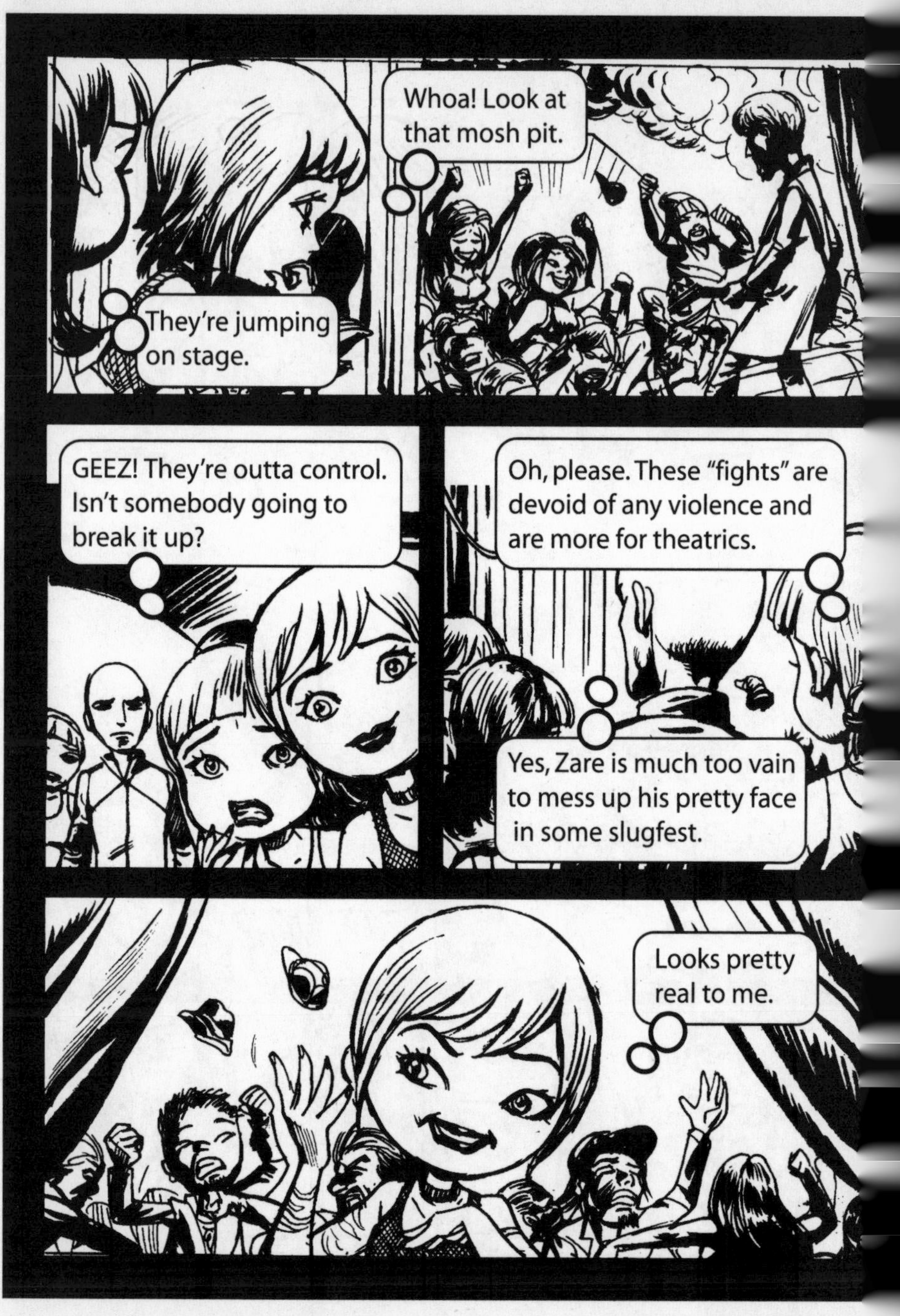
They're jumping on stage.
Whoa! Look at that mosh pit.
GEEZ! They're outta control. Isn't somebody going to break it up?
Oh, please. These "fights" are devoid of any violence and are more for theatrics.
Yes, Zare is much too vain to mess up his pretty face in some slugfest.
Looks pretty real to me.

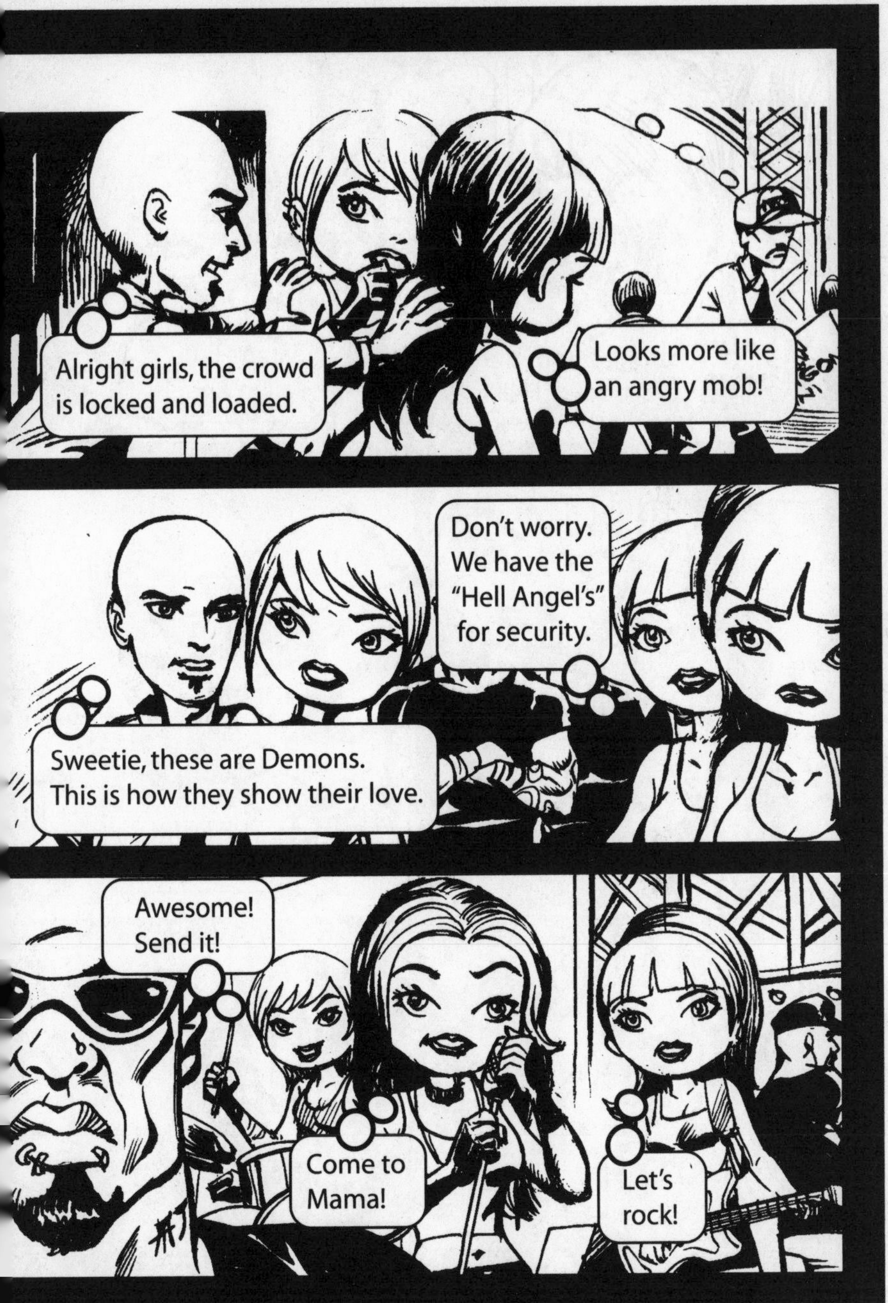
Alright girls, the crowd is locked and loaded.
Looks more like an angry mob!
Sweetie, these are Demons. This is how they show their love.
Don't worry. We have the "Hell Angel's" for security.
Awesome! Send it!
Come to Mama!
Let's rock!

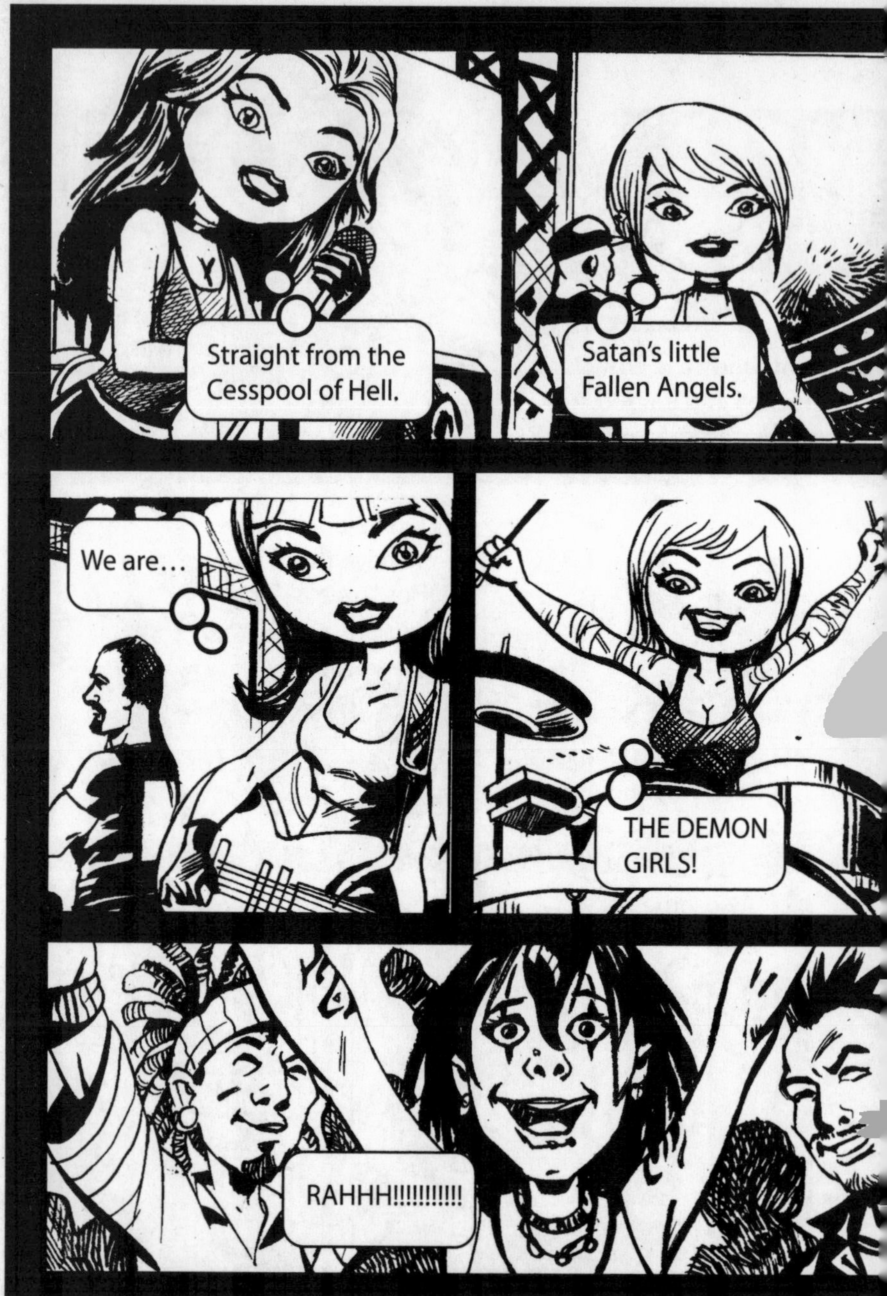
Straight from the Cesspool of Hell.
Satan's little Fallen Angels.
We are…
THE DEMON GIRLS!
RAHHH!!!!!!!!!!!

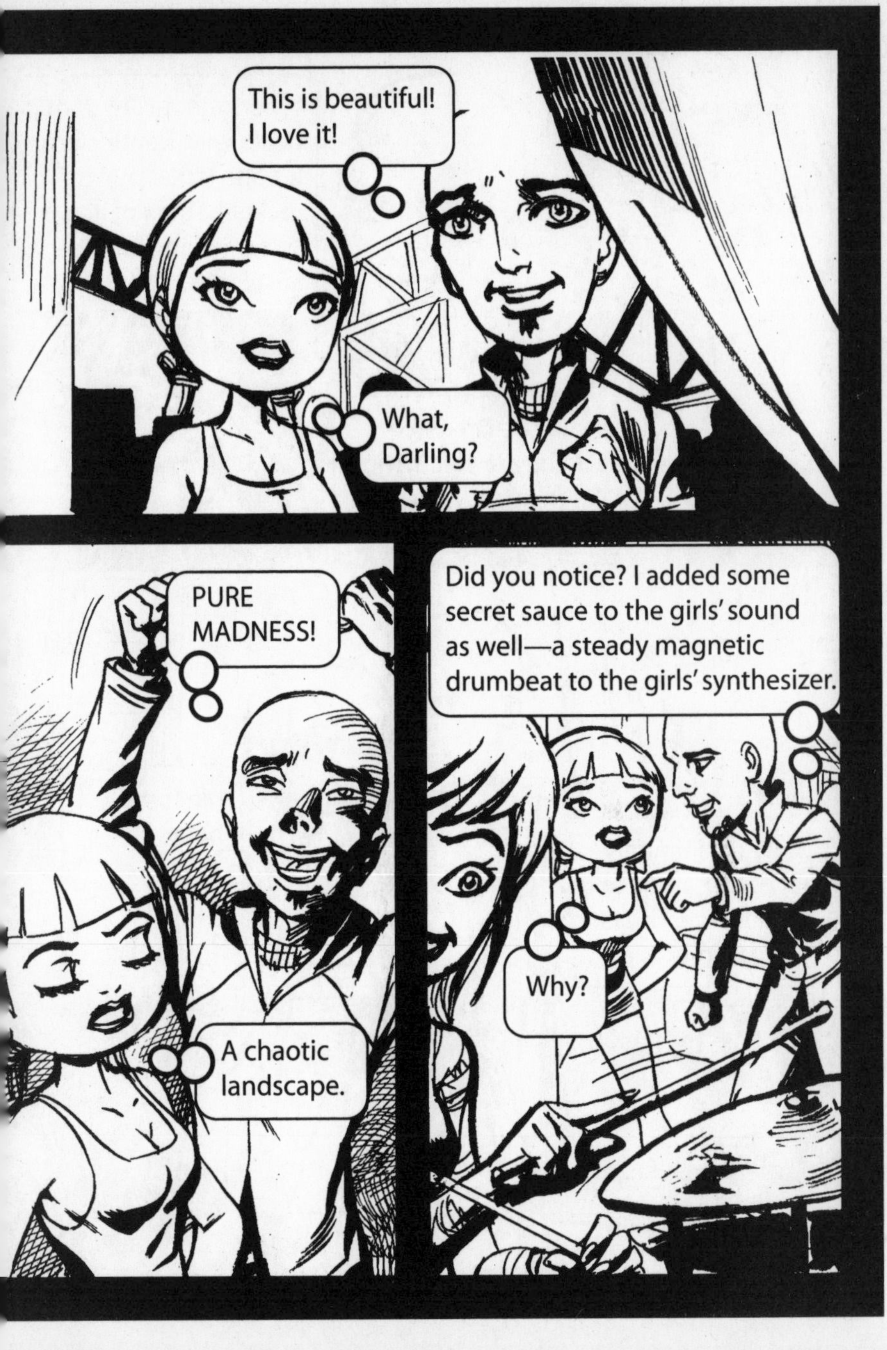
This is beautiful! I love it!
What, Darling?
PURE MADNESS!
A chaotic landscape.
Did you notice? I added some secret sauce to the girls' sound as well—a steady magnetic drumbeat to the girls' synthesizer.
Why?

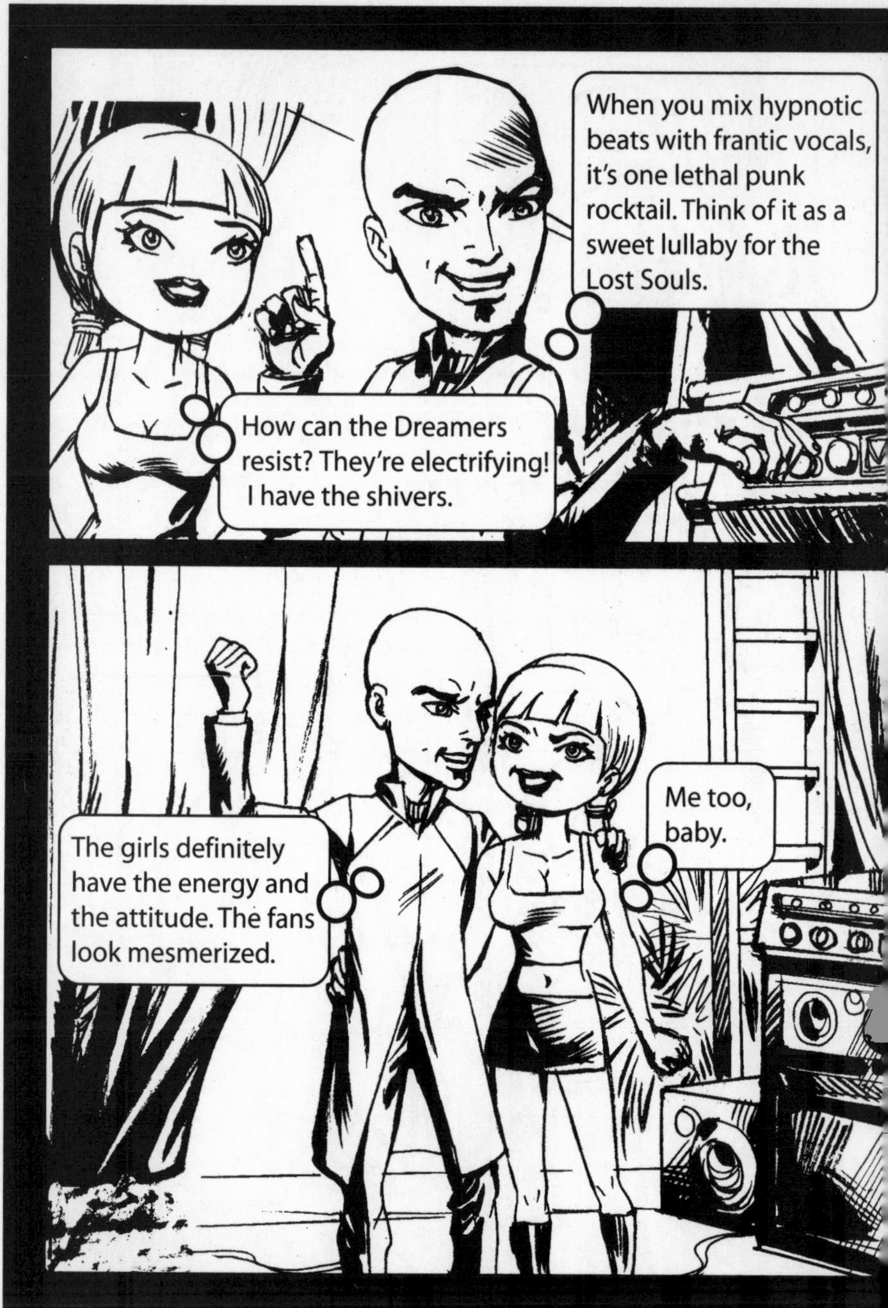
When you mix hypnotic beats with frantic vocals, it's one lethal punk rocktail. Think of it as a sweet lullaby for the Lost Souls.
How can the Dreamers resist? They're electrifying! I have the shivers.
The girls definitely have the energy and the attitude. The fans look mesmerized.
Me too, baby.

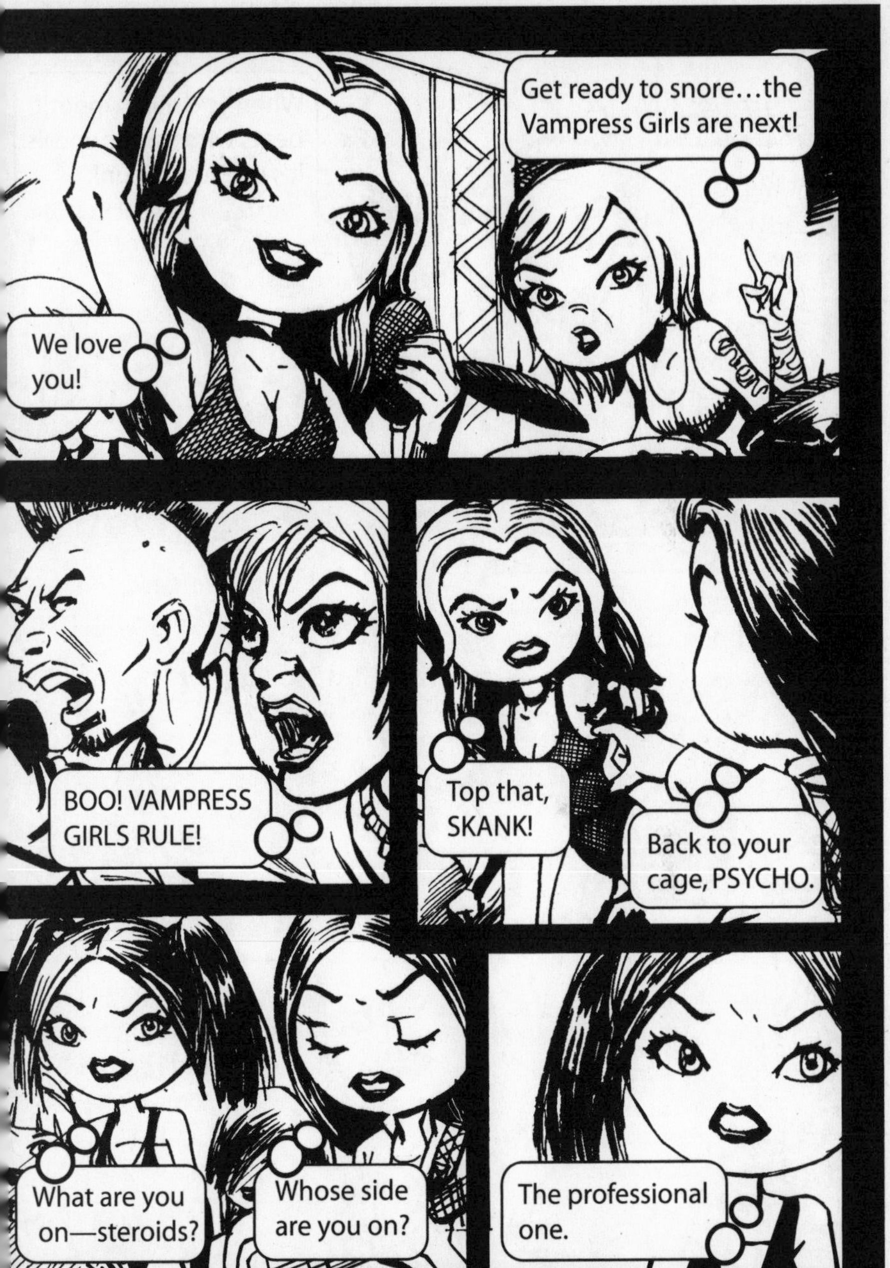

We love you!
Get ready to snore…the Vampress Girls are next!
BOO! VAMPRESS GIRLS RULE!
Top that, SKANK!
Back to your cage, PSYCHO.
What are you on—steroids?
Whose side are you on?
The professional one.

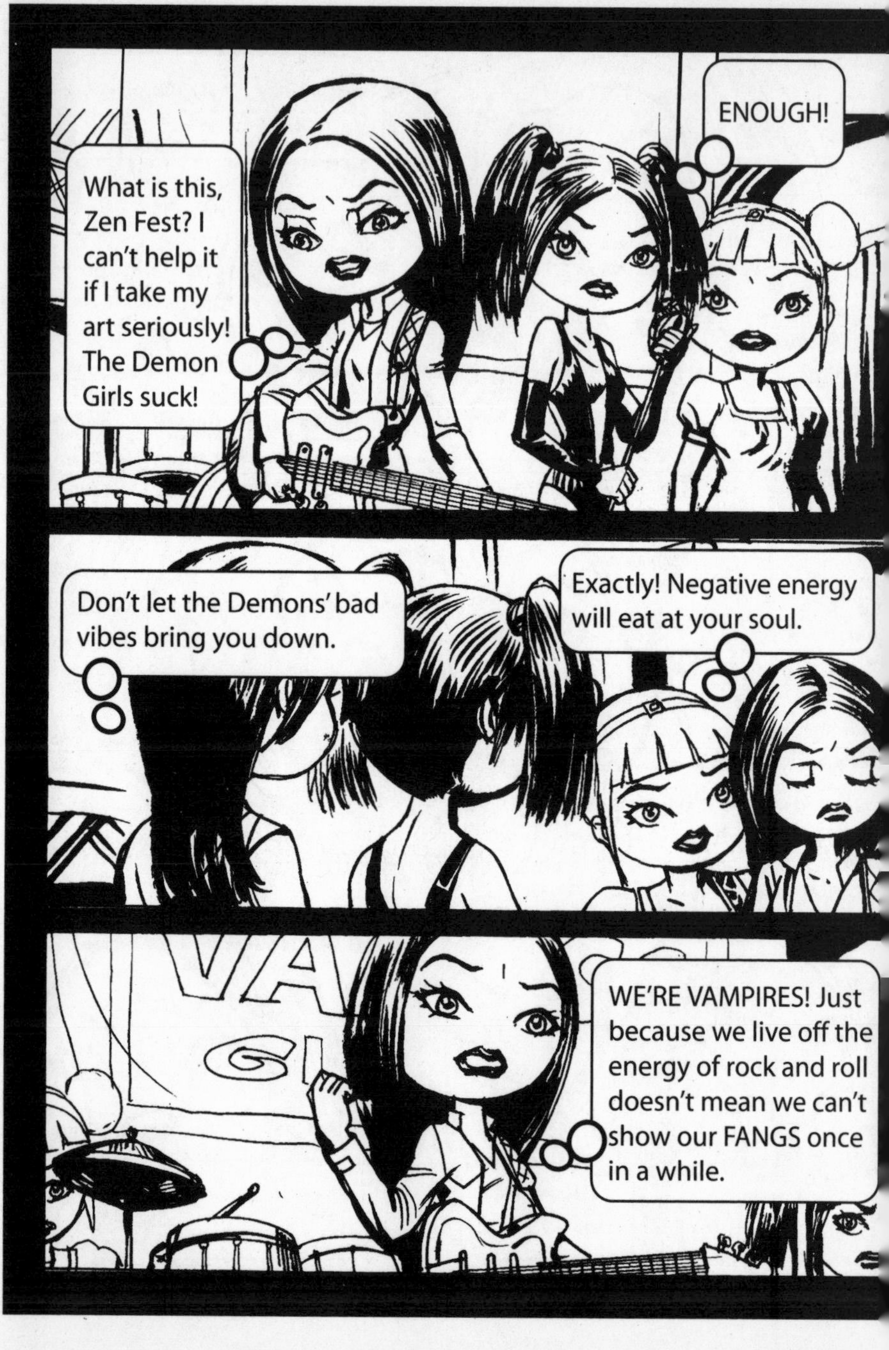
What is this, Zen Fest? I can't help it if I take my art seriously! The Demon Girls suck!
ENOUGH!
Don't let the Demons' bad vibes bring you down.
Exactly! Negative energy will eat at your soul.
WE'RE VAMPIRES! Just because we live off the energy of rock and roll doesn't mean we can't show our FANGS once in a while.

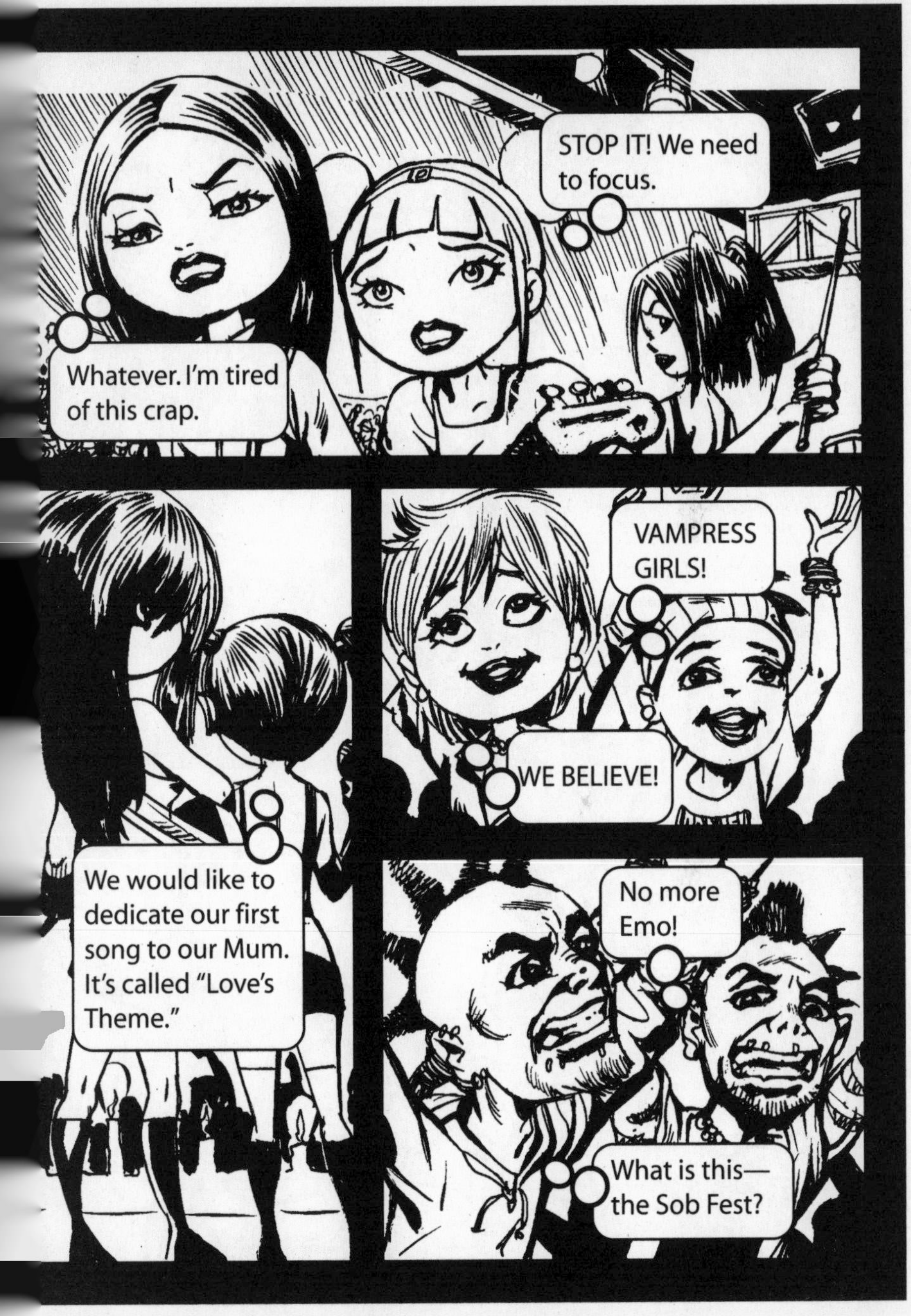
Whatever. I'm tired of this crap.
STOP IT! We need to focus.
We would like to dedicate our first song to our Mum. It's called "Love's Theme."
VAMPRESS GIRLS!
WE BELIEVE!
No more Emo!
What is this—the Sob Fest?

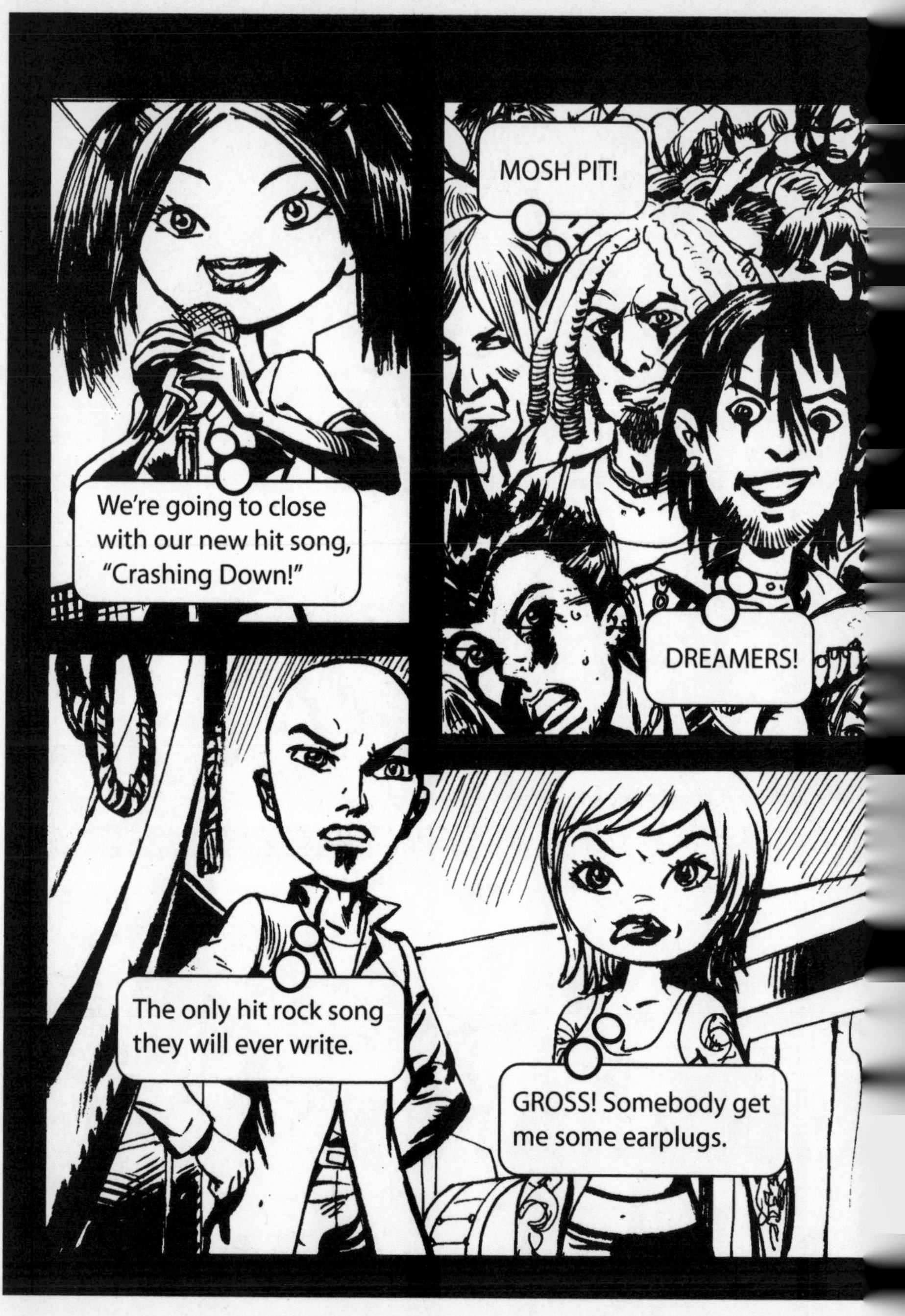
We're going to close with our new hit song, "Crashing Down!"
MOSH PIT!
DREAMERS!
The only hit rock song they will ever write.
GROSS! Somebody get me some earplugs.

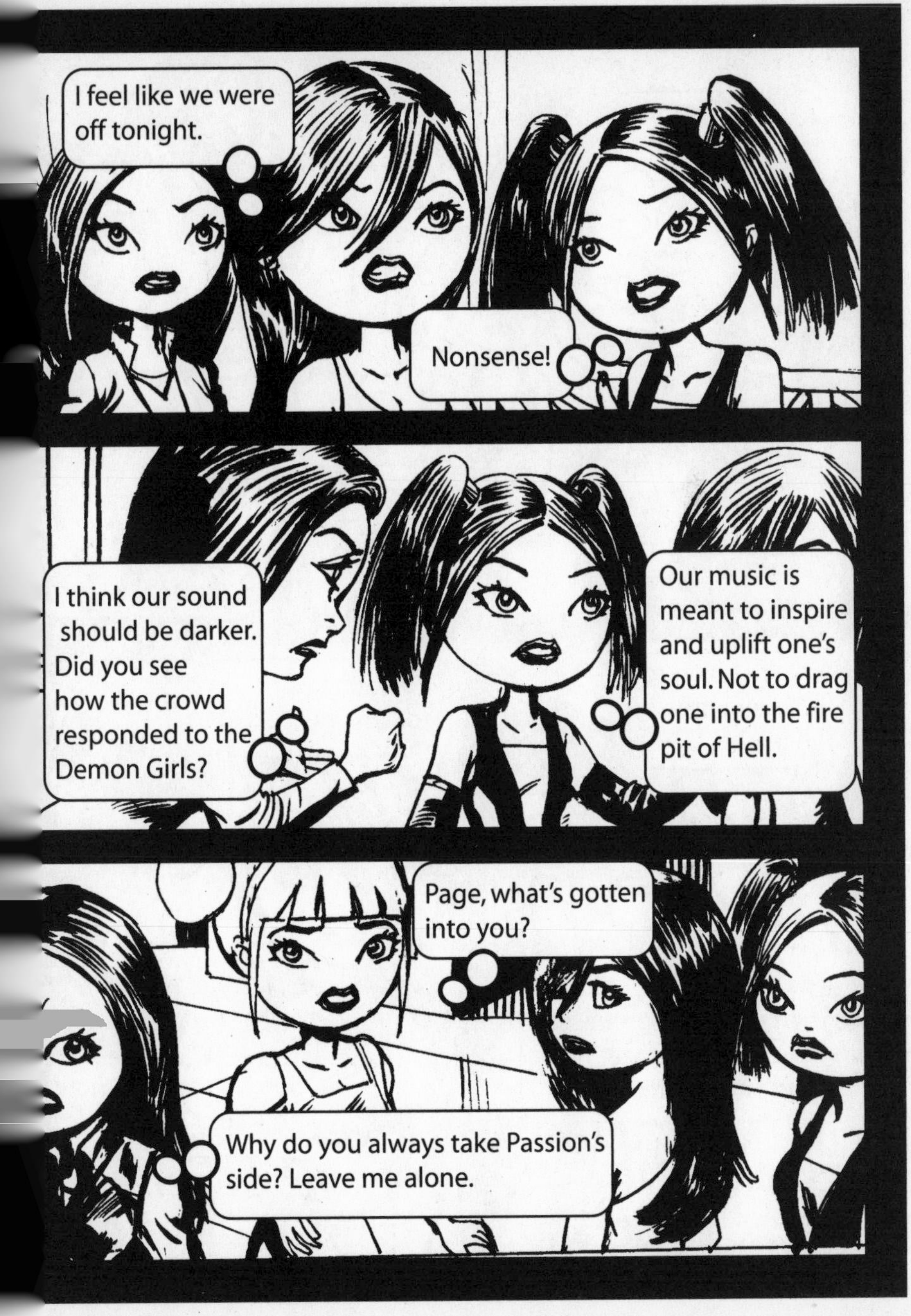
I feel like we were off tonight.
Nonsense!
I think our sound should be darker. Did you see how the crowd responded to the Demon Girls?
Our music is meant to inspire and uplift one's soul. Not to drag one into the fire pit of Hell.
Page, what's gotten into you?
Why do you always take Passion's side? Leave me alone.

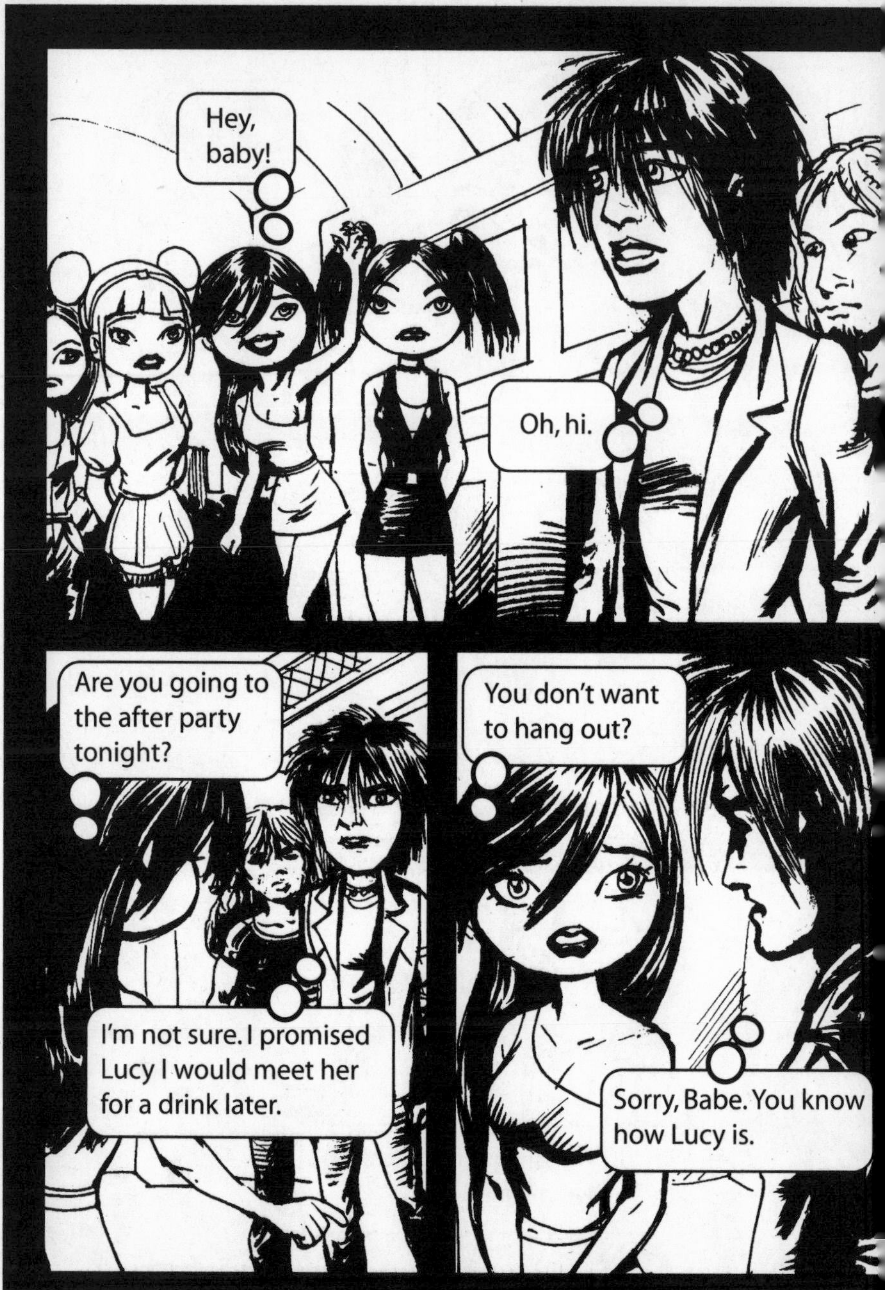
Hey, baby!
Oh, hi.
Are you going to the after party tonight?
I'm not sure. I promised Lucy I would meet her for a drink later.
You don't want to hang out?
Sorry, Babe. You know how Lucy is.

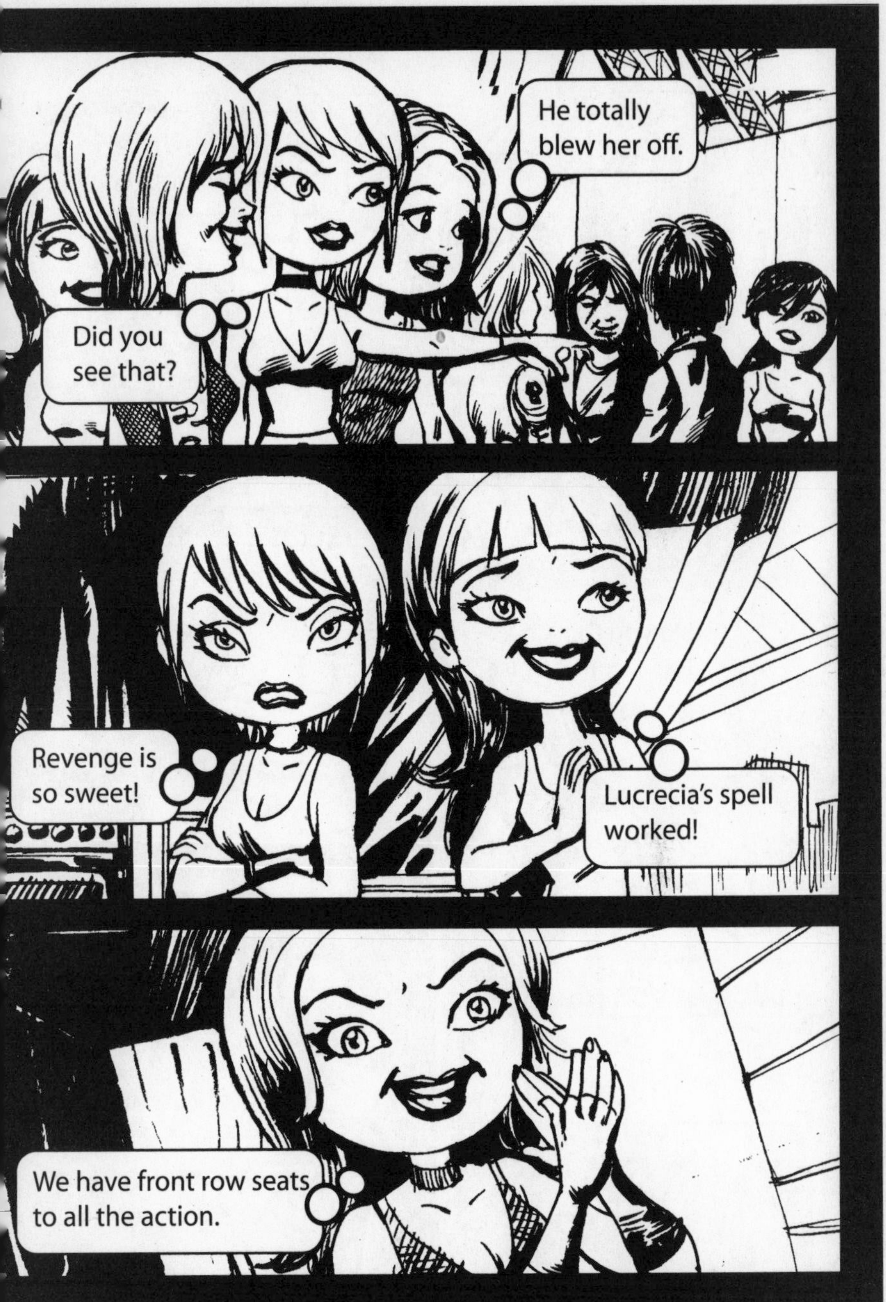
He totally blew her off.
Did you see that?
Revenge is so sweet!
Lucrecia's spell worked!
We have front row seats to all the action.

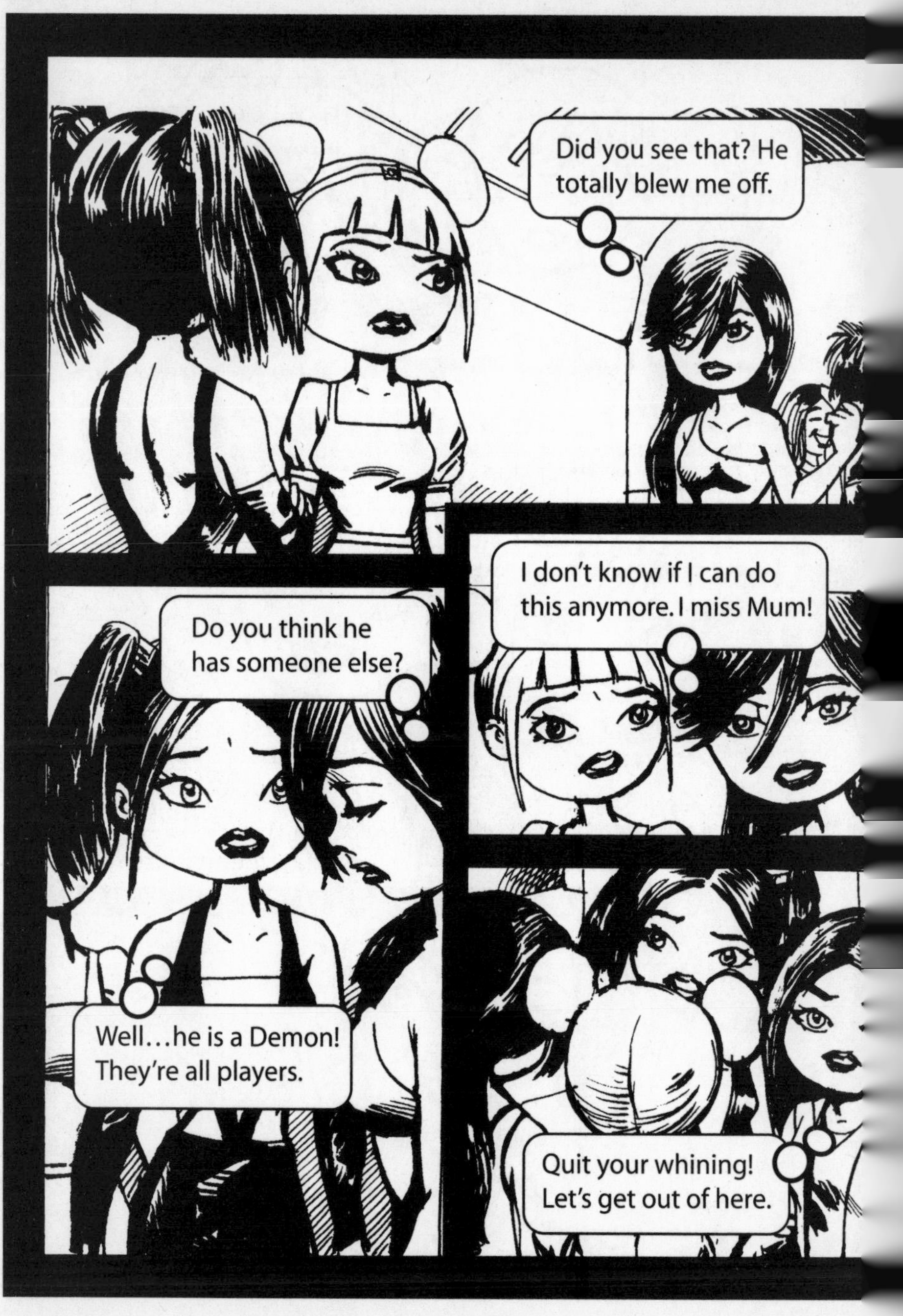
Did you see that? He totally blew me off.
Do you think he has someone else?
Well…he is a Demon! They're all players.
I don't know if I can do this anymore. I miss Mum!
Quit your whining! Let's get out of here.

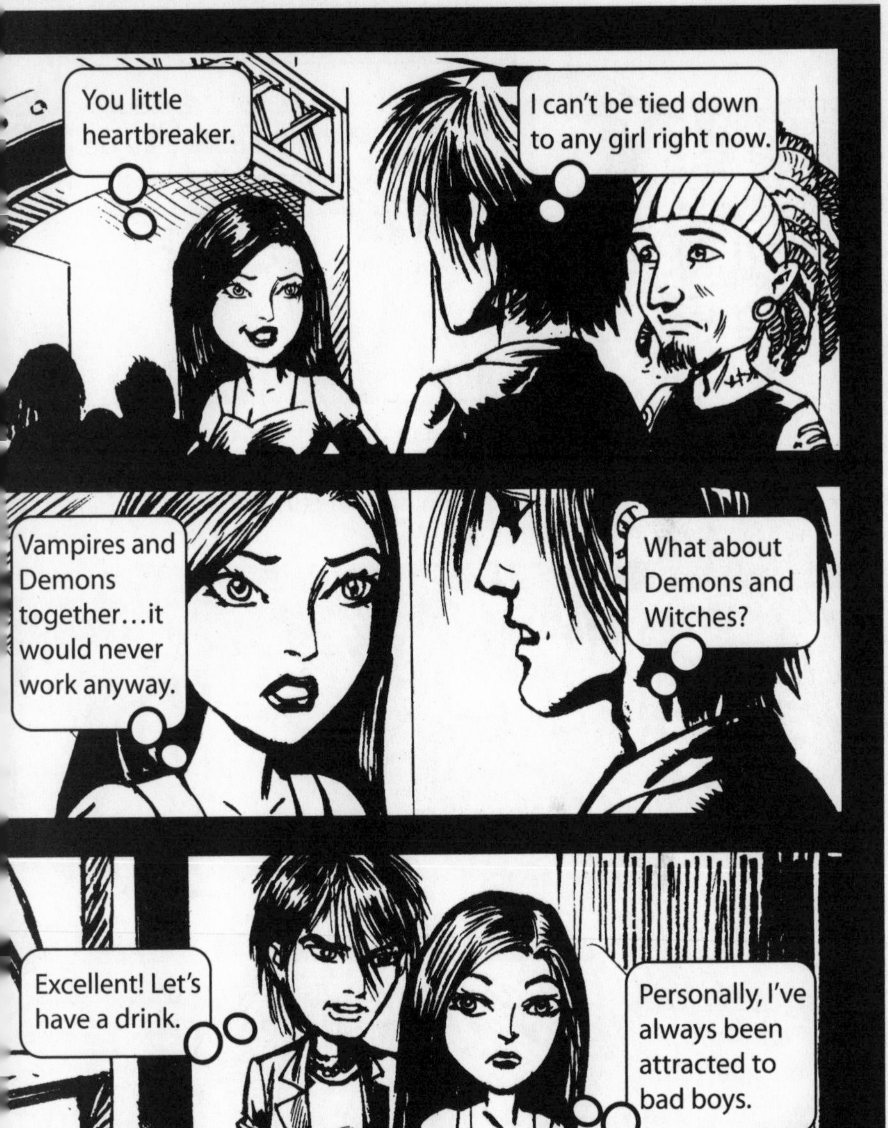
You little heartbreaker.
I can't be tied down to any girl right now.
Vampires and Demons together…it would never work anyway.
What about Demons and Witches?
Excellent! Let's have a drink.
Personally, I've always been attracted to bad boys.

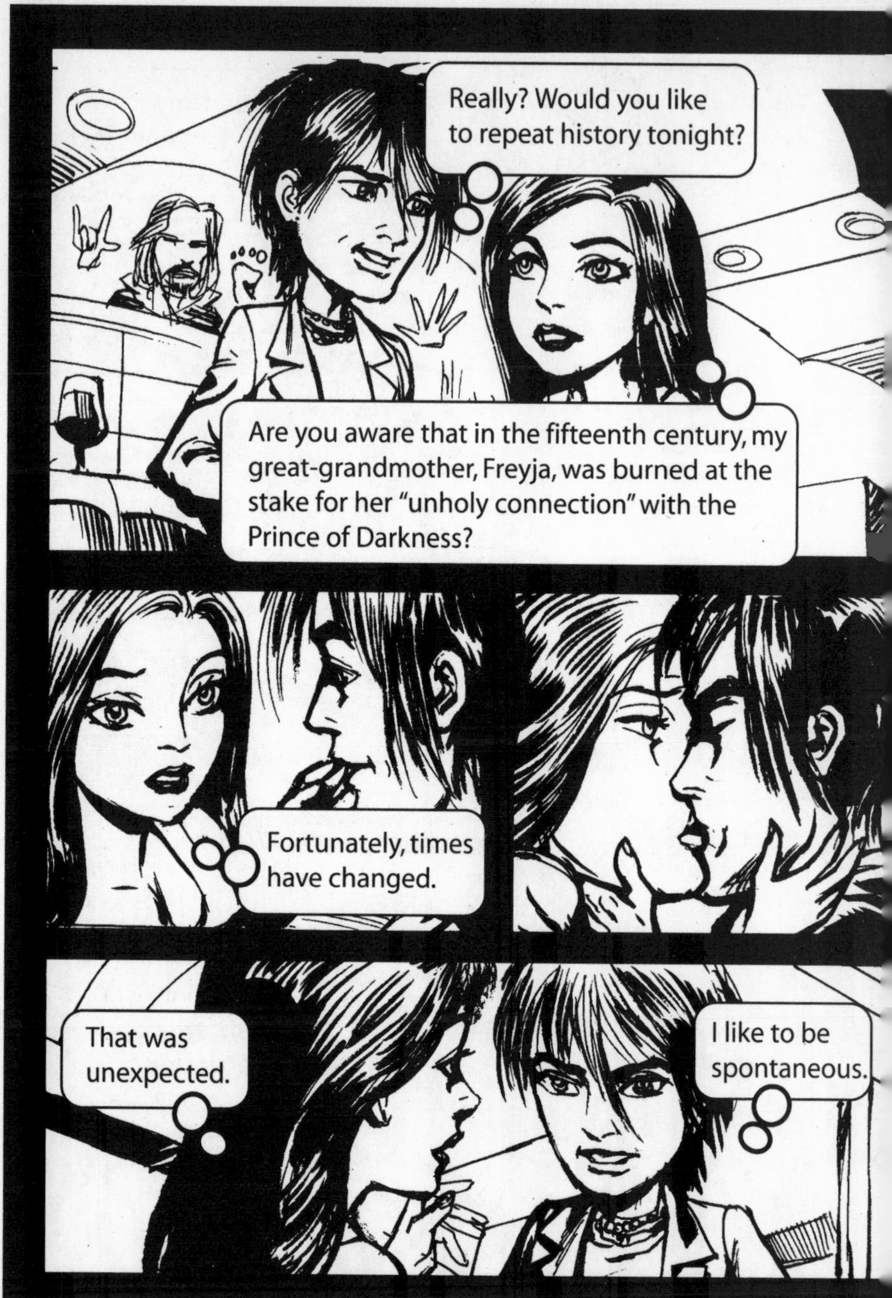
Really? Would you like to repeat history tonight?
Are you aware that in the fifteenth century, my great-grandmother, Freyja, was burned at the stake for her "unholy connection" with the Prince of Darkness?
Fortunately, times have changed.
That was unexpected.
I like to be spontaneous.

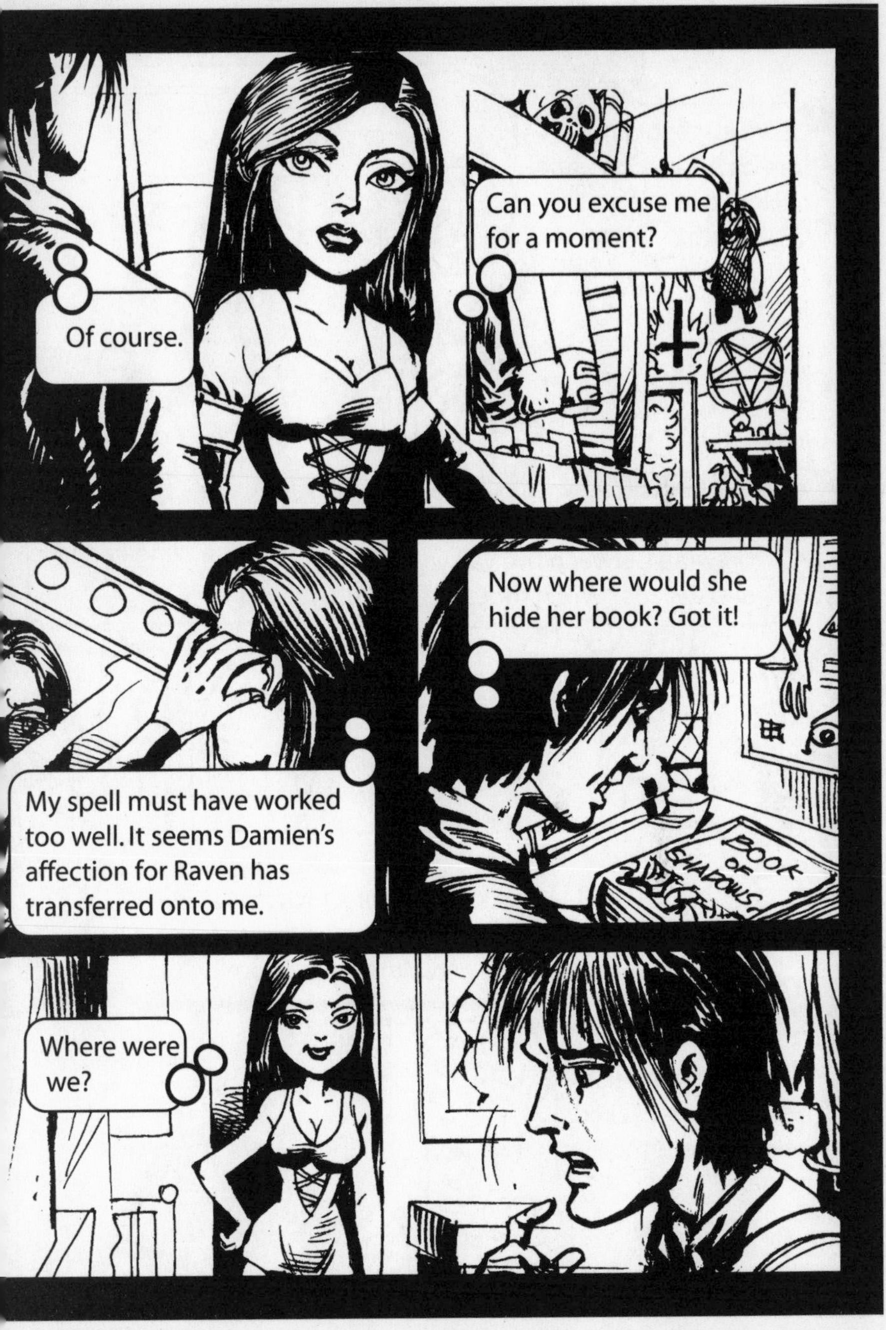
Of course.
Can you excuse me for a moment?
My spell must have worked too well. It seems Damien's affection for Raven has transferred onto me.
Now where would she hide her book? Got it!
BOOK OF SHADOWS
Where were we?

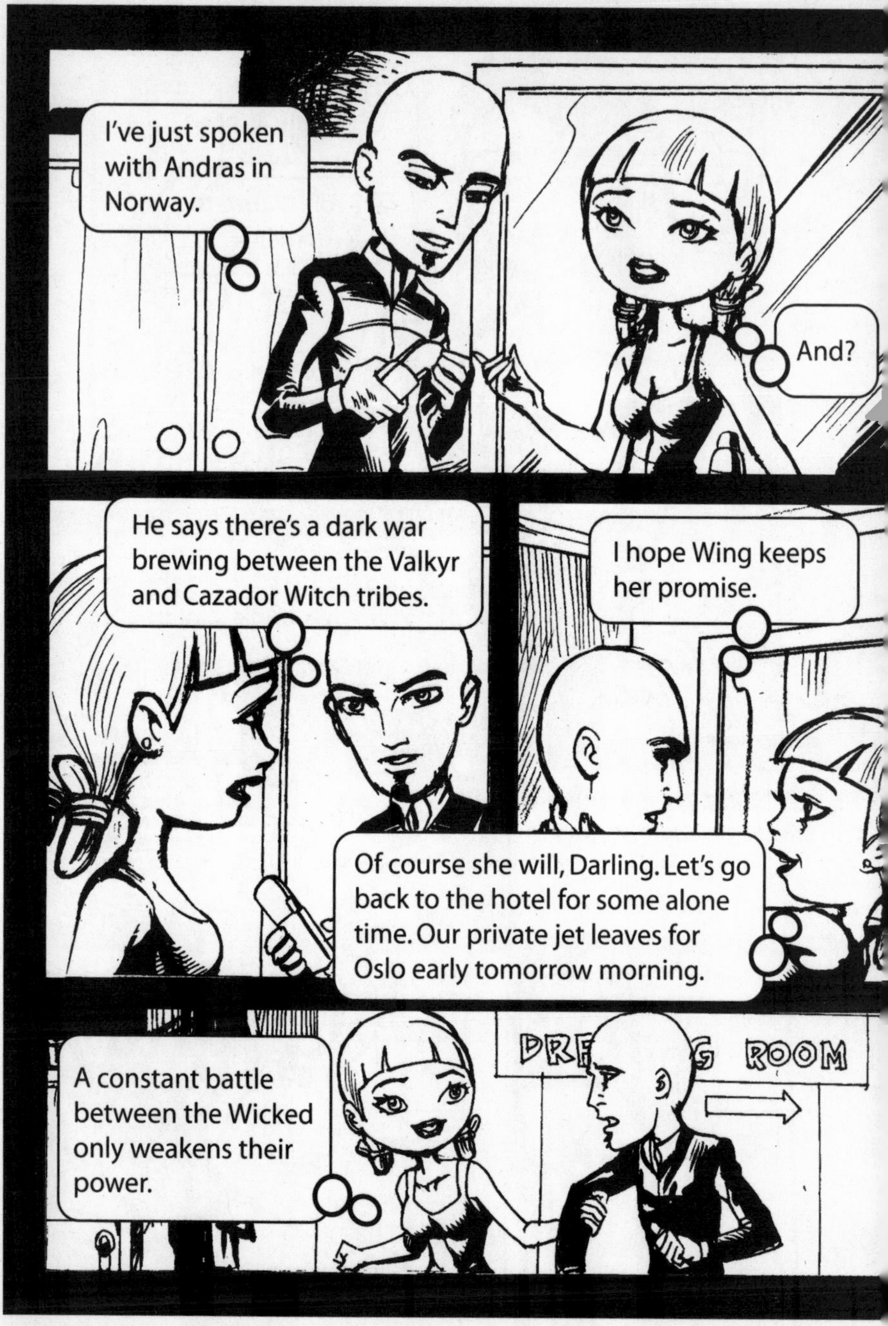
I've just spoken with Andras in Norway.
And?
He says there's a dark war brewing between the Valkyr and Cazador Witch tribes.
I hope Wing keeps her promise.
Of course she will, Darling. Let's go back to the hotel for some alone time. Our private jet leaves for Oslo early tomorrow morning.
A constant battle between the Wicked only weakens their power.

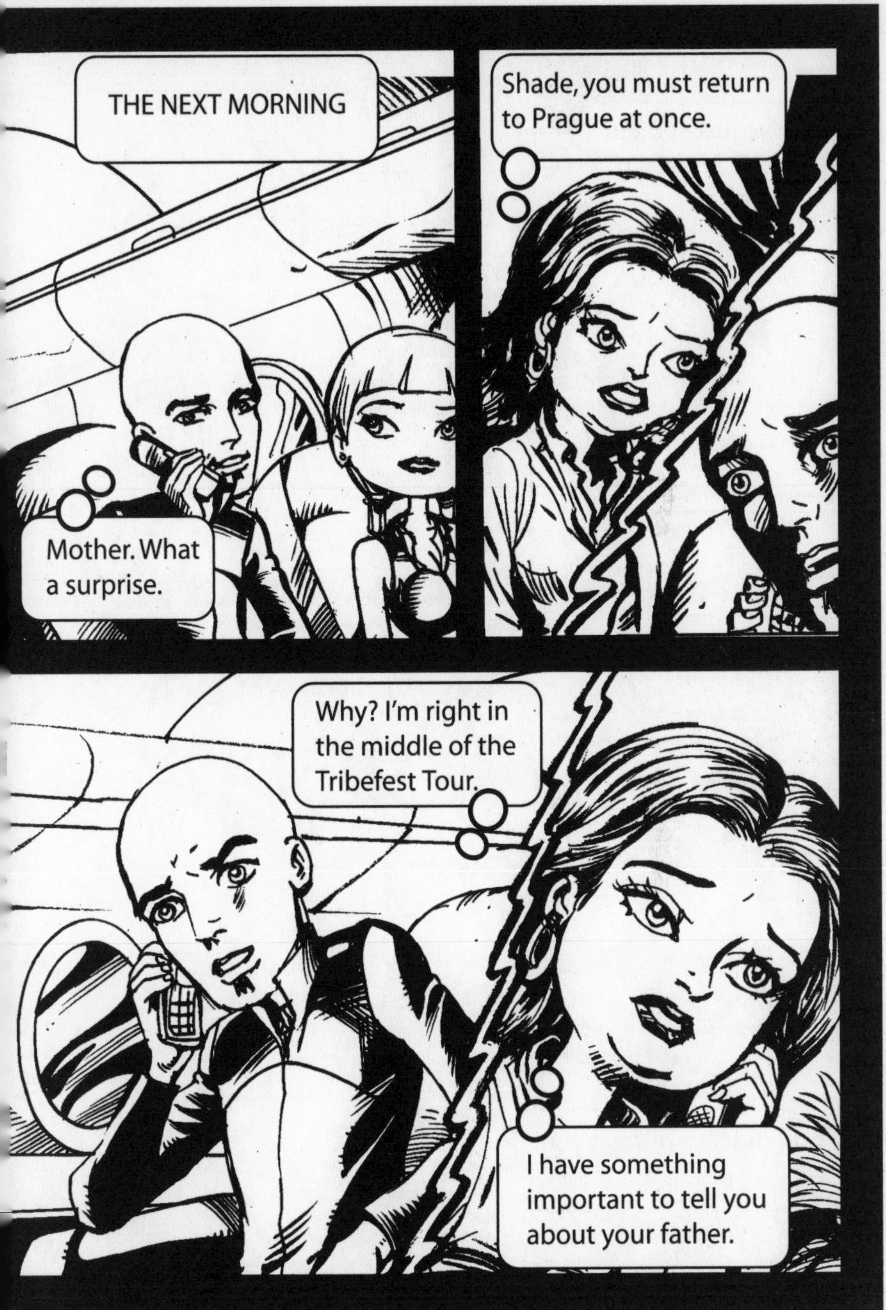
THE NEXT MORNING
Mother. What a surprise.
Shade, you must return to Prague at once.
Why? I'm right in the middle of the Tribefest Tour.
I have something important to tell you about your father.

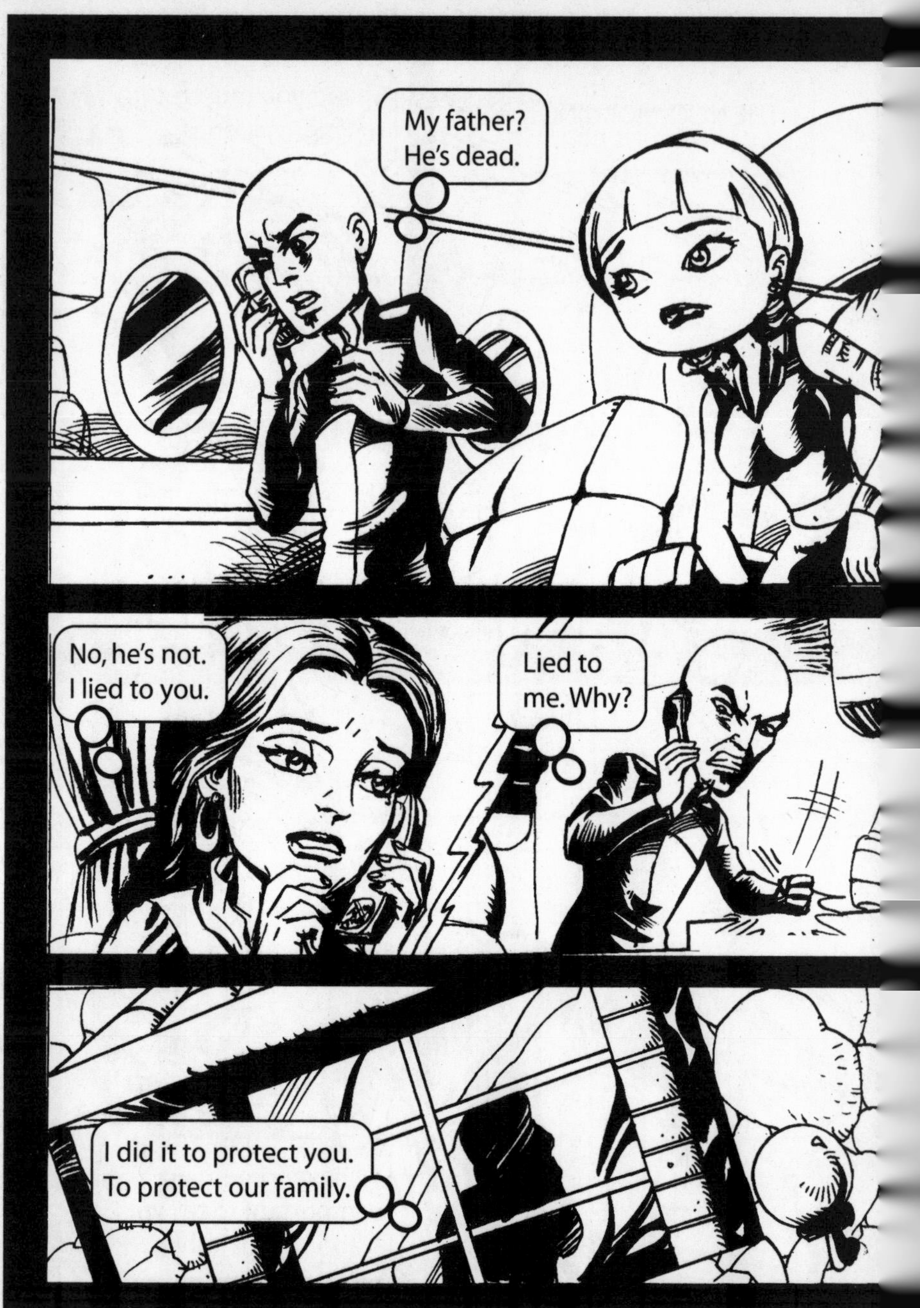
My father? He's dead.
No, he's not. I lied to you.
Lied to me. Why?
I did it to protect you. To protect our family.

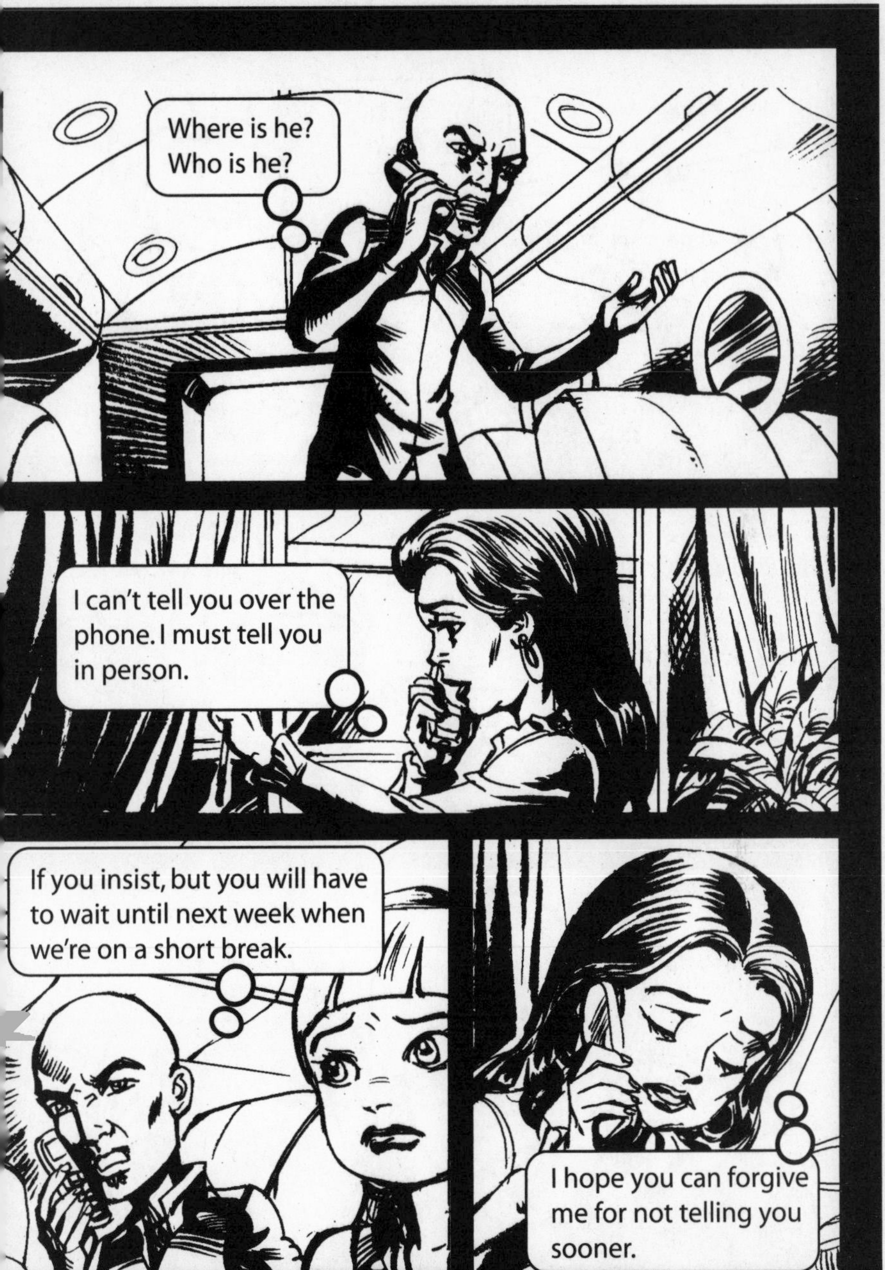
Where is he? Who is he?
I can't tell you over the phone. I must tell you in person.
If you insist, but you will have to wait until next week when we're on a short break.
I hope you can forgive me for not telling you sooner.

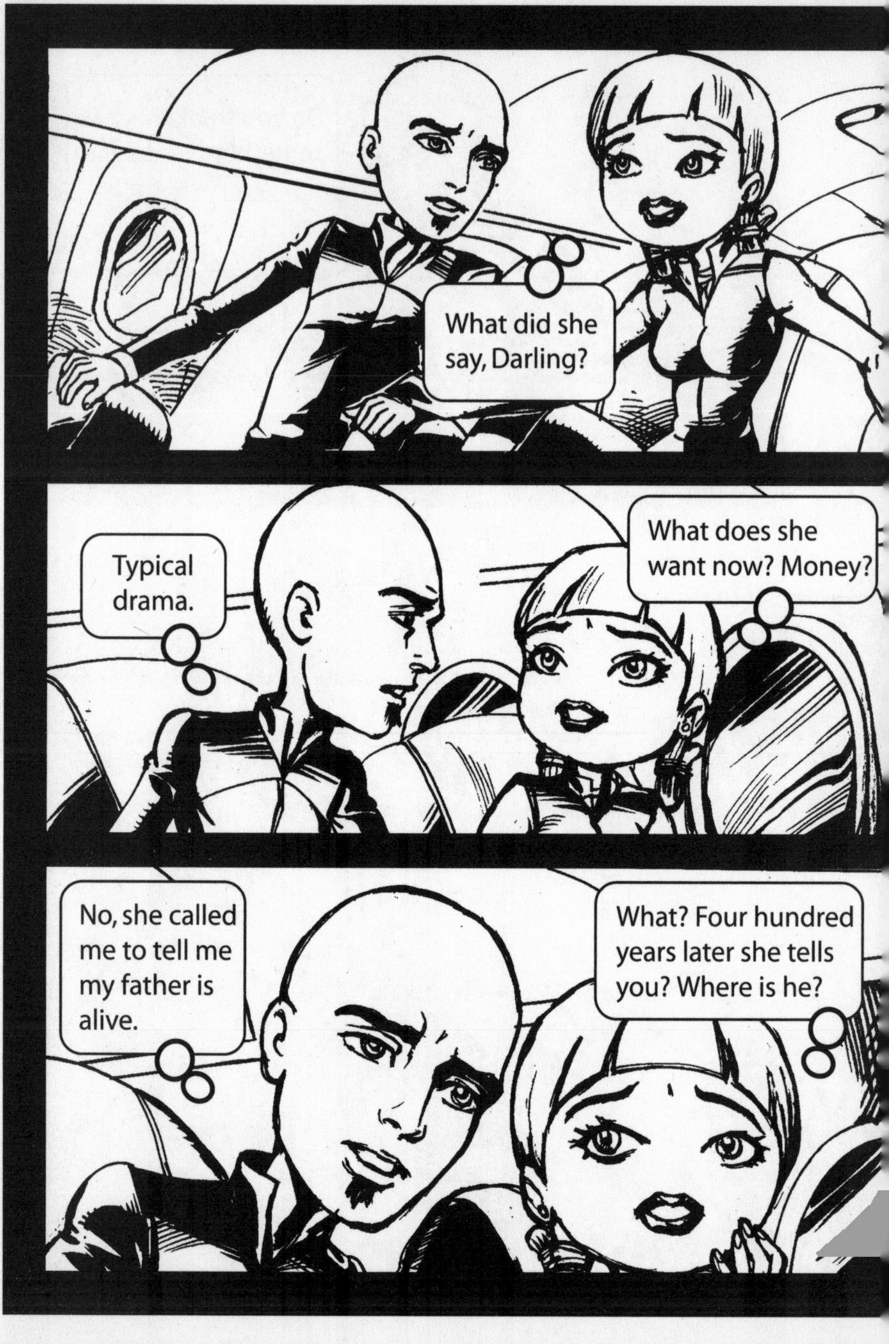
What did she say, Darling?
Typical drama.
What does she want now? Money?
No, she called me to tell me my father is alive.
What? Four hundred years later she tells you? Where is he?

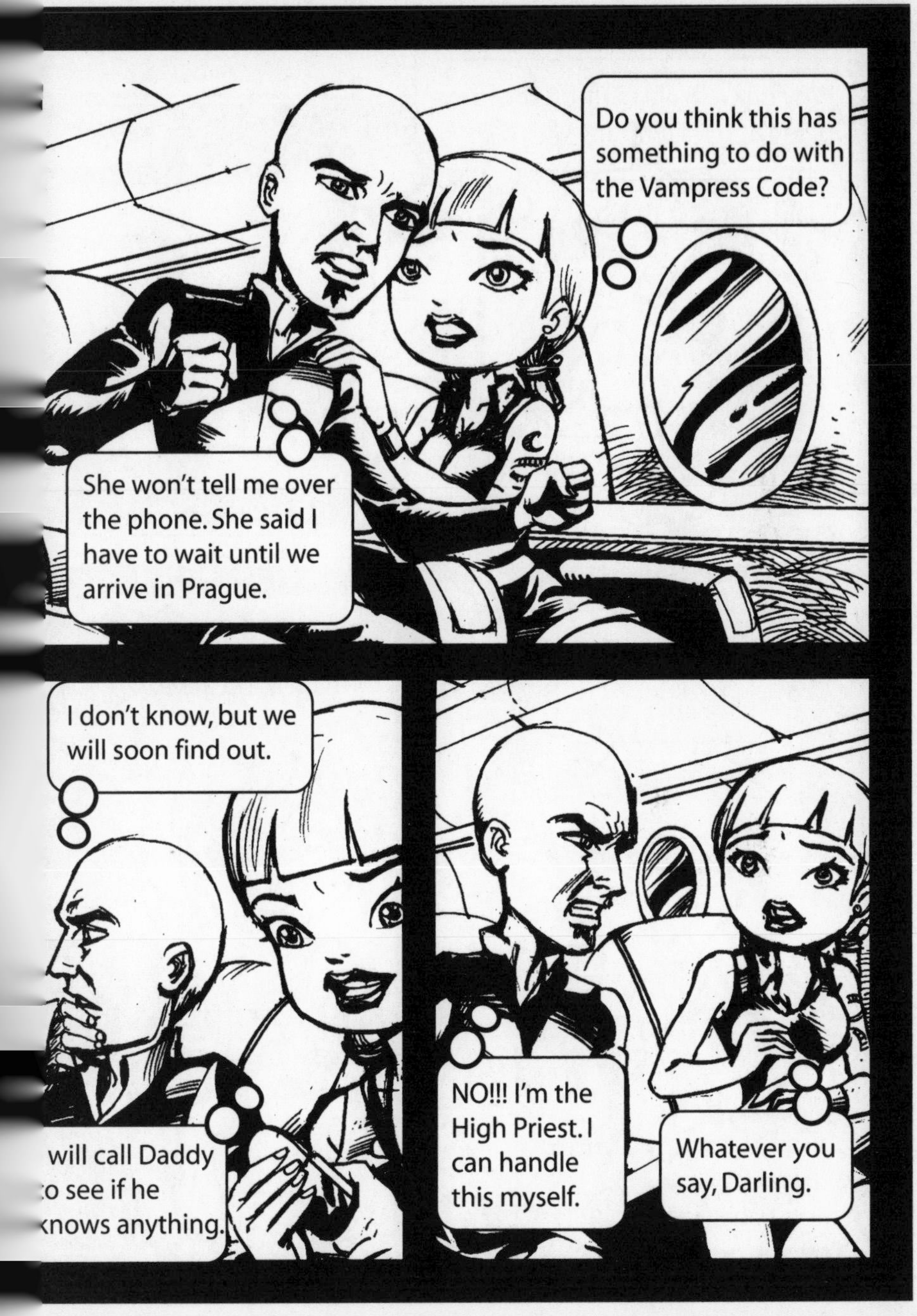
Do you think this has something to do with the Vampress Code?
She won't tell me over the phone. She said I have to wait until we arrive in Prague.
I don't know, but we will soon find out.
will call Daddy o see if he nows anything.
NO!!! I'm the High Priest. I can handle this myself.
Whatever you say, Darling.

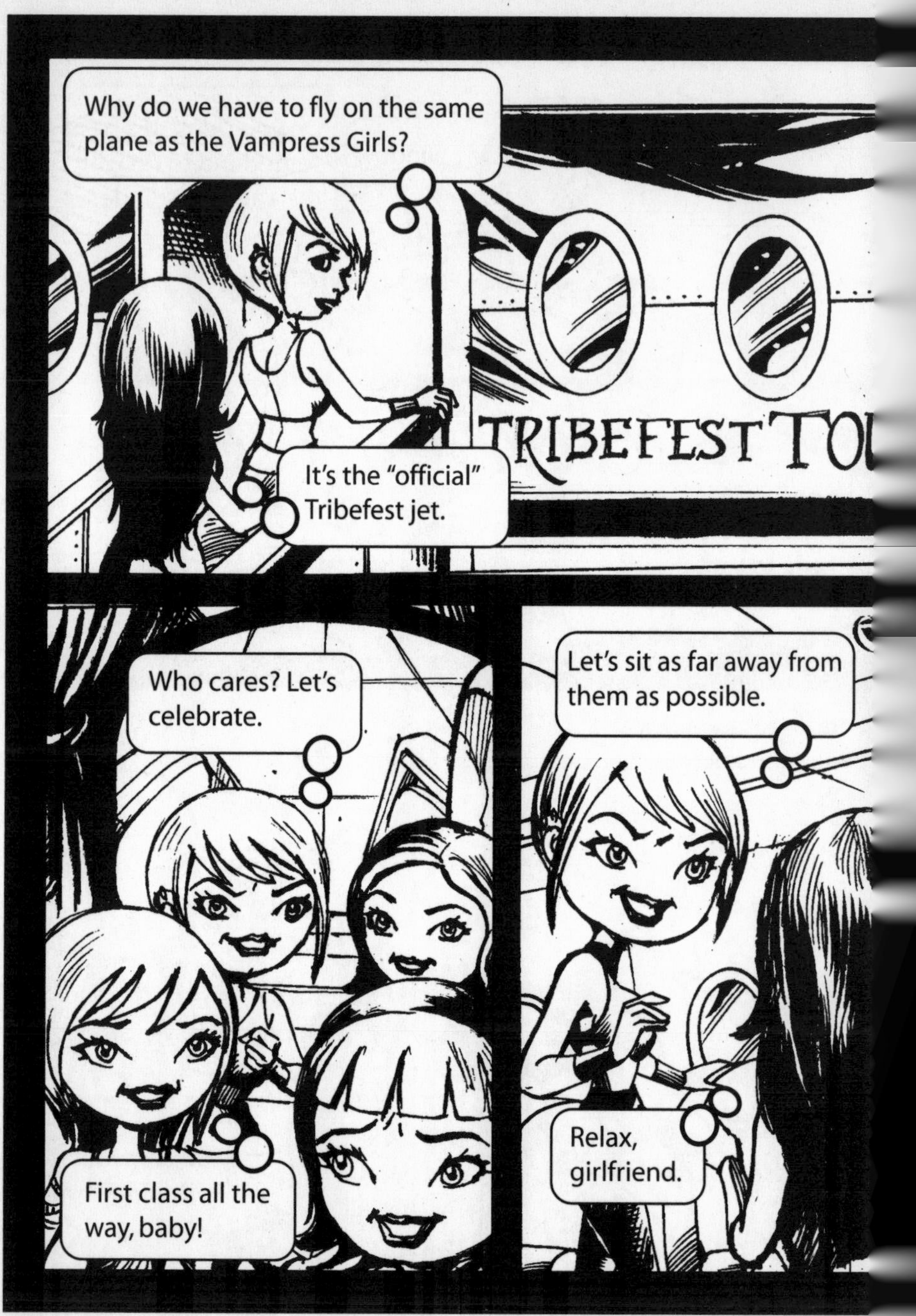
Why do we have to fly on the same plane as the Vampress Girls?
TRIBEFEST TOU
It's the "official" Tribefest jet.
Who cares? Let's celebrate.
First class all the way, baby!
Let's sit as far away from them as possible.
Relax, girlfriend.

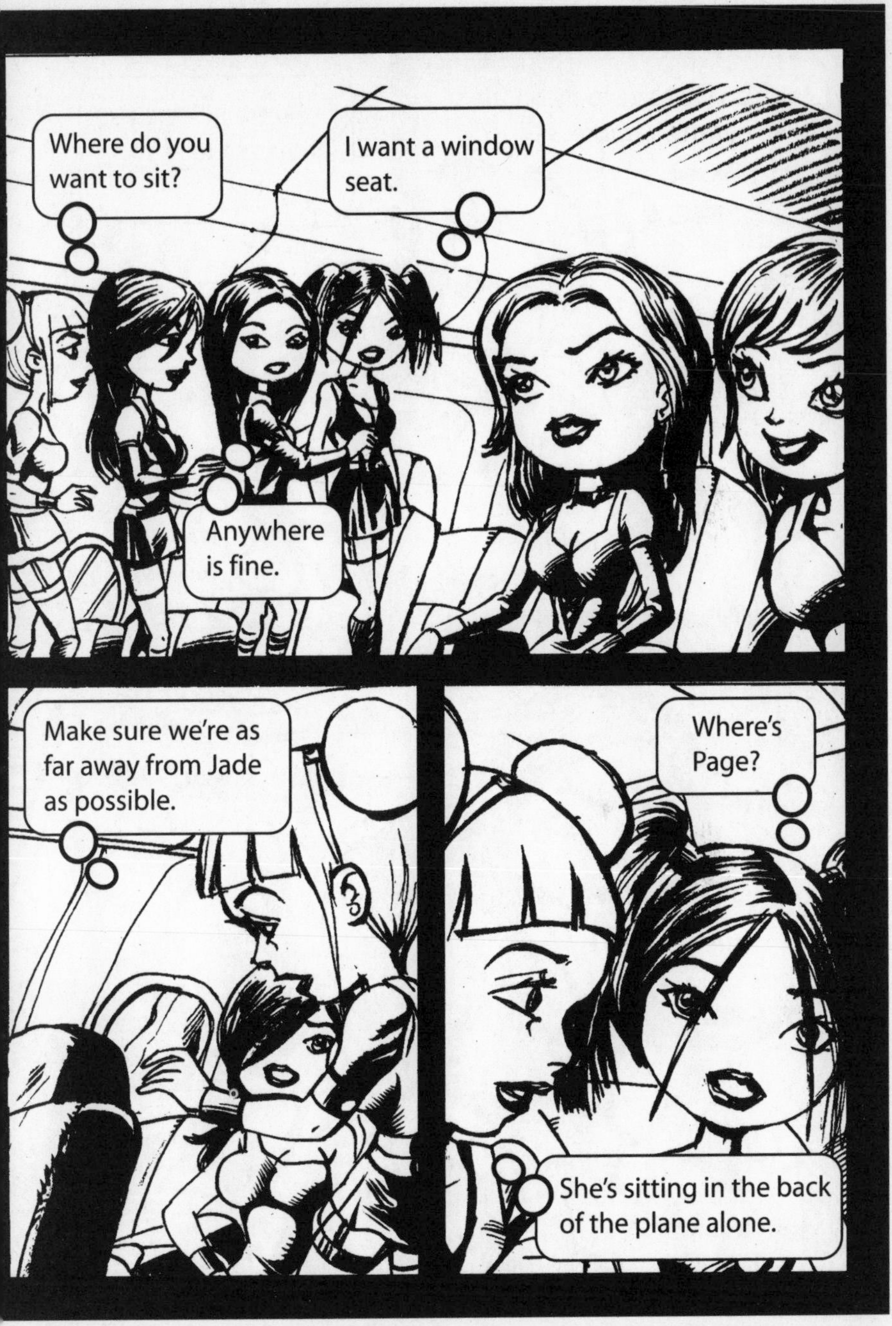
Where do you want to sit?
I want a window seat.
Anywhere is fine.
Make sure we're as far away from Jade as possible.
Where's Page?
She's sitting in the back of the plane alone.

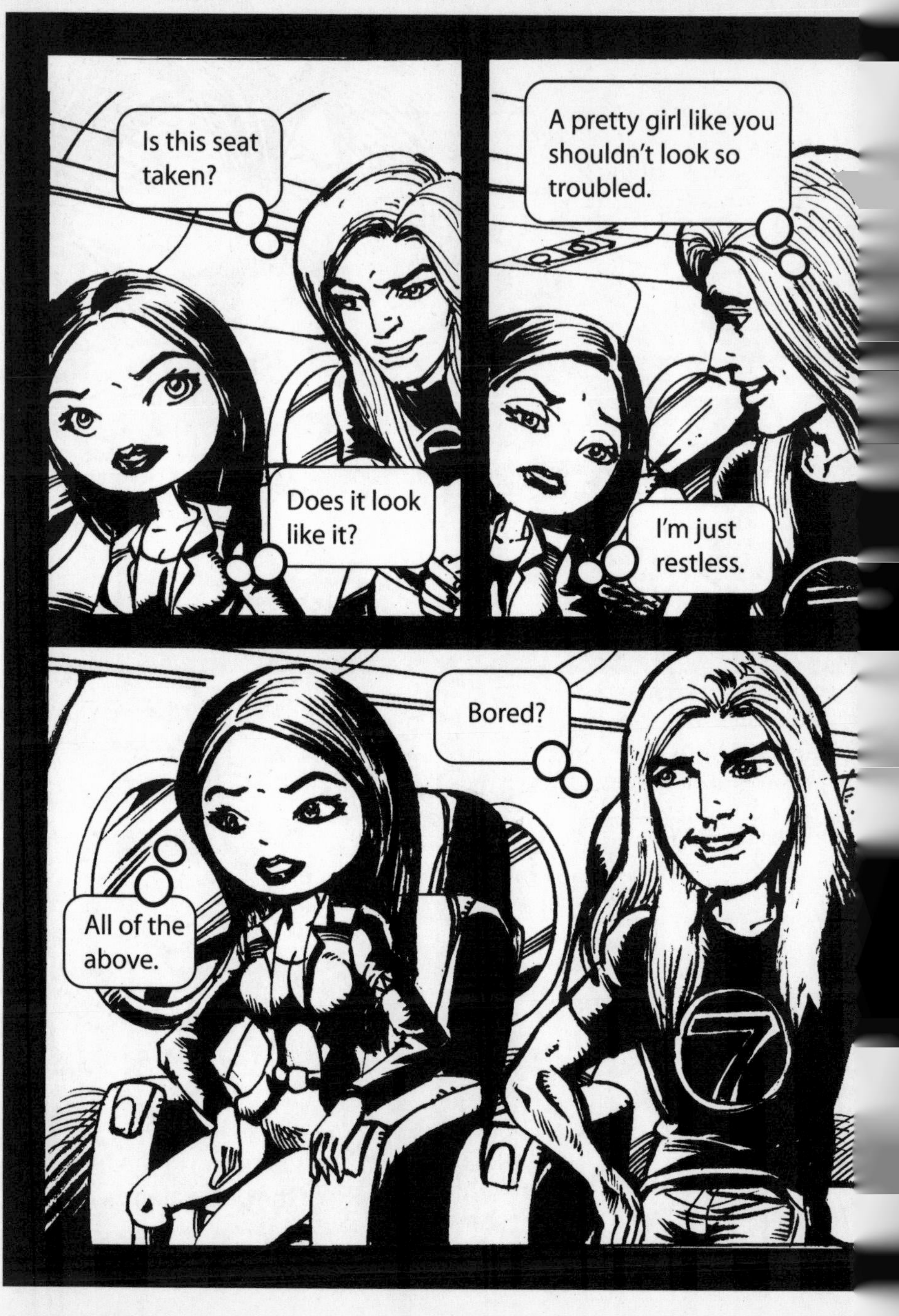
Is this seat taken?
Does it look like it?
A pretty girl like you shouldn't look so troubled.
I'm just restless.
Bored?
All of the above.

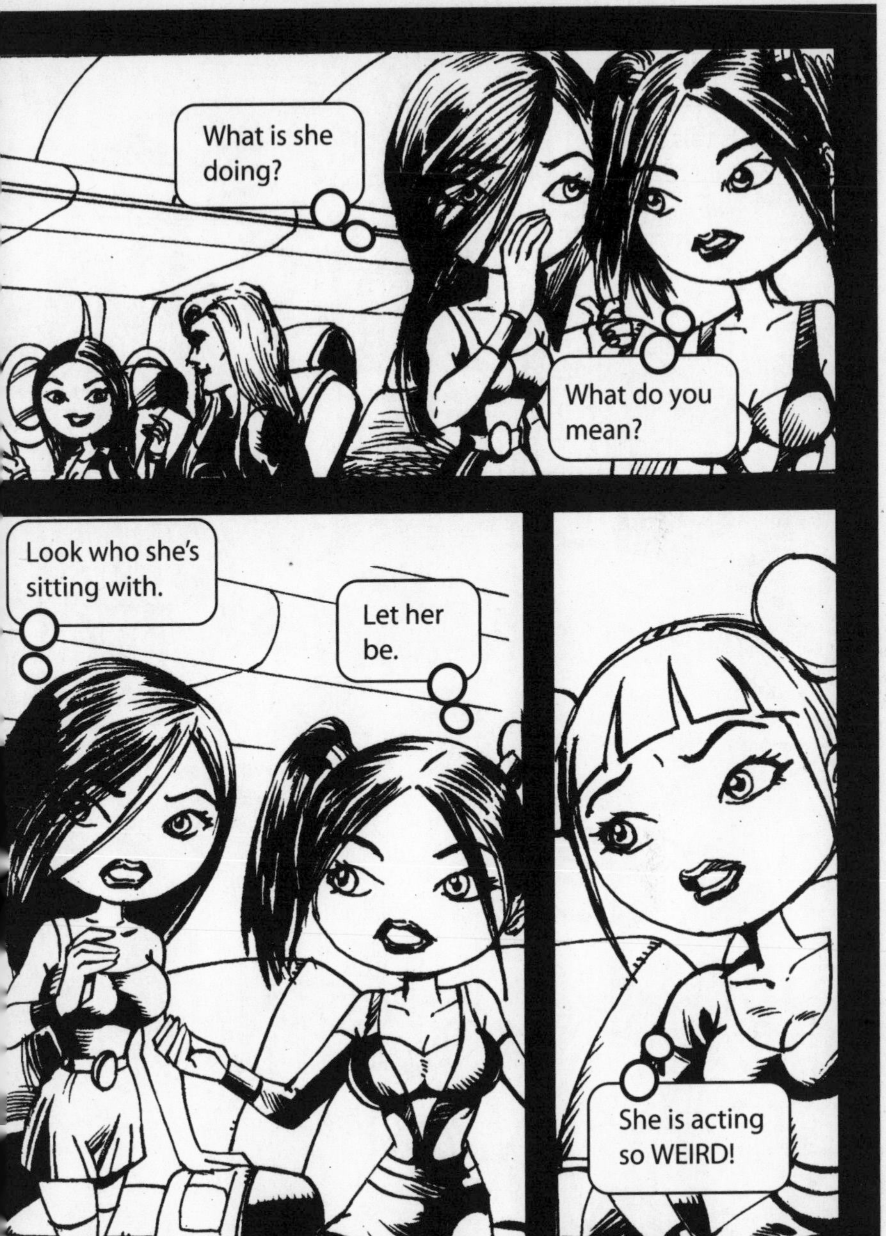
What is she doing?
What do you mean?
Look who she's sitting with.
Let her be.
She is acting so WEIRD!

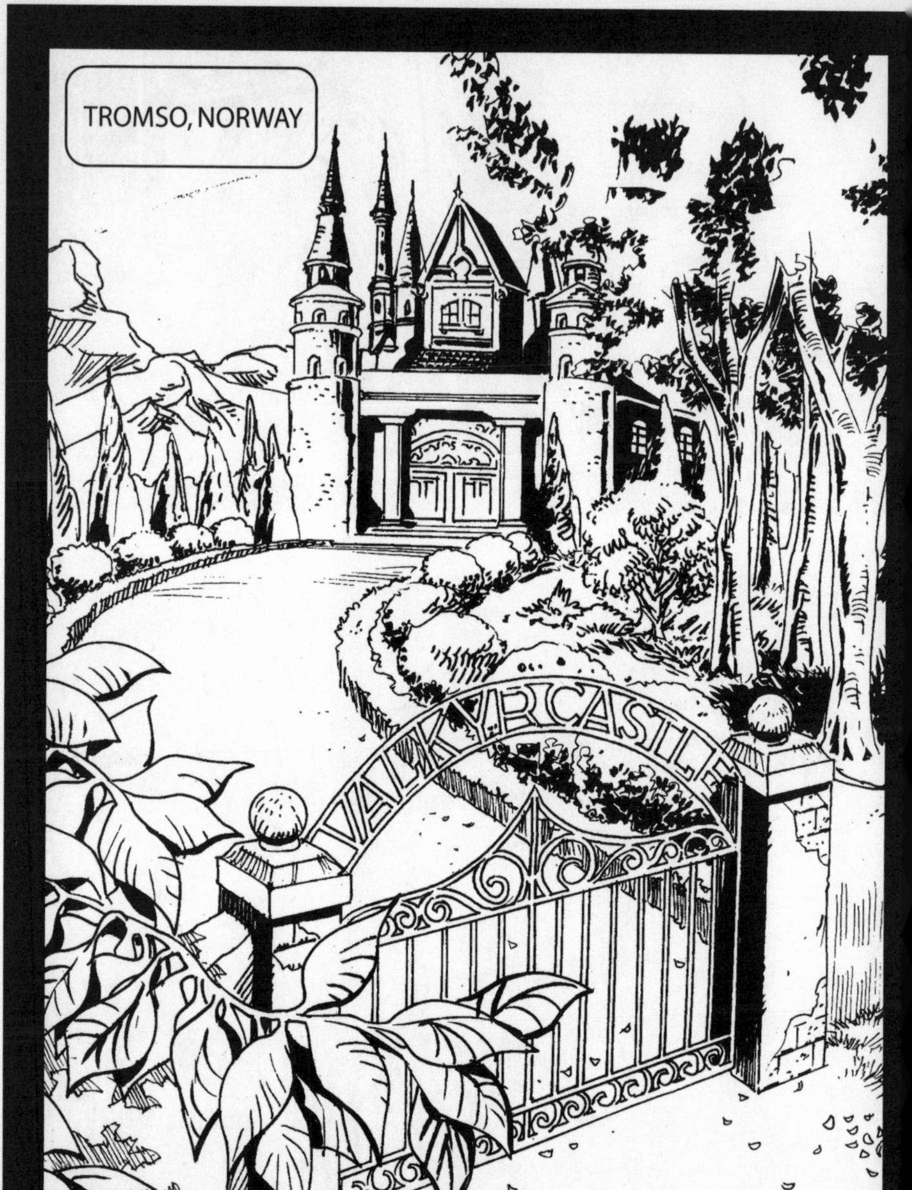
TROMSO, NORWAY
VALKYR CASTLE

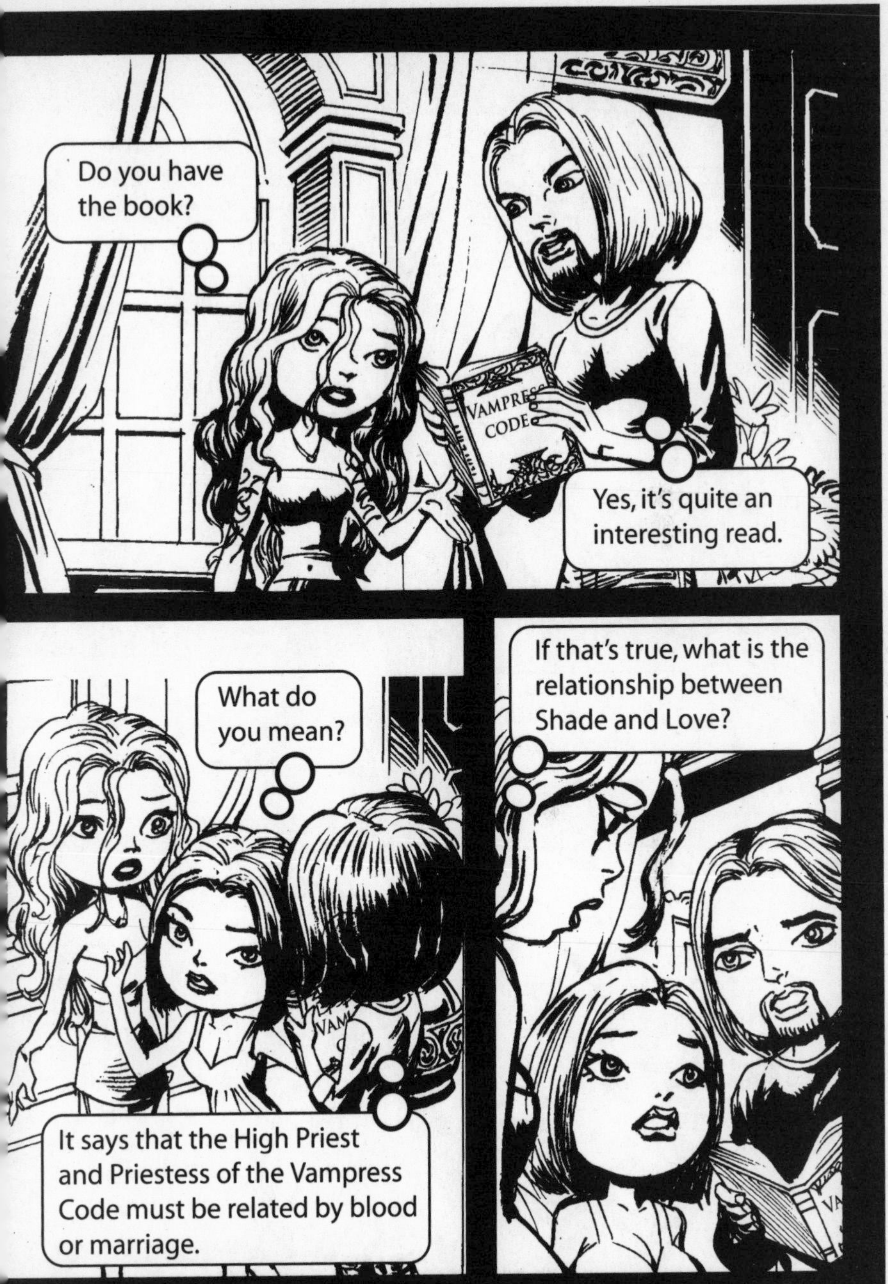
Do you have the book?
VAMPRESS CODE
Yes, it's quite an interesting read.
What do you mean?
It says that the High Priest and Priestess of the Vampress Code must be related by blood or marriage.
If that's true, what is the relationship between Shade and Love?

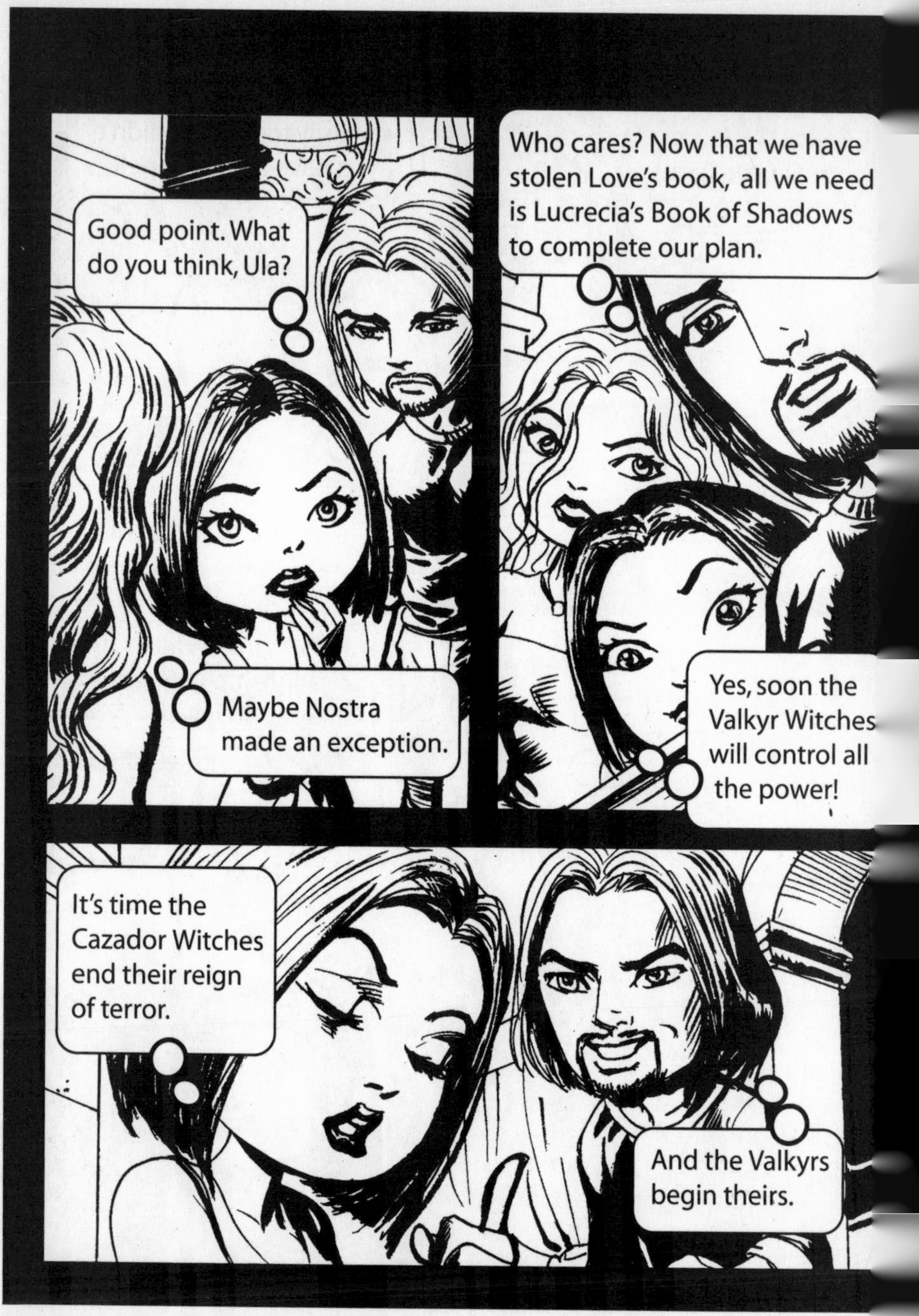
Good point. What do you think, Ula?
Maybe Nostra made an exception.
Who cares? Now that we have stolen Love's book, all we need is Lucrecia's Book of Shadows to complete our plan.
Yes, soon the Valkyr Witches will control all the power!
It's time the Cazador Witches end their reign of terror.
And the Valkyrs begin theirs.

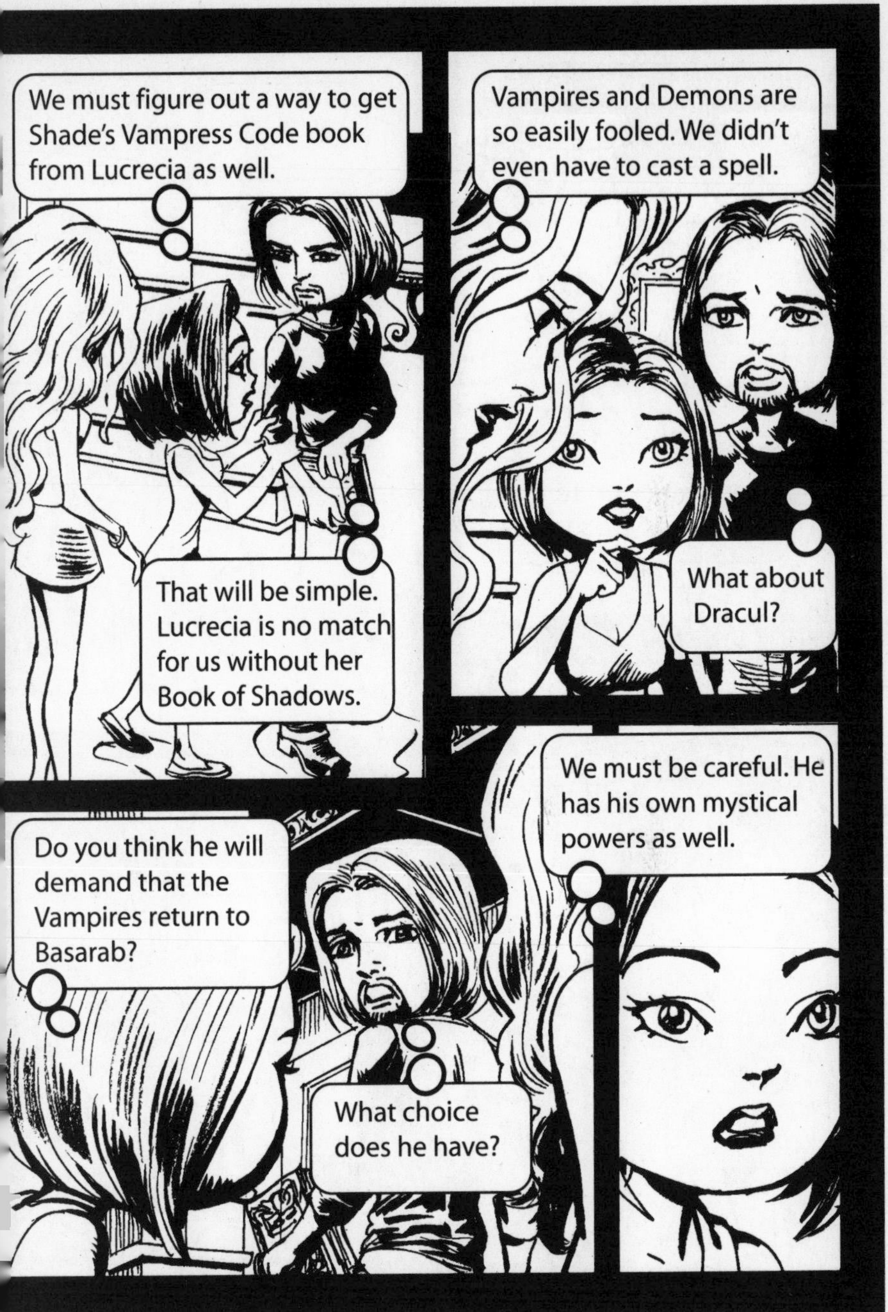
We must figure out a way to get Shade's Vampress Code book from Lucrecia as well.
That will be simple. Lucrecia is no match for us without her Book of Shadows.
Vampires and Demons are so easily fooled. We didn't even have to cast a spell.
What about Dracul?
Do you think he will demand that the Vampires return to Basarab?
What choice does he have?
We must be careful. He has his own mystical powers as well.

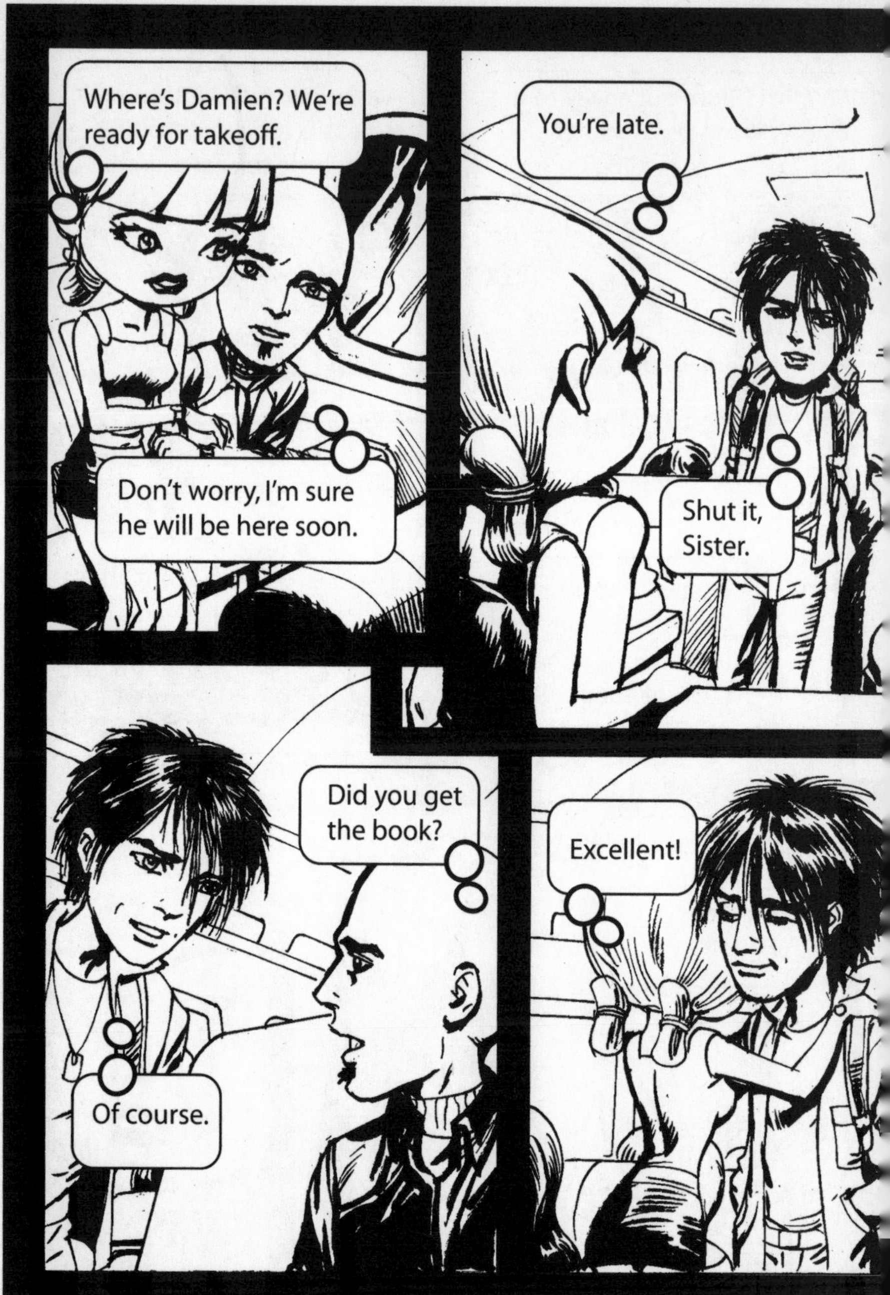

Where's Damien? We're ready for takeoff.
Don't worry, I'm sure he will be here soon.
You're late.
Shut it, Sister.
Did you get the book?
Of course.
Excellent!

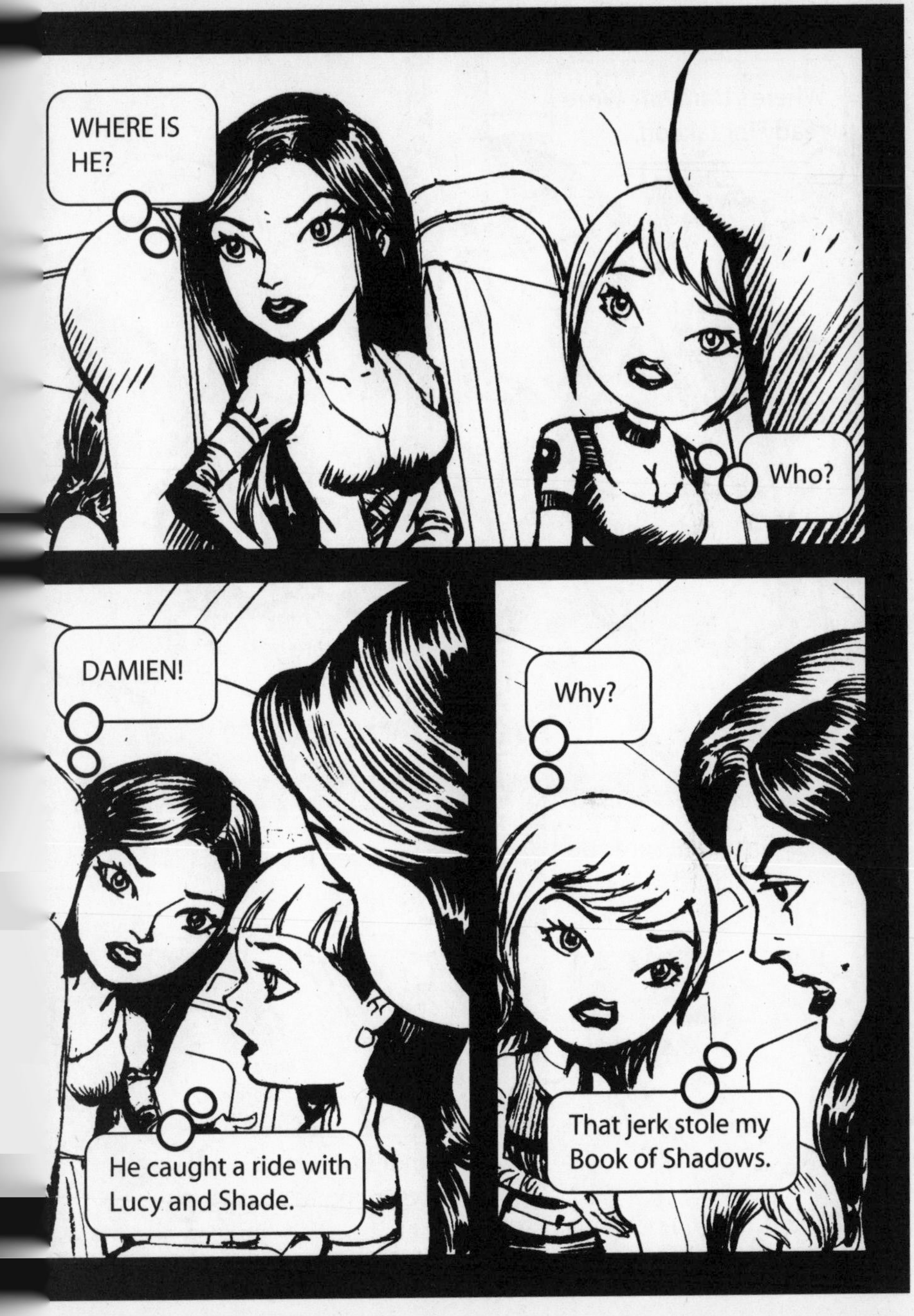
WHERE IS HE?
Who?
DAMIEN!
He caught a ride with Lucy and Shade.
Why?
That jerk stole my Book of Shadows.

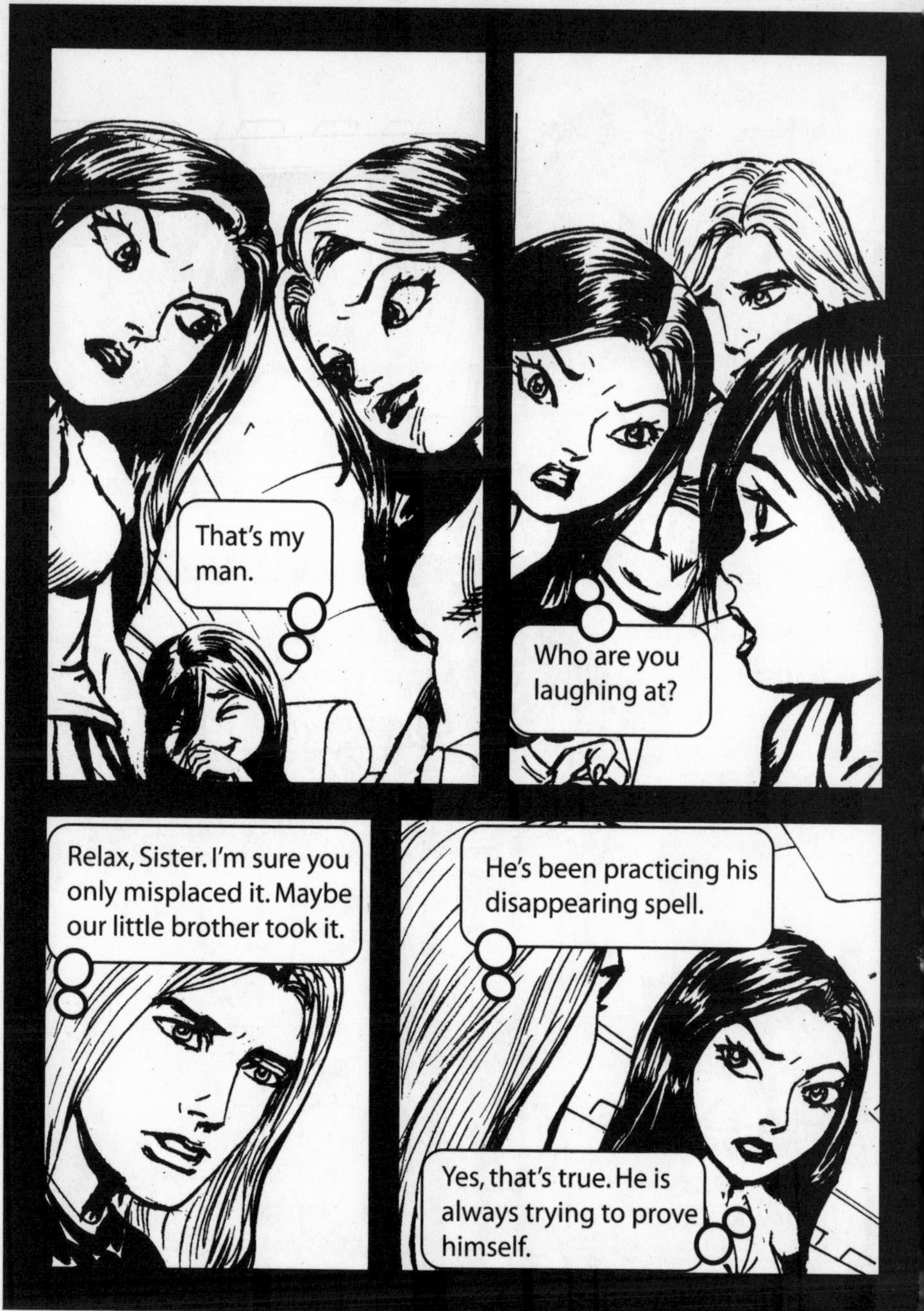
That's my man.
Who are you laughing at?
Relax, Sister. I'm sure you only misplaced it. Maybe our little brother took it.
He's been practicing his disappearing spell.
Yes, that's true. He is always trying to prove himself.

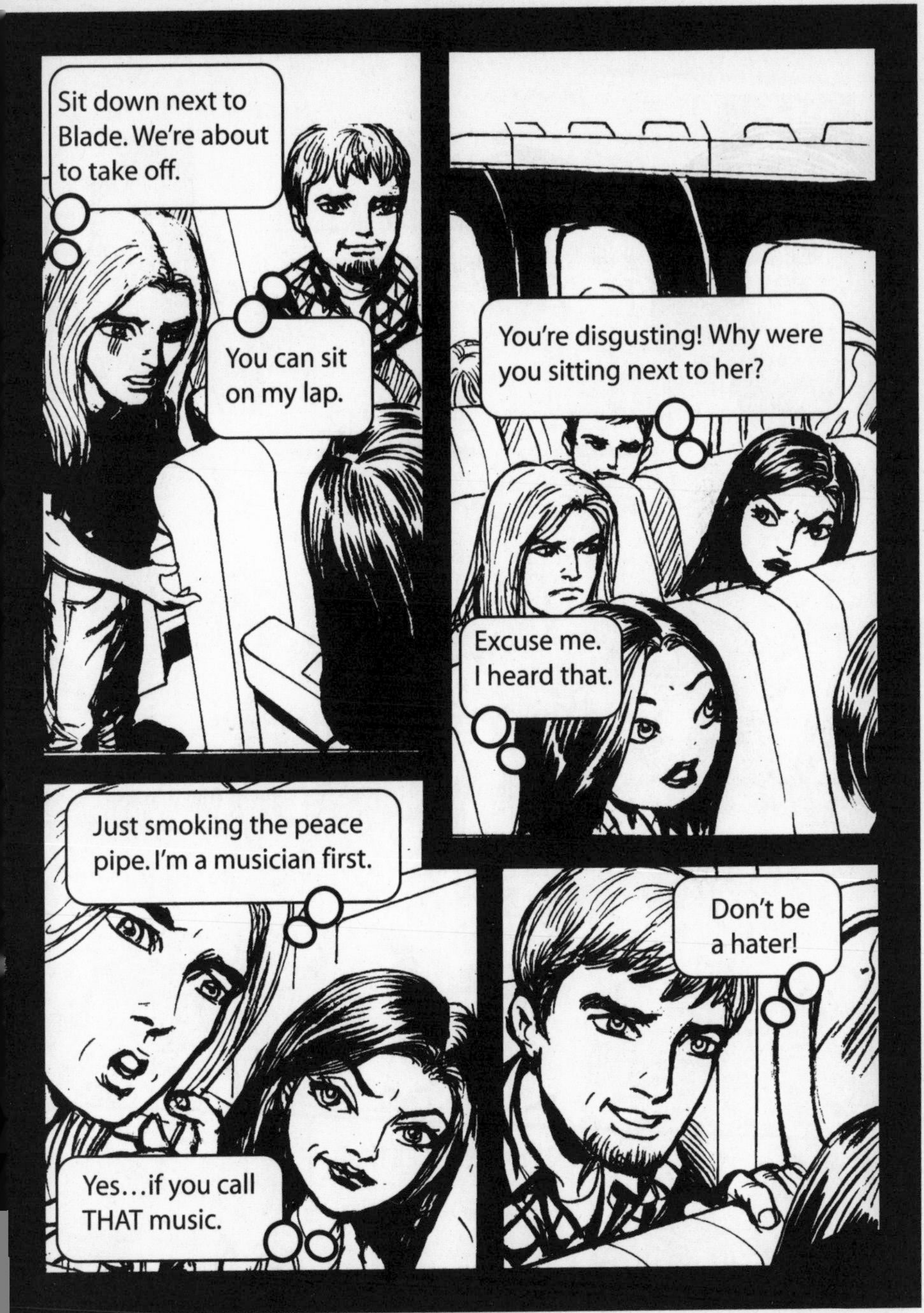
Sit down next to Blade. We're about to take off.
You can sit on my lap.
You're disgusting! Why were you sitting next to her?
Excuse me. I heard that.
Just smoking the peace pipe. I'm a musician first.
Yes…if you call THAT music.
Don't be a hater!

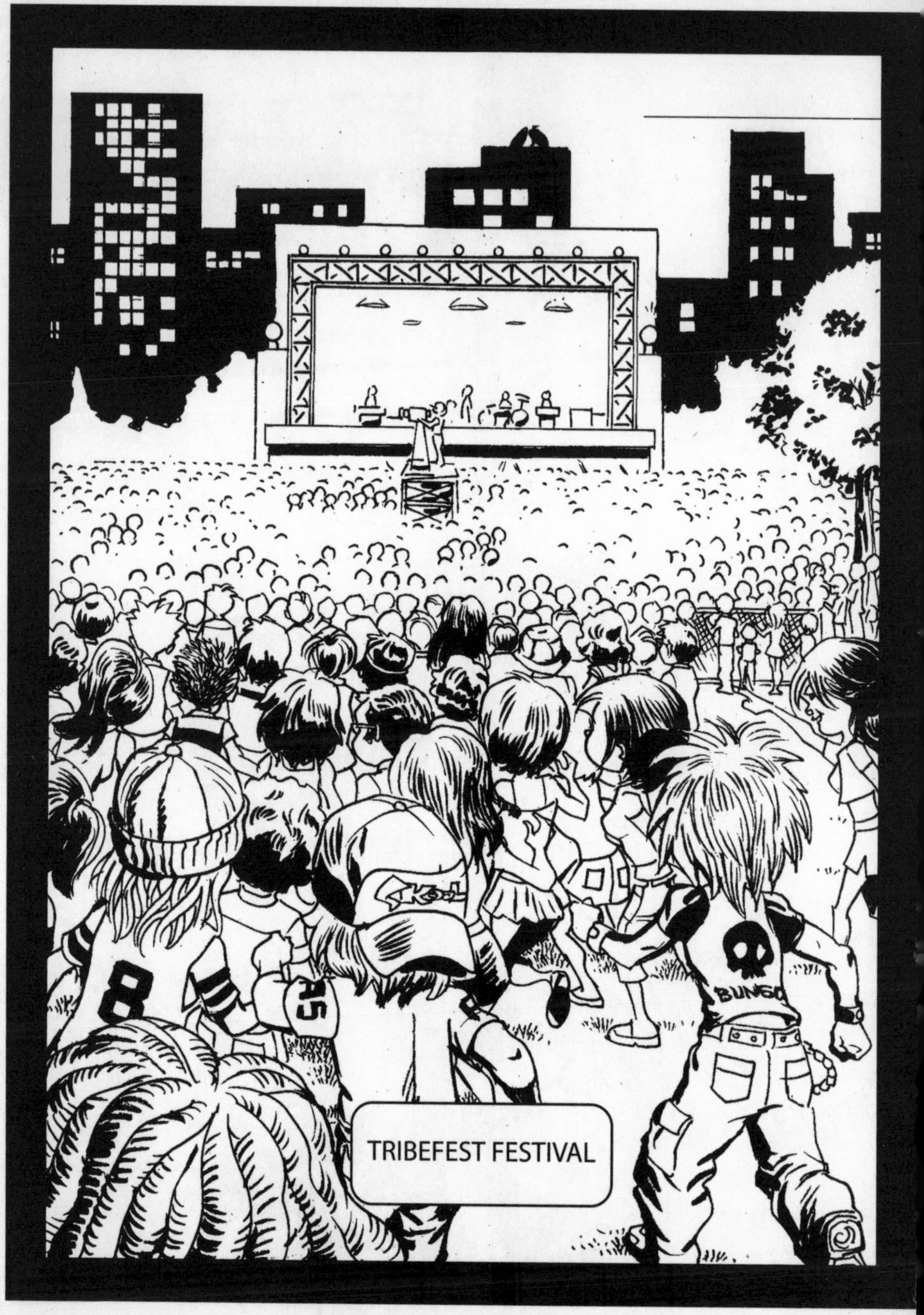
TRIBEFEST FESTIVAL
BUNGO

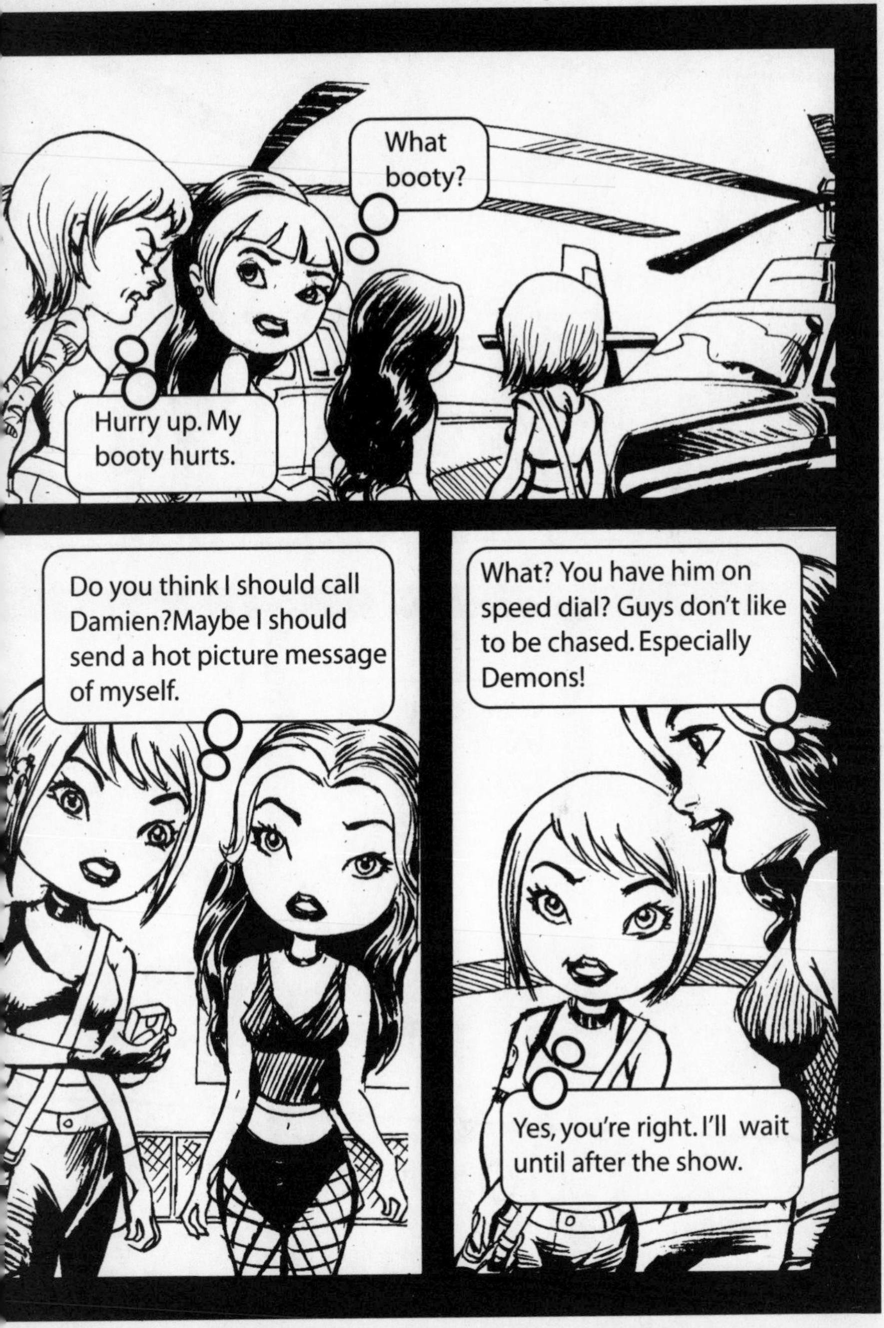
What booty?
Hurry up. My booty hurts.
Do you think I should call Damien?Maybe I should send a hot picture message of myself.
What? You have him on speed dial? Guys don't like to be chased. Especially Demons!
Yes, you're right. I'll wait until after the show.

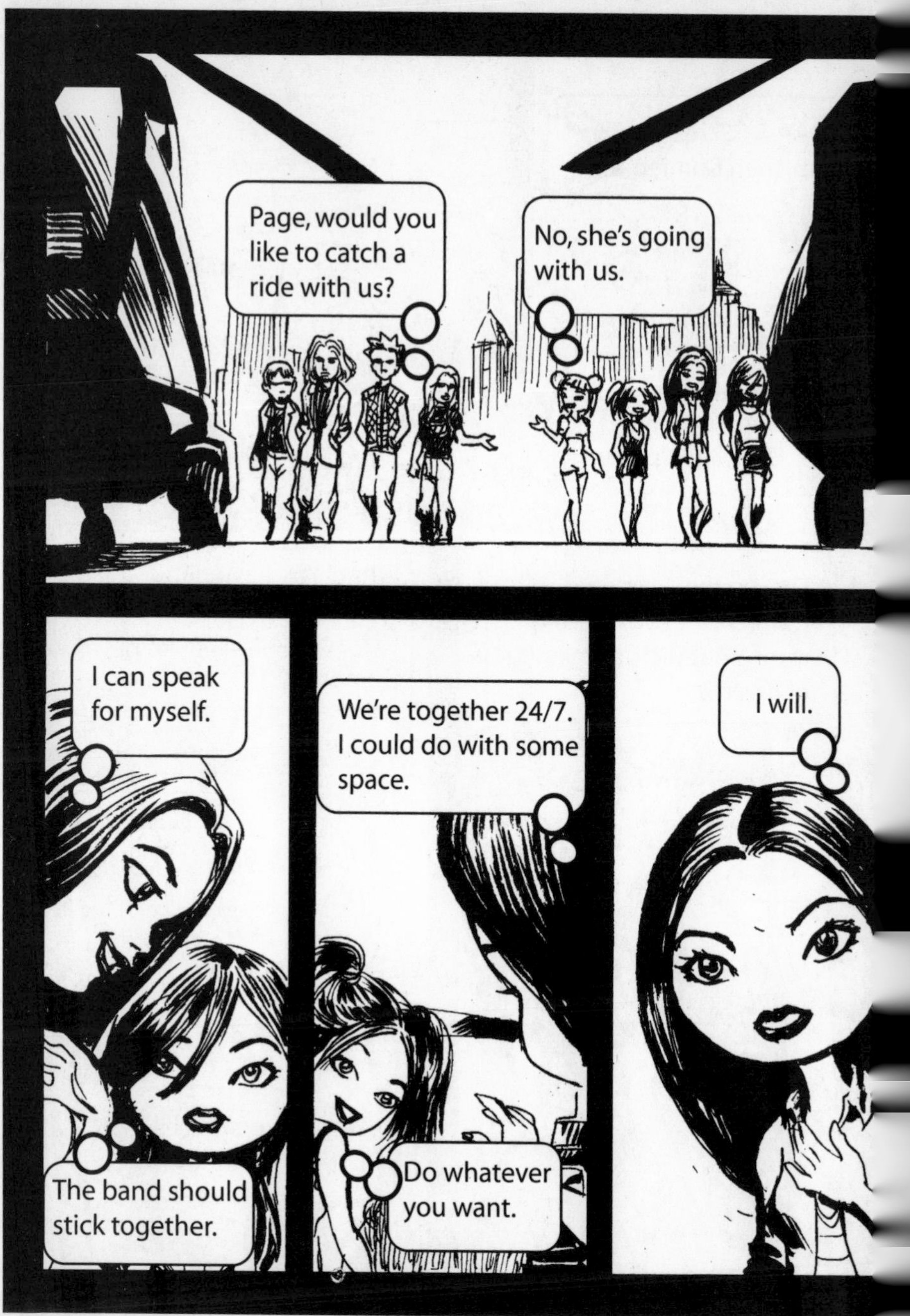
Page, would you like to catch a ride with us?
No, she's going with us.
I can speak for myself.
The band should stick together.
We're together 24/7. I could do with some space.
Do whatever you want.
I will.

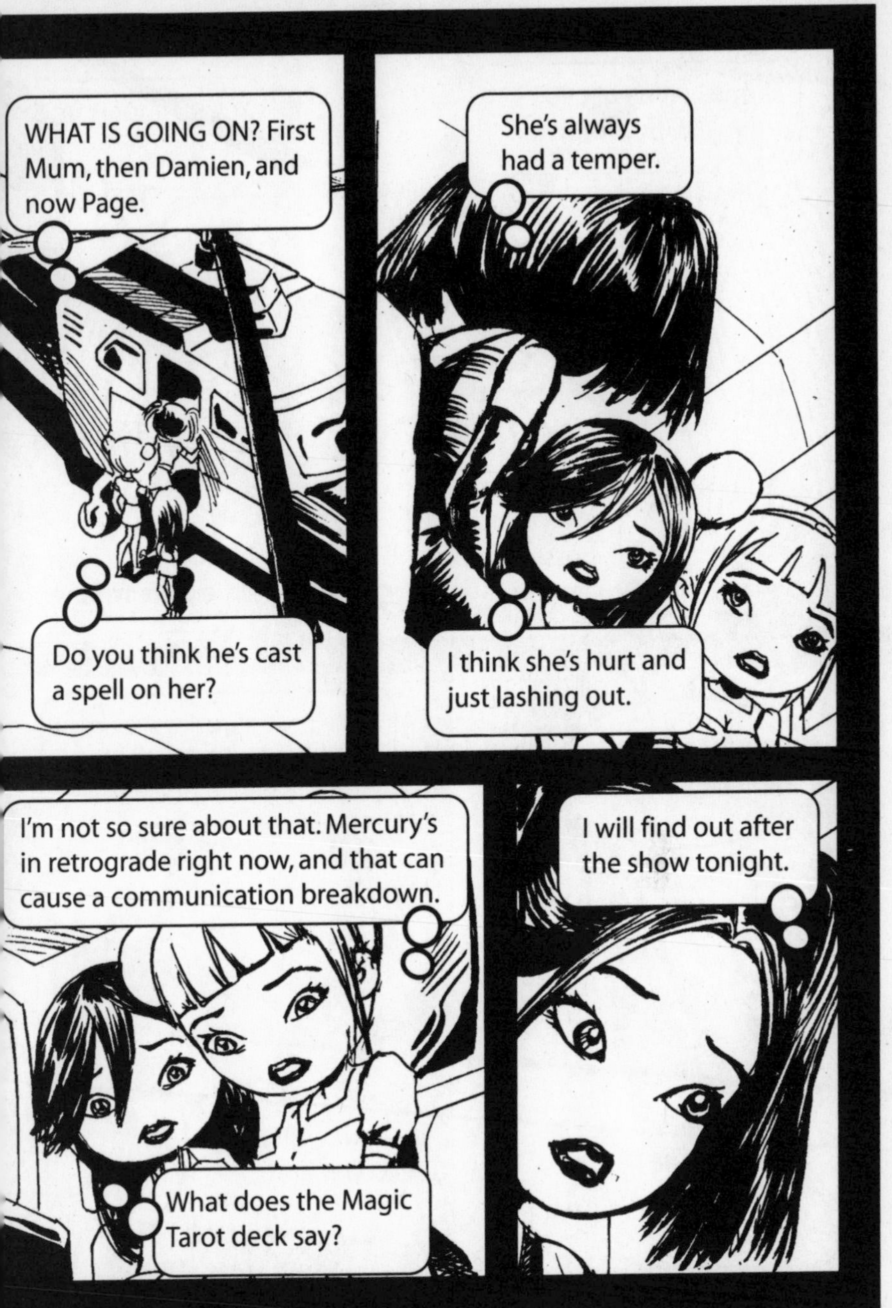
WHAT IS GOING ON? First Mum, then Damien, and now Page.
Do you think he's cast a spell on her?
She's always had a temper.
I think she's hurt and just lashing out.
I'm not so sure about that. Mercury's in retrograde right now, and that can cause a communication breakdown.
What does the Magic Tarot deck say?
I will find out after the show tonight.

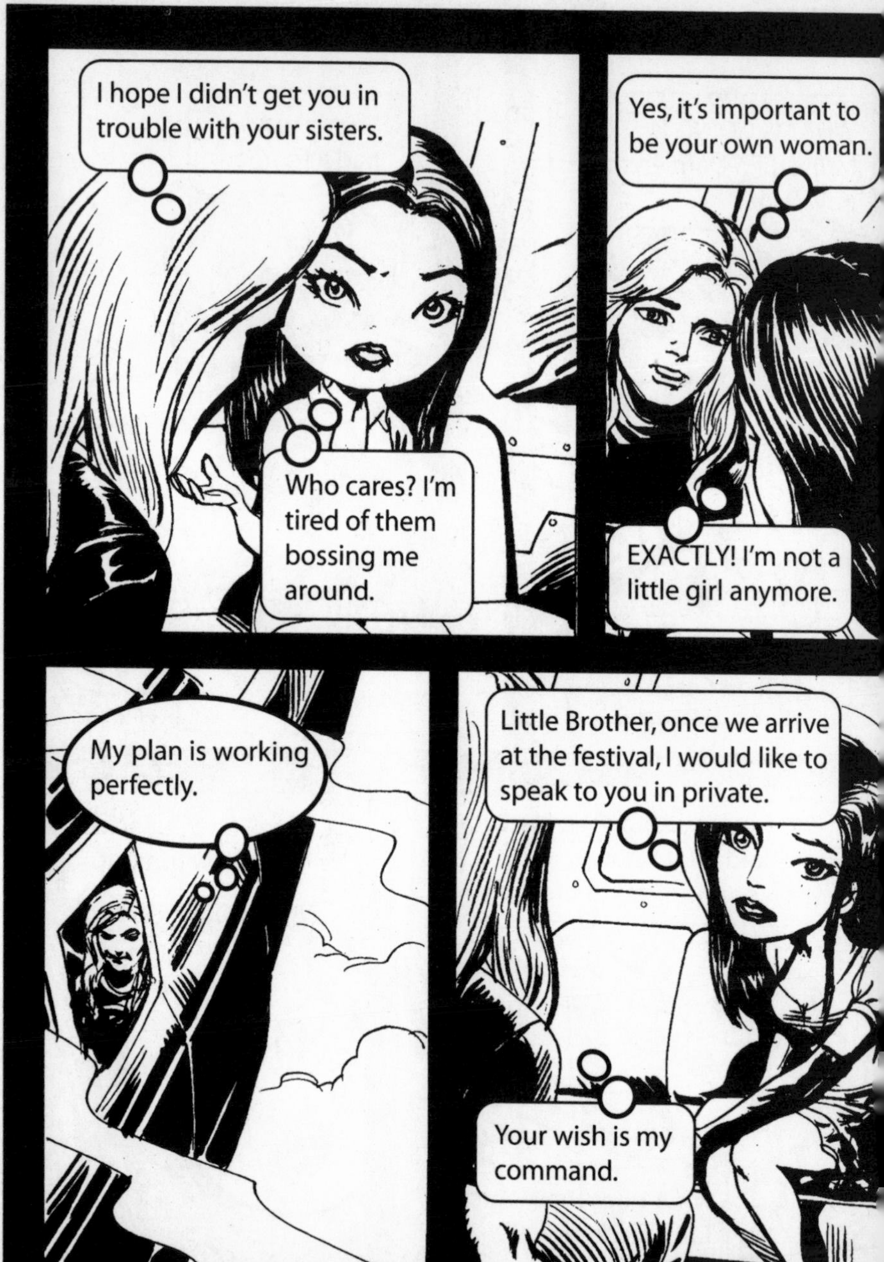
I hope I didn't get you in trouble with your sisters.
Who cares? I'm tired of them bossing me around.
Yes, it's important to be your own woman.
EXACTLY! I'm not a little girl anymore.
My plan is working perfectly.
Little Brother, once we arrive at the festival, I would like to speak to you in private.
Your wish is my command.

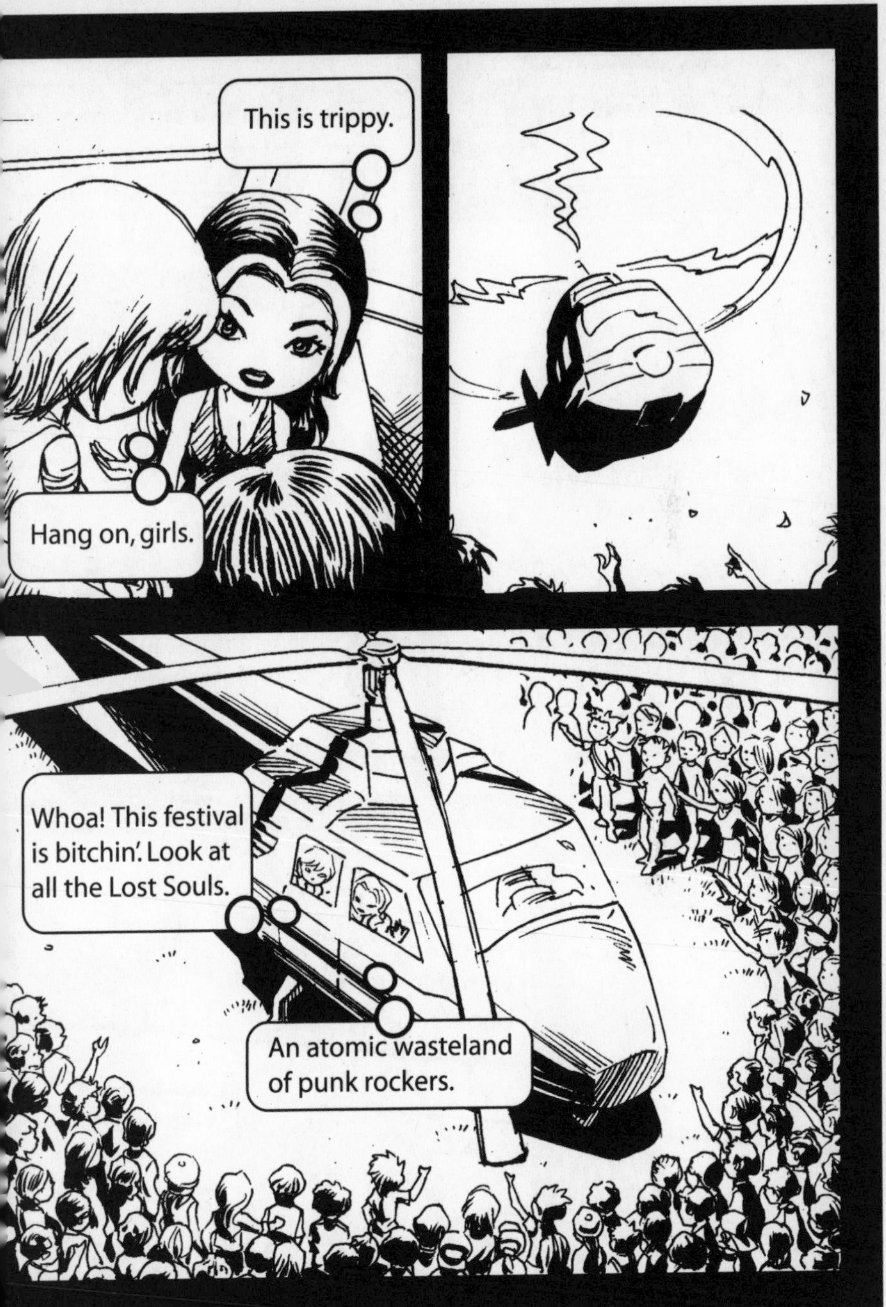
This is trippy.
Hang on, girls.
Whoa! This festival is bitchin'. Look at all the Lost Souls.
An atomic wasteland of punk rockers.

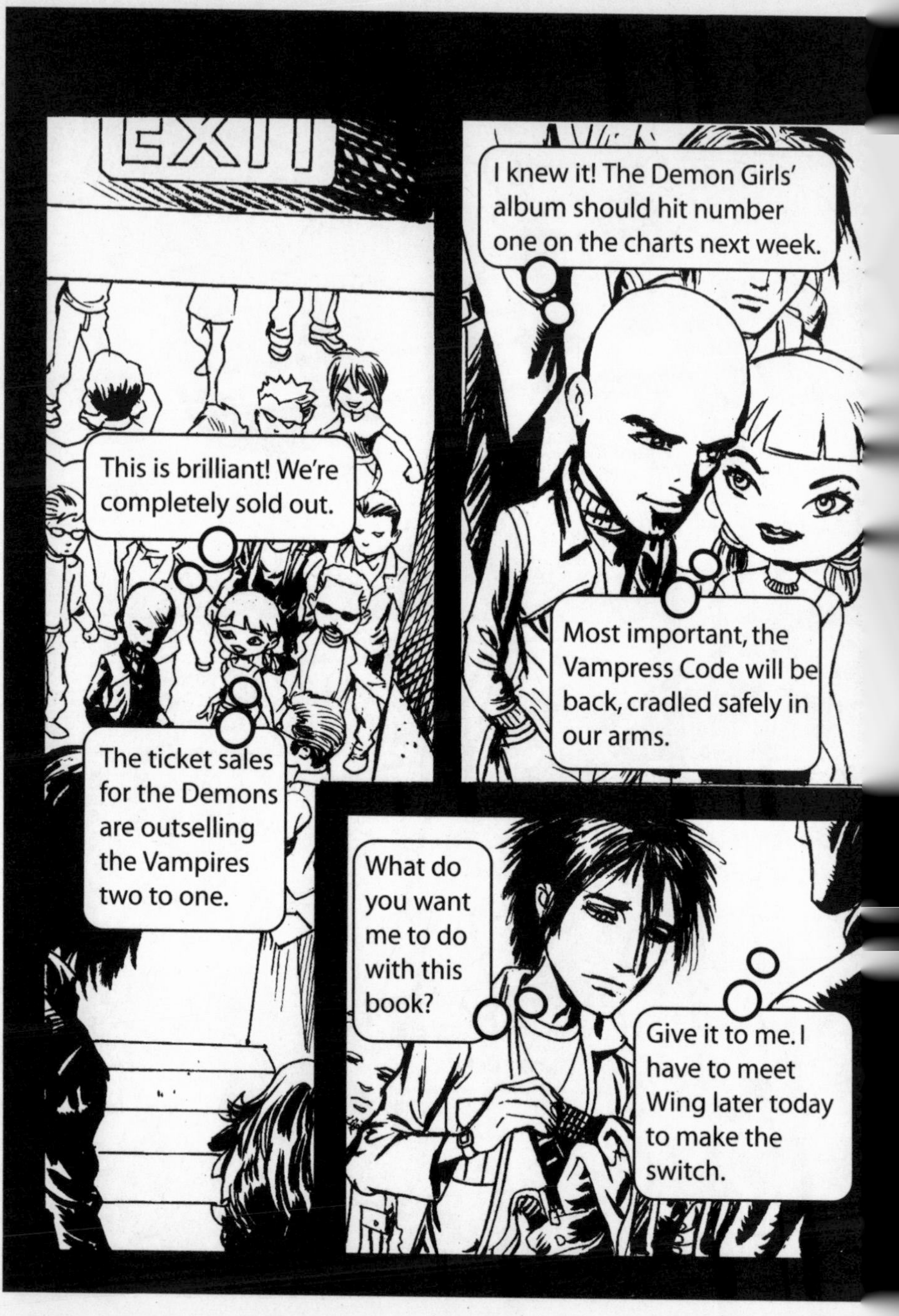
EXIT
This is brilliant! We're completely sold out.
The ticket sales for the Demons are outselling the Vampires two to one.
I knew it! The Demon Girls' album should hit number one on the charts next week.
Most important, the Vampress Code will be back, cradled safely in our arms.
What do you want me to do with this book?
Give it to me. I have to meet Wing later today to make the switch.

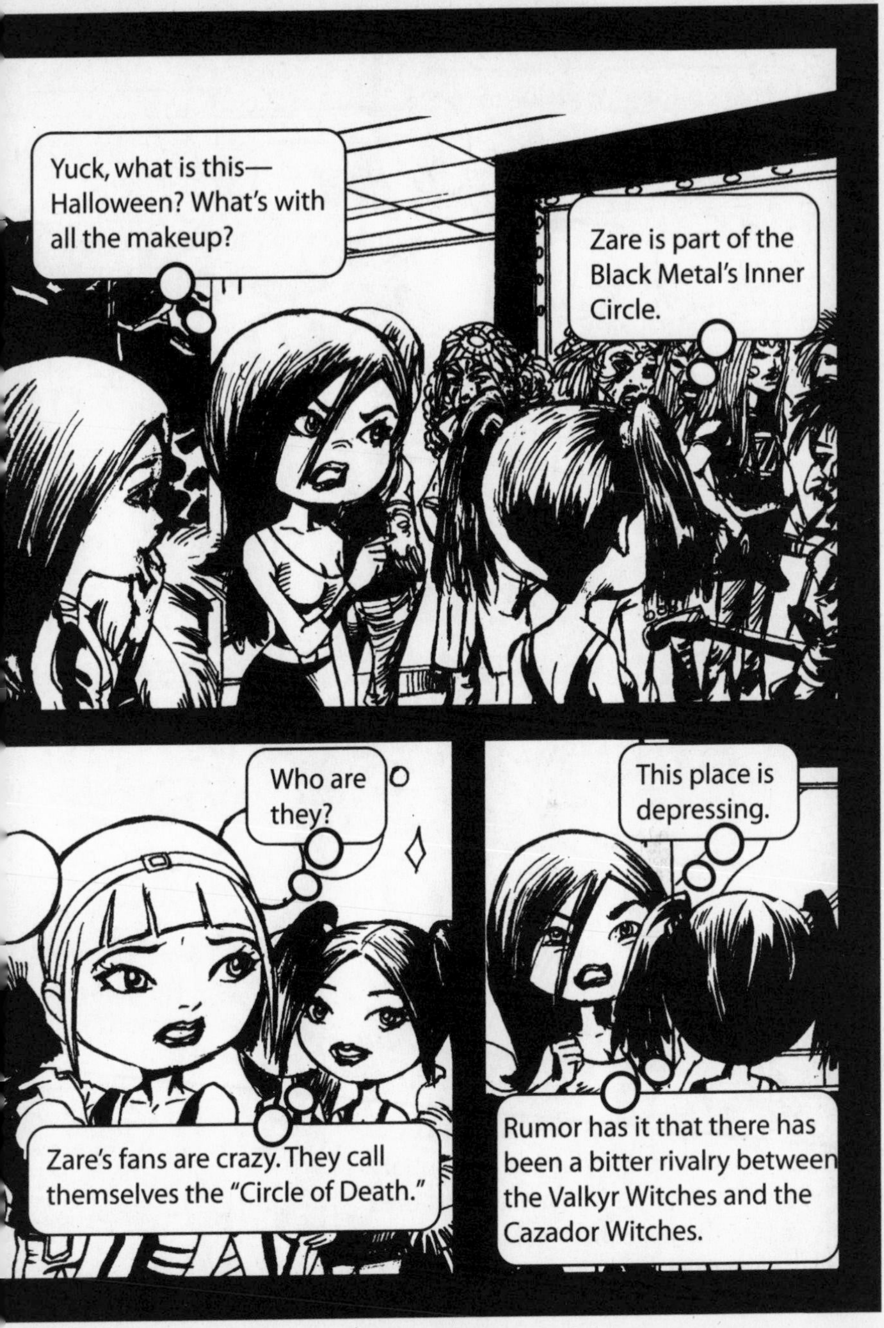
Yuck, what is this—Halloween? What's with all the makeup?
Zare is part of the Black Metal's Inner Circle.
Who are they?
Zare's fans are crazy. They call themselves the "Circle of Death."
This place is depressing.
Rumor has it that there has been a bitter rivalry between the Valkyr Witches and the Cazador Witches.

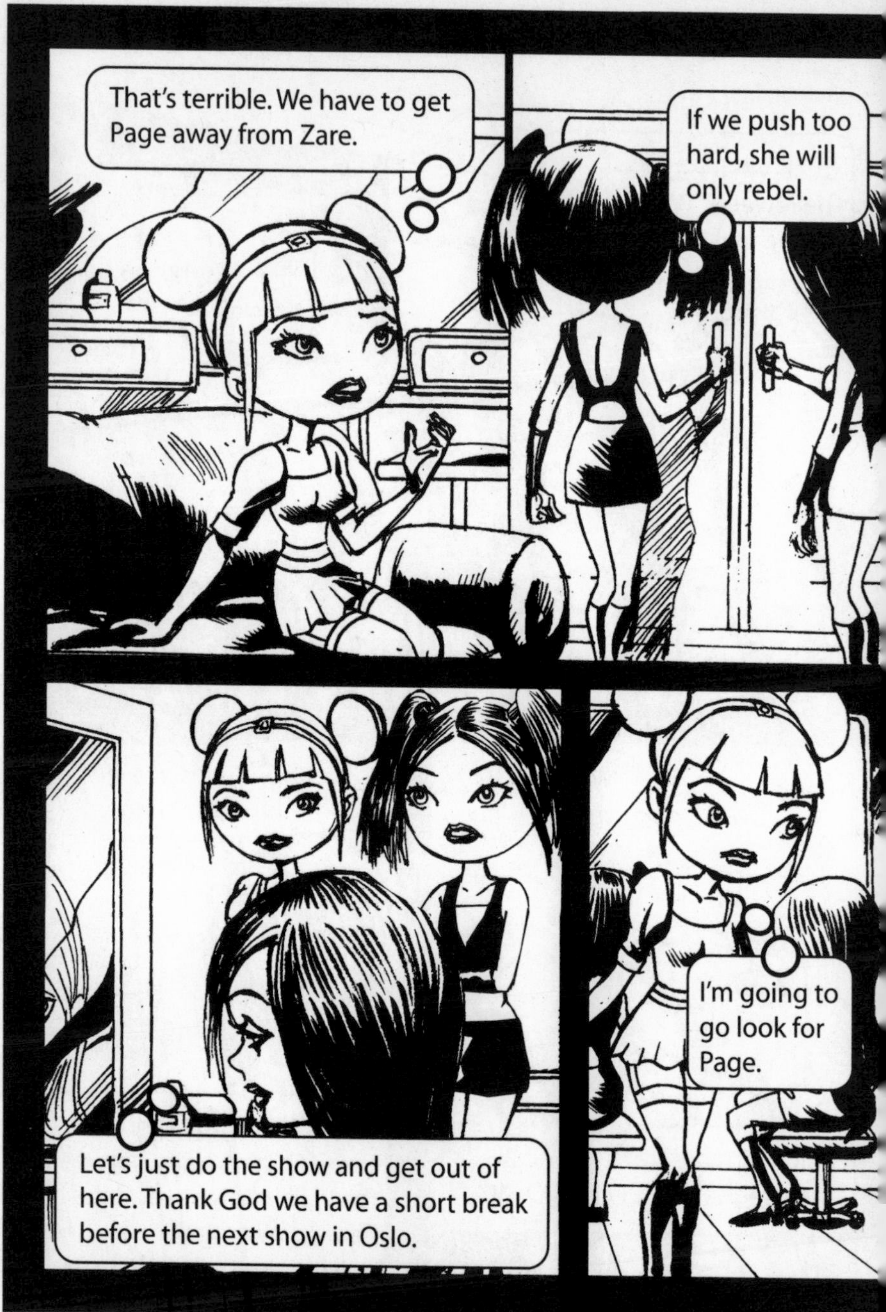
That's terrible. We have to get Page away from Zare.
If we push too hard, she will only rebel.
Let's just do the show and get out of here. Thank God we have a short break before the next show in Oslo.
I'm going to go look for Page.

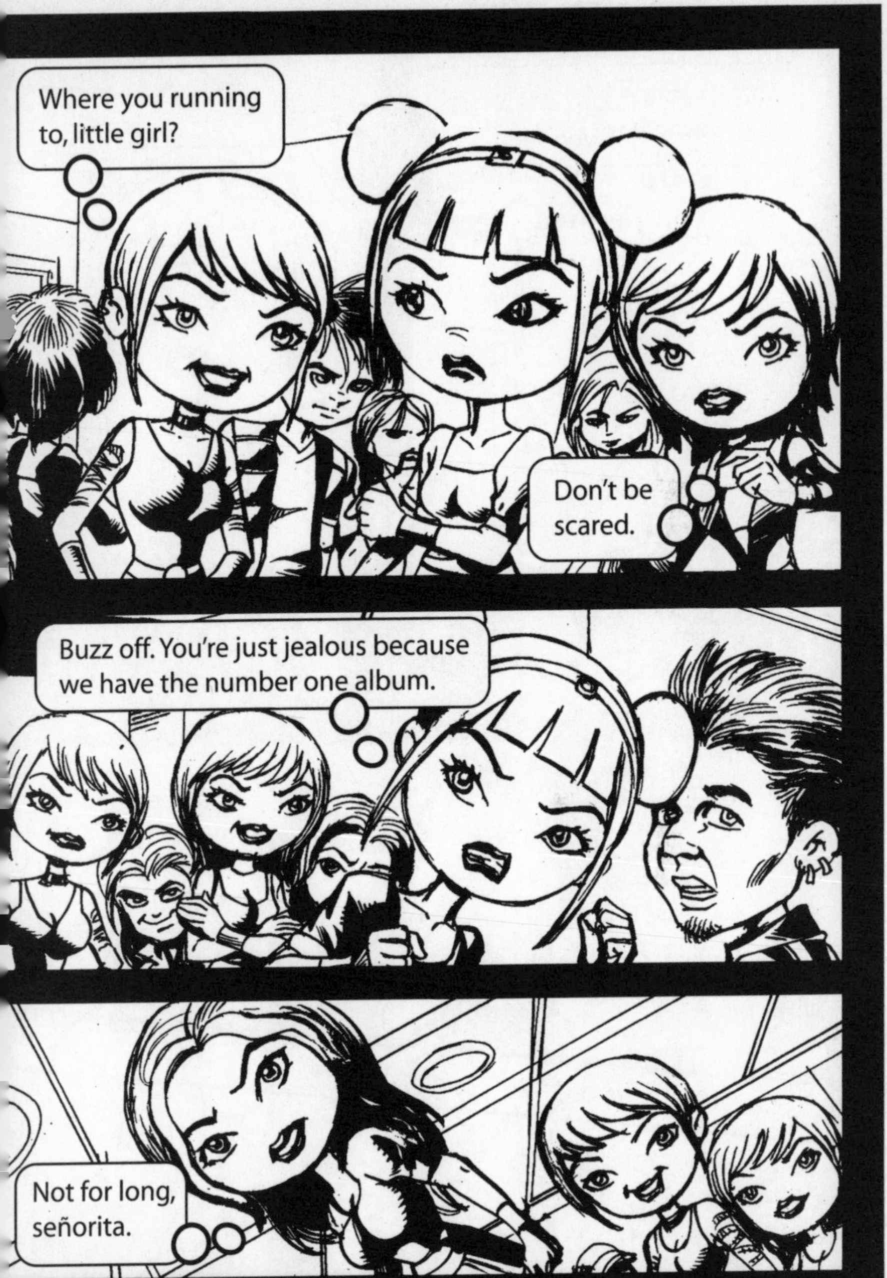
Where you running to, little girl?
Don't be scared.
Buzz off. You're just jealous because we have the number one album.
Not for long, señorita.

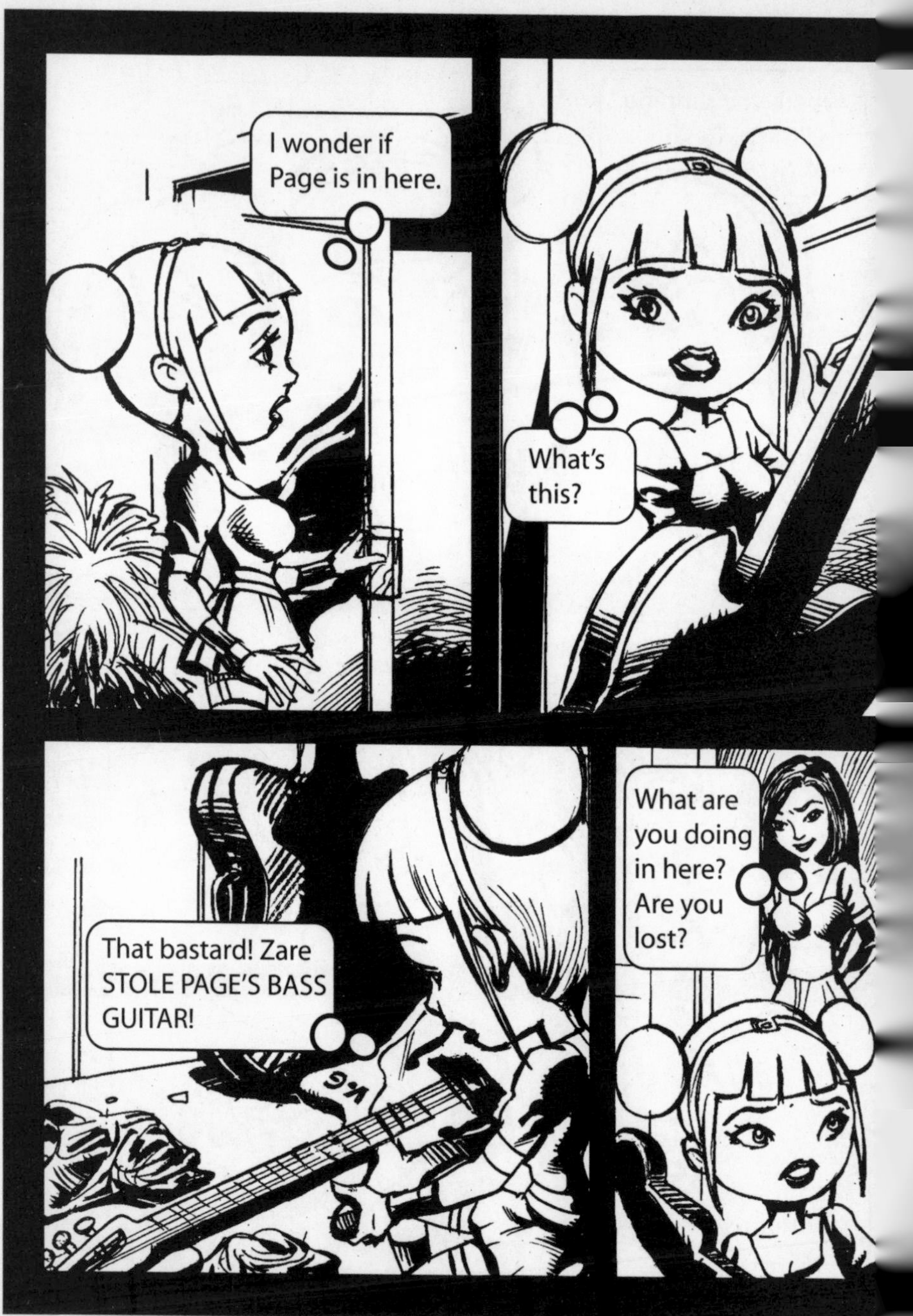
I wonder if Page is in here.
What's this?
That bastard! Zare STOLE PAGE'S BASS GUITAR!
What are you doing in here? Are you lost?

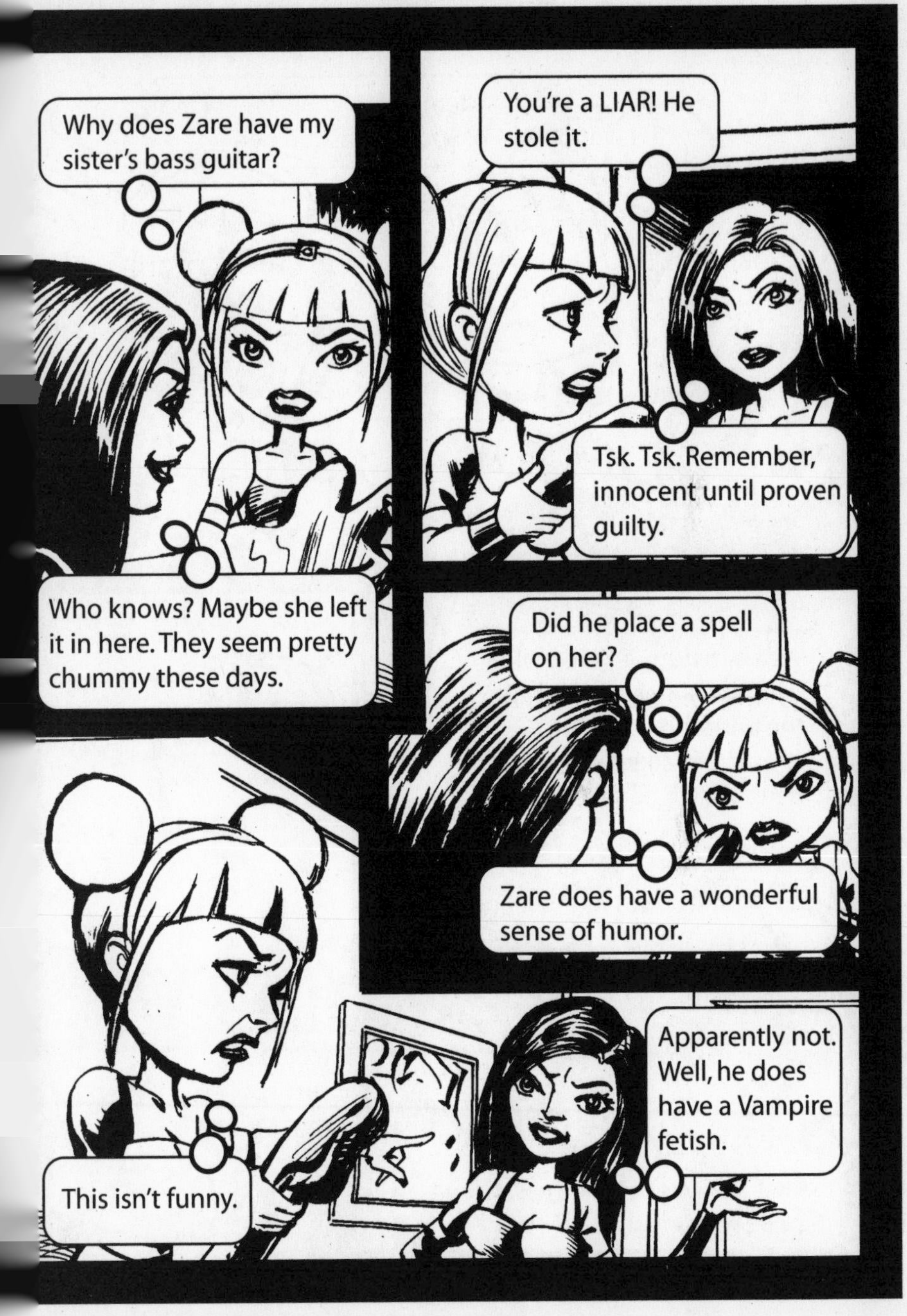
Why does Zare have my sister's bass guitar?
Who knows? Maybe she left it in here. They seem pretty chummy these days.
You're a LIAR! He stole it.
Tsk. Tsk. Remember, innocent until proven guilty.
Did he place a spell on her?
Zare does have a wonderful sense of humor.
This isn't funny.
Apparently not. Well, he does have a Vampire fetish.

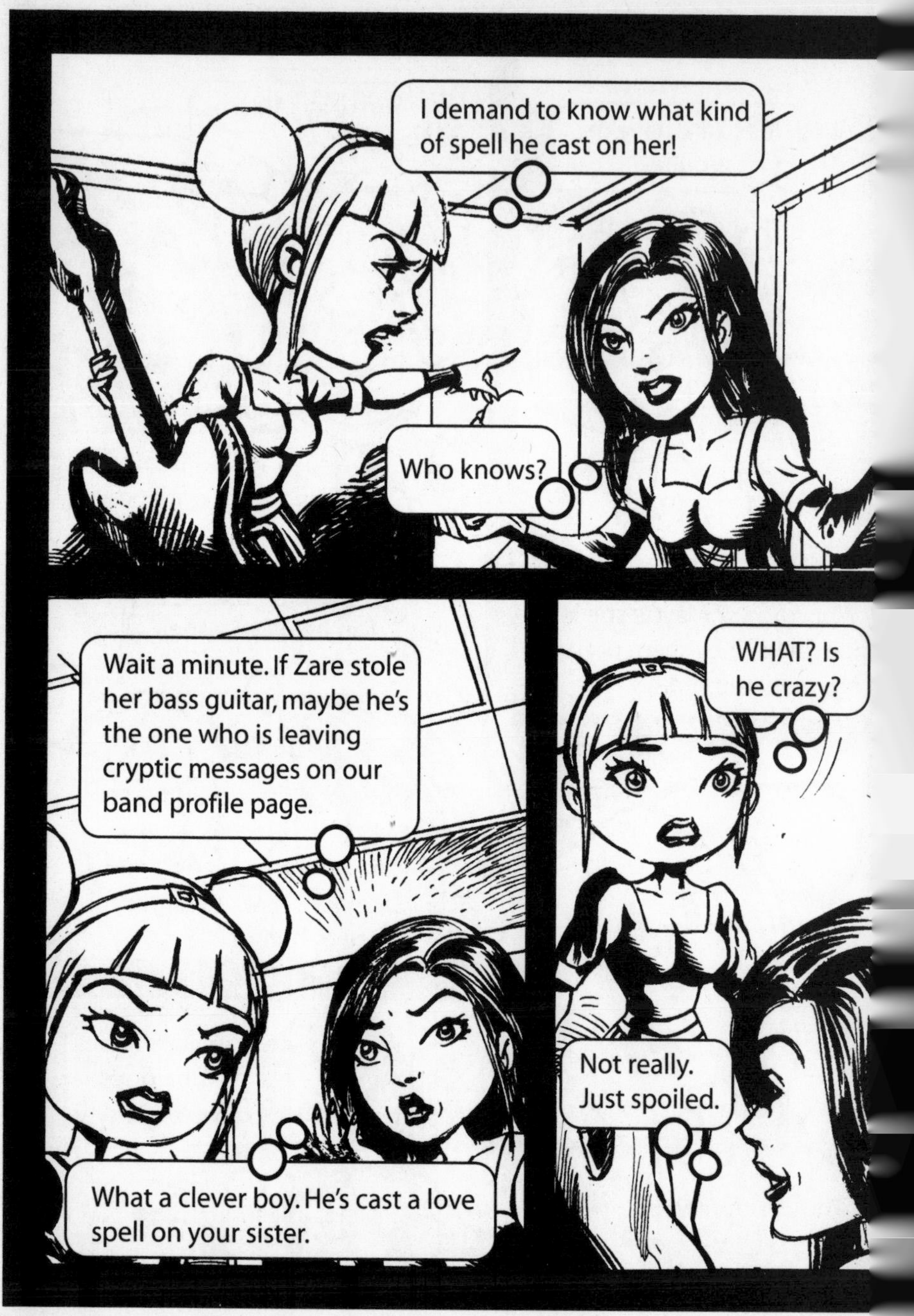
I demand to know what kind of spell he cast on her!
Who knows?
Wait a minute. If Zare stole her bass guitar, maybe he's the one who is leaving cryptic messages on our band profile page.
What a clever boy. He's cast a love spell on your sister.
WHAT? Is he crazy?
Not really. Just spoiled.

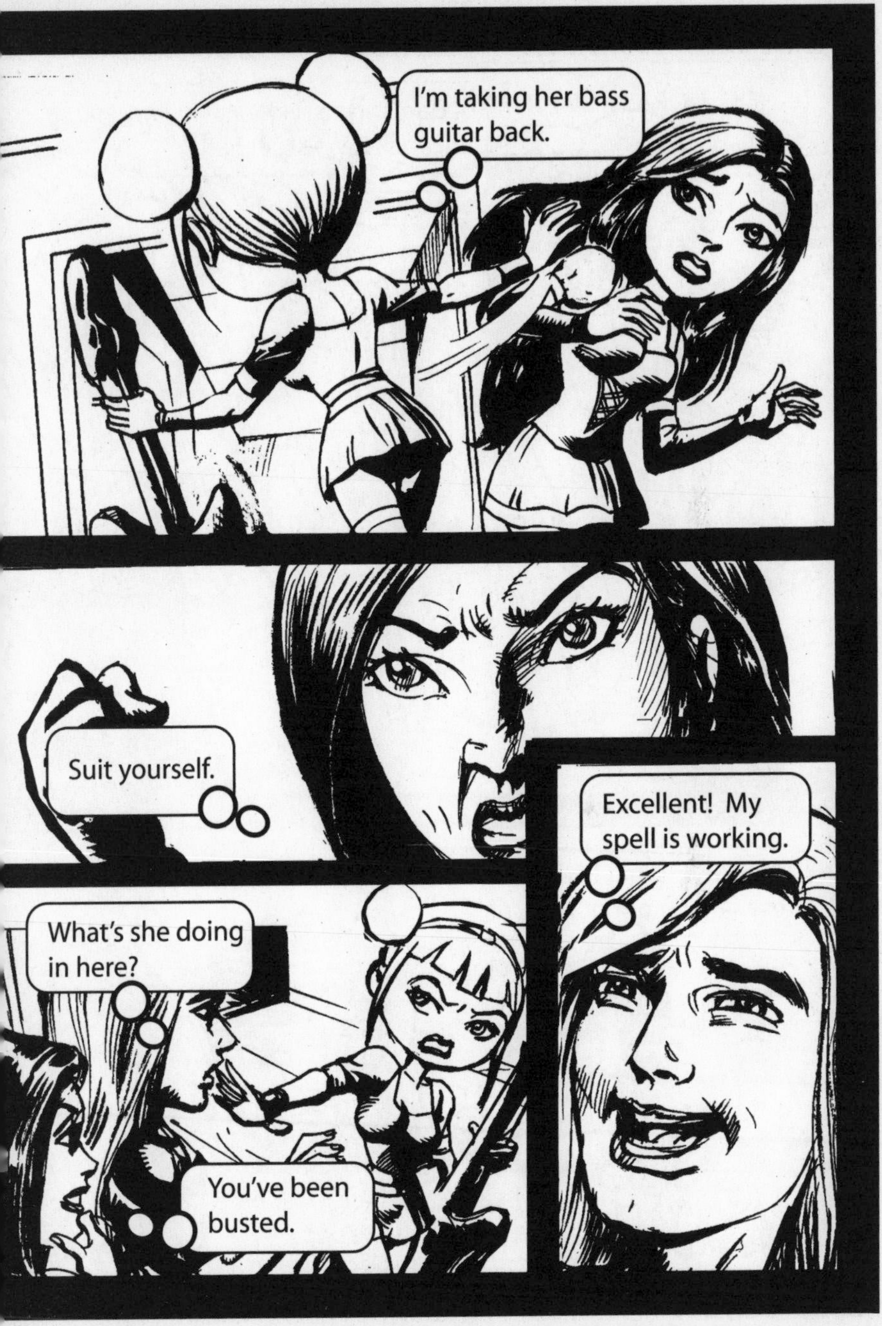

I'm taking her bass guitar back.
Suit yourself.
What's she doing in here?
You've been busted.
Excellent! My spell is working.

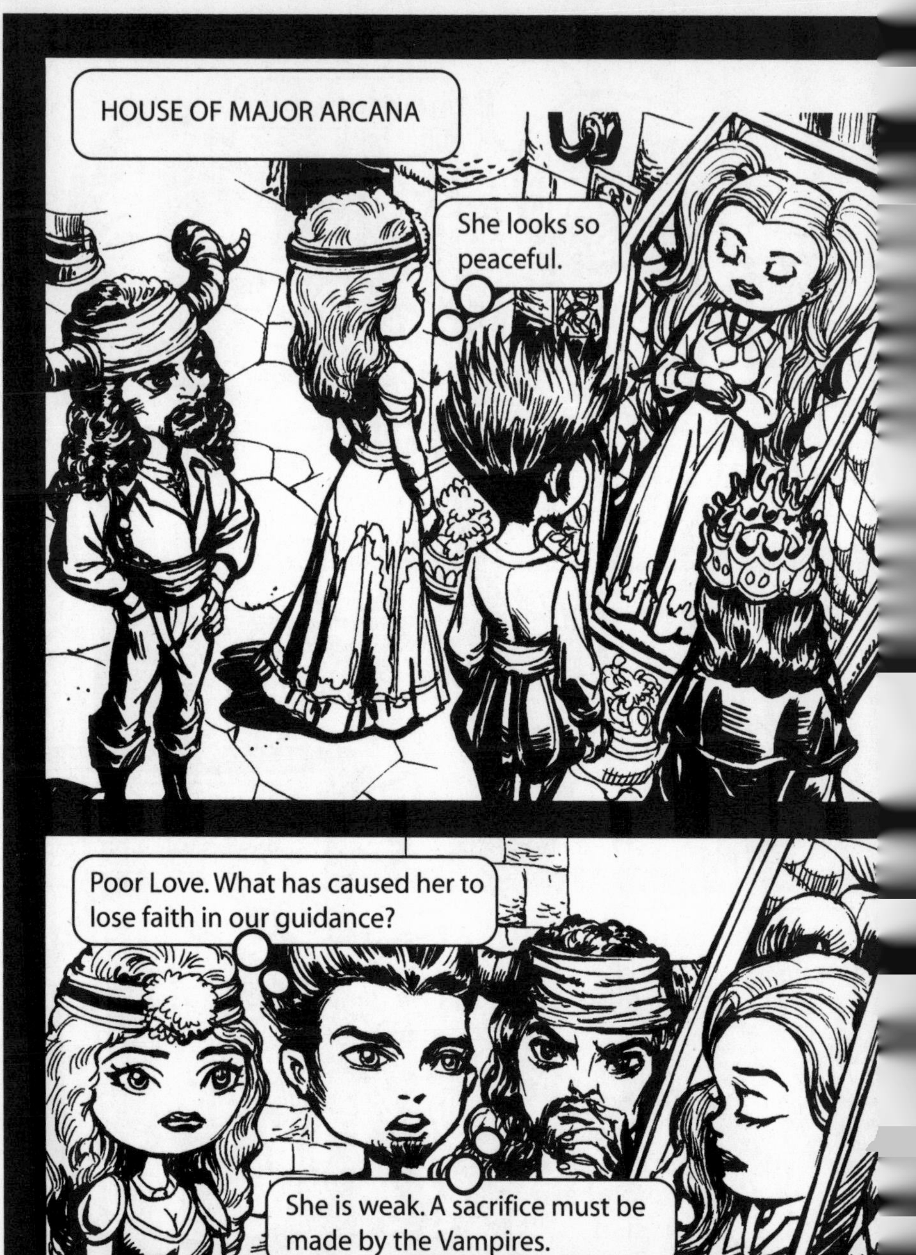
HOUSE OF MAJOR ARCANA
She looks so peaceful.
Poor Love. What has caused her to lose faith in our guidance?
She is weak. A sacrifice must be made by the Vampires.

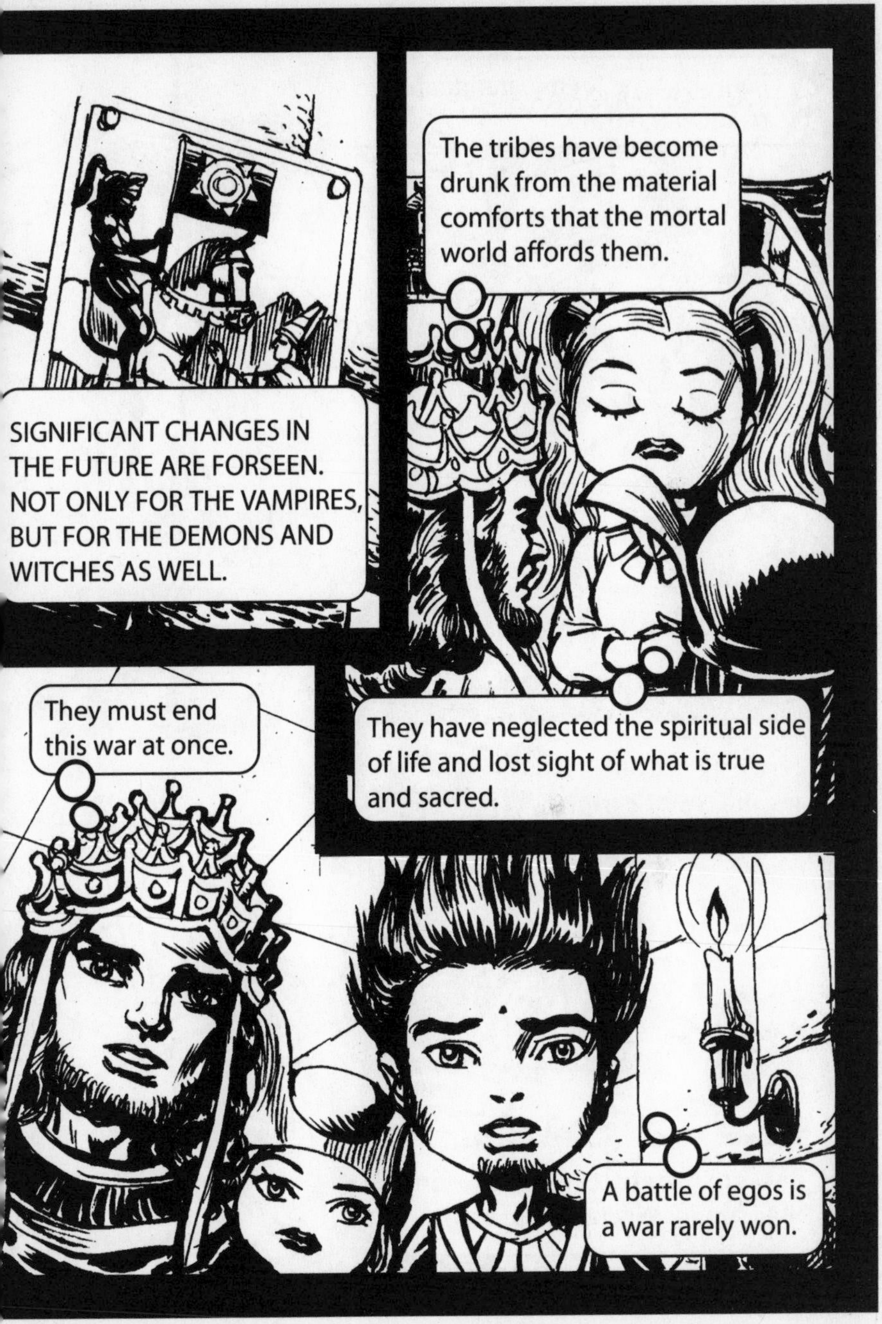

SIGNIFICANT CHANGES IN THE FUTURE ARE FORSEEN. NOT ONLY FOR THE VAMPIRES, BUT FOR THE DEMONS AND WITCHES AS WELL.
The tribes have become drunk from the material comforts that the mortal world affords them.
They have neglected the spiritual side of life and lost sight of what is true and sacred.
They must end this war at once.
A battle of egos is a war rarely won.

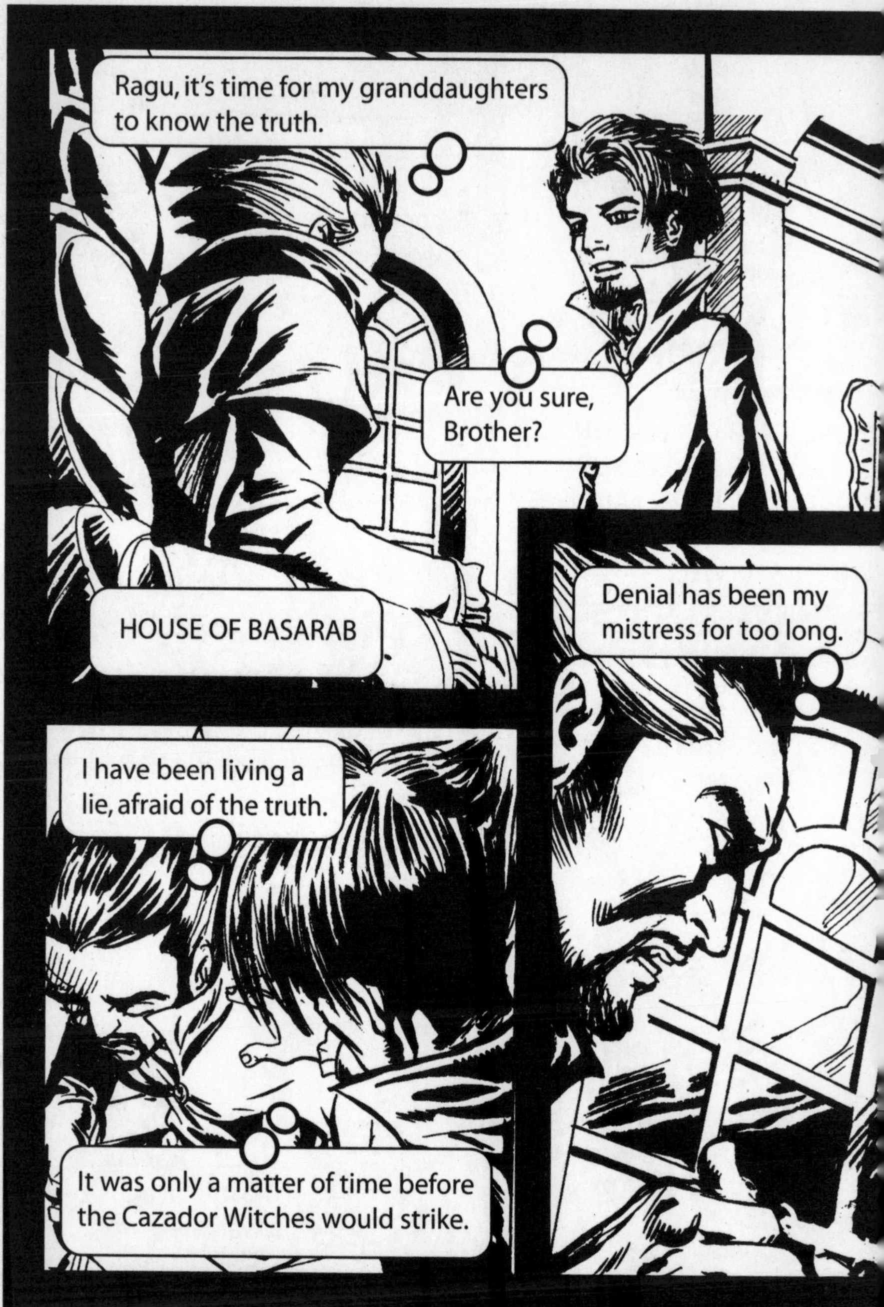
Ragu, it's time for my granddaughters to know the truth.
Are you sure, Brother?
HOUSE OF BASARAB
Denial has been my mistress for too long.
I have been living a lie, afraid of the truth.
It was only a matter of time before the Cazador Witches would strike.

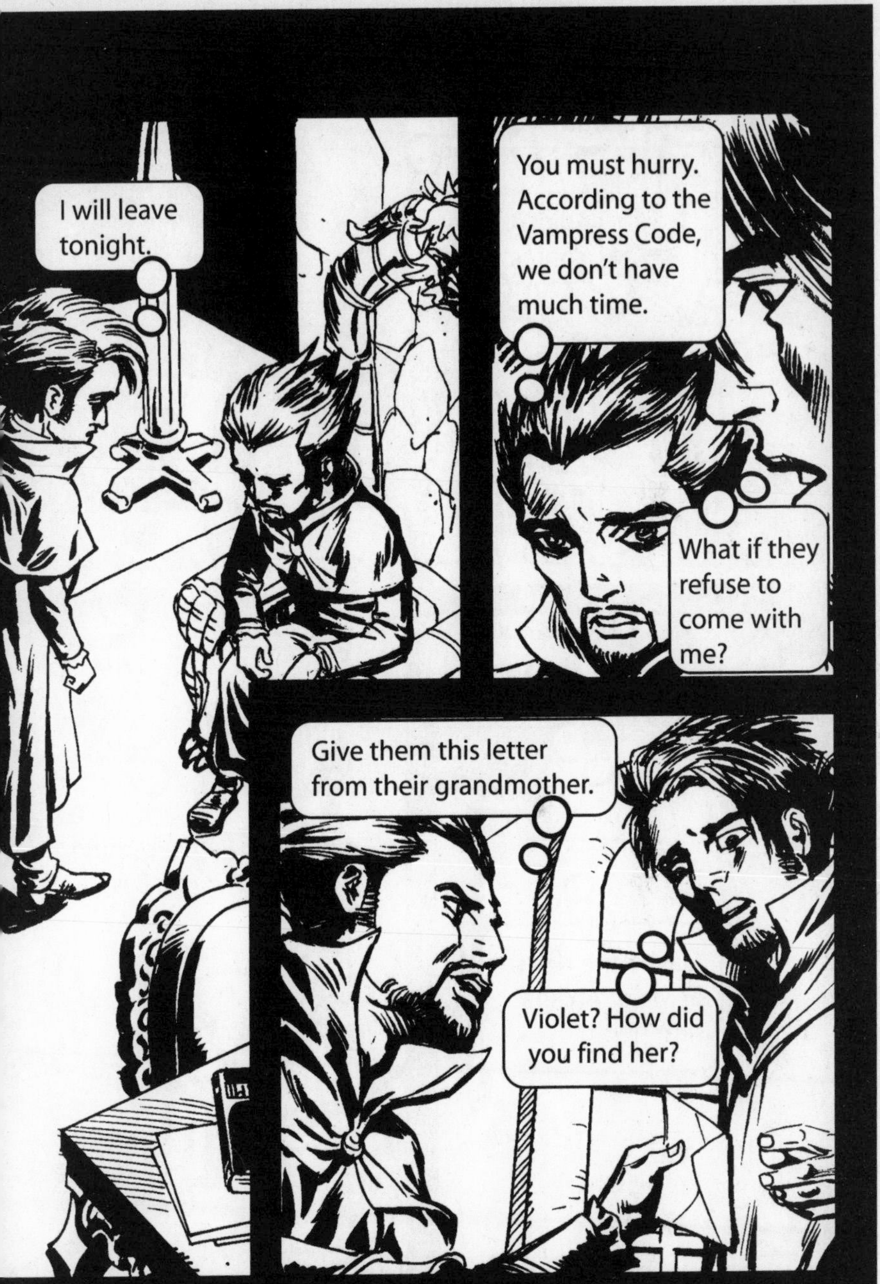
I will leave tonight.
You must hurry. According to the Vampress Code, we don't have much time.
What if they refuse to come with me?
Give them this letter from their grandmother.
Violet? How did you find her?

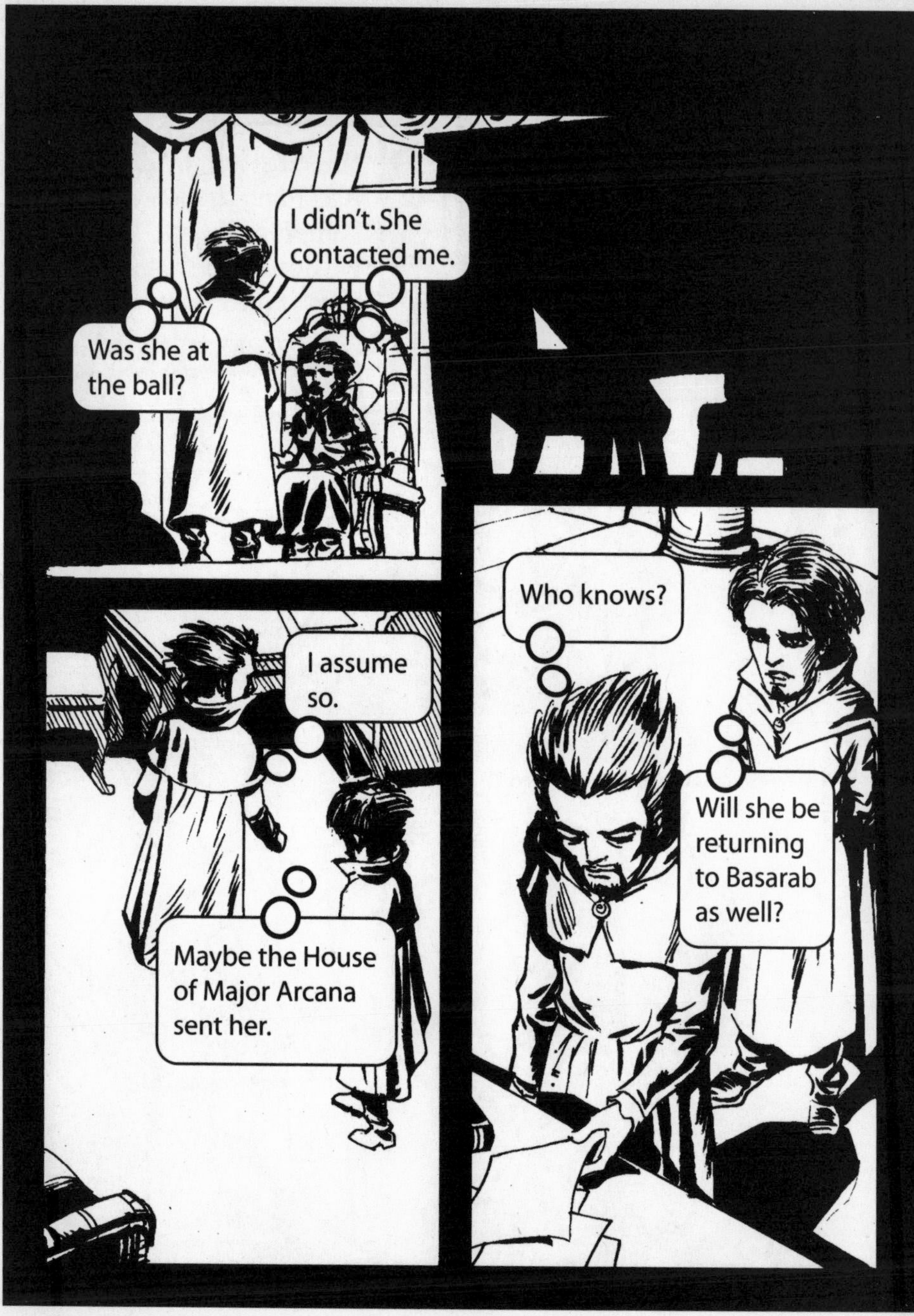
Was she at the ball?
I didn't. She contacted me.
I assume so.
Maybe the House of Major Arcana sent her.
Who knows?
Will she be returning to Basarab as well?

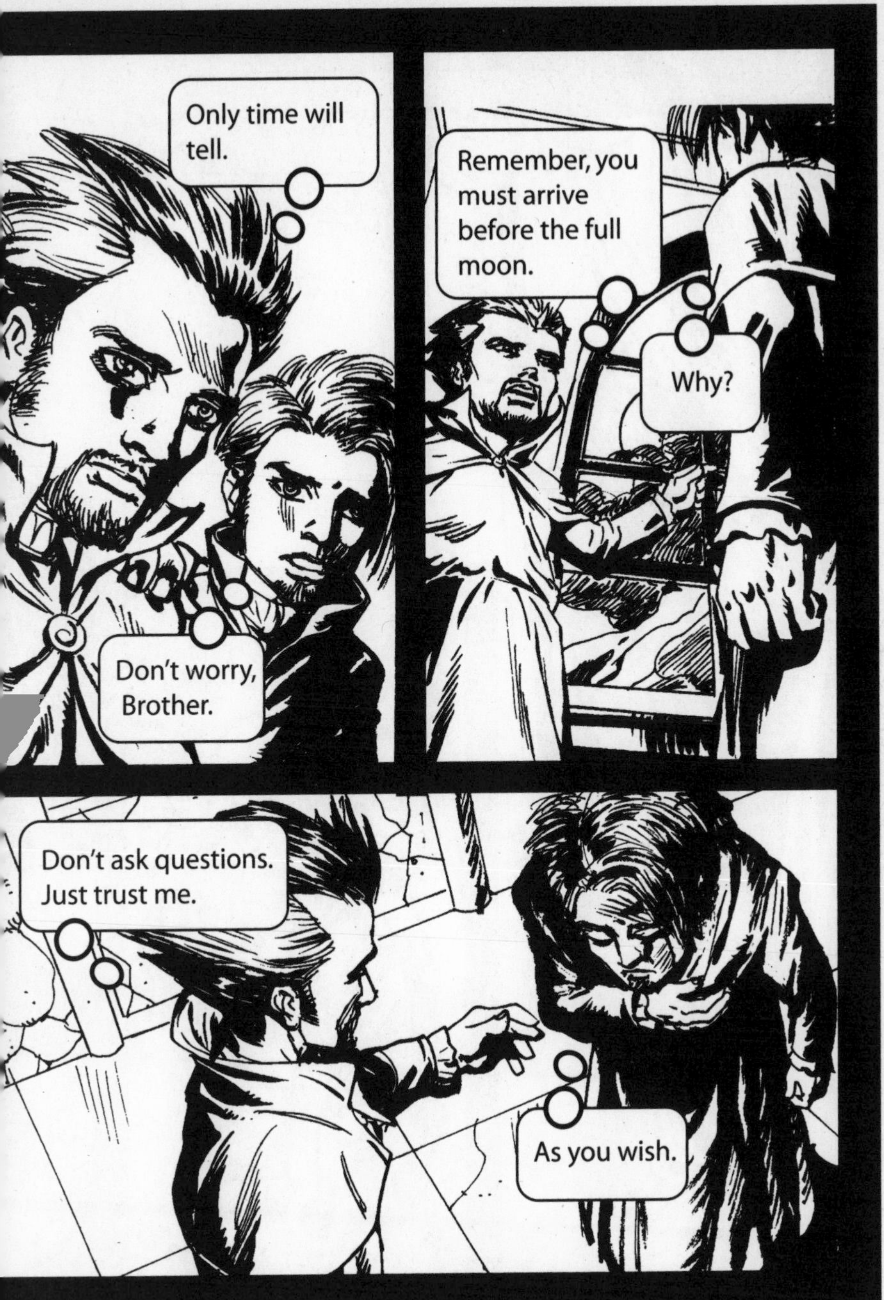
Only time will tell.
Don't worry, Brother.
Remember, you must arrive before the full moon.
Why?
Don't ask questions. Just trust me.
As you wish.

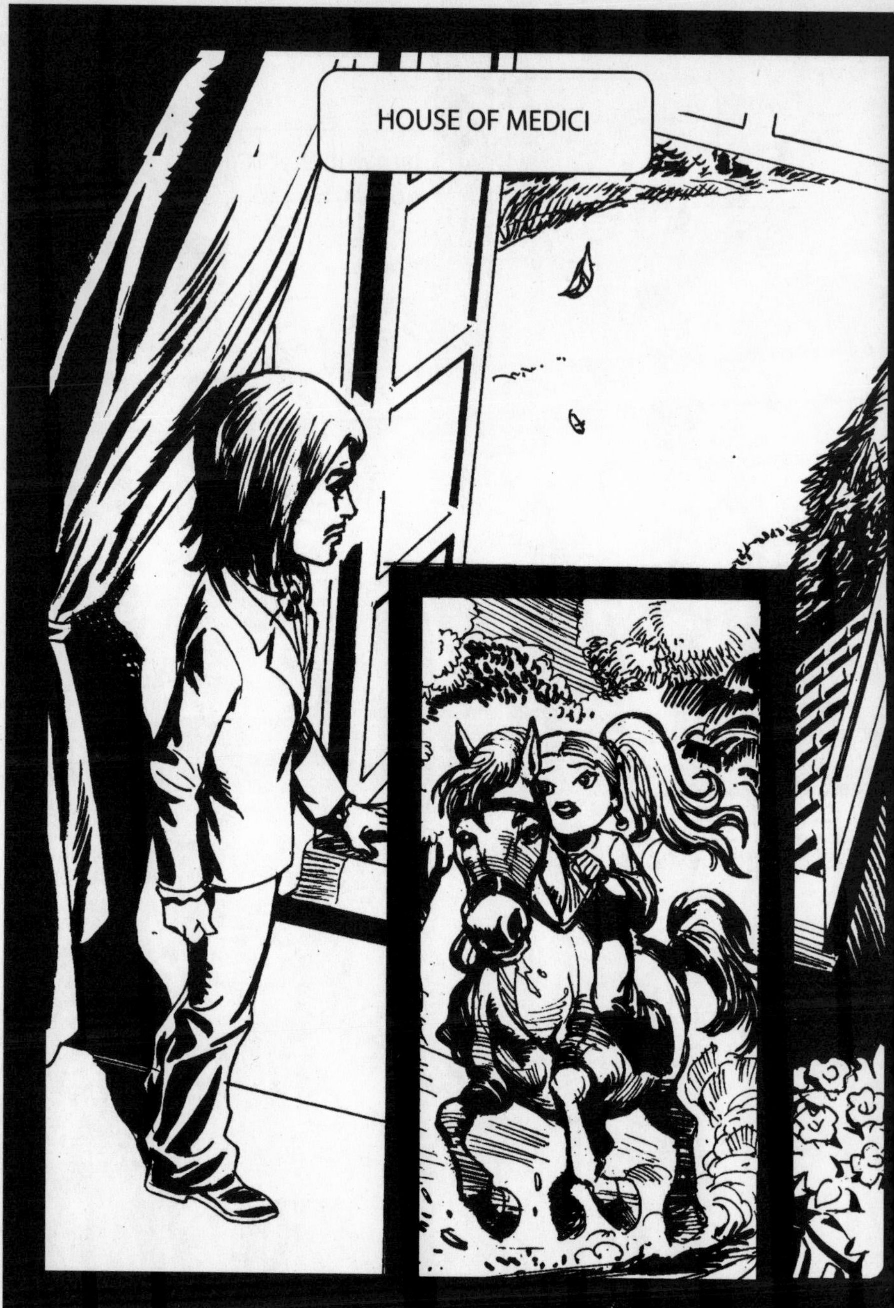
HOUSE OF MEDICI

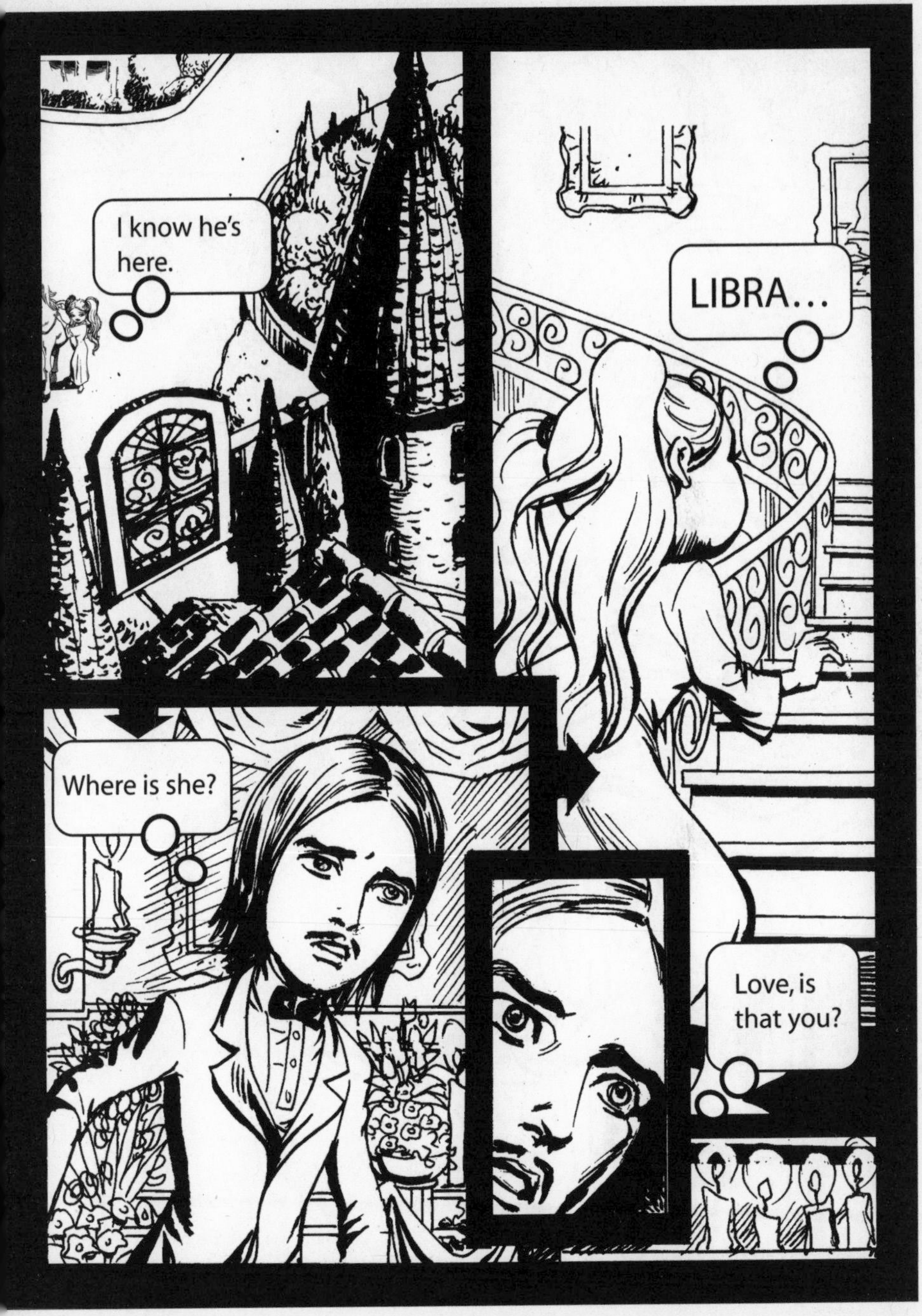
I know he's here.
Where is she?
LIBRA...
Love, is that you?

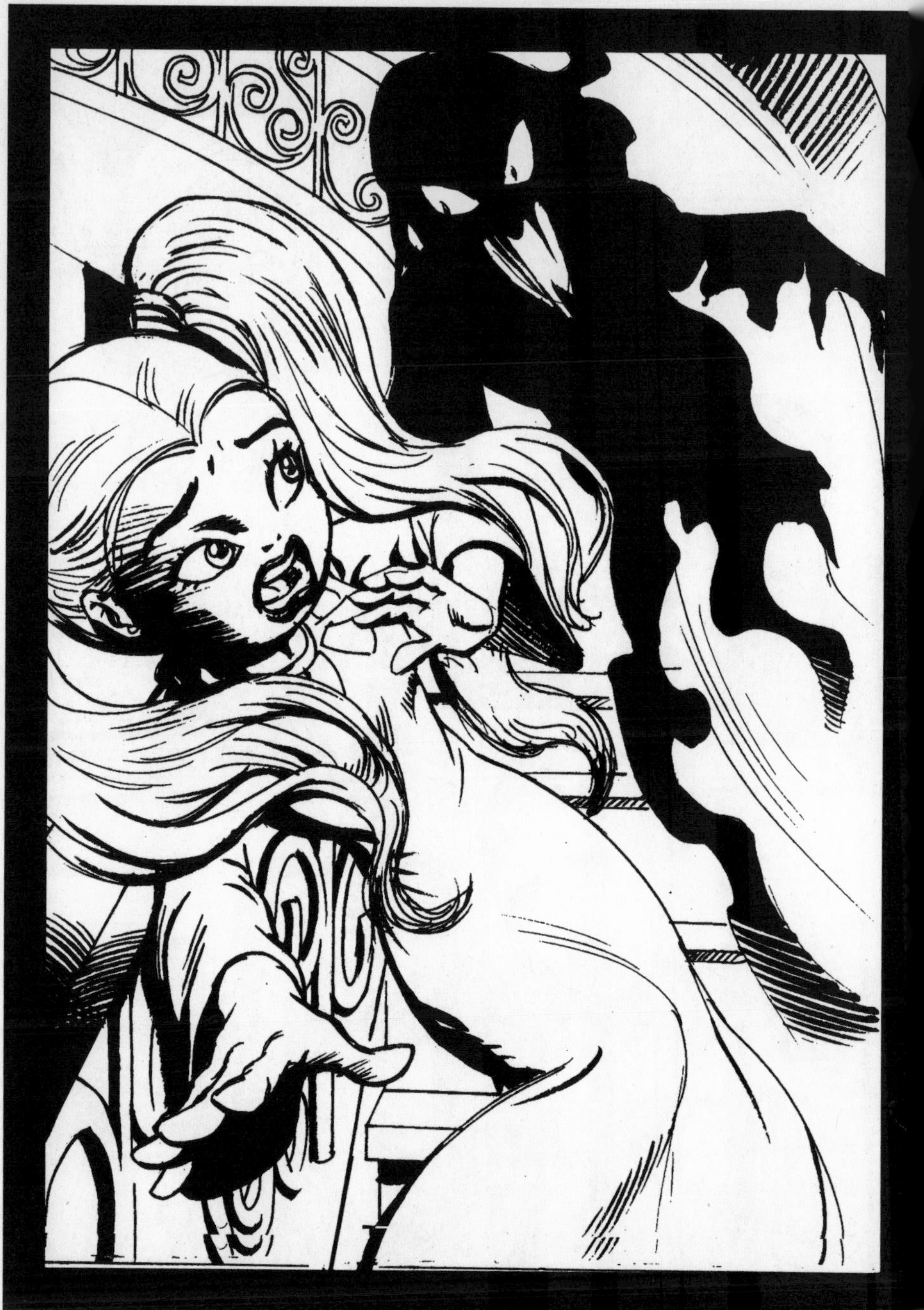

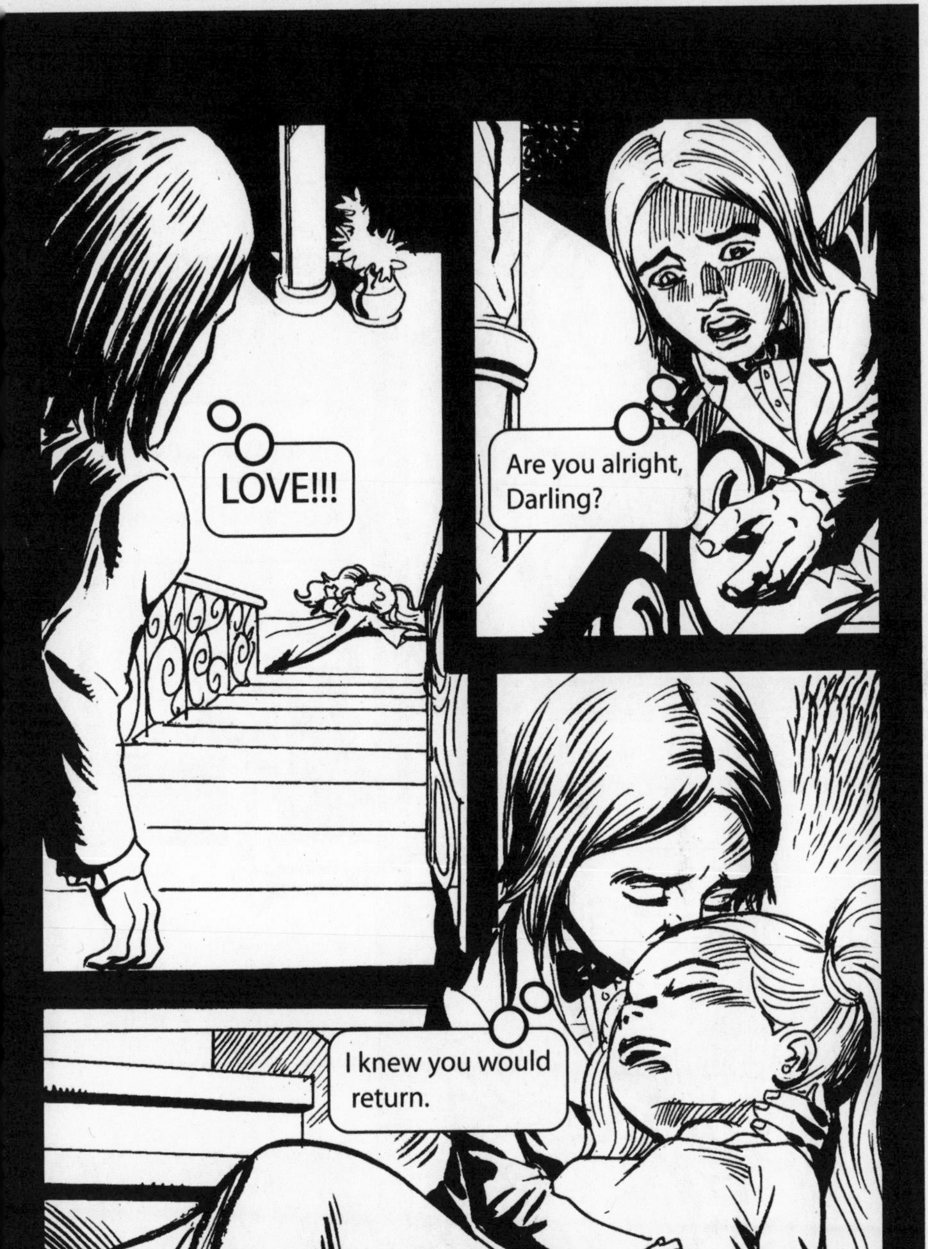
LOVE!!!
Are you alright, Darling?
I knew you would return.

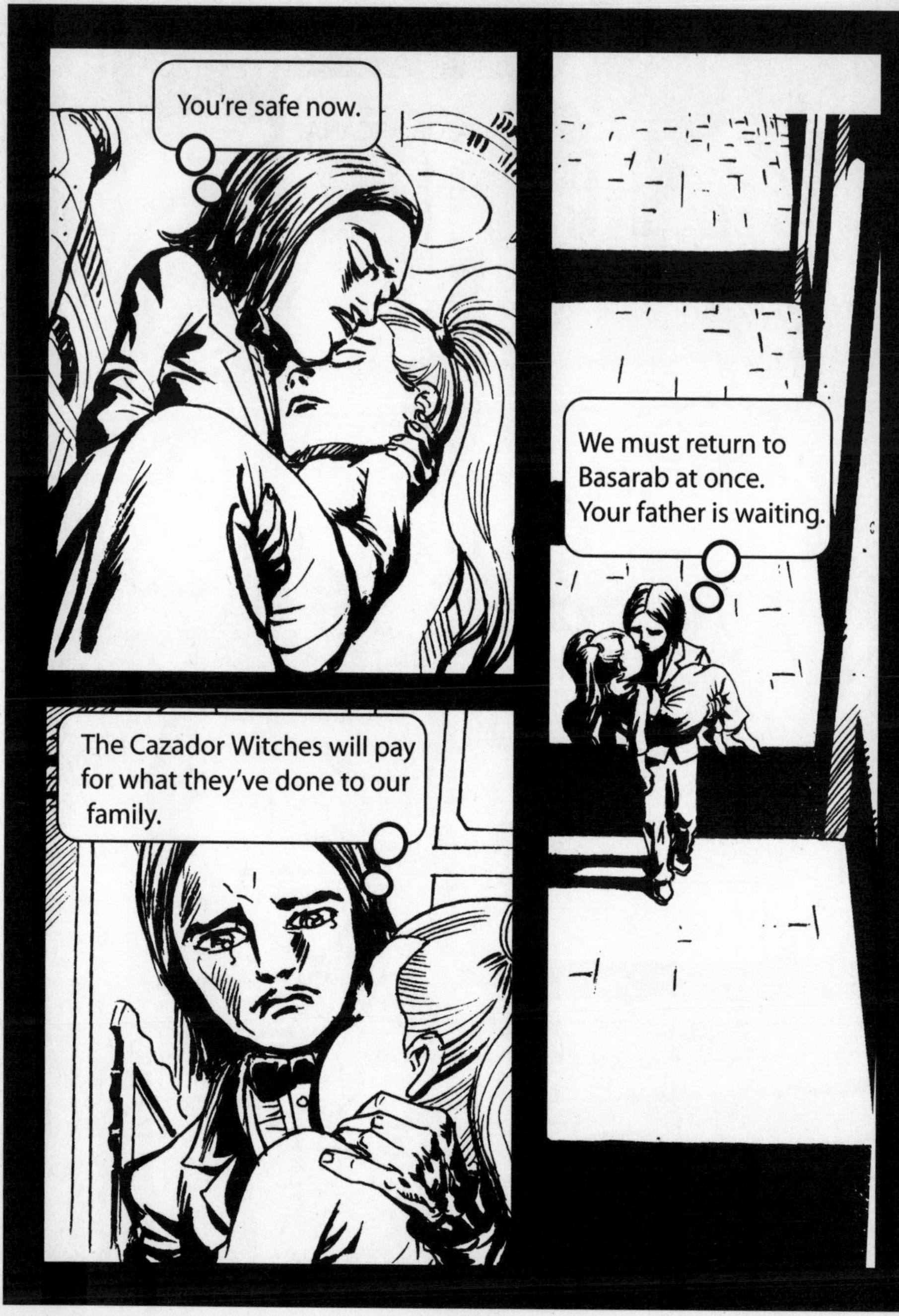
You're safe now.
The Cazador Witches will pay for what they've done to our family.
We must return to Basarab at once. Your father is waiting.

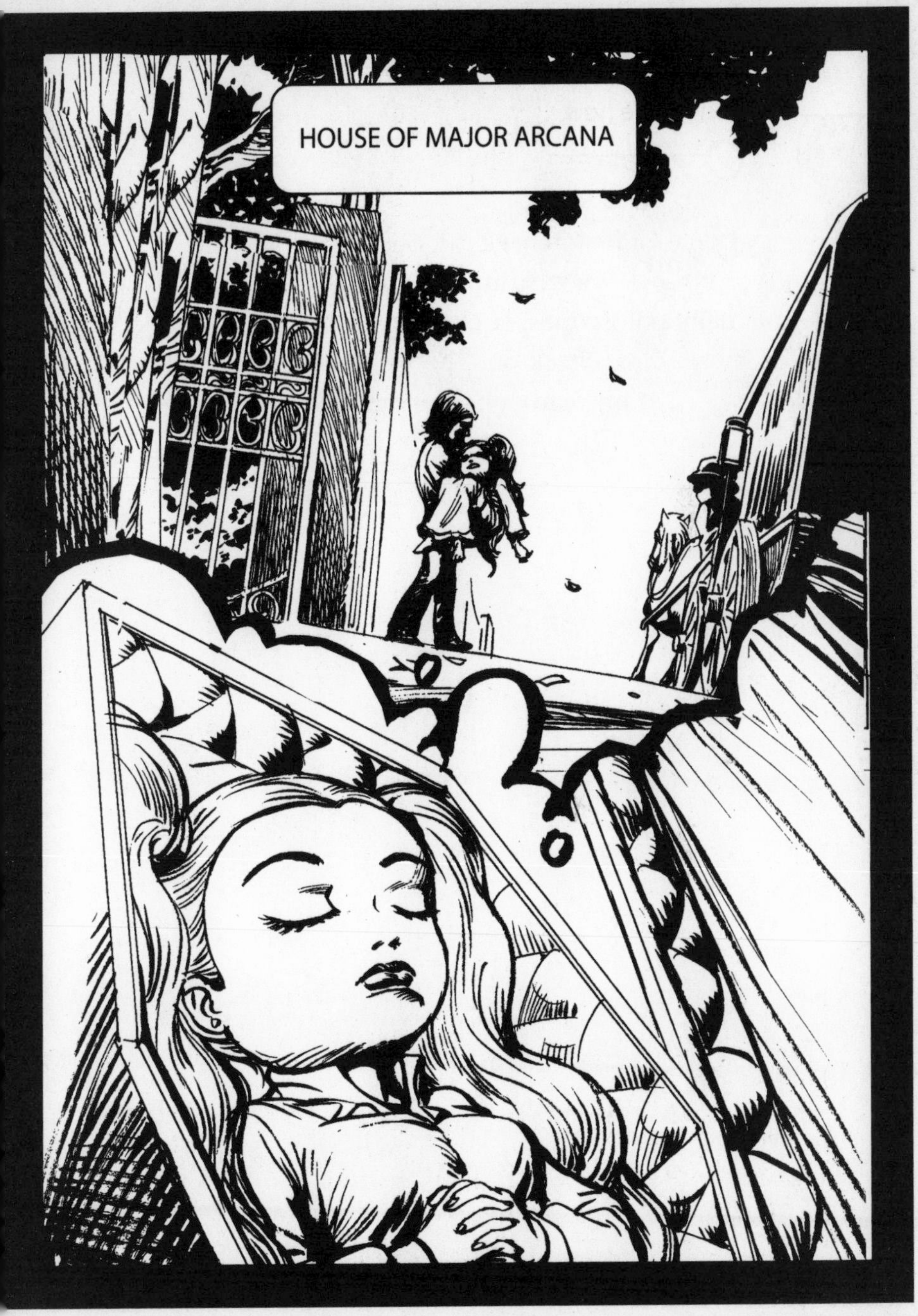
HOUSE OF MAJOR ARCANA

Don't forget to check out our official website at
www.vampressgirls.com.
Free daily horoscopes, tarot card readings, screen savers,
and more. Also, check out The Vampress Girls band page
at myYearbook.com/vampressgirls.

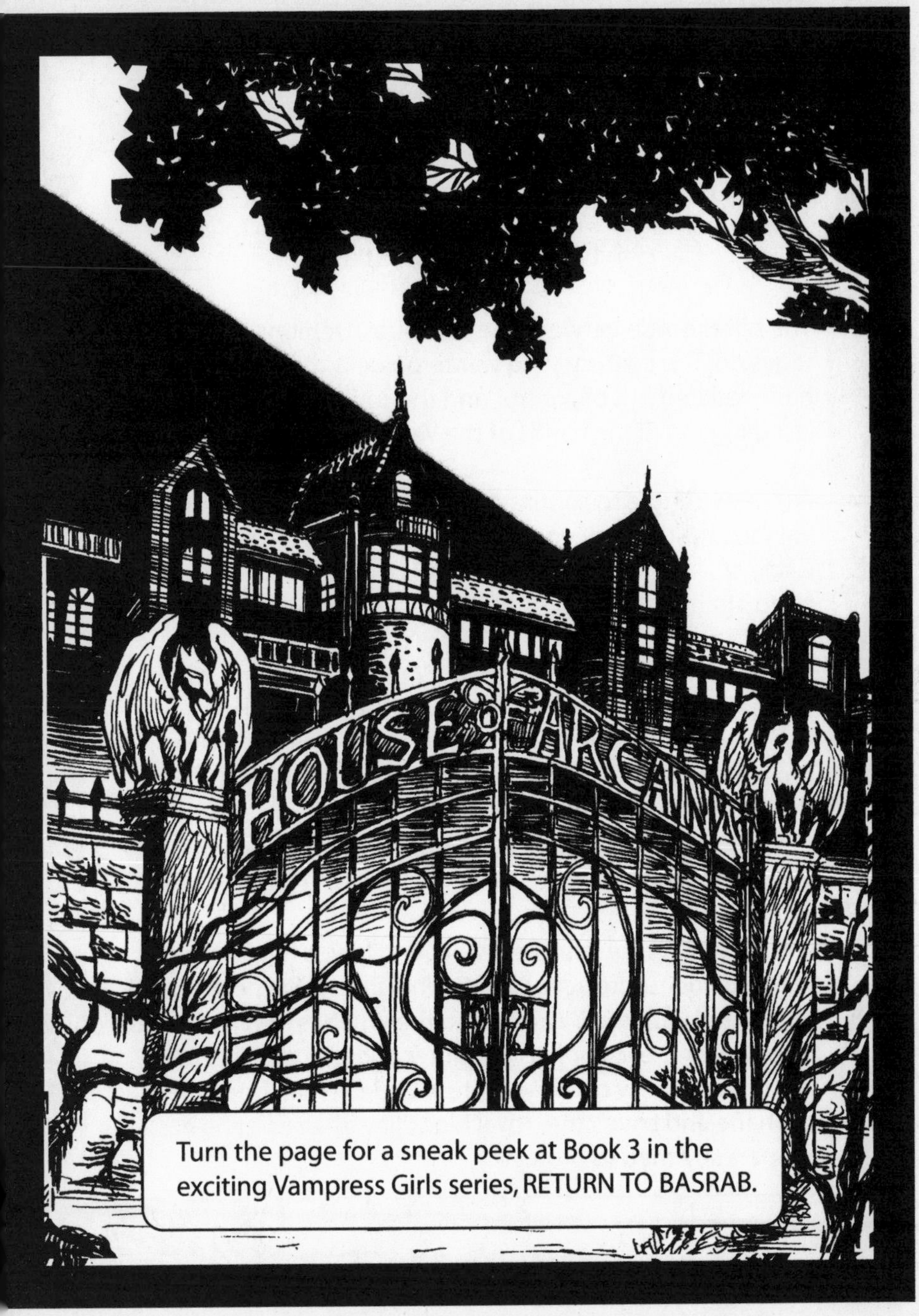
HOUSE ARCANA

Turn the page for a sneak peek at Book 3 in the exciting Vampress Girls series, RETURN TO BASRAB.

THE VAMPRESS GIRLS
Return to Basarab

The bitter battle between the Vampires, Demons, and Witches rages on. The century-long war to possess the Vampress Code has escalated out of control, and the souls of the Dreamers are left dangling in the hands of the Vampress Girls.

As they struggle to continue their rock tour, the Vampress Girls are faced with many unexpected obstacles. Zare has drawn his Circle of Death around Page, and his evil presence has torn the band apart.

In desperation to save his family, Count Dracul has summoned the leaders of the Vampire Tribe to return to Basarab at once. His daughter, Love, who has narrowly escaped death, has traveled through a secret passage in time left open by the House of Major Arcana. Reunited with her one true love, Libra, together they must find a way to undo the evil spell cast by the Witches of Cazador.

The Dreamers', the Vampress Girls', and Love's fates hinge on the past and future actions of Count Dracul. Will he end his bitter feud with the Demons and the Witches? Will he be able to win back the love of his daughter and grandchildren? Or will the prophecy of the Vampress Code reveal the hidden fact of Shade and Love's true royal bloodline, the secret he has desperately tried to protect?

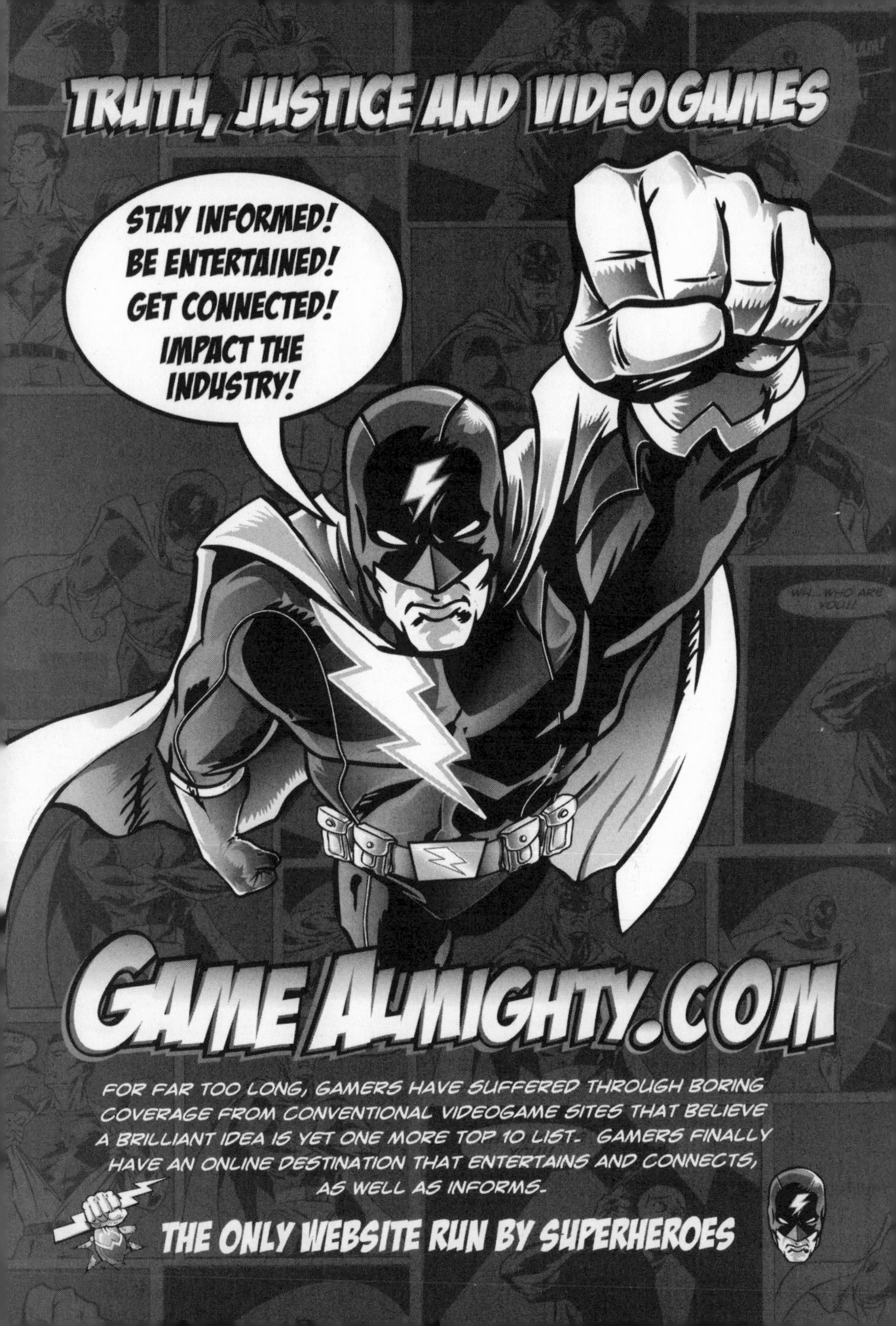
TRUTH, JUSTICE AND VIDEOGAMES
STAY INFORMED! BE ENTERTAINED! GET CONNECTED! IMPACT THE INDUSTRY!
GAME ALMIGHTY.COM
FOR FAR TOO LONG, GAMERS HAVE SUFFERED THROUGH BORING COVERAGE FROM CONVENTIONAL VIDEOGAME SITES THAT BELIEVE A BRILLIANT IDEA IS YET ONE MORE TOP 10 LIST. GAMERS FINALLY HAVE AN ONLINE DESTINATION THAT ENTERTAINS AND CONNECTS, AS WELL AS INFORMS.
THE ONLY WEBSITE RUN BY SUPERHEROES